H16

Please return this book on or before the date shown on your receipt.

To renew go to:
Website: **www.slough.gov.uk/libraries**
Phone:   **03031 230035**

# MISS NIGHTINGALE'S NURSES

**From the docks of Liverpool to a distant battlefield, can one girl find her brother and save herself?**

Ada Houston's life is shattered when her brother Frank goes missing following an accident at the docks. She hears a rumour that he survived and left Liverpool to fight a foreign war, so she boards a ship to bring him home. But the battlefields of the Crimea are a hostile place for a penniless young woman. Then one day she is offered the chance to train as a nurse under the famous Florence Nightingale. Ada shows great aptitude as she cares for her injured countrymen, makes new friends and finds romance. But Frank is still missing and she needs to find him before it's too late...

# MISS NIGHTINGALE'S NURSES

# MISS NIGHTINGALE'S NURSES

*by*

Kate Eastham

**Magna Large Print Books**
Gargrave, North Yorkshire,
BD23 3SE, England.

British Library Cataloguing in Publication Data.

A catalogue record of this book is
available from the British Library

ISBN   978-0-7505-4724-6

First published in Great Britain by Michael Joseph 2018

Published in Large Print 2019 by arrangement with
Penguin Books Ltd.

Magna Large Print is an imprint of Library Magna Books Ltd.

Printed and bound in Great Britain by
T.J. (International) Ltd., Cornwall, PL28 8RW

The Crimean War was one 'in which women, so long confined to the domestic sphere, finally found an active and indispensable role as nurses, and one that would ultimately make nursing an acceptable profession for their sex. It was also the last war in which British army wives were allowed to accompany their husbands on campaign, and thus bear witness to and share the terrible catalogue of suffering, death and disease that war brings in its wake.'

Helen Rappaport, *No Place for Ladies: The Untold Story of Women in the Crimean War*

# Prologue

*'Live life when you have it. Life is a splendid
gift – there is nothing small about it.'*
Florence Nightingale

## *Liverpool, 1837*

'I might be in luck,' muttered the midwife quietly
to herself as she delivered the baby safely on to
the bed. And she was right: the child's face was
indeed covered by a thin, silvery membrane. It
was a caul, so rare that this was the first she'd ever
seen. It was a valued talisman and she knew full
well that she'd be able to get good money for it. In
all the time she'd been delivering babies in these
streets, in all that time, she'd never had a caul.
And the moment she saw it she knew exactly what
she would do: she wouldn't say a thing to the
mother; she would have that caul for herself. She
had only ever heard stories from other women
who attended births about how much you could
get for one. They were so rare that no one she
knew had ever had one for themselves. But this
would be hers and she knew plenty of sailors who
would be interested in buying such a powerful
token to keep them safe on a voyage. After all,
everybody knew that a man who carried a caul
could never drown.

She grabbed a piece of clean cloth from the side

of the bed and pressed it flat to the baby's face, hoping that the transparent membrane covering the child's nose and mouth would stick fast and not scrunch up. She took her time with this, trying to get the best position on the cloth.

'Why isn't the baby crying?' said the mother from the other end of the bed.

The midwife didn't reply; she was at a crucial stage: the caul was just starting to stick to the cloth.

'Mrs O'Dowd?' said the mother more urgently.

'Just a moment...' muttered the midwife as the caul started to peel off the baby's face.

'Mrs O'Dowd,' said the mother with rising panic in her voice, 'is the baby all right?'

At last the caul was safe and Mrs O'Dowd laid it carefully aside before turning her attention to the baby. It was still a bit blue and didn't seem to be breathing so she picked up a piece of flannel and wiped out its nose and then gave its body a bit of a rub. Still nothing, so she got a towel and used it to rub the baby all over. Then it started to snuffle.

'Baby's fine, Maggie, she's just fine.'

'Is it a girl?' said the mother.

'It is indeed a girl,' said Mrs O'Dowd, looking up with a smile, 'and she's a bonny baby girl as well.'

Maggie laid her head back down on the pillow with a sigh of relief.

'Now I'll just cut the cord and you can have a hold of her,' she said, fishing in her pocket for two pieces of apron string. 'I need to tie these very tight or there'll be blood squirting everywhere.'

When the pieces of apron string were tied tight about an inch apart on the cord, the midwife took the sharp knife that she always carried for the purpose and sliced it through, separating the baby from its mother with one clean stroke. That's when the baby started to cry, to properly cry. Maggie looked anxiously down the bed again as Mrs O'Dowd took a knitted blanket and laid the writhing baby on it, wrapping her firmly and then cradling her expertly with one arm before walking up to the top of the bed and handing the sticky, crying bundle to the mother.

'You did very well there, Maggie,' said Mrs O'Dowd as she stood with her hands on her hips watching the mother soothe her baby, then seeing the baby open her dark eyes to look at her mother for the very first time. There was no crying now.

'Will you look at that, Maggie, she knows you already.'

Maggie smiled and spoke a few words to her daughter.

Mrs O'Dowd stood for a few moments more, sharing this special time with mother and baby, and then she roused herself and said, 'Now, Maggie, you might remember from when your first was born, we need to get the afterbirth out.'

Moving back down to the bottom of the bed the midwife thought all was progressing as it should, so she readied herself, only to find that there didn't seem to be anything moving but there was quite a lot of blood and it was starting to pool on the bed.

'Maggie,' she said, trying to keep the rising panic out of her voice, 'you're doing very well but

11

could you try and bear down a little to push the afterbirth along?'

'I'll try,' said Maggie but she had no strength left to push and seemed to be getting a bit sleepy.

The midwife looked again between the woman's legs; the bleeding was steady and there was still no sign of the afterbirth.

'How are you feeling?' said Mrs O'Dowd, looking up to her face, an element of unease creeping in. Maggie gazed at the midwife and tried to speak but stumbled on her words. 'Not so good,' she said at last, her voice very quiet. 'Take the baby ... will you...' she murmured, her voice slurring then tailing off.

To her credit, Mrs O'Dowd stayed calm enough to swiftly remove the baby from the mother's limp grasp. But after she placed her in the wooden crib, carefully prepared with a spotlessly clean sheet, she turned back to the bed to see with alarm that blood was flowing more heavily now, soaking into the mattress. Within seconds there was blood dripping from underneath the bed on to the scrubbed wooden floor.

In full panic, her mouth dry and her heart racing, Mrs O'Dowd did her best to try and grasp the afterbirth and deliver it. When this didn't work she stuffed a ball of cloth up the birth canal to try and put some pressure on to stop the bleeding. But nothing could be done. The afterbirth was stuck fast, the bleeding was torrential, and within minutes she was watching in horror as Maggie's face and hands turned white and her life ebbed away.

Mrs O'Dowd stood helpless, a sob rising in her

chest. This had happened to her before, more than once, a woman bleeding right in front of her eyes, and she knew that there was absolutely nothing she could do about it. Nothing at all, except go to the top of the bed and hold on to the woman's hand, hold her fast. And in no time at all Maggie was gone and the room was silent except for the drip, drip of her blood on to the wooden floor.

The midwife stood for some time with her head bowed, still holding Maggie's hand. When she came to, knowing there were things that needed to be done, she looked down and saw the baby girl wriggling in the crib, already loosening the blanket around her. Poor little mite, she thought, starting out in this world with no mother. Poor little thing. And then she thought grimly that the caul hadn't brought the little one much luck so far, but then who knew what the future might hold? And as she stood there looking at the baby, Mrs O'Dowd felt goose bumps on her arms and a prickling at the back of her neck and she knew for sure that the little girl was going to be a special one.

Letting go of Maggie's hand, Mrs O'Dowd reached over and gently closed her eyes. Death in childbed was common but all the midwives she knew took pains to conduct decent and proper rituals for preparing the mother's body. Now, we need to get things in order, she said to herself, pulling the sheet up to cover the dead woman's face.

Seeing the caul by the side of the bed, Mrs O'Dowd drew in a sharp breath; she wasn't sure she would be able to take it with her now. Then

13

again, what would they do with it here? There was only Maggie's father and he would be completely overwhelmed by all of this. It would be the last thing on his mind. He might not even want to see it, not after what had happened. So she reached out and took the caul, quietly slipping it into her bag before she could change her mind.

Maggie's father had been out to work on the docks that day. He knew his daughter was labouring and was hoping to come home to find the job done. After all, it was the second child to be born to his only daughter and from what he understood the labour should be quicker. The first, when Frank was born, had lasted for days and he had been coming and going to and from work with the sound of her wailing and screaming in his head.

As he approached their small home he was relieved not to hear the screams out in the street; all seemed quiet and calm in there. Closing the door behind him, he could hear movement in the one room that they had upstairs but no excited chatter of the women or the sound of a baby crying. A feeling of heaviness gripped his heart and his voice would not come out properly as he called up the stairs.

'Everything all right up there, Mrs O'Dowd?'

He heard a gasp from the midwife and within seconds she was clattering down the stairs, her face ashen, trying to hold back the tears. He knew instantly something was badly wrong.

'Is the baby...?' He couldn't get the words out.

'Yes, yes, the baby is safe, Mr Houston, but Maggie, she ... she...' Her words broke on a sob.

'I'm so sorry, there was nothing I could do.'

Padraic Houston had lived long enough to know that many women died during childbirth. That, in fact, women who found themselves with child carried the prospect of their own death alongside the joy of bringing new life. But that's what happened to other women; this was his Maggie, his little girl.

He stood in the small parlour of his own home, his hand across his mouth, holding back the sobs. Mrs O'Dowd stood in front of him, unable to find any words of comfort, but gently placing her hand – still stained with Maggie's blood – on his arm. It was the tentative cry of the baby girl lying alone in her wooden crib upstairs that did it in the end and the man crumpled as if someone had punched him. Mrs O'Dowd grabbed him and held him close as he stood there crying, patting his shoulder and trying to find some soothing words. Padraic nodded a few times but could not speak, his voice strangled back in his throat. He pulled away from the midwife and went out through the door.

No one knew where Padraic Houston went that day and he could not remember. He walked and walked and was gone for three hours. Mrs O'Dowd did not worry; she had seen this reaction before and knew that he would be back. What's more, she had known Padraic for years; he was a good man, a steady man with regular employment on the harbour, a freight clerk who needed to wear a collar and tie for the job. He would be back for the grandchildren.

She stayed with the baby and took care of Maggie's body, cleaning off as much of the blood as she could. She knew that they would need a clean mattress under her; it had been drenched with blood and was completely ruined.

The women from down the street had already been in. They always knew, without being told, what was happening in each of the houses. They had helped Mrs O'Dowd mop up the pool of blood under the bed; they had brought scrubbing brushes and had a good go at the stain that remained, but no amount of scrubbing could clear it and the blood had soaked through between the floorboards, becoming a part of the fabric of that house forever.

Then they helped Mrs O'Dowd roll Maggie's body and pull the clean mattress under her. It had been borrowed from two doors down where Mrs Regan was looking after Maggie's little lad, Frank. He was too young to know properly what was going on but they would take him up to see his mother when he came home. They would let him sit on the bed and touch her cold skin and say goodbye, so that he would have some under-standing of what had happened and, in time, know that she was gone.

When Padraic returned he had the strength to see Maggie's body and to give a name to his new granddaughter. He called her Ada, after his own mother. And the next day he set off with a heavy heart to see the priest and arrange not just a christening, but a burial that would take place on the same day.

# 1

*'There is no part of my life, upon which I can
look back without pain.'*
Florence Nightingale

## *Liverpool, 1844*

Padraic relished the Sunday afternoons that he
could spend at home with the children. From their
small house they could hear the noise of the port
and sometimes smell whatever cargo was in dock.
He liked to be able to hear the ships loading and
unloading, the hum of the harbour, occasional
shouts, and know that for one day, he did not need
to be involved, he did not need to be recording
numbers in a ledger or arguing over tallies.

On these days Ada would sit on his knee and
chatter away to him as he told stories of sailors
and mermaids and pirates. Frank would be sitting
at his feet playing with some wooden blocks and
the carved figures that Padraic had made for him.
The boy seemed to be able to spend endless
hours stacking and restacking the blocks, moving
the figures around, completely lost in a world of
his own.

Ada, now seven, was sitting on her grandfather's
knee one Sunday, snuggled up to his waistcoat
where she could hear the tick of his watch, when
she looked up at Padraic and said, 'Mary Regan

17

says that I'm a bastard.'

'What did she say?'

'She said that I'm a bastard.'

'Well, you tell Mary Regan that you are not a bastard. You have a father but he is a sailor and he is out at sea.'

Frank turned from his play with the blocks and asked, 'Is he, Grandfather, is he?' Padraic had never seen young Frank as interested in anything ever.

'He is indeed and a very good sailor too.'

'See, Ada,' said Frank, 'I told you so.'

It seemed that there had been all kinds of conversations going on that Padraic had not been party to. Not wanting to disclose any more information about the man who had given his daughter two children but never married her, Padraic tried to change the subject.

'Well, Ada, did I tell you about the man who saw a mermaid sitting on the harbour wall?'

'I knew that anyway,' said Ada, slipping from Padraic's knee and confronting her brother. 'I knew that, I just didn't want to talk about it.'

Frank stood up and glared at his sister. 'You did not, you said it wasn't true.'

'I never did,' Ada snapped back at him.

'You did so,' Frank replied, leaning down and bringing his face close to Ada's.

Padraic could see that Ada wasn't going to back down. Her breath was coming quickly and her shoulders were held square. 'Now then, Ada,' he said steadily, but she wasn't having any of that and in the next moment she was running upstairs and throwing herself on to the bed.

He gave her a minute then followed her up.

Sitting down on the creaky iron bedstead, still covered with the patchwork quilt that Maggie had made, he was forced to acknowledge that he should have taken the lead with this stuff and made sure the children had the story before others started telling it to them.

'I'm sorry, Ada,' he said, 'I should have talked to you about your father. It's just that when your mother died I was sad for a very long time and then we just got on with things and it never seemed the right time. Is it all right if I tell you a little bit about him now?' Ada nodded her head with her face still pressed into the pillow.

He took a deep breath, stroking his grand-daughter's hair as he spoke. 'Well, Ada, your father was a sailor. A strong, handsome fella with dark, curly hair and a bit of a swagger about him. You have his hair and your mother's eyes. And Frank has his father's eyes.'

Padraic glanced down the stairs. He could see Frank sitting on the bottom step, all ears.

'Well, your father once told me that he had sailed all around the world and seen many wonderful things: huge whales; dolphins leaping at the side of the boat; night skies so full of stars that you could hardly put a pin between them; pearls found by divers in the depths of the ocean. And he probably saw a few mermaids as well.'

'When is he coming back?' asked Ada, turning over and propping herself up on her elbows, with that adorable scrunch between her brows when she asked a question. Which was often.

'Well now, Ada, I just don't know, because when

the ships go out you never know when they might come back. They have so many adventures out there and sometimes they decide to stay longer.'

Padraic knew for a fact that the children's father, Francis, had been back into Liverpool at least twice since Ada was born, and each time he had sent word asking if he could see the children. But Padraic had not liked the man when Maggie was alive and he certainly didn't want to see him now, not with the life that he led, with the drinking and suchlike. He didn't want him near the children. Especially since he was sure that some of the things he remembered about Francis were beginning to show in Frank, a certain moodiness and stubborn streak, things that he didn't want to be reinforced by contact with the lad's father. The man was best away.

Ada was still scrunching her brows, not convinced, but Padraic didn't want any more questions about her father, and so again he tried to distract her.

'Well now, Ada, about that man who saw a mermaid sitting on the harbour wall...' Ada's eyes widened, and Padraic saw with relief that she was ready for a story.

'What colour was her hair, Grandfather?'

As Padraic launched into the story he began to feel tired, very tired. There was no doubt looking after the two youngsters was no easy task for a man of his age. Of course he wanted to care for them – while there was breath left in his body he would look after Maggie's children – but sometimes it was exhausting. And at times like these he missed his wife, Edna, more than ever. Yes, he was lucky to have Mrs Regan to mind the children while he was at work and she did a good job, but how much easier it would have been to still have Edna, to share in this life with the grandchildren. They had wanted to have more themselves but she had been sickly when they married, with a weak heart, and so they only had Maggie and then one winter she caught some fever that was doing the rounds and she was gone. As easy as that. How she would have loved to have been here now with these children.

Padraic felt a familiar tightness in his chest when he thought about Edna and, as he continued to tell the story, repeating the words that he had memorized when Maggie was a girl, his voice began to tremble and he felt a lump in his throat and then tears started to well up in his eyes. Ada missed nothing and she was soon scrunching her brows again. 'This isn't a sad story, Grandfather,' she said. 'Why are you crying?'

'Oh, I'm not crying, Ada,' he said, his voice thick with emotion. 'I think that mermaid must be giving me some salt water from the ocean, that's all.'

Ada reached up to wipe his tears with her small hand. He could tell she didn't believe him for one minute and in that moment he could feel her sympathy reaching out to him – as young as she was she seemed to understand and it helped him, it really helped. What would he do without Ada? Who would have thought that a child born on such a tragic day would turn out to be so sweet-natured. Yes, you'd expect her to be resilient and she was that too, and of course she could be

21

stubborn, just like her mother, but she was as smart as a whip and you could always talk to Ada and she would listen. And she loved a story. He would never have told anyone, not even Mrs Regan, but Ada was the reason he was able to keep going. Yes he loved Frank as well but, for Padraic, there was something very special about Ada.

## *Liverpool, 1855*

More years went by and Padraic's steel-grey hair turned to silver, but apart from a slight stoop of his shoulders he was still very much the man he used to be. Ada was proud of her grandfather's hair and loved to brush it for him, sweeping it back from his forehead with a flourish. She had just had her eighteenth birthday and he had given her a small silver and mother-of-pearl brooch with a clasp and a tiny chain to pin it to her blouse so that she would never lose it.

Ada loved to feel the smooth mother-of-pearl and see the shimmering colours dance in the light. She no longer believed in mermaids but if she had then this beautiful and exotic substance, which her grandfather had told her was found inside the shell of an oyster, would adorn the combs that they pulled through their hair.

She wore the brooch as she worked in the tiny kitchen of the house from where she could hear the noise of the port. She had wanted to find some work herself when she grew old enough but her grandfather had strongly opposed this, telling her that he needed her to work in the house, taking over the jobs that he had till then to pay for – the washing, the cooking, the cleaning. In truth he hated the thought of his beautiful Ada going out to work, scrubbing floors or cleaning up inside the ships after they had unloaded. He didn't want that for her; she was his precious girl.

Frank had grown tall and very strong and was proving to be a good porter, off-loading all kinds of cargo from the ships. Ada loved to hear about the merchandise and the places they came from, but Frank didn't talk much so her grandfather usually had to fill in the details of the silk and the brandy, the tea and the coffee and the bales of cotton.

Padraic was proud that Frank had found work on the docks, although he had been hoping the lad might follow him into the Dock Traffic Office as a clerk. But as Frank grew more muscle and began to look like a man who would need physical work, Padraic realized he had a good deal of his father in him and would need something that taxed him physically. He had mentioned to Frank that there was a position going but he knew what the answer would be. He knew that you could never force a lad like Frank to go in a certain direction; you had to let him find his own way and Frank's way turned out to be the harbour side. This was dangerous work. Padraic had been on the docks all his working life; he knew how many accidents there'd been. He made sure that Frank was aware of the risks, then he had to let him go, to do what some young men feel that they have to do. Padraic also saw that Frank had a quick temper and could have angry outbursts, and he knew, for sure, that he had already been in a number of scraps. He hoped that the lad would learn to control his temper.

That particular day, Ada was making a beef and carrot stew for their supper. It was cooking over the fire and she kept taking the lid off the iron pot to give it a stir. She was pleased by the quiet bubble of the meaty liquid.

There was a knock at the door and Ada shouted, 'Come in.' She knew that it would be Mary Regan. Although a couple of years older than Ada they had remained firm friends since childhood, despite their numerous spats and wrangles. Mary was already with child and each time that Ada saw her she was surprised by how much her belly had grown.

'Sit down, Mary,' she said, not able to take her eyes off her friend's swollen midriff. 'Take the weight off.'

Mary sat but she couldn't get all that close to the table. Ada couldn't stop laughing.

'We're going to have to cut a piece of the table out for you.'

'Hopefully it will be any day now,' said Mary, relief at this thought mingled with genuine fear.

'You'll be right enough with it,' said Ada, looping her arms around her friend's neck and giving her a bit of a snuggle. In truth she was terrified for Mary. She had helped out with other women in the street and having seen a birth she had no idea how any woman could manage such a terrifying feat. She kept thinking about the neighbour who had come to her door with terrible labour pains saying the baby was about to be born. She had had to drag the woman home and wait with her for Mrs O'Dowd to come. By the time the midwife got there the woman was screaming and pushing and there was a lot of blood. The baby was born dead. Ada pushed the thoughts away and told herself that Mary would be fine, she would be just fine. 'Now, Mary, I'm brewing some tea, and we have cake.'

They hadn't been sitting long in that warm and cosy kitchen when they heard an almighty crash from the direction of the docks. They knew what it meant, and it wasn't good – a load had been dropped from one of the new hydraulic cranes, and it sounded like a heavy one. The next minute they could hear frantic shouting and the sound of their neighbours opening their doors to look out.

These incidents happened every now and then but this sounded like a big one. Ada and Mary both knew instantly that the crash would mean that men had been harmed.

'Do you think...?' said Mary, her face white.

'No, we'll stay here,' said Ada firmly. 'I don't want you going down there in your condition. With that big belly you'll be knocking something else over.' Ada made herself smile to keep Mary relaxed but her face felt tight and there was a gnawing anxiety in the pit of her stomach.

'Do you want some more tea?' she asked, not waiting for her friend to respond before pouring it from the pot.

'Thanks,' said Mary, too distracted to continue with any other conversation. Ada flinched as they heard another smaller crash and both girls strained their ears to try and hear what might be going on. This time, ominously, there was no shouting. Then, as expected, they heard the sound of feet pounding up the street. Someone was running for the doctor. That was how it went.

Ada felt sick to her stomach. She knew that her grandfather worked inside at his desk so she wasn't too worried about him, but Frank was always out on the harbour side and today he was unloading a big ship full of timber. He'd gone out with a whistle that morning, thinking that he would be able to earn some extra.

The two girls sat tight at the kitchen table, the remains of the cake left on the plate. They continued to attempt some kind of conversation while listening out for what was going on.

They soon heard the pounding of feet going back the other way, towards the dock, and then the brisk, measured steps of the doctor.

Ada got up again to stir the stew and this time she took a small spoon and tasted it. It needed a bit more salt. She scooped some up from the small dish where it sat close to the fire and plopped it in without thinking. The next taste confirmed that the stew was very salty indeed. Irritated with herself now – Ada was proud of her cooking and liked it to be perfect – she bustled across the kitchen to a wooden box in the corner. She pulled out some sewing that she and Mary had been doing for the baby and, after a while, when there was no more noise from the docks, they both began to relax. 'No news is good news,' said Mary.

Time passed; Mary went home. It was the hour at which Grandfather was due to return. He didn't come. He was usually on time but sometimes could be held up with a miscalculation of cargo. Ada had known that happen before but there was no sign of Frank either and, strangely, none of the neighbours had been in to talk about the cargo that had been spilled or who had been injured at the dock.

The gnawing feeling in the pit of Ada's stomach was growing now in leaps and bounds. She knew there was something wrong.

She left the house. There was no one out on the street but she felt like she was being watched as she marched towards the dock. The place was full of ships packed together and there was a pile of broken timber on the side and a big piece of stone cracked in half where the crash must have taken place. There were plenty of men about on the harbour, people that she knew, but they didn't greet her and they looked away when she glanced in their direction.

She walked straight to the Dock Traffic building where her grandfather had worked since it opened. She loved this building, with its grand columns in front and the tall chimneys reaching up to the sky, but today she didn't see any of it. She walked straight in past all the men to the door of the office where the lower-ranking clerks had their desks and looked in through the round glass at the top of the door. He was there. The only one left in the room. Sitting with his back to her.

All of Ada's fears were made real in that moment as she stood outside the door, seeing her grandfather slumped in his chair with his head in his hands. She knew then that something terrible had happened and that once she opened the door and walked into the room she would become a part of it. She summoned up all her strength, took a few deep breaths and then grasped the door handle and quietly entered the room. 'Grandfather, do you need to tell me something?' she said gently.

He turned slowly in his chair and she gasped when she saw his face. He looked like he had aged by twenty years, his face hung with lines, his eyes drained of life.

'Grandfather,' she said again.

He could not speak; he kept opening and closing his mouth but no words would come. She went to him and crouched down in front of him, taking his hand.

'Tell me the story of what happened,' she said, feeling suddenly strong because he, for the first time in her life, seemed so weak.

'It's Frank,' he said at last.

Ada squeezed his hand; she had known it must be.

'He was on the deck of the big ship that came in and there was a sudden collapse of the cargo. They had a huge piece of timber, an oak tree, on the hydraulic crane and the chains slipped. It swung round, knocking some men into the harbour. Then it slipped and crashed on to the deck and down on the quay, crushing poor Tommy Simpson, crushing him to death.'

Padraic paused, gasping for air. Ada realized that she was squeezing his hand so tightly now that it hurt and she was staring at the floor. She released the pressure a little, glancing up to his face, a face that she no longer recognized.

'Go on,' she said, looking down at the floor again.

'No one really saw what happened to the men knocked into the harbour. The ships were packed in so tight that it was almost impossible to see where they fell. One was pulled out alive, but one man is still missing. Frank is missing.'

Ada squeezed her grandfather's hand even harder and felt a huge sob rise in her chest. She bowed her head for a moment to make sure that she locked that sob deep down. If she let it out now she would be of no use to him.

Padraic slumped forward as if all the breath had been knocked out of him. Ada got up and walked round behind his chair. She put her hand on his shoulder, standing behind him now with her head bowed and her heart pounding so fast and hard in her chest that she thought she might explode. She knew she had to try and calm herself; she had to take charge. She took a deep breath. It was hard to breathe in: her heart seemed to have taken over all the space inside her young body. She took another breath, insisting that her heart would calm. She battled with her frozen mind, until at last she was able to speak, but her voice sounded thin and strange to her ears. Not her voice.

'Have they been looking for him?'

At first he did not – could not – reply, but then he made a gasping sound and sat up a little straighter. 'All afternoon,' he said. 'No sign.'

Then he grabbed his hair with both hands, spitting out anguish with his next words: 'I told him not to get too close to those cranes, especially

29

when they were using chains. I told him, I warned him how easy it was for the load to swing round. I kept telling him.'

Ada felt that she was only half listening and couldn't react to what he was saying. Still trying to make some kind of plan, she snatched at thoughts and tried to patch them together.

'Somebody must know what's happened,' she said. 'Let me speak to them.'

'He must be dead,' said her grandfather, slumping forward again on to his desk.

'No,' she insisted. 'He could have ended up on another ship. Have ships gone out today?'

'Yes, plenty,' said her grandfather, his voice quiet.

Ada took another deep breath. 'Well, we need to search again, we need to ask around, he might be lying injured somewhere, he...'

'Ada, listen to me. There is no sign of him. He must be dead.'

'I don't believe it!' she said, feeling suddenly angry. 'And neither should you.'

She made towards the door but he shot up from his chair, coming back to life at last.

'Ada,' he said, his voice getting stronger, 'I need you to take me home.'

Hearing the pain in his voice, she stopped in her tracks and felt the sob in her chest rising up. Still fighting to control it she had to let some tears start to flow, spilling down her cheeks. Turning to him, she went to his side and took him by the arm, supporting him as he walked unsteadily out of the office while the other clerks stood by, their heads bowed, as if watching a funeral pass.

It seemed to take an age for Ada to get her grandfather back to their small home. She felt that she was moving as if in a play, acting out a part as though this was happening to someone else. She was there but not there. Ada could feel the weight that he was putting on her and knew how much he was struggling. It felt like the street was empty but there must have been some passers-by.

As they got closer to their own front door she saw one or two standing, looking at them, their faces sombre. Ada hated it already, being the centre of attention, and she felt furious that these people were standing and staring and not down on the harbour looking for Frank.

Ada felt the weight ease a little as one of the Regan lads took Padraic's other arm. She looked over and recognized one of Mary's brothers, the one who had tried to kiss her last Christmas. He glanced across at her but said nothing. Together they manhandled her grandfather into the kitchen and sat him at the table, where he slumped forward again, his arms cradling his head.

Once the Regan lad was released he removed his cap and folded it, then stood by the table with it in both hands, turning it over as if not knowing what to do with it. 'Sorry for your loss,' he said, instantly regretting his words when Ada threw a sharp glance at him.

'Not yet,' she said. 'He is missing, that's all.' All the while feeling the sickening lurch of her stomach and the tight pounding of her heart.

Seeing the stricken look on the lad's face, Ada thanked him and said that they would be fine.

The lad nodded and mumbled something before shoving his cap back on his head and leaving as swiftly as he could without showing disrespect.

Ada went to the fire and lifted the lid off the stew. It was dried out and starting to burn. She removed it from the plate and put the kettle on to boil, brewing them a cup of tea that neither of them could drink.

Eventually Padraic stood and spoke softly to Ada. 'I'm going to bed. Will you be all right, lass?'

'I will,' she said, glad that he seemed calmer.

'We'll see what tomorrow brings,' he said, setting a foot on the stairs then climbing heavily as if the weight of all the world rested on his back. Ada watched him go and held her breath.

Two steps from the top his foot slipped. She gasped and shot up from her chair. He made a sound, not even a word, and held his right hand out towards her with his fingers splayed. Ada sat back down and let him continue. She had to leave him; he needed to be alone up there at one side of the partition that they had made when Frank was getting older. A flimsy divide that gave each of them some private space when Frank was getting too big to share a bed with Padraic.

She sat and listened to him move slowly around the room upstairs, heard the belt of his breeches hit the floor as he took them off, letting them fall to the ground rather than folding them neatly over the chair back as was his usual practice. She heard the heavy sound of the bed as he slumped down on it and then the creaking of the bed frame as he tossed from side to side, trying to get to sleep. Then it went quiet and she was left sitting alone at the kitchen table with two cups of cold tea, feeling exhausted but with all kinds of thoughts singing through her head: anger for what she thought might have been Frank's reckless behaviour starting to seep in.

She felt that she would never sleep again but knew that she had to try to go to bed. So, leaving the cold tea on the table she slipped out of her clothes and into a nightgown, then drew back the curtain of the small bed space that nestled under the stairs.

This was usually one of her favourite moments of the day. The outside of the curtain was a plain brown fabric, serviceable stuff that all the houses used. The inside, however, provided a magical space. She had made it from a spoiled bolt of cloth that her grandfather had brought back from the docks one day. They weren't sure but they thought it was silk from China. It had fallen from a cargo on to the deck and had been mostly ruined by sea water, but Ada had found just enough to make a panel for her curtain and, for her, it was like a porthole into another world.

She lay there now looking at the square of pale yellow silk, a patch of sunshine in her time of need. She remembered the day Grandfather had brought it home, how excited they both were unrolling it on to the kitchen table, finding a section unspoiled and seeing for the first time the splendour of the embroidery, the pale pink and luscious blues and reds woven into flowers and butterflies and exotic birds, all on a background of the warmest yellow. Just the right colour to give calm.

As Ada lay there she looked at the woven scene

33

and moved her gaze from butterfly to flower to bird as she often did. That night though she didn't see it in her usual way, creating stories in her head as she went. That night she used it to try and calm herself by counting the number of pink flowers, then the butterflies and so on, until she felt some kind of relief coming over her body. Then and only then could she let out the deep sobs inside her chest and let flow the salt tears that she had been struggling to hold back. She lay on her side and let them flow and flow into her pillow.

There was no sound from upstairs; at least her grandfather had settled.

Ada slept fitfully, and woke listening for something, although she didn't know what. The house was quiet, just the noises of the next-door neighbours raking the fire and the dull mumble of morning voices.

It took a second or two for Ada to recall what had happened, and when she did the shock came back to her with new force. She shot up in bed, straining her ears for the sound of Frank's snore or anything that might indicate that it had all been a mistake; that he had made his way home in the night and would be wondering what all the fuss was about.

But there was no sound from upstairs, no sound at all.

Grandfather must be exhausted, she thought as she made herself get up to start the day. She needed to light the fire and start breakfast before he came down. She pulled on her clothes and nipped out through the back door to the shared privy. She was expecting to see some of the neighbours waiting in line, but there was no one. It must be a bit later than I thought, she said to herself.

She knew that she would never get used to the shared privy. She hated it, preferring to use the chamber pot if she could, but that was under her grandfather's bed and she didn't want to disturb him yet.

Taking a shovel of coal on the way back into the house, she set to and raked the cinders. She felt empty and sore inside, and her hands were shaking as she placed a few sticks in the grate. Doing her usual work helped a little and she knew that she would have to keep busy, to stop herself thinking about Frank. When she'd made sure that her grandfather was all right she would go back down to the dock and try to find out what had happened and what needed to be done next.

She knew that Padraic wouldn't be going in to work, but she thought that she should now go and wake him; he needed to be getting up and having his breakfast. He might want to go down the street and make some enquiries about Frank himself.

She climbed the stairs, gently calling his name.

He must have been exhausted and still be sleeping, she thought, when there was no reply. Yes, that's it, she thought, seeing the line of his back under the covers as he lay on his side facing away from her.

Unwilling to disturb him from the sleep that was protecting him from shock and sorrow, she stood for a few moments gazing down on him.

35

Asleep in the same bed that her mother had lain in to give birth to her eighteen years ago and that she had shared with Frank when they were little. It still had the same patchwork quilt and the same simple crucifix on the wall over the bed head. She glanced to the other wall and saw the small black iron grate where she had played at keeping house, a stack of coins and a comb resting on the mantel that Padraic had taken from his pocket before undressing, and his breeches on the floor, the only thing that was out of place in this well-loved environment.

He was still flat out so she moved quietly to shake his arm.

The flesh beneath his shirt felt soft and his arm flopped back behind him at a strange angle.

'Grandfather,' she said, shaking him harder. Then: 'Grandfather!' much louder when she got no response. She rolled him back towards her and he slumped over, his face blotched dark red, his lips white and his unseeing eyes staring at the ceiling.

Ada started to scream, then to wail, and she continued to shake the poor, lifeless corpse of Padraic Houston until those next door and a passer-by in the street broke through the front door and ran up the stairs to help.

Someone with strong arms grabbed her from behind and tried to pull her back from the bed, but Ada fell to her knees, ragged sobs escaping from her body as she held on to her grandfather's arm. She felt someone – it must have been Mrs Hanlon, the neighbour from next door that she hardly knew – place a hand on her shoulder. A hand that seemed to understand something of what she was going through but could offer no comfort for Ada.

'Fetch the doctor, fetch the doctor!' she screamed, and the voice of Mrs Hanlon replied, telling her that someone had gone for him. It wouldn't be long.

It seemed to take forever before Ada heard the sound of a leather-soled shoe on the wooden stairs and the doctor was there by the bedside, confirming the news she had been dreading.

Ada glared at him, shouting, 'No, no!' and grasped her grandfather's hand more tightly.

The doctor stood for a moment then shook his head and indicated to Mrs Hanlon that he wanted to speak to her downstairs. They left the room and Ada continued to kneel by the bed. She vowed to herself that she would not move from the side of that bed until someone could do something about this.

She could hear the murmur of voices from downstairs and felt that she needed to know what was being said. Standing up from the bed, she took another moment to look at her grandfather's beloved face and then leant down and pulled the cover up to his chin. Not over his face, not yet, but up to his chin.

Her legs were weak and her heart was racing but she managed to climb down the stairs. The doctor was just leaving and gave her a sorrowful look as he went through the door.

Mrs Hanlon turned to her and repeated what the doctor had said: 'They think his heart gave out, just gave out, what with the shock of what happened yesterday.'

Ada found herself crying again and starting to sob.

'Go back upstairs,' said Mrs Hanlon gently. 'Go back up and spend some time with him while you can.'

Ada nodded and then she was climbing the stairs and kneeling beside the bed, reaching out to hold on to her grandfather's hand.

She couldn't even think about Frank now. She pushed the thoughts away and tried to cling to a happier version of events: he was missing, he would be back, and she would need to tell him about what had happened to grandfather, and how he had given her such a scare.

But it was starting to sink in: there would be only bad news to tell Frank. Their grandfather was gone. He was gone and there would be no more stories, and no more of his wonderful smiles. She would never hear the sound of his voice again or feel the warm touch of his hand. She felt completely devastated, all alone in the world, an orphan.

At some stage she felt a hand on her shoulder and turned to find Mary's shocked face looking down at her, tears in her eyes. She got up and Mary hugged her as closely as she could with her pregnant belly. Ada could feel the baby kicking frantically. How strange, she thought, it feels like it knows that something is wrong.

Mary's mother came to help her daughter's stricken friend, saying a prayer for a man that she thought very highly of, a man that she had known all of her married life. When she was finished Mrs

Regan pulled herself up from the bed and looked down at him, scarcely able to believe the bad luck that had struck his family. 'Well, Padraic Houston, you've been a good man and no man could have done a better job with those two grandchildren. May you rest in peace now, Padraic, and don't you worry, we'll help look after your Ada.'

# 2

*'So I never lose an opportunity of urging a practical beginning, however small, for it is wonderful how often in such matters the mustard-seed germinates and roots itself.'*
Florence Nightingale

After the priest had said his final Amen and gone, Ada went back up the stairs to find some money for the coffin. As she entered the room she was almost surprised to find her grandfather still lying there on his back with the two big pennies over his eyes where she had laid them herself.

Wiping away her tears, she went to the fireplace and pulled out the tin with a picture of Queen Victoria on the lid from the space in the chimney. She couldn't remember how old she was when he had showed it to her but it was a few years back and she had felt very special as she stood there with him swearing her to secrecy and instructing her to tell no one where it was hidden, not even Frank. It was a bit dusty on top but in there she found some notes and coins. She didn't know how much a coffin cost but took out a handful of notes. As she did she saw a piece of yellowed paper folded at the bottom of the tin. It crossed her mind that she should be wondering what it was, but she felt so strange and slowed up she couldn't even bring herself to lift the paper out and examine it.

'Thanks, Ada,' said Mrs Regan, counting out the notes she needed then telling her to put the rest back and not tell anyone where she kept it. 'Not anyone,' she said emphatically. 'There have been too many cases of the recently bereaved being robbed around here for us to take any chances.'

Recently bereaved, thought Ada, mulling the phrase over in her head.

Later that day the coffin was brought and it just fitted up the stairs and into the bedroom. The joiner had a couple of his men with him and they lifted Padraic into the box, leaving the lid propped at the side, leaning against the wall.

Ada told Mrs Regan to make all the arrangements at the church and things were done around her. The Regans stayed close with her all through that day and during the wake of the night. Someone brought in a bottle of whisky and a few glasses were drunk. Ada would have none; she had once had a sip and had disliked the strong burning liquid that made her gasp. Neither did she want anything to do with the substance that could turn normal hard-working men into the violent beasts that she sometimes heard and encountered out on the streets of Liverpool.

Time passed in a blur, and by the morning of the funeral Ada had entered some other kind of existence. She walked with Mary behind the coffin on the way up to the church, the neighbours standing out in the street with their heads bowed and caps off, the street quiet apart from the whimper of a child and the noise of the port as the world continued to turn. She heard the sound of crying and then she realized it was herself and Mary.

Four strong men from the Regan family carried the coffin on their shoulders over the short distance to the church. A real mark of respect, everyone knew that – if it had been someone of lesser standing they would have needed to pay for the wheeled cart to trundle him up the cobbles. But Padraic Houston was held in high esteem. He had been a very good man.

She would recall snatches of the mass and the final lowering of the coffin into the grave that held Padraic's Edna and his daughter, Maggie. Then the priest's voice saying ashes to ashes and the heavy, broken sound of the handful of soil that she threw down on to the lid.

In the days that followed the funeral Ada tried to make sense of her situation but her thoughts did not seem to be able to connect. She attempted to keep up with her daily cycle of chores but somehow things got mixed up. She found herself standing staring out of the window or holding a book that was her grandfather's, or sitting at his place in the kitchen holding one of his shirts.

She kept thinking that she was doing all right, that she was managing well, and then her eyes would fall on something that belonged to him or she would find a small item, like a stub of a pencil, and she would burst into tears. Floods of tears.

She struggled to sleep at night but found herself needing a nap during the day and dozing off almost anywhere, sometimes lying on his bed or wandering into Frank's room. She was completely disconnected from the reality of Frank's disappearance, not making any effort to go to the dock, ask any questions or find anything out, still telling herself that he would turn up one of these days 'like a bad penny'. Mary and Mrs Regan had told her that they would listen out for any news and let her know. But although they regularly came in with food and to relight the fire for Ada when she forgot to put more coal on, there was never any news about Frank.

Ada sometimes fancied she heard the sound of her grandfather upstairs: a creak of a floorboard as he moved around; the sound of him getting out of bed, especially in the early morning, as if he was getting ready for work. She would wake hearing this, having forgotten overnight that he was dead and gone.

She would hear his voice calling down to her, with the rising intonation on her name, about to ask her a question. Sometimes she would almost shout back, and then the reality would hit her. As she sat at the table she could hear his conversation and him regularly telling her not to be afraid, that she was strong and clever and who knows what she might achieve.

'You are here for a reason, Ada.'

Then she would hear him ask her if he had told her the story about the ... but he would never say what. And, like he'd always told her, 'One day you will tell your own stories, Ada.'

Sometimes she would dream that she was sitting on his knee and they were talking. She was trying to tell him one of her made-up, childish stories. He would say she had a good imagination. 'What's imagination, Grandfather?' And he would tell her and then write the word down for her with the stub of a pencil he always carried in his pocket, spelling it out and breaking it down, 'I-mag-in-ation', and then repeating it, making sure that she got the new word. 'I like that word, Grandfather.' And she would add it to all the other words that he had given her since he first showed her the letters and taught her the sounds, making sure that his Ada, and her brother Frank, would be able to read.

Well-meaning neighbours and acquaintances called in to offer their respects and give advice, sometimes telling her – trying to make her feel better – that there were deaths all the time, every day, in Liverpool. People were falling under carts, setting themselves on fire, drowning in the harbour, falling down stairs, being murdered. Someone told her that the other day a woman had slipped on an orange peel in the street and fallen to the ground, broken her thigh bone and died from the injury. As easy as that. So don't be surprised at anything that can happen, Ada. At least the old man died in his bed, peacefully sleeping, at least there was that.

But he is still dead, she wanted to scream at

them. And no matter how he died the pain for her was the same. She knew they meant well, the people who came back and forth through the house at that time, but young as she was, she knew that she would have to go through this terrible pain on her own and try to grieve in the best way she could.

Mrs Regan came in to tell her that Mary's baby had been born, a healthy baby boy, and Ada smiled and asked about her friend but could not feel any real joy. She was just numb.

She wandered around the house with her mother-of-pearl brooch pinned to her blouse, all the time using up the stash of coins that her grandfather had hidden for a rainy day along with his funeral money. This felt like much more than a rainy day; this felt like the end of the world.

Anyway, she kept pottering along and the money kept going down until some weeks later, when the people had stopped coming in with food, she found herself feeling a bit hungry. She went to the stash to get some money so she could go up to the shop, but there was only one penny coin left, just one.

As she stood over the bed where she'd placed the empty tin, holding the single, last penny in her hand, she looked into the box again. It was completely empty apart from that piece of yellowed paper lining the bottom. Lifting it out to check if there was any chance of more money beneath it she unfolded the paper and found that it had some writing on it. The ink had faded and the letters were badly shaped but when she went over to the window, she could just make out the words:

*Dear Maggie Houston,*

*My man Francis cannot marry you. He has a wife and a child all ready.*

*Signed,*
*X*
*(the mark of his wife Marie)*

Ada reeled back. Seeing her mother's name and then the name of her father was a shock. With everything that had happened over the last few weeks she had forgotten about her past life and besides, no one had told her much, even about her mother, the woman who had died in this room, in this bed, bringing her into the world.

Why had she not asked her grandfather more questions when she had the chance? She should have asked. But then she remembered the few times that she had questioned him about Maggie, how it had set him off crying and she had felt bad. She couldn't bear to see him upset and so she had stopped asking. She had kept quiet and if she had any questions she'd asked Frank. But he'd been too small to remember their mother; he was useless.

Mary had told her that Mrs Regan always said what a grand woman Maggie Houston was but there was no detail, so Ada had no picture of her in her head. Seeing the letter in her hand now brought a flood of regret. She sagged with it and sat down heavily on the bed, lying back across the mattress with the letter resting lightly on her

45

chest. As she stared up at the ceiling she felt helpless and even more alone and the tears began to flow down the sides of her face and drip on to the patchwork quilt. How must Maggie have felt when she got this letter? There was no date on it – when did she get it? All these questions flying around in her head and no one in the world who could answer them. Except, of course, the person who had sent the note, this Marie, this other woman. But there was no address on the letter; it would be impossible to find her. Did she even want to find her and her child, someone who could be her half-brother or -sister? And this Francis, this father of hers whom she hadn't even known by name, was he still alive? Even if he was, why should she seek him out? He had never shown any interest in her or Frank; he had never been near!

Ada continued to lie on the bed until the tears stopped flowing and then she sat up. Seeing the letter in her hand she used all her strength to scrunch it up into a ball and then throw it hard against the window. It bounced back and rolled under the bed and that's where she left it.

Feeling her belly growl with hunger she scrabbled around for the money that had slipped from her hand on to the bed. Then she ripped the patchwork quilt off, sending the tin box clattering on to the floor. She didn't even hear the noise or bother that she had left it discarded as she pulled at the quilt, dragging it behind her down the stairs.

That same quilt, the one that had been hand-stitched by her mother, was the first item that she took to the pawn shop. The first of many. She was ruthless in the way that she pulled pots and pans and cutlery out of the cupboards and the covers and ornaments off the surfaces of the house, angrily ripping apart the life that she had there, the life that she could no longer share. Each time she came back from a trip to the pawn shop she felt emptier inside but also lighter and it was with some satisfaction that she put the pawn tickets into a teacup. The only things that she couldn't touch were Grandfather's pocket-watch, her mother-of-pearl brooch, the red shawl that had been her mother's, the silk-lined curtain and the stuff in Frank's room. The rest was fair game as far as Ada was concerned, even down to the crucifix over the bed head and then the bed head itself.

As she worked her way through the house, she left drawers pulled out and debris lying on the floor. She stripped the old place down until in the end she had three full teacups of pawn tickets and not much else.

So what now? She couldn't think of where to go next. And that's when the people started coming back into the house, tutting a bit, saying they were sorry, saying they were worried about her. She still wasn't really listening, not until Mrs Regan spoke to Mary and Mary came to see her.

Mary tapped on the door as she always used to, like she had done on the day of the accident. It felt like that was years ago now. Ada heard the familiar tap and shouted, 'Come in.'

Mary found her best friend sitting at the table with teacups full of pawn tickets, an empty grate and hardly anything left in the house that made it look like a home.

Ada looked up and Mary was hard-pressed to recognize her old friend.

'What the blazes have you been doing in here, Ada Houston?' said Mary, her eyes darting round the kitchen and taking in the dirt and the disorder.

'What do you mean?' said Ada with a note of defiance rising in her voice. 'Somebody had to sort this lot out and unless you've forgotten what's happened here I'm the only one left.'

'I can see that,' said Mary, picking up a tea cloth discarded on the floor and going over to one of the drawers and shoving it to. 'Indeed I can.'

'What do you mean?' spat Ada, pushing back her chair and squaring up to Mary.

'This place is a tip, an absolute tip.'

'How dare you,' said Ada, glaring at her friend. 'How dare you, Mary Regan.'

Mary stood and looked at her friend for a moment. Her hair was wild and unbound, her clothes were grubby and she had the light of a maniac in her eyes.

'I know it's been hard for you,' she said in a much gentler voice. 'I know it's been hard but I'm here to help you now. Just have a look round this place, Ada, what would your poor grandfather think?'

'What would he think?' shouted Ada. 'What would he think? He's dead!'

Mary crossed herself and muttered, 'God rest his soul,' then she looked at Ada standing in the wreck of her own kitchen with her fists balled and knew that she had to take things in hand.

'Yes, he's dead,' said Mary, raising her own voice, 'but that doesn't mean you can let things go to wrack and ruin.'

'What do you know?' shouted Ada back at her. 'What do you know? He's gone and left me here all alone, without Frank, with nothing!'

Mary took a step back, unsure whether Ada was going to fly at her like a cat with its claws out, just as she'd done when they were little.

'Yes he has,' she said from a safer distance, 'but he didn't mean to die, Ada, he didn't mean to die. The last thing he would have wanted to do was leave you here on your own. You know that, Ada, don't you? You know how he felt about you.'

Mary waited, standing completely still in front of Ada, and then gave an inward sigh of relief as she saw her friend unclench her fists and look around the kitchen as if she was seeing it for the first time. Then Ada's head sank and she started to cry, big sobs coming out of her small body.

Mary was straight there, putting her arms around her, holding her tight, almost squeezing the breath out of her. She let her cry and then she loosened her embrace and stood back a little, taking a look at her friend close up.

'You know what my mam always calls you, Ada? Little Ada with the big heart. And it's true. Sometimes things that happen are too much for people like you, but you know what, me and you are from the same stock. You remember the story of our people coming off the boats from Ireland, starving hungry with nothing but the clothes on their backs? We have the same blood, Ada, the same blood, and we can get through anything. We

Regans and Houstons, we've always had it tough and that's how I know you will come through this, Ada, you will come through.'

Ada drew back, still unsure, but starting to really listen to what her friend had to say.

Mary laid a hand on her arm. 'All right then, Ada. All right. Let's get this place tidied up.'

Ada nodded.

'That's my girl,' said Mary, moving instinctively to give her friend another hug, then looking down at her. 'But you might want to give your face a bit of a wash first,' she said, seeing the smudges of grime on Ada's tear-stained face. 'And maybe do something with that mop of hair: you could have a bird nesting in that lot and you wouldn't even know about it.'

Ada looked up and smiled for the first time since her grandfather had died; she actually smiled. Her face felt tight with the strangeness of using muscles that had become set with grief and she began to realize where she was and what had happened.

'I don't know where I've been,' said Ada, staring down at the floor.

'Well, don't worry about that. It takes us different ways, but we come out of it, we come back. So chin up ... I'll put some of this water in the kettle and go and see if I can scrape up some coal to light the fire. You get a cloth round your face and wash off that muck and for God's sake do summat about your hair,' said Mary, brushing some of the dark brown curls away from her friend's face. 'That's better. I can see you now.'

Once Ada was cleaned up and ready for work it

didn't take long for the girls to go through the small house and set things straight. By that time Mary had the fire lit and the kettle on and the water was boiling. Telling Ada to sit down at the table, she went to the cupboard to find the cups then cracked up laughing when she found it empty.

'What?' said Ada.

'It's a good job you used the teacups for your pawn tickets cos there's nowt in the cupboard to make a brew with,' said Mary.

Ada started laughing and then emptied two of the cups out on to the table, piling the pawn tickets up.

'I don't even know what I've been eating or drinking these last few weeks,' she said.

'Well, it's time to start now,' said Mary. 'Mam sent us some scone to have with a brew, so let's get you started on a thick slice of Mrs Regan's driest offering.'

Ada giggled, remembering Mrs Regan's baking.

'It's like flint grit, this stuff,' said Mary, 'but it'll fill your belly.'

Ada felt good to be sitting back at the kitchen table with Mary. She still felt the dark shadow of the last time they had sat there but just for now it was pushed back into the corners of the room. At first she found herself sitting tensely, listening to Mary but very aware of the sound of the docks, a sound that she'd been trying to blot out for weeks. She knew what she was listening for, she knew what she was dreading and every time there was some sort of crashing noise from that direction she felt her stomach clench. But Mary carried on with her chatter about the baby and the new house that she had with her husband over the other side of the city away from the docks. He was a tailor and Mary had been helping him out, said they were starting to get busy, they might need to take on another pair of hands to help out.

'You could come and live with us, Ada,' she heard her friend saying. 'You could come and help out until you get something else sorted.'

'What?' said Ada. 'Sorry, what did you say?'

'I said you could come and help us out. We're getting busy and there'd be enough work for you as well. We couldn't pay you owt but we could give you board and lodgings till you got yourself sorted.'

'Oh no, I can't move from here, Mary. I can't move; I need to be here for when Frank comes back.'

'But what if he doesn't come back, Ada, what if he never comes back? There's been no word from the docks, nothing's been found... And besides, if he did come back he'd go straight to Mam's and she'd know where you were. And you need to be in work.'

'Well, I was thinking of asking down at the docks, see if there was anything going there.'

'You're not doing that, Ada,' said Mary straight out. 'The work is rough and it will ruin you. And the men who work there are rough as well, so if the work doesn't ruin you then the men certainly will. Your grandfather would never have wanted that for you.'

'I suppose you're right,' said Ada, staring at her teacup.

'And the other thing is the rent. I know your grandfather always paid up in advance but Mam thinks that will be coming to an end soon. The landlord will be at the door, Ada, and you know what that means.'

Ada sighed. 'I hadn't even thought about that,' she said. 'Of course ... I need to get work fast so I can pay the rent and get sorted.'

'Ada, I'm sorry to have to tell you this but I might as well come straight out with it. They won't let you stay here, a single lass on her own. They won't do it; they'll chuck you out on the street if need be. And they'll want the next lot of rent straight away. There'll be no time to look for work; you'll be out on your ear.'

Ada looked at her friend. She couldn't speak.

'Mam thinks you'll have to the end of this week and they might give you a few days' grace seeing as you've been here for all these years and Padraic was a good man and well respected round here. But you will have to go.'

Ada felt as if the solid wood of the kitchen table that she was leaning on was starting to tilt and slide from under her. She put her head in her hands to try and keep it steady. This place was the only home she'd ever known. She'd been born here, Frank had been born here, her grandfather had died here and her mother had gone before. She wanted to fight to keep it but she was too exhausted, drained of everything, and she knew that Mary was right: she had seen with her own eyes many a family turned out on the street when they couldn't pay the rent.

She sat with her head bowed as the realization

53

washed over her. Then she heard her grandfather's voice in her head again, telling her it would be all right, that she needed to make her own life now, her own stories. Telling her again that she was clever and strong, that she could do it.

'I don't know about that,' she mumbled to herself, but then her grandfather said, 'You can, you can. You have to.'

'What was that?' said Mary.

'I can do it,' said Ada, straight out. 'I have to do it.'

Mary smiled. 'Right then, what we need to do now is clear out all of the furniture and your stuff. If it's still here when the landlord comes they'll take the lot.'

'How can we...?'

'The Regans have it in hand, Ada, don't worry. You just get yourself packed up; we'll do the rest.'

'All right,' said Ada, standing up from the table.

'We've got some time,' said Mary. 'They won't be here just yet. We don't have much furniture at ours so we can take what you have up there if you want and we'll keep hold of it until you get yourself settled.'

'Yes, yes,' said Ada.

Over the next couple of days Ada worked hard in the house. She lit the fire every day, cooked herself a bit of food, and she cleaned through, wanting to leave the place looking decent. That's what Grandfather would have wanted: leave it decent for the next folk to come in. She hadn't packed Frank's stuff yet, leaving it till last, just in case he did come back before she moved. In the end she had to go into his room and put his clothes and his few belongings into a box. Mary had told her she could take everything up to their house, and she would squeeze it in somewhere.

On the day she was moving, the Regan lads came with a handcart and easily lifted her few sticks of furniture and boxes of belongings on to it. They all worked down the docks and had plenty of muscle. Ada exchanged glances with Martin, the one who had helped her with Grandfather on the night of the accident. She gave him a small smile and he immediately looked away, a red flush coming to his cheeks. 'I think Martin's a bit sweet on you,' whispered Mary, giving her a gentle poke in the ribs. 'And he's my favourite brother, but don't tell the rest.'

As they went to get the bed from the room upstairs Ada felt a lump in her throat and tears well up but she pushed them back down again. There was work to do. As the bed was lifted the lads started laughing: Ada had forgotten to move the chamber pot and there it sat, on full display. Thank goodness she had remembered to empty it that morning.

Once the lads had clattered away down the stairs in their work boots, Ada spotted a rolled-up ball of paper lying in the dust where the bed had stood. She knew what it was straight away and picked it up. Straightening it out and looking at the faded letters once more she felt the hairs prickle at the back of her neck. She thought about her poor mother, with child a second time and deserted by a man who was already married. She vowed there and then that she would never find herself in that situation. She folded the letter this time and shoved it in her pocket.

'You ready?' said a voice behind her and she turned to find Martin.

'Yes, yes, I think so,' said Ada, feeling her face flush a little. 'Just give me a moment.'

As Martin clattered down the wooden stairs Ada stood in the tiny room for a few more moments. She wanted to remember it, make sure it was ingrained on her mind so that she would never forget. But now that the furniture had gone, already it had begun to feel like a different place, a place set for new people and their different lives. Glancing around, she spotted Grandfather's comb on the mantelpiece. How could she have missed that? She grabbed it quickly, not wanting to leave any remnant of their lives in the house for some-one else to find. Then she walked down the stairs, one step at a time, not too fast, not too slow, making each one count as she went down them for the last time. And as she reached the bottom she carried on walking, brushing past the ghost of her grandfather as he stood crying at the foot of the stairs on the day that she was born.

As she walked up the street following the hand-cart she felt a pain in her heart; the house seemed to call out to her and try to draw her back. But she knew that she had to keep on walking up that street and the more distance she put between herself and the walls of that place the less it would be able to draw her and the better she would feel. She could see neighbours looking out and the children who were playing stopped in their tracks for a few seconds to stare at them. Everybody round here knew what had happened; everybody had seen this kind of thing many a time before. First the coffin would go up the street, then days or weeks later the handcart with a few sticks of furniture and a few bags of clothes would trundle over the same cobbles with a pale-faced family dragging behind.

Ada was determined not to be a straggler and not to lose her dignity. So she walked with seeming purpose and tried to hold her head high, keeping up with the handcart and the gaggle of Regans who had come to her rescue. She had no idea what to expect at Mary's house, but she had nowhere else to go so she would have to try and make the best of it. She didn't even know if she would come back to the street at all. But then if Frank came back – when Frank came back – maybe they could move back in there, the two of them making a new home together.

# 3

*'Were there none who were discontented with what they have, the world would never reach anything better.'*
Florence Nightingale

Life at Mary's house was strange. Ada had never lived with other people before. Yes, she had known Mary Regan her whole life but she had never slept in a house with those who weren't her own kin and she had never shared a place with a new baby. And Mary's son could cry. He had the gripes or something, and he howled and screamed most of the time, or so it seemed, with his small face scrunched up into a fierce ball and his tiny fists clenched. Nothing could soothe him.

Mary was feeding him from the breast but he butted at her and messed around and never seemed to settle. Ada tried as best she could to help out but she was useless with babies. If anybody ever handed her a sleeping one, within no time at all it would be screaming or puking. But at least the ready commotion in Mary's house took her mind off things; she didn't have any space in her head to start dwelling on feeling sad: the baby's screaming made sure of that.

She'd only been there two days and she'd not had any sleep. Mary seemed to stand up to it very well – after all, she'd grown up in a house full of screaming children – but Ada could see that her new husband was walking around like a ghost, with dark circles under his eyes, and he was tetchy and sharp with Mary, telling her to settle the baby, and to do this, do that, to help him out as well. Ada felt for her friend but couldn't warm to her husband. On the morning of the third day Ada pulled her grandfather's pocket-watch out of one of the boxes where she'd carefully packed what was left of their possessions and put it in her pocket. Then she told Mary that she needed to go out to the pawn shop and get some more money. Mary looked a bit surprised but said of course, it was time she went for a stroll into the city.

In fact, she had also made the decision to go down to the docks and ask about Frank. It was the only thought that had been in her head since she'd left the street and it went round and round and probably always would until she could get some answers. And the only way to try and get answers was to start asking questions. She hadn't had the strength or the head for it before now but it's what her grandfather would have wanted. Yes, Mary had said that her brothers were listening out and if they heard anything at all they would let her know, but she had to be sure for herself that the men down there remembered that her brother was missing.

Also, she couldn't stay at Mary's, she just couldn't. So that meant she needed to be looking for some work. She would ask at the docks. She knew Mary wouldn't like it but beggars couldn't be choosers and perhaps she might join one of the teams of women who cleaned out the ships.

Another thing as well: Mary had been hinting that Martin was thinking of settling down. She'd kept nudging Ada with her elbow and whispering that he'd be looking for a wife soon. But Ada knew that the last thing she wanted right now was some red-faced boy for a husband and a house full of screaming babies. There had to be something else out there for her and now that she was feeling more like her old self she wanted to go and see if she could find it.

Ada was surprised at how calm she felt as she made her way through the city towards the docks. Even as she walked down her old street she still felt all right. But then, as she came closer to their house, she realized that the door was wide open and somebody was moving in. The place had new tenants already. Ada's stomach gave a lurch as she passed the open door and glanced in. She could see a woman and a child and a man in there and she met the woman's gaze for just a few seconds as she walked past with her heart pounding.

'Well, Ada, it's like to be,' said her grandfather's voice in her head. 'That young couple are like me and your grandmother moving in with our Maggie. The world continues to turn, Ada, it certainly does.'

It felt strange. Not only could she hear his voice but as soon as she had passed the door of their house she felt as if her grandfather was walking beside her, as if he'd just come out of the front door and decided to join her. Memories came flooding back and she found herself smiling inside but at the same time feeling the sorrow of what had happened that day of the accident. She never knew that these two things could be held together at the same time. She had been grieving so hard that she had been unable to feel anything else and had begun to feel that she would never be warm or contented ever again, yet as she walked along she felt her grandfather walking beside her and it gave her strength. She felt like she was a little girl again, walking confidently beside him, holding his hand. Back then she had had no cares in the world.

As she drew nearer to the harbour gates, the sound of the dock grew stronger: the clanking of cranes and cargo and the shouting and mur-murings. A group must be disembarking from a ship, she thought. She could smell coffee in the air, and knew that coffee beans were being unloaded and would be stacked in one of the huge warehouses that were right there on the quayside.

At the gates she saw people pouring through, new arrivals to Liverpool. She knew by the state of the poor souls, even before she could catch their accent, that they were her people, the Irish. They were ragged and thin, almost starving, with pale faces. Grandfather had told her about the plight of these people who continued to follow the route chosen by his own family, people who had suffered what was called the potato famine. He was angry in that year before he died, angry at the ships that packed the Irish people into the holds, too many of them, dying on the way over to Liverpool. They called them coffin ships.

Ada stood still and let them flow around her, men, women and children. Some were old and looked worn down; all were thin. Some of the younger ones had a spark and she could see the light of hope in their eyes. As they passed her she silently wished them well and hoped that they would find what they were looking for. But sadly, she knew, as they all poured in one direction, that these people, fresh from the boats, were forced to live in terrible over-crowded conditions in the worst part of the city.

Once the crowd had passed by, Ada made her way to the Dock Traffic building. She had not been back since the day of the accident and she felt again some of the tension that she'd had that day, remembering how she had clenched her jaw tight as she walked to stop her teeth chattering.

She was calmer now and ready to ask her questions, but it did feel odd to go in through that door knowing that her grandfather would not be at his desk, that he would never be at his desk again.

She saw one or two familiar faces as she made her way to her grandfather's office. She peered in through the round window at the top of the door just as she had done before, and for a moment she almost saw him there slumped forward on his desk. But instantly he was gone and all she could see was the straight, thin back of the young clerk who must have taken his job.

Tapping on the door she walked into the room and went straight to the desk of the senior clerk who had known her grandfather. She stood for a few moments as he finished an entry in his ledger and then he looked up and frowned at her.

'Can we help you, Ada?' he said. 'I did tell one of the juniors to take your grandfather's pens and such from the desk up to your house.'

'Oh yes of course, that's fine,' said Ada. 'I'm here for something else. I just wanted to ask you if there'd been any news of our Frank or if anybody had any idea at all what might have happened to him.'

'Well, young lady,' said the senior clerk, drawing himself up to his full sitting height, 'I don't think you should be troubling yourself with that. There is no information and even if there was I don't think we would be at liberty to share it with you.'

'But I am his only family,' said Ada.

'That may be so, young Ada, but this kind of thing is no issue for a young lady like you. It needs to be dealt with by a man.'

'Stuff and nonsense!' said Ada before she could stop herself. 'And besides, there are no men, there is just me.'

The clerk cleared his throat and adjusted his collar and put his head back down to make another entry in the ledger. 'There is nothing to tell you,' he said. 'Nothing at all.'

'Thank you for your time,' said Ada, trying not to sound as furious as she felt, and she turned from the desk, strode through the office and back out to the harbour side. Glad to be out of the stuffy interior and taking deep breaths of salt air, she thought: How ridiculous, and she knew for a fact that her grandfather would never have treated a young woman like she had just been treated. Stupid, stuffy old man, she muttered to herself as she went in search of somebody who might be able to talk straight to a woman.

Seeing a porter she recognized, someone she knew for sure had worked with Frank, she went over to where he was leaning against the base of one of the hydraulic cranes having a smoke.

'All right, young lady?' he said. 'You're Frank Houston's sister, aren't you?'

'Yes I am,' she said, glad to find someone who seemed ready to talk to her on a level.

'Bad business what happened with your grandfather. Sorry to hear about that. He was a good man, very fair and very honest. He's been missed, he has for sure – some of those fellas in that Dock Traffic Office don't know their arse from their elbow.'

Ada couldn't help but smile. 'I think I've just met one,' she said.

The old docker laughed and coughed a bit on his pipe. Then, after spitting out a bit of bacca, he dropped his voice to say, 'And that thing with your Frank, well, me and the lads, we've been grieving over what happened that day and we've been going over it nearly every day since. And to be honest ... we were all expecting his body to be found somewhere in the harbour or washed up further down the estuary...'

Ada felt her stomach lurch and she bowed her head.

'Now, lass,' he said, 'the reason I'm tellin' you is because it's a bit of a mystery... We've been fully expecting to find your Frank so we could give him a decent burial and all that. But the thing is ... there's been nothing.'

Ada still stood with her head bowed.

'There's been nothing and we old dockers, we sometimes get a feeling in our bones, and it doesn't feel right that Frank's body has never been found,' he said, reaching out and giving her arm a bit of a shake, causing her to look up at him. 'That means there's still a chance that your Frank might be alive.'

'Really?' said Ada, feeling a surge go through her body. 'Is that what you lot think?'

'Yes we do, we do indeed ... but of course we don't really know ... but we think that he might have been knocked on to another ship.'

'Right,' said Ada. 'I mean, that did cross my mind as well... Is it possible? Have you known that kind of thing happen before?'

'Well,' said the man, pointing out across the harbour with the stem of his pipe, 'see how tight those ships are packed together? Like that one over there, unloading heavy stuff right next to a ship as it is getting ready to set sail? Well, that day it was just the same, all the ships were jammed in together and then when the chains slipped on that lump of timber it all happened so quick nobody could see who went where, and what with it all landing on poor Tommy Simpson, everybody was running to him on the quayside so nobody saw what happened to the rest, and your Frank could have been knocked on to another ship, knocked out cold. And there was a ship next to them that was moving off – we all remembered that all right. The crew would have been busy and they wouldn't have found him till they were too far out to sea to turn back. It has happened before that, once or twice, that some poor bugger's ended up on another ship, usually dead, mind, not knocked out.'

'Where was the ship going, do you know?' asked Ada, narrowing her eyes as she looked out across the harbour.

'I do know, yes. It was the army ship.'

'Army ship?' said Ada.

'Yes, heading out to the Crimea.'

'The Crimea?'

'Yes, the Crimean War. Where they just had those big battles and that Charge of the Light Brigade. So many of our lads killed out there, so many, and for what?'

What if Frank's found himself out there? Ada was thinking. What if he's got himself shot and can't get back home?

'See that ship there,' said the docker, 'that's the

65

*Golden Fleece.* It's going to the same place. Think it's called Scotari or summat. It's where that Florence Nightingale is. Y'know, she's that nurse.'

Ah yes, thought Ada, I remember Grandfather coming home full of some story from the *London News.* It seemed so long ago but it must have been only a few months back. She remembered thinking how marvellous it was that a woman could go out there and do that work, helping so many soldiers. She recalled seeing the picture of Miss Nightingale with a lamp, tending the sick. It had moved her to tears.

'So, as I say,' continued the docker, 'me and the lads, we just hope he might have been knocked on to that ship. It seems like the only way he could have survived that day.'

'So that ship there,' said Ada, pointing to the one he had indicated. 'That ship, the *Golden Fleece,* is going to the Crimea?'

'It is that,' said the docker. 'It's leaving tomorrow late morning. There'll be a hell of a commotion down here when that lot are boarding. It'll be chaos... Yep, it's going off tomorrow to them poor sods out in the Crimea.' Then he spat on the ground and moved off down the quay.

'Thanks,' she said, calling after him, but he was already gone.

Ada stood for some time staring at the ship, all kinds of thoughts going through her head. Determined now that Frank must have fallen on to a ship, she couldn't let herself consider any other explanation. Then she turned and made her way to the pawn shop with Grandfather's pocket-watch and as she walked she began to realize exactly what she needed to do and she knew for sure that Mary would not like it one bit.

She must have spent longer out on the docks and at the pawn shop than she thought, for as she was passing back through her old street the light was beginning to fade. She steeled herself to go by their house again but this time it felt like something had fallen into place inside her somehow and she felt stronger. As she passed by she saw a new lamp shining in the window and caught a glimpse of the couple with their child sitting at the table. She knew in that moment that she would have to follow her heart and never give up her search for Frank and that the kind of life she could see there, through that window, her window, wasn't what she wanted right now. It wasn't a husband, it wasn't children, it wasn't a small kitchen of her own, but something that would be a different life, a different story.

# 4

*'But rather, ten times rather, die in the surf,*
*heralding the way to that new world,*
*than stand idly on the shore!'*
Florence Nightingale, *Cassandra*

'Are you stark raving mad!' shouted Mary. 'No, you can't go off on some wild goose chase after Frank. That thing about him ending up on a ship going out to the Crimea, it's only a rumour that's been going round! Nobody knows for sure.'

'So you knew! You knew and you didn't tell me!' Ada shouted back, her face flushing red.

Mary stared at the floor for a moment before lifting her head and saying in a much quieter voice, 'I didn't tell you cos I knew exactly what you'd do. And it's the wrong thing.'

'It's not up to you to decide what's the wrong thing or the right thing for me, Mary,' said Ada, trying to get some control.

There was silence for a few moments as the two women stared at each other, their breath coming quickly. Then the baby started to whimper and then to cry in its crib and Mary went over to pick him up. As she stood rocking the baby, trying to lull him back to sleep, they stood quietly, looking at his face that was beginning to contort, a sure sign that he would soon be screaming blue murder.

'Have you any idea what it's like out there?' said Mary, rocking the baby frantically now. 'Have you heard any of the reports? So many men dead, blown to bits or catching cholera and all sorts. It's no place for a lass, Ada, no place at all. And what will you do there?'

'I was thinking I might try my hand at being a nurse.'

'Try your hand!' shouted Mary above the rising wail of the baby. 'Try your hand? You can't even cope with the baby screeching and writhing. How will you cope out there? There's men coming back horrible and mutilated.'

'I've made my mind up and that's that,' said Ada, not wanting to lose face and trying to cover her own concerns about what Mary had just said. 'And I might find Frank. And if I don't I'll come straight back.'

'You might come straight back in bits,' said Mary. 'And what about money for the journey – have you thought about that?'

'I've taken Grandfather's pocket-watch to the pawn shop. They've given me a good price and that should be enough for the ticket and leave a bit more besides.'

'I don't think you can even buy a ticket for a ship like that. It's an army ship; you can't just stroll up there and buy a ticket. How are you even going to get on board?' Mary was almost bellowing above the screaming of the baby.

'I will find a way,' said Ada, keeping her voice steady.

'Oh, Ada,' said Mary, dropping her voice, 'you've no idea what you're doing, no idea.'

'I'm going, Mary, I'm going. Frank's my only kin,' said Ada firmly.

Mary slumped down in the chair, the baby still howling on her lap. Looking over at Ada, she said at last, 'All right then, all right, but you have to promise me that you'll look after yourself and not fall in with the wrong crowd, and if you don't find Frank you turn round and come straight back to Liverpool. Do you hear?'

'I hear,' said Ada, getting up and walking over to put an arm around her friend. 'I'll get going first thing, just before it gets light, give myself plenty of time to get on to the docks and work things out,' she said, tightening her arm around Mary just a little and reaching down to stroke the baby's head as he lay now guzzling his milk.

'You take care going through the city. I couldn't bear it if something happened to you. I've got plenty of kin, as you know, but you're like a sister to me, you truly are. There's no one like you.'

Ada felt her eyes welling up with tears and tried to mumble a few words, but she just found herself squeezing Mary's shoulder a bit tighter and muttering, 'I know, I know. I'll be back.'

In the early hours of the morning Ada pulled her mother's old red shawl from a box and wrapped it round her as tight as she could. She'd already packed a canvas bag with a few belongings and now she pulled it off the bed and tiptoed through the house to make her way out. For the first time, the baby had been quiet for most of the night, so she crept out, not wanting to risk any slight noise that might set it off.

As she gently clicked the door shut behind her she felt a sense of relief mixed with a tightness in her belly and a jangling in her head that kept screaming, 'What the heck are you doing now, Ada Houston?' She'd never been out unaccompanied in the city at this time of day and she was surprised at how cool the air was even though it was now late spring. Spring already; the year seemed to have gone quickly but then it felt like a lifetime ago since she had been seeing in the new year with her grandfather. She would never have imagined that this year of 1855 would see him gone, and her creeping off in the early morning to try and get a passage on a ship, never in a million years.

In the cool air the smoke of the city hung in the

pale, yellow light of the gas lamps, and although Ada felt more alone than she'd ever been in her whole life as she walked away from Mary's house, she also felt excited. She felt alive.

Stopping just down the street, she made sure that the bag was secure and that her mother-of-pearl brooch was pinned firmly to her blouse. Then she pulled the red shawl up over her head and held it tightly under her chin in order to hide as much of her face as possible. Mary had told her to do this – it was the safest way for a young woman to get through the city – and she had told her to walk fast and strong and look like she knew exactly where she was going. And not to stop. But she'd already done that.

She had never walked this route in the early morning light before and once she was out of Mary's street, it felt much harder to see her way along the pavement and she began to worry that she might take a wrong turn and end up in a bad area of the city. Already she could see shapes of people huddled in doorways or others standing with a smoke. She moved quickly past, knowing they were just vagrants, poor people with no refuge and no hope, huddled on cold stone trying to get some sleep. She knew this but she still feared what desperation might lead these people to do. Checking that her bag was secure again and hidden under her shawl, Ada ploughed ahead, keeping a steady pace.

She felt sure that she would need to turn off soon down a narrower street – or should she have turned by now? As she got deeper into the poor side of the city she felt her feet sliding and slipping through stuff on the path and the smell that crept through the smoky air was foul. She tried not to think about what might be underfoot or who might be lurking in the shadows.

Then from out of nowhere three boys stepped in front of her, blocking her way. They must have been in a doorway, keeping very still. She couldn't see their faces but she could tell by their harsh, breaking voices that they were after money. She was forced to stop; they were not going to let her pass. Ada pulled the shawl closer around her face and held it tight.

'Can ye spare a few pennies, missus,' said the biggest boy, stepping up a little closer to her. Ada knew that if she made a move to her bag to get out a coin she would be lost. They would be on her and who knew what might happen. She had to think fast, so she slumped her shoulders and mustered a cough, then spoke in as croaky a voice as she could: 'Let me by, lads, let me by. There's cholera at our house and I think I'm starting with it.'

Instantly the boys stepped back. 'Show us your face then,' said the ringleader.

Ada coughed again, and managed a wheezy, 'I don't want to do that, that's the way it's spread. It's spread by the miasma, by the air that I breathe out.'

The boys stepped further back, then one of them said, 'Come on, Mickey, let's get out of here. We don't want the cholera.'

Then they were gone, stepping back into the smoke and slipping away as quickly as they had appeared.

Instantly Ada straightened up, pulled her shawl tighter and marched off. She could feel her heart pounding and, spurred on by fear, walked with a new urgency, feeling stronger and braver than she actually was. She followed her instinct for direction and was soon on the right road.

It was almost dawn when she reached the street where she had been born. There was a light on in her old house and she felt her stomach lurch with grief as she walked by almost holding her breath. But once she had got past and was on the familiar path to the harbour she felt able to relax a little, although this time she had no sense of her grandfather walking with her. She was completely on her own.

The noise of the harbour, as it grew ever stronger, was so familiar that it did hold some sense of home for her and as she passed through the gates it felt like she was heading towards something that was understood, something that held promise. The smell of the salt air and the clank of the machinery stirred her and she instantly picked up again the excitement that she had felt when she'd come down here with Padraic, when he'd had time to show her around and they had walked by the ships and he had told her where each one was going or where they'd just come back from. She felt her heart swell with pride at how much he had known about the world and its people just by living and working on the harbour.

She found herself stopping in her tracks to admire the great Albert Dock that had been opened just a few years ago, and remembered Grandfather telling her that it would make

Liverpool the finest harbour in the land. In the early morning light, the huge slabs of granite that had built the quayside seemed to glow, and the cast iron and brick of the warehouses soared above her. She felt almost overwhelmed by the beauty and the strength of it all.

She stood for a good five minutes just looking.

The waterfront was packed with a forest of masts but she could easily pick out the *Golden Fleece*, the ship that the old docker had told her about yesterday. She could see that it was busy with men loading goods, and there seemed to be some commotion going on in front of it. As she walked closer she could make out a clump of women on the quay who seemed to be arguing with someone.

She moved closer to see what was going on. The party had a number of big bags packed with bottles, some packages and a trunk. The seaman that they were arguing with seemed to be telling them that they could not take all of the luggage on board the ship. They would have to leave the bags with the bottles that looked like brandy or some other strong liquor.

'But we are only five now,' said one of the women. 'One of our party is missing, so that means there is one less body on board so we should be able to bring all our bags.'

'Not these,' said the seaman, pointing again at the bottles.

Ada knew what he was up to; she could see it in his eyes and the way he looked at the bottles poking out of the bags. And she also knew that this might be her chance to blend in with some travelling companions.

She stepped forward and called to the group, 'Yoo-hoo! I'm here, sorry to be late.'

The women looked round as one, all with blank expressions.

Ada knew that she would have to be quick so she moved in straight away and squared up to the seaman.

'Is there some problem with our arrangements?' she said.

'There is indeed,' he said, trying to make the most of his height as he stood above Ada.

'So what exactly is the problem?' said Ada. 'And before you answer, my man, I want you to know that a close relative of mine has a very important position in the Dock Traffic Office, so unless you have something to say that is an official order, I suggest you keep quiet and allow me and my party to board the ship.'

Ada did not know where that speech had come from but she seemed to have modelled her approach on Frank's description of some of the grand ladies he had seen on the harbour, how they spoke and how they looked down their noses at a young ruffian like him. He had made her laugh many a time taking off those women. The seaman looked flabbergasted and tried to answer back, but clearly could not find the right words.

Ada was straight back at him. 'I suggest you allow us to board then, my man, and we will, of course, be taking all of our luggage with us.'

He stood back and the party of women followed Ada up the gangplank.

As soon as they were below deck and out of

earshot, the women turned to Ada and started laughing.

'Who are you?' she said when the laughter at last died down.

The women burst out laughing again and one of them said, 'You've gone and done it now, miss! We're army wives, off to the Crimea, to the war.'

'What!' said Ada, although she knew exactly where the ship was going – she just didn't want them asking any questions about her decision. A decision that she wasn't beginning to regret, exactly, but one that she knew, in her heart of hearts, she should have taken more time to consider. She knew that if they started questioning her then her resolve would weaken further and she wanted to do this; she would not be able to live with herself if she hadn't done all that she could to find her only kin. Even though that brother of hers could be so bloody moody and annoying at times, he was still her brother.

'Do you still want to come with us?' said one of the women.

'Yes,' said Ada as firmly as she could. 'And what's more I have money here to pay my way.'

The women didn't argue as Ada tipped out most of the coins from her pocket, the last of her grandfather's money. Then they rallied round her, telling her not to worry, they'd look after her. They were on their way to a place called Scutari; that's where most of their husbands had ended up. And it was the place where that nurse, Florence Nightingale, had her hospital.

'I know about Florence Nightingale,' said Ada, remembering again how impressed she'd been by the stories her grandfather had told her. And at least she could take some strength from the story of Miss Nightingale; if she could go out there with her lamp, then any woman could. Despite this, her mind was still flying all over the place, wondering what she had done.

'Are you a nurse?' one of the wives asked.

'Not really,' said Ada. 'No, I just need to get away from Liverpool.'

Sensing that Ada did not want to tell them any more, and with a woman's understanding of how many reasons there might be for someone to flee, the group seemed to be satisfied with that.

'Just one question,' said another of the women, 'are you with child?'

Ada blushed instantly. 'No, definitely not,' she said.

'That's all right then,' said the woman, and, seeing Ada's red face, continued, 'I just had to ask because where we're going you certainly don't want to be birthing a child.'

'One more question,' said another of the group, who had stepped forward and looked like she might be in charge, 'what's your name?'

'Ada, my name's Ada Houston.'

'Well, Ada, don't let this lot riddle you with questions – sometimes they don't let up. I'm Sarah ... this is Emma, and this one, the one that's trying to delve into all your private affairs, she's Greta. Now, let's get you sorted, see if we can find you a bunk. And any minute now the purser will be down to take all our names and put them in the record. Just let me do the talking.'

Ada nodded. She already felt that she could

trust this group of women.

They soon had her settled with them in the cramped conditions deep in the bowels of the ship. The women had food, drink and some blankets. Sarah told her that she was lucky not to be going out with the first wave to the Crimea – they had really packed the passengers in and some had died as a result. They were expecting a few more to join them down there but the biggest party on board would probably be the horses.

'Horses?' said Ada. 'I didn't know they could travel by boat.'

'Oh yes,' said Emma, 'so many have been killed, the army need more.'

As soon as Ada was settled on her bunk she fell into a deep sleep and didn't wake up until they started to bring the horses on board. Not even in her exhausted state would she have been able to sleep through the shouts of the men, the sound of the hooves and the frightened neighing of the creatures. One of them must have broken loose because she could hear a huge commotion with hooves crashing and slipping on the wooden decking.

'It's just the horses,' said Greta, handing her a mug of cold tea, and then Ada remembered that Mary had given her some biscuits for the journey and she brought them out for all to share. They were very dry and Ada smiled to herself as she realized that Mary had inherited Mrs Regan's curse when it came to baking. The women didn't mind though; they seemed to be easily pleased. It was early days yet with them but Ada had the impression that this lot didn't worry about much.

She did wonder, however, how anyone could get used to the noise of terrified horses and splintering wood.

Once the horses had boarded and the noise had settled, Sarah told her that they would soon be underway. Ada felt her stomach tighten and her heart miss a few beats. Even though she had lived by the harbour her whole life she had never actually set foot on a ship, not even when it was moored, let alone when it was actually sailing. She had seen plenty of them coming in and going out every week and she had imagined what it would be like to be on board. And as a child of course she had been enthralled by her grandfather's stories of mermaids and dolphins and had yearned with a passion for the chance to set sail across the oceans, making up stories in her head about stowaways and pirates. Then as she got a bit older and began to know that it was very unlikely that some young lass who kept house like she did for Grandfather would ever get the chance to go on a voyage, she had ruled it out and accepted that she probably would never see much beyond her city of birth. But what had happened over the last weeks had turned all that upside down and here she was, here she was at last, thrilled and terrified all at the same time.

She felt the first lurch of the ship under her as it began to move out into the estuary, and Greta grabbed her and hugged her, saying, 'Here we go, here we go,' and then, 'Come on, everybody, let's go up on top and say our goodbyes.'

Ada had no choice; she was carried along with the group and before she knew it she was up on deck with the women, waving at the shore and watching Liverpool retreat. As she stood there, her city growing smaller and smaller, leaving all that she had known behind, Ada felt a shiver go right through her body. Some of the wives were excited, some were crying, all of them were leaving Liverpool and all that they had there, and Ada couldn't help but feel sad. When they were too far out to see much of the city any more she moved with the group back down below to their quarters.

As soon as she was in her bunk exhaustion hit her again. All of the grieving and then the sleepless nights at Mary's had drained her of everything. It felt good to lie down in her own space, her own bunk, and be rocked to sleep by the movement of the ship; it felt so good.

When she woke again the ship was creaking around her and her narrow bunk was swaying from side to side. The women were sleeping and when she looked down there were a number of wooden pails standing ready. Wonder why they've provided so many buckets for our toilet, she thought, before drifting off to sleep again.

Ada had the answer to her question the next time she woke, cold and clammy with a heaving in her belly and her mouth watering. She slid quickly off the bunk and grabbed the nearest pail. Side by side with two of her new friends she heaved her guts up into the bucket, then heaved some more. Climbing back on to the bunk, she thought she was probably done, that she had cleared everything out, but she was mistaken. She was soon back with the bucket again, and then again and again.

She had heard about seasickness but didn't realize that it was so violent. She had imagined that it was a gentle clearing of the system, then all would be well. In fact, all the passengers down in steerage were at it and for her it lasted a full week. One of the poor women continued to puke, on and off, all the way to Scutari.

After a full week, Ada began to think that she had entered some new world where she would never stop the sickness and never be able to eat again. She could hardly keep a sup of water down. If it hadn't been for the army wives taking turns to help her when they weren't puking themselves she thought that she might well have died.

Just when she had started to get to a place where she had made her peace with everything and was fairly sure that she would never stop puking and didn't even care any more, somehow, miraculously, she started to feel better.

She could keep down some water and even a bit of food but her legs were so weak and she was so unused to the roll of the ship that she had to cling on to something even to stand. Walking was a whole other thing that she didn't attempt at first. But after a few days she had to get out of the pit where she now lived that smelt of puke and sour breath. She thought that if she didn't get up to see the sky and smell the air, she might die.

Greta was regularly up on deck having a bit of banter with the sailors or the soldiers. She offered to take Ada up the first time, not wanting her to go overboard or fall foul of one of the lecherous men who felt it was their right to make use of a young girl on a long voyage.

'Hold on to me,' said Greta as they made their way to the ladder that took them up to the next level and the next ladder. As Ada started to climb the second ladder she could feel the air coming down the hatch and gulped it in. It was fresh and salty. It was the elixir of life.

Once up on deck Greta took her to the side of the ship and told her to hold fast. Ada felt the vessel's motion even more strongly here and there was a breeze that blew the fallen strands of hair away from her face and made her feel refreshed, alive. She looked up to see the sails of the ship billowing out as they glided over the water. Looking down over the side, she loved the way that the ship cut so cleanly through the water, the way that it rode the waves. She felt exhilarated, born again.

Still clinging to the side, she looked down the boat and saw a man with his back to her that she thought she recognized. Then her stomach squeezed tight as she looked again. The man she could see holding lightly to the side and chatting to one of the sailors was Frank – surely it was Frank.

She felt her heart beating fast and started to feel a bit sick again, telling herself that she was light-headed, she was seeing things. But when she looked back again, the young man had the same colour hair and the same build. She rubbed her eyes to make sure that she wasn't seeing things but that just made them blurry, so she started to edge her way, hand over hand, closer to the young man.

When she was right up behind him, she waited

for a moment before tapping him on the shoulder.

He turned and Ada held her breath, disappointment flooding through her. It wasn't Frank. It was a young man with the same hair and same build but he had the sharp features of a very different face. He looked puzzled or worried and started to say, 'Are you all right...?' but she was already moving away, hand over hand back down the boat, muttering her apologies. She felt ridiculous and more than a bit heartbroken – just for a few minutes her heart had soared and she had really thought that it could be her brother. Now she felt like a fool. She glanced back and the young man was still looking in her direction but, thank goodness, was making no move to come down the deck towards her.

When she got back to the spot where Greta had left her, she leant over the side a little, gulping in air, trying to stop the grief hitting her hard in the belly like it had done over and over again since her grandfather died. Her knees went weak and she started to slump against the side of the ship. She was grateful when Greta saw her and broke away from her conversation with one of the sailors to come and rescue her, saying, 'That's enough for your first time, let's get you back below deck.'

She let herself be led back down, just about able to manage the steep steps of the ladders and feeling her foot slip a number of times. Once back in the dark pit of the boat, she began to feel safe again, despite the stink and the heat.

'Are you all right?' said Greta.

'Yes, yes, thank you,' said Ada, feeling that she just needed to sit down before her knees gave way. The woman frowned, sensing that there was more to it than that as she guided her over to the bunk, then sat beside her.

'Look, Ada, what is it? You can tell us lot anything; it won't go any further.'

When Ada didn't reply she said, 'Is he your lover?'

'Who, what?' said Ada, not connecting to what she was saying.

'The handsome young man up on deck, the one in the brown tunic. It's just that I saw you tap him on the shoulder and speak to him and then I saw your face. You looked like you were going to cry. Was he your sweetheart? Has he broken your heart?'

'No, no, nothing like that,' said Ada. 'I've never seen him before.'

'So why did you look so sad, then, when he turned round?'

Ada sat for a moment, not saying anything, but when she realized that Greta would wait as long as it took to get a reply she started to speak. 'I thought he was my brother. He had his back turned to me but he looked just like him and I thought it was him.' Once she had started talking she felt a river of words starting to pour out as she told Greta all about Frank and how she had come to be on the ship.

'Whew,' said Greta, 'you must think the world of him if you're prepared to do that. It's my first time going, but the others have been warning me that it's Hell on earth out there. Hell on earth.'

Ada felt a bit sick; this was exactly the reason she hadn't wanted to share her story before the ship was on the move, before there was no going back. She had no choice but to continue now. She sat on the bunk next to Greta and wondered what she had done, coming out here like this. What had she done?

'If he's anywhere he's most likely in Scutari – that's in Turkey,' said one of the other women, who had been listening to every word Ada said. 'If he's any sense he wouldn't go anywhere near the front line – that's Balaklava. Scutari's miles away, takes about another week in a ship to get up to Balaklava from there. And who's to say that he wouldn't just stay on the ship and go straight back to Liverpool or on to another place?'

Ada's heart sank. Of course that was possible, but in her rush to head off and find Frank she had pushed back all other thoughts except that she needed to follow the route he might have taken, to go there, to try to find him and bring him back. Maybe Mary had been right, she was 'stark, raving mad'.

'Well, it's too late now,' she said to no one in particular as she swung her legs up on to the bunk and pulled the blanket over her.

After two weeks at sea Ada lost touch with time and simply lived within the daily rhythm of the ship and the roll of the sea. She was beginning to feel a little bit at home on the boat and pleased that she had beaten the worst of the seasickness. Then they hit a storm.

Ada would learn later that they had been in the Aegean Sea, tantalizingly close to their first port of call, Scutari. She knew that the army wives had been relieved when they had come through the Bay of Biscay, a place where they were fully expecting to be thrown around a bit. It was the early hours of the morning, just after daybreak. They were asleep – well, as asleep as you can be in the bowels of a noisy sail ship. Ada woke fully and suddenly when she fell off her bunk. They all fell off their bunks at her side of the ship: banged down on to the boards of the floor, then were thrown back against the bunks as the other side of the ship came up.

Ada had the breath knocked out of her; she couldn't speak, but some of the women were screaming and shouting and there was water pouring in through the hatch, sloshing down each time the boat lurched. She could hear the wind howling and screeching outside like some demented creature. It was terrifying.

Ada managed to scrabble round and found a fixed piece of wood to hold on to, then grabbed Emma who was sliding back and forth along the floor. She got her, lost her, then got her again and this time pulled her in a bit closer using her legs.

Poor Emma seemed to be out of it, and not responding. Ada could see that her left arm was twisted out of shape but somehow she managed to get her more secure and was able to stop her crashing back and forth.

All the time the noise above them was terrifying. The horses were screaming and shrieking with distress, and there was the sound of breaking wood and crashing hooves. Men were shouting. Then they heard what sounded like heavy objects moving back and forth, with everything crashing around them.

Ada concentrated on holding on with one hand and keeping Emma steady with the rest of her body. She managed to wedge her in and block her but was unable to prevent her twisted arm from getting caught time and time again. Thank goodness that Emma was unconscious.

Ada held fast for what felt like hours, until finally the movement of the ship settled and the water stopped slopping down through the hatch. It was still rough out there and the wind still howled but she was able to loosen her grip between lurches and start to look around.

All of their belongings were strewn around and there was broken glass and the sound of people groaning. Emma was still unconscious, her arm definitely broken, although Ada daren't look too close.

Things seemed to have quietened down on the deck above but heavy objects were still sliding and dragging around. And then, as if from another world, they heard the sound of a man weeping. Ada felt for him, felt for all of them and the horses that had surely died up there. But as far as she could see all souls on this lower deck were still breathing and it wasn't long before they felt another shift in the movement of the ship as they entered calmer seas. It was soon possible to stand and move around a bit and come to terms with how their small world had been smashed to pieces.

The other wives came straight over to check on Emma.

'You did well there, lass,' said Sarah. 'Without you keeping hold of her, she would have been a goner. You might not be a nurse but you certainly have the makings of one.'

Ada helped to move Emma over on to her side, into a better position with her injured arm uppermost, and Sarah produced a small knife from her boot and started to rip at the woman's sleeve so they could have a look at the injury, saying, 'We need to get this done before she wakes up and starts feeling the pain. It will hurt like hell.' The lower arm was red but looked normal; the upper arm was swollen, twisted and out of shape.

Ada's stomach heaved again.

'Now,' said Sarah, looking straight at Ada, 'find me a big square of cloth, will you?'

Ada scrabbled in the debris that lay all around and at last found a brightly patterned square of cotton. She brought it across to Sarah, who was still feeling up and down the injured arm, and waited for further instruction. 'Right then,' Sarah said at last, 'we need to set this arm as best we can. I'm going to twist it back the right way and straighten it. Then I want you to hold it in position while I fix it with a sling.'

Ada understood immediately. Sarah twisted the arm round as quick as she could; it made a scraping, crunching sound that made Ada feel sick but she managed to grab the arm and keep it in position.

'Good job,' said Sarah, giving Ada a quick smile, just as Emma woke up screaming her head off.

They both shouted at her: 'Keep still, keep still! We need to put the sling on,' but she was beside herself with pain and starting to thrash around.

Instantly all of the other women were there,

holding their friend down, ignoring her screams. The piece of cloth was folded into a triangle, the point of the triangle was laid at the woman's elbow then the cloth was knotted round the woman's neck.

'Now get her some brandy, quick,' said Sarah, planting a big kiss on her injured friend's tear-stained cheek. 'This is going to hurt so bad for such a long time that you might want somebody to chop it off, but it will get better,' she continued. 'And hopefully you'll still have some use left in it.'

As soon as the women were finished and the injured party was laid on her bunk, Ada crawled on to her own bed and wrapped herself tightly in her red shawl. Greta came to her and offered her a tot of brandy, but she said, 'No thank you, I don't drink liquor,' before falling into a deep sleep that was more like being dead than anything else.

# 5

*'There might be employment for a lady Superintendent here as well if you would prefer it... I can hardly define the work ... other than the moral control of Nurses & Sisters.'*
Florence Nightingale

'Wake up, wake up! We've landed, we're in Turkey!'

'No, not yet,' said Ada, pulling the blanket over herself and turning her back on Greta.

'Yes, yes, we're here, Ada, we're in Scutari, you need to wake up,' said Greta, shaking her now more strongly than ever.

That can't be right, thought Ada, I can still feel the roll of the ship beneath me, doesn't feel like we're in the harbour. I just need to get some more sleep.

'Come on, lass,' said the army wife with a tone in her voice that meant she wouldn't stand any messing. 'You need to get off here with us; this ship's going up to Balaklava, near the front line. It's a godforsaken spot up there. And the most likely place your brother might be is here. Come on!'

Ada had to wake up or fall on the floor, so she roused up pretty quick and managed a sleepy smile through tousled hair for the woman who was shaking and dragging her to God knows where.

'All right, all right,' she said. 'Just let me get my things.'

As she turned back to push her one or two belongings into her canvas bag, Greta cracked up laughing. 'Ooh, Miss Ada, maybe you should have brought a much more commodious valise.'

Ada couldn't help but laugh and this made her wake up properly. She took the comb back out of the bag, raked it through her hair, twisted her thick locks into a knot, then secured it with a comb. 'Right,' she said, still a bit bleary.

'Not really,' said Greta, taking a rag out from her sleeve and spitting on it. 'You've got some dried stuff on your face and your eyes are full of sleep.' Using the rag she rubbed a bit too vigorously on

Ada's cheek and then wiped her eyes. She glanced at the hair but had to leave it – too many patches of what looked like dried vomit.

'You'll do,' she said, taking Ada's arm to prevent her turning back once more to the bunk. 'You'll have to do.'

At the last moment Ada remembered her shawl and raced back to the bunk to pull it free from the blanket.

'Come on!' said Greta. 'The rest of them are already on dry land.'

As Ada climbed up the ladder into the bright light, the heat of Scutari met her. She had to narrow her eyes as she came up on deck and wasn't able to see at first. Greta grabbed her again and they proceeded down the gangplank. Ada was very glad of her companion; her legs were weak and her balance seemed off. She clung to the army wife.

They quickly found the rest of the group, who had been joined by another woman Ada didn't recognize. It was so noisy on the dock, with people and cargo being unloaded and the push of the crowd all around, that the wives had to shout to be heard. And what was that smell? With so many distractions, her legs still feeling for the roll of the ship, and with the heat, Ada had no idea what was going on.

At last, the shouted conversation seemed to have come to an end and Greta grabbed her by the arm and they moved off as one unit. Once away from the crowd, Ada was more able to make sense of what was being said. It seemed that the wives had some concern that she would not be able to stay with them in their lodging. That meant she would not have anywhere to stay, while she looked for her brother, but they thought she would be able to make her way up to the hospital and try there, see if they needed any volunteers or anyone to work.

Ada felt panicked, her mind flying all over the place, but she knew that she didn't want to get packed off back to Liverpool before she'd even had the chance to ask around about Frank.

'All right,' she said, 'but can you all keep your eyes and ears open for my brother? His name is Frank Houston and he's tall and strong with dark blond hair and blue eyes, very blue eyes.'

'We've got that,' said Greta, giving her friend a quick hug. 'We'll do our best for you. Now go with this man,' and she pushed her in the direction of a loaded cart hitched to two mules, adding, 'You stand a better chance of finding something up at the hospital with Miss Nightingale. If you come with us they'll work out straight away that you're not with the army and send you back on the next ship leaving for England.'

Ada didn't want to leave the group but hearing the mention of Miss Nightingale's name again she felt a small thrill of excitement.

'Go, go!' shouted Sarah. 'You'll do well up at the hospital. If you need us, just ask for the house where the English army wives are staying. Everybody knows where that is.'

There was no time to say goodbye properly as Ada scrambled up on to the cart beside a mule driver who stared straight ahead. She shouted to the women she had grown so close to and waved goodbye frantically, tears not far away, but they were already swallowed up by the crowd.

Swaying along beside the driver of the cart, Ada began to feel like she was back on board ship and therefore more steady, but when the cart came to a halt in front of a large building and the driver indicated that she should jump down, her legs almost gave way and she had to cling to the rough wood at the side of the cart for support.

Fortunately a woman in a grey dress and starched, white apron had seen her stumble and came to her aid. 'You must have just arrived – still got your sea legs,' said the woman with a grim smile.

'Yes,' said Ada, starting to laugh. 'How could you tell?'

Her helper was not amused and immediately pursed her lips. 'Are you a nurse?' she asked. 'Have you got a letter?'

'Well, not exactly,' said Ada, using her unsteady gait and reeling head to her advantage as she exaggerated a stumble in order to avoid giving a proper answer. The woman grabbed her and pulled her up with strong arms. Ada stole a glance at the woman's face; it was severe, her mouth a firm, straight line.

Somehow the woman managed to get her in through the door of the building.

'Do you not know where you are? Who sent you?'

Ada saw a chair, slumped down on it and closed her eyes, shutting out the woman's questions, not wanting to answer, trying to think up what her story was going to be, trying to give herself time.

93

But the woman would not let up. 'Are you a nurse? Where is your letter?'

Ada thought quickly. 'There was a storm at sea,' she said. 'All my papers were lost.'

'Really,' said the woman, looking down her nose at Ada as she sat in the chair. 'Well, we'll see about that. Miss Nightingale is busy today; you will meet her tomorrow. We will find you a bed for the night and then *we will see*. Wait here and I will find someone to take you.'

Well, this is going well, thought Ada as she sat gently swaying on the chair in the entrance of Scutari hospital. She was already missing the easy company and ready acceptance of her travelling companions.

'Right, young lady,' said another woman's voice. Ada looked up to the welcome sight of a round, smiling face. A rush of relief flooded her body – thank goodness for human kindness. She smiled in return, but it must have been a strange smile because the kind face immediately showed some concern.

'You're in a bit of a state, dearie,' said the woman. 'You probably just need to get some rest and you're in luck: there is only one spare bed in this whole building tonight and it's with me. I'm Elsie, by the way, one of the washerwomen.'

'Ada. Ada Houston. Nice to meet you.'

Ada allowed Elsie to lead her through a number of corridors to her quarters. She was so glad to see the small bed already made up with clean sheets that she fell down on to it immediately, burying her face in the pillow as she had done as a child.

'I was going to offer you some food or maybe you need to freshen up, but I can see that you are exhausted. You sleep as long as you need,' said Elsie. 'I'll make sure you're up in plenty of time to see Miss Nightingale in the morning.'

However, Ada needed but a few minutes of complete relaxation away from the questions and steely glare of the woman in the apron before she was ready to turn over, prop herself up and listen to what Elsie had to say.

'So, young lady, it looks like you had a tough crossing,' said Elsie. 'I'll never forget my passage here, thought I was going to die, puked most of the way, lost so much weight nobody recognized me when I got here. Made up for it since, though,' she said, taking both hands to grasp the round belly that bulged under her apron and give it a bit of a shake. 'So, I guess you want to be a nurse,' she went on. 'Hope you've got a strong stomach, not just for the stuff you have to see and smell but the discipline. It's strict here. Granted, Miss Nightingale has got this place running like a tight ship, but she's all about the men, the sick and the injured. If I was one of them, I'd want her looking out for me. Don't get me wrong, she's not there washing and bandaging and turning up with her lamp at night, none of that; but she is in charge here and all the nurses are trained by her and carry out her instructions. She sets a very high standard. Such a strong and respectable lady, is Miss Nightingale.'

'But I thought she sat on the ward at night with her lamp. There are stories about that in the paper. She sits with the soldiers, like an angel.'

Elsie laughed. 'Well, you know what, the men

who write those papers don't always get the story straight. Yes, she does come down to see the patients and she will sometimes sit beside a soldier who she has concerns about. Her heart is in her work, you see. But that thing with the lamp at night – well, she does come down, but only to check that the nurses have heeded the curfew and are gone from the wards. She won't stand for any messing between the nurses and the men. You know what men are like once they start to feel a bit better.'

Ada sat for a moment mulling over this new information. Suddenly the world did not seem anywhere near as straightforward as when she'd imagined asking for work from the Miss Nightingale she had in her head. She would have had no worries about meeting that compassionate woman, who worked selflessly with the wounded soldiers, mopping brows, sitting up all night, who would smile and tenderly thank her for coming to the Crimea, who would offer her work tending the sick and maybe tell her personally that she would do all she could to help find her dear brother. But the woman Elsie described sounded quite different.

'Don't you be worrying,' said Elsie, sensing Ada's concern. 'If you're right for the work, Miss Nightingale will make a good nurse out of you, she will that. I remember when we first arrived here: there was nothing but dirt and squalor on those wards. Now look at them – clean and light. She gets the air moving through. You'll have a challenge, though, doing the work. That first winter the nurses were treating soldiers with frostbite and when they unrolled the bandages toes came off with the dressings. I even found some in my laundry.'

Ada gave a slight groan and started to feel sick.

Elsie laughed. 'You'll see all sorts round here. You'll get used to it.'

Sensing that she needed to change the subject Elsie launched into another story. 'Have you heard of Mrs Mary Seacole?'

'No,' said Ada, interested.

'Well, she's a nurse as well and I had her here staying with me one night. Such a lovely, warm person and a wonderful nurse. She came here to meet Miss Nightingale, not looking for a job like you – she'd already asked before she left London and they'd said no. But even though she'd been told that she couldn't have a job she still came out here anyway under her own steam and now she has her own place in the Crimea, near the front line. She is doing such good work up there. What a woman!'

Ada agreed heartily, though by now exhaustion from the journey was hitting her hard and she felt herself sinking fast into sleep.


'Is Miss Houston still with you?' It was morning and the woman who had helped Ada from the cart was standing in the doorway.

'Yes she is, Sister,' said Elsie, standing aside, so that Ada would be in evidence.

'Ah, there you are,' said Sister crisply. 'Miss Nightingale will see you now.'

'Good luck, dearie,' said Elsie as Ada got up to leave.

97

'Thank you for your kindness,' said Ada, giving Elsie's hand a squeeze as she passed by.

'Come along,' said Sister. 'Miss Nightingale is a very busy person. Her time is precious.'

Ada followed along behind Sister. She really did set quite a pace, and her own legs were still a bit wobbly. They went along several corridors, then through a long room with beds down the side occupied by men, some with bandages round their heads or legs. All seemed quiet. There was a very bad smell.

She tried out a small smile at one of the men, who seemed to be staring at her, but his expression did not change and it made her feel silly and uncomfortable.

Then they were out through the long room and into another corridor and then a different area of the hospital, where the smell was less obtrusive. Sister stopped abruptly at a door and bowed her head as if listening for something inside. Then she knocked on the door and Ada heard a faint voice call for them to come in.

Sister opened the door and stood to the side for Ada to enter.

'Miss Nightingale, this is the girl who arrived yesterday. As I mentioned, she has no papers.'

Then she was gone, closing the door behind her. Ada stood, still rather unsteady, in front of a slender woman in a dark grey gown who was writing in a large leather-bound book. Something about the woman's sharp demeanour made Ada understand that she must be quiet and still and wait.

Miss Nightingale took her time completing the entry in her book. It looked like some kind of ledger with numbers and calculations but Ada couldn't be sure. She found herself staring at the neat hair and perfectly placed lace cap. Ada felt her heart racing.

At last Miss Nightingale placed the pen decisively on a pad next to the ledger. Ada was impressed by her precision of movement. Then she looked up and fixed Ada with a gaze so piercing that she thought this earnest woman with a pale face might be able to see right through to her very soul.

Ada could not speak. She was completely at the woman's mercy.

'Sit,' she said at last, indicating a chair to Ada's left.

Ada sat, making an effort to straighten her back and look alert.

'I am Florence Nightingale,' said the woman, fixing Ada again with those bright eyes that shone with intelligence. 'I believe you are looking for work here as a nurse and that your letter of introduction has been lost on the ship.'

'Yes,' said Ada, unable to get out more words before Miss Nightingale ploughed on.

'I am afraid that we have no positions vacant for nurses at present, and, in fact, I have had no correspondence whatsoever with regard to your appointment. Therefore there is nothing here at Scutari for you. I'm sorry.'

Ada felt very strongly, now that Miss Nightingale's eyes were upon her, that she knew everything there was to know about Ada Houston and the real reason why she was seeking work at the hospital.

'What I can do,' Miss Nightingale continued more kindly, 'is give you a letter to take up to Balaklava hospital. They are always looking for nurses up there.'

Ada tried to say, 'No, I need to be here,' but Miss Nightingale held up a hand to silence her. Then she opened a small drawer at the side of her desk and neatly slipped out a piece of paper, picked up her pen and dipped it in the ink pot.

Turning her bright gaze back to Ada she simply said, 'Full name?'

For a moment Ada thought she might have forgotten even that and she stumbled a bit with her reply.

'Sorry: Miss Ada Houston.'

'Training?'

Now Ada really was stumped. 'Well, I've not had any real training but I did look after someone in their own home who was sick.'

Miss Nightingale held up her left hand and Ada fell silent. 'No training,' she said as she wrote the detail into her letter. 'You see, that's the difference. All my nurses are properly trained. We feel here that it is important. We need to set the right standard. You should be all right in Balaklava, though; they take all sorts. However, Sister Mary Roberts is up there. She was one of mine. Excellent nurse. Miss Smith is up there also; she is in charge, but I will address this letter to Sister Roberts – she knows more about what is going on and what needs to be done.'

Miss Nightingale then signed the letter with a well-controlled flourish, blotted the ink, folded it with precision and slipped it into an envelope.

Handing it to Ada, she called for Sister, who must have been waiting at the other side of the door.

'Please make sure that Miss Houston is escorted back to the harbour. She is going up to Balaklava and I believe that there is a ship leaving this afternoon. Thank you, Sister,' and Miss Nightingale turned back to her ledger, immediately renewing her focus on whatever important work lay before her.

Ada opened her mouth to try and speak but there was nothing that she could say and Sister gave her a terrifying glance. As Ada left the room her mind was reeling. I will have to go, I will have to go up to Balaklava, to that circle of Hell! I must get a message to the army wives and let them know where I am going, ask them to send me word straight away to Balaklava hospital if they hear anything of Frank.

'Do you have any luggage?' Sister asked as they walked.

'No, just this bag,' said Ada.

Sister twisted round to see the canvas bag slung over Ada's shoulder. 'Highly irregular,' she said. 'I suppose your trunk was lost at sea also.'

'Yes it was,' said Ada with a touch of defiance in her voice. 'Terrible storm that was.'

Ada noted a slight squaring of Sister's shoulders as they continued to walk, all the time knowing that somehow she would have to get a note to the army wives. How could she do it? Then she saw the shape of Elsie heading down another corridor and she broke step from Sister to chase after the washerwoman.

'Elsie, Elsie!' she called after her, like she was

some long-lost friend.

'Yes?' said Elsie, turning around. 'How did you get on? Did you get a job?'

'No, not here but they're sending me up to Balaklava.'

Elsie immediately crossed herself and then opened her mouth to speak but Ada had to cut her short; it was only a question of time before Sister realized that she wasn't in tow and came looking. 'I need you to do something very important for me, very important. Please, please can you get a message to some friends who came in with me on the last ship from Liverpool. They are staying at the home for English army wives. Do you know where it is?'

'Yes, yes, I know the one. What's the message?' said Elsie with a conspiratorial gleam in her eye.

'Tell them that Ada has been sent up to Balaklava so that if they do hear any news about my brother – Frank Houston – they must send word immediately to Balaklava hospital.'

'Got it,' said Elsie, just as Sister shouted down the corridor: 'Come here at once! This is highly irregular. Miss Nightingale has ordered you to leave immediately for Balaklava. Immediately!'

'Good luck, dearie,' said Elsie, 'and don't worry. I'll get the message delivered for you. Frank Houston, your brother, send a message to Balaklava, right?'

'Yes,' said Ada, giving the washerwoman a big kiss on the cheek before hurtling back down the corridor to meet the glare of Sister, who looked just about ready to explode with rage. 'Very irregular,' she said yet again. 'You will be well suited to Balaklava.'

As they continued their march to the door of the hospital Ada began to feel relieved that she was being shipped out to another place. Even though it was on the front line, close to the fighting, it might not be quite as hostile as working here in Scutari.

# 6

*'Beggars in the streets of London were at that time leading the lives of princes, compared to the life of our soldiers in the Crimea when I arrived.'*
Florence Nightingale

Back at the harbour, Ada found that the ship going up to Balaklava was, of course, the *Golden Fleece*. She clambered aboard and found the deck busy with sailors preparing to set sail. It looked like she had got back just in time. The purser saw her straight away and made his way over, and immediately Ada produced the letter from her bag so that he would know exactly what she was doing. She smiled to herself. She didn't even know what she was doing yet; she had no idea if going up to the front line was the right thing to do – the thought of it was already terrifying – but she recognized that she didn't seem to have any other option. She needed some kind of accommodation and a means of supporting herself and at least she trusted Elsie to get word to the army wives. And, who knew, maybe Frank was in Balaklava after all.

And there was another thing: she had the letter that was a recommendation for work, and it had been given to her by Florence Nightingale, the famous Lady with the Lamp. And what if she could help out and maybe learn to be a proper nurse? What if she could do something good to help with the injured soldiers while she was looking for Frank? She could almost see herself in the uniform, the grey dress and the starched apron, carrying her own lamp and sitting by a bedside, and for the first time in a long while she began to feel a sense of real purpose.

Maybe she was a complete fool to think that she might be able to do that kind of work, but there was one thing for sure: if she was to have any chance of finding her brother she could not go back to Liverpool without giving it a go.

As she leant on the rail and stared down into the harbour, she felt the presence of someone nearby. Glancing to the side she saw the young man in a brown tunic whom she had mistaken for Frank. She was glad to see him, his vague familiarity making her feel better. He still looked a bit like Frank but this time it was no shock to her and she was pleased to see him.

'How far is it to Balaklava?' she asked one of the sailors.

'Well, miss,' he said with a serious face, 'that all depends on how the weather goes. There can be bad storms in the Black Sea and we need to sail right the way up to the Crimea. It's quite a distance, you know, quite a way.'

'How many days would you expect then?' asked

Ada, trying to get some idea.

'Well now, last time I made this run, it took us about six days, yes, about six days, I think.'

Ada had had no idea it would be so far. Seeing her concern the sailor added, 'But it might be less. As I say, it depends on the weather. At least you'll have plenty of room down there, miss, we aren't taking any other passengers apart from a few soldiers who have come out of the hospital. Poor buggers have got better so they're being sent back up there to go and get shot at all over again.'

Ada flinched at his grim humour.

'They won't be bunking down with you, miss, they'll be with the lads. And we still have some of the horses to deliver up to Balaklava, plus supplies. That lad over there, the one as keeps looking at you, he's one of the grooms for the horses.'

'Is he?' said Ada, feeling her face flush and not needing to look over to see which young man the sailor was referring to. 'Thank you,' she said, 'I'll go down below now and sort out my bunk.'

The sailor gave her a small salute and she headed straight below decks without glancing up.

Ada lost track of how many days the journey took, but thought in the end it was five. She was pleased that she didn't need the bucket this time – she seemed to have maintained her resistance to sea-sickness – and they didn't hit any more storms.

The day they arrived in Balaklava, the excited shouts of the sailors told her they were coming into harbour. Gathering her things together and making sure she had the red shawl, she took one last look below decks before climbing up the ladder for a final time.

The bright light of the Crimean sun shone down on her as she came through the hatch, and as she squinted up into the blue sky she felt that she was climbing through to a new life.

Up on deck, her legs began to feel weak again and she needed to cling to the side of the ship. The light was strong and very bright and she was blinking like some underground creature. Looking around she could see that the small harbour was bristling with the masts of dozens of ships moored close together. The town itself seemed to be made up of a number of squat buildings surrounded by low hills. Strangely, she couldn't see any trees. Ada was eager to get on dry land and gazed longingly at it, but the dock area was so packed with people she wondered how on earth she would be able to get through. The crew had spilled out on to the harbour and were busy unloading. She waited as long as she could but when she started to get bumped and jostled by the crew as they carried stuff ashore she knew it was time to make a move.

Gingerly, she made her way down the gang-plank. Then she stood on the dock at Balaklava, clutching her canvas bag and struggling to remain upright, as the smell of horse muck, rotting fruit and effluent and a barrage of noise hit her full in the face. Her legs, once more unused to solid ground, felt for the roll of the ship.

The heat of the sun beat on her face and without the shade of a bonnet she was unable to see much at first. Then, as her eyes began to adjust to the bright full sun, brighter than any summer that she could have imagined back home, the chaos around her began to feel more real. The horses that had survived the journey danced around, snorting, wide-eyed and slicked with sweat, throwing their heads up in fear, and yanking at their halters. A woman screamed as one pushed into her, knocking her off her feet as it backed away from its handler and almost fell into the waters of the dock. Men in uniform shouted; women stood in groups arguing. All around Ada there seemed to be laughter and people jostling one another, tussling with their bags, bumping into each other.

Desperately trying to find a focus, Ada searched for the groom. She couldn't see him at first, but then a couple of the horses shifted and Ada spotted him quietly talking to one of the terrified creatures, running his hand slowly down the animal's neck, stroking and soothing. While others shouted and twitched at theirs, increasing the distress, he stayed calm and so did his horse.

At this distance he looked even more like Frank and she started to scan the others gathered on the quay, hoping against hope that her brother could be there and it would be that easy to find him, to simply see him in the crowd and he would come walking over to her with a smile or a scowl, depending on what mood he was in. She knew that there was next to no chance of that though. And then again, maybe Mary had been right, she was stark, raving mad to come out here, to a place where she knew no one and nothing was familiar. Even the light was different here – and what was that smell?

Just for a moment her head sank and she had to fight back the tears; but she knew that she could not be seen to be weak in this strange place. Who knew who might be watching her. She could not appear vulnerable. So, she used the sight of the groom, with his dark blond hair curling at the base of his neck and his strong back, to ease her sorry state as she stood on the quay. As he soothed and calmed the horse Ada began to regain some control. She felt her mouth begin to set in a determined line, and some strength return to her body. She would not give up now, not after coming all this way. She had come here to find Frank and she would not go soft now.

Then, suddenly, someone grabbed her arm saying, 'Nurse, nurse! We need you over here – quick, quick now, the doctor needs some help.'

It was only a boy and she tried to tell him that she wasn't a proper nurse, but she had no strength to resist him as he pulled her staggering through the crowd towards a bloody patch of ground in a shaded area of the quay.

Too dazed to react with her usual quick wit, she took a moment to take in the scene. The small patch of shade was littered with bodies, some lying on filthy blankets, others propped against a wall.

The voice of her assailant broke through again. 'I've brought her, doctor. Here's that nurse. You won't need me now.' And with that he was gone, running through the crowd.

Ada opened her mouth to protest but no sound came out. Instead she found herself looking in silence at a thin man in a blood-soaked apron with a knife in his hand. She saw that his arms were soaked up to the elbows in blood. Surely this man was a butcher not a doctor.

The man lying stretched out before him on a makeshift table was muttering softly to himself and rolling his head from side to side, his face burning red and blistered in places, his hair matted with mud and dried blood. Still wearing the remains of an army uniform, he appeared ripped and mangled as if recently mauled by some giant beast.

The doctor glanced at her fiercely and said, 'Right, nurse, don't dither, I need you to hold this leg for me, hold it very steady.'

Ada could see, even in her exhausted state, that the man lying on the makeshift table needed all the help that he could get. She was not a nurse, she had no idea what she could do, but she had to do something. She put down her bag and moved to take the strangely inhuman leg that was being presented to her. A sickly, overwhelming stink met her nostrils and her stomach heaved but she held on to that leg; she wanted to do everything she could to help the poor man who lay before her.

So she clung to that leg and stood ready. The doctor seemed completely focussed on the task in hand and two other men were there at the man's head, holding him down. Ada saw the doctor gripping the knife more firmly in his bloodstained hand and then loudly, as if making an announcement in church, he stated his intention. 'As you can see, nurse, this man has gas gangrene affecting his left lower limb. Therefore I am about to perform an above-knee amputation.'

Ada swayed a little.

'Keep it still, nurse, keep it still!' he said, and through sheer strength of will she managed to steady herself. He continued as if completely unaware of her inexperience. 'As you can see, the line of demarcation is just below the knee and we need as wide a margin as possible, therefore I'm making the incision here.'

He drew a finger across the man's leg to mark the line and Ada nodded.

'As soon as I finish cutting through the soft tissue, you must pass me that saw.'

What saw? she thought desperately, determined to do whatever was required but starting to feel a bit light-headed.

Then he swept the blade towards the leg and the sharp knife slipped into the man's flesh. The patient struggled, yelled and cursed, trying to twist his body away from the pain with all his remaining strength, but the two men at the head of the table increased their grip and used their weight to hold him down.

As the first dotted flush of bright red blood sprang from the wound Ada swayed but continued to cling to that leg. Somehow she managed to pass the saw to the doctor when he asked, and continued to cling to the leg until finally she felt it come away from the man's body. And then, completely overwhelmed, she slumped and hit the ground in a dead faint.

In her dream Ada was warm, safe, being gently rocked from side to side. She felt completely at peace for the first time in so long.

Then something started to tug at the corners of her mind.

A voice. A shouting voice.

She felt heavy, sleepy, couldn't rouse herself; it was like being under a thick muffled blanket. She was sure she could hear a fly buzzing and felt the tickle of an insect crawling over her face but was unable to move her hand to brush it away.

The buzz and the drone of flies continued and the voice became clearer and then insistent, shouting and arguing with another voice, a woman's voice.

'Bloody nurses, can't even stay on their feet! Where do they get these blasted women from anyway ... couldn't finish, couldn't tie off the artery properly... Look at this mess – he bled everywhere.'

Then the smell hit her again – sickly, heavy, the smell of death – and she remembered where she was, where she had willingly come.

# 7

*'No man, not even a doctor, ever gives any*
*other definition of what a nurse should be*
*than this – "devoted and obedient". This definition*
*would do just as well for a porter.*
*It might even do for a horse.'*
Florence Nightingale

Slowly opening her eyes, Ada tried to sit up but was forced back down by a firm hand and a commanding voice, a woman's voice.

'You lie still a while, dear, you've had a nasty

shock and bumped your head. That doctor was completely out of line to get you working straight off the ship. He had the audacity to complain that you had compromised his sutures. Stuff and nonsense: he should be able to sew up under canvas in the dark and in a storm. And they should be using chloroform like the French to knock the poor buggers out before they start cutting. Poor man probably died of shock.'

As Ada was trying to make sense of these words, delivered rapidly and with force, she became aware of the bulky frame and smell of lavender water that accompanied the speaker.

'Don't you worry, dear, I gave him what for. And what about the state of my poor horses? Not one of them would have survived the journey without that boy. They'll need to be tended if we want them back on form. I can't begin to tell you what the heat and the flies and the poor fodder have done to my horses. Then they take them out to the front line and get them blown to smithereens...'

Ada opened her eyes and looked into the face of the speaker: a woman of generous middle age with arched eyebrows split by a deep frown line and a large determined mouth that now broke into a wide smile to reveal a remarkable set of straight white teeth.

'Hello there, young lady, welcome to Balaklava. I'm Mrs Fitzwilliam. Now, you just have a swig of this and we'll have you back on your feet and shipshape in no time. Come along, do as you're told.'

Ada had only once had a tiny sip of alcohol so

the smell and the burning taste of what was thrust to her lips now via a hipflask was quite a shock. She coughed and spluttered as it burned its way down her gullet but, to be fair, it did have the desired effect and she was suddenly awake and able to move.

Mrs Fitzwilliam hauled Ada up from the ground, declaring that there was nothing like a bit of brandy in times of need, then continued in her forthright manner to warn against the drinking of any water in the Crimea unless thoroughly boiled. Having witnessed the fate of those who did she felt sure that no one wanted to end up like that. Best to stick to spirits, wine or beer.

Once standing, Ada began to feel that her legs had regained the possibility of holding her upright, but as she looked up she was immediately overshadowed by the sight of the tallest woman that she had ever seen. Mrs Fitzwilliam towered above her as she checked Ada over. Then, swiftly moving on to practical matters, she said, 'Right, dear, where are you commissioned, which hospital? Or are you going up to the front?'

Ada was unable to speak following the assault of the brandy, so it was fortunate that Mrs Fitzwilliam never seemed to require a reply. Instead she took the opportunity to give Ada's left cheek a vigorous pat.

'Come on, dear, come on, we need to get going before that ghastly man comes back. Are you stationed at Balaklava?'

Still bewildered but wanting to avoid further attempts to rouse her, Ada nodded her assent. Within seconds she was marched out of the small harbour building to which she had been conveyed when she had fainted. Coming back out now into the bright sunlight was a shock but she was calmer and more able to take in the detail of the scene around her.

During the period of time she had been absent the frenzy she'd experienced when she got off the ship had ended and the area was calmer. Around her the warm air was filled with the sounds of the wagons being loaded with cargo from the ship and voices shouting, but the horses had gone and the groups of soldiers were beginning to disperse. Although it was still oppressively hot, Ada could feel a gentle breeze on her face. She inhaled more deeply to try and revive herself and found that the smell was less of an affront now that she was starting to get used to it.

The injured men who had lain pitifully in the shadow of the building were being loaded on to wagons, carefully handled by the two heavy-set men who had been present at the operation. Ada was at first puzzled by how quiet the soldiers were – surely they must be in pain – but then she saw the haunted look on their faces and began to understand something of what the men must have been through.

Thankfully there was no sign of the doctor but her heart tightened momentarily and the hairs prickled at the back of her neck when she saw a blanket shrouding the body of the man that she had attended on the makeshift surgical table.

Ada realized that she was moving, being irresistibly pulled along by Mrs Fitzwilliam, who had spotted a stern-faced woman wearing some kind of uniform and a large bonnet directing the operation to move the wounded men.

The transaction was efficient and Ada was received by the woman at the insistence and on the recommendation of Mrs Fitzwilliam. No words were spoken by the woman other than, 'Come along, nurse,' but at least Ada had the feeling of being required to do something.

As she saw the impressive figure of Mrs Fitzwilliam stride away Ada couldn't help but admire her speed and vigour. She watched as her rescuer untethered and skilfully mounted a large black horse with a flowing mane and tail. Then with a jolt she realized that Mrs Fitzwilliam was not wearing a skirt but a garment that was loosely divided into legs that tucked into her strong leather boots. Mrs Fitzwilliam was wearing breeches! She sat astride the horse and used her strong legs to squeeze the animal into action; then she was off at some speed, twisting round in the saddle and shouting back to Ada, 'You take care, young lady, and if you need anything you can find me at the Commandant's House.' Then she was gone, raising the dust as she went.

Ada followed the woman to whom she had been assigned, trying not to think about where it might lead. Her legs had begun to feel weak again and she was still feeling slightly dizzy, so she was relieved to find that they seemed to be heading for one of the wagons. As they approached, the woman turned to her with a stern expression and said in a much gentler voice than Ada had expected, 'I'm Sister Mary Roberts. I'm in charge of two wards at the hospital, and you must refer to

115

me as "Sister" at all times.'

Ada tried to tell her that she had heard of her from Miss Nightingale but her words wouldn't come out. She fumbled in her bag for the letter but Sister Roberts motioned for her to put it away and told her to climb up on to the driver's seat behind a thin, brown horse with a scrappy mane, which was standing resting one of its back legs.

'I'll look at your letter of recommendation later,' she said.

Sister Roberts took a long time to check the load on the back of the wagon against a list that she produced from her pocket. The load looked like it contained sacks of food or cereals, but other packages were carefully bound and marked with a red cross and Ada assumed that they contained medical supplies.

As she did her checking, Sister Roberts kept frowning, tutting and shaking her head. It seemed that all was not well with the consignment and this was causing some confusion or frustration.

The longer Ada sat, the more uncomfortable she felt in the heat of the sun. Her face began to burn and she reached down into her bag to take out the red shawl. Pulling this over her head, she was able to sit, still hot, but at least with some protection from the blaze of the sun.

At last, with a big sigh and a final shake of her head, Sister Roberts jumped up on to the seat, settled herself and straightened her uniform. With a practised flick of the reins, the old horse stumbled into action and they were moving.

She glanced across at Ada with the red shawl

around her head.

'You should have brought a bonnet,' she said as a statement of fact rather than a criticism.

Ada looked at her and nodded, trying to smile but beginning to feel a bit sleepy and swimmy in the head.

As they started to move faster, Ada lurched in her seat and grabbed hold of the side of the creaking wagon to stop herself from swaying too violently. Thankfully they could only move at a very slow rate but their route was uneven and potholed with many stops and starts. As they jolted and lurched along she saw countless small buildings amid the rocky terrain. What a strange land, she thought.

Her attention was caught momentarily by a soft thud and boom in the distance, like the sound of heavy machinery moving suddenly. She glanced across at Mary Roberts, who understood the question. 'That's the big guns at Sevastopol starting up, as they do, any time of day or night.'

The noise continued to echo back and forth as they rattled up a rocky incline and Ada felt terrified. She had never heard a big gun before. How far away were they? Could they reach them here as they bumped along this track? Sensing her alarm, Sister Roberts spoke again in a gentler voice: 'No need to worry, those guns are miles away. We are safe at present.'

Ada felt relieved and her body relaxed a little. She hadn't liked the 'at present' part of what Sister said but she had to let that worry go for the time being. She let herself settle into the erratic rhythm of the wagon as it bumped over every hole in the road and concentrated on not falling out.

By the time they got to the hospital Ada's head was resting on the firm shoulder of Sister Roberts. She vaguely remembered a hand shaking her and someone speaking to her but then she was being unloaded by strong arms and carried. She opened her eyes to see the face, she was almost sure, of one of the male assistants at the operation. Ada tried to smile but she couldn't feel her own face any more.

Then she floated or was carried away as she heard the voice of Sister Roberts ordering her removal to the nurses' sick ward.

# 8

*'These women had the true nurse-calling –*
*the good of the sick first, and second only*
*the consideration of what is their "place" to*
*do – and that women who wait for a housemaid*
*to do this or a charwoman to do that, when*
*the patient is suffering, have not the making*
*of a nurse in them.'*
Florence Nightingale

'Nurse Blackwood, we have a new admission to the nurses' sick ward. Please can you attend immediately.'

Nurse Rose Blackwood looked up from her patient and nodded. This was an inconvenient time because they were busy straightening up and trying to get the men settled for the night, doing what they could in the very crowded and dirty wards to keep up some semblance of care. The soldiers were fractious and more demanding because they knew that the nurses would all be disappearing by eight o'clock.

Looking about her now, Nurse Blackwood felt sorry for most of these poor souls and would have liked to have kept vigil overnight. Some of the men constantly called out for a drink or other small comfort or just needed to know that somebody was there. Most of these poor beggars would be hard pressed to be a significant threat anyway, weakened as they were by wounds and infections. Working nights would also allow some control over the ill-disciplined hospital nurses, who spent the evening getting as drunk as possible from any form of alcohol they could lay their hands on. For Rose this had been very shocking at first but in comparison to the horror and suffering she bore witness to every day it had now become a mere inconvenience.

The best way to exit the ward without fuss was to move at speed, otherwise one became too embroiled with minor detail and final adjustments. This required a certain amount of hardness on her part but she always promised herself that those she ignored on the way out she would give that extra bit of attention to the next day.

She picked up her wool skirt and, with a flash of fine stocking, skilfully flitted her way through a sea of needy faces and a murmur of 'Nurse, nurse, please, nurse.'

As she reached the area of the ward where the beds were, she automatically scanned under each one; sure enough, dark huddled shapes and the glint of an eye indicated that the rats were back in. At the sight of them her stomach turned and she moved faster. She would let the other staff know so they could have a go at them with brooms and clubs. Some of the fitter patients kept bayonets within reach for that purpose but most were too sick to even notice the scurrying of these vile beasts under and over beds and mattresses.

At last she reached the door and ran full pelt into Mary Roberts.

'Ah, Nurse Blackwood,' said Sister with a great deal of amusement twinkling in her brown eyes. 'We have a new nurse, just arrived off a ship from Scutari, in a bit of a state and not really rousable. I think it's sun stroke but with all the fevers going round we can never be too sure. Would you go along and have a look at her? I need to get on and sort out the supplies. We seem to be short again – they never send on what they should from Scutari.'

Rose had stood quietly listening, concern for the new recruit growing. 'Yes, Sister, of course. Do we know anything about the new nurse?'

'Ah yes,' said Sister Roberts, pulling Miss Nightingale's letter out of her pocket. 'I spoke to her only briefly but there is a letter of recommendation here. Her name is Ada Houston. She has no training; they have nothing for her at Scutari. The thing is we weren't expecting anyone – there has been no correspondence. Miss Smith may know something about her but I doubt it. Anyway, nurse, you get along there and see what you can do for the poor girl. At this rate we might lose her anyway.'

Nurse Blackwood nodded and walked to what would be, hopefully, her final duty of a very long day.

On reaching the sick bay Rose took stock of the situation. A hospital nurse who yesterday had developed a high fever and had been projectile vomiting now lay quiet, a bit too quiet for her liking, in the far bed. One thing that Rose had learnt very quickly about these fever cases was that beyond sponging them down there was little that one could do. Either the fever would break and the patient would recover or the infection would be unstoppable and lead quickly to death.

Nurse Blackwood's heels clipped on the wooden floor as she went across the room to make her assessment of the new patient. She seemed to be sleeping and, as Sister Roberts had reported, she was hardly rousable and clearly had a bad case of sunburn on her face from standing out without a bonnet. Rose noted a pretty face with delicate cheekbones, a small but full red mouth and the longest black eyelashes that she had ever seen. The girl's hair was struggling to escape from its restraint and although spattered with what looked like dried vomit, it fell luxuriant on the pillow as Rose removed the combs that held it in place. Someone, probably Sister Roberts, had already removed a worn but carefully darned red shawl that now lay neatly folded at the end of the bed.

First Rose felt the girl's face and neck to check for heat, observed the depth and strength of her breathing and looked for the beat of a rapid pulse beneath the delicate skin of the young woman's neck. She was sunburnt but there was no sign of a major fever. Beneath the thin blanket the girl was fully clothed in dress that was suited to the cold streets of some English town, not the summer heat of the Crimea, and so Rose removed the girl's outer garments for comfort. She was surprised to find that the girl had a rather lovely mother-of-pearl brooch pinned to her blouse. Best secure that to her shift, she thought, so it doesn't get lost.

Finding a bowl of water and a cotton cloth by the bed, she gently sponged the girl's face, neck and hands. As she turned the hands over she noted finely shaped fingers and delicate palms covered in very rough skin. It looked like this girl was more than used to hard work. Then finally, as she had been taught, using the last dregs of water for the most soiled area, she soaked and then sponged the dried vomit from that glorious mane of dark brown hair.

Rose always liked to perform these simple offices for people. It made her feel as well as know the reason she had come out to this godforsaken place. The tenderness with which she wiped the girl's skin, taking extra care around her eyes and laying the cloth for a few moments across the forehead, had become, for Rose, almost like a meditation. It was a ritual that she had performed many times within the walls of this hospital, but each time it was done with as much care and respect as she could muster. She felt that the more battered, weather-beaten or maimed the face, the more deserving of this small comfort. She had known hardened soldiers' eyes fill with tears on receipt of this tender care.

She knew by the girl's responses that it would be a waste of time sourcing a bowl of beef tea or a piece of bread for her – she wouldn't be taking solid food just yet. So she simply offered a sponge soaked in drinking water first to the lips and then to the girl's mouth. The girl drank readily, so Rose offered some sips of water from a spouted cup, carefully propping her up with her free arm. The girl muttered thank you and then opened her eyes just for a moment. She gave Rose a beautiful smile that felt like a glimpse of the sun. Rose smiled back at her and then squeezed her hand before saying goodnight.

The ward was rapidly darkening; Rose found a lamp and lit it with the tinder. This was the time she should be finding her way back to the nurses' quarters and taking her rest, but she was reluctant to leave this girl with the lovely smile. She remembered what a state she herself had been in when she first arrived and how grateful she had been for one of the nurses at Scutari sitting with her; she would probably get into trouble with Sister Roberts for this but she knew what her instincts were urging her to do.

The welcome glow cast by the lamp flickered around the room and in the corner she saw a chair. She would sit here tonight by the girl, then she could give her drinks overnight and make sure she was safe.

She laughed to herself as she carried the Turkish lamp across to a small table between the beds. She felt like Florence Nightingale with her lamp, but knew that back in Scutari Miss Nightingale was also known as the 'lady with the hammer' after an incident where she had been denied access to a storeroom of medicines that were needed for her wounded men. And she had taken a hammer and smashed the lock off the door. Rose smiled when she remembered the story and felt so proud of the woman who had inspired her to come out to the Crimea.

Beginning to feel sleepy, Rose found herself drifting off and began to doze in the chair by the girl's bed. And as the night passed, her waking and sleeping became muddled and she entered a strange state of awareness.

She found herself back home watching again the spectacle of the troops as they embarked, their bright red jackets, shining buttons and military hats dazzling and delighting the huge crowd that had gathered to see them off. No one, except her father, really seemed to know where the Crimea was but everyone was certain that the men would be back soon and they would be victorious. In her sleep she also visited again that cold drawing room in her father's house where, under the tick of the mantel clock, she had requested permission to apply to join the contingent of army nurses gathering for transfer out to Balaklava. She saw again her mother's look of pain as she glanced up from her embroidery then put down her needle.

Rose would like to think that this was due to concern for her daughter's safety but she knew, in truth, it related to the probable loss of a love match that her mother had been working on between Rose and a local landowner's son.

But Rose's imagination had been caught by the prospect of doing something good for others – not taking flowers round to an ailing relative or visiting the poor house, but doing something that would make a real difference.

Conditions for the soldiers in the Crimea had been reported for all to see in *The Times,* and with the journalists now having access to that new telegraph, the people of England could get the news very readily, almost before the blood had dried on the battlefield. This had made Rose feel close to the events of the war and to the plight of the men and she had begun to have vivid dreams of being dressed as a nurse and carrying a lamp like Miss Nightingale. And the more afternoon teas she had to sit through, or invitations to balls that she received, or, worst of all, the stitch after stitch that she was required to make with her embroidery needle, the more she wanted – no, needed – to do something real.

# 9

*'The very first requirement in a hospital [is]*
*that it should do the sick no harm.'*
Florence Nightingale

In the doctors' quarters at the other side of the hospital building, John Lampeter paced up and down the restrictive length of a barely furnished room. He ground his teeth in frustration and talked out loud, going through the surgical procedures he had been required to perform during another busy day of receiving casualties from Sevastopol. One of the above-knee amputations had gone smoothly but that last procedure was a complete mess. The man shouldn't have bled like that. It would be easy to blame his incompetent assistant but he reluctantly and angrily acknowledged that his sheer exhaustion and repeated exposure to a series of demanding tasks had compromised his performance.

Damn and blast it, he could feel again the artery slipping from his grip as the useless ligature tightened on nothing. He had been left frantically clawing around in a haemorrhage of blood for the blasted vessel as the poor blighter exsanguinated before his eyes. He hadn't even realized that the new nurse had fainted until after he'd finished. I mean, where did they get these women from anyway? Any nurse with the right experience should be able to stay on her feet during a routine operation. Not that it would have made any real difference; these procedures were difficult even in the best of circumstances, and when an injured man had been left so long before he was seen by a doctor, when infection had set in, it was even worse.

Lampeter was always hard on himself and he hated it when things didn't work out for the best. He had been a doctor long enough to know that was often the way, but even so he still despised himself for what he regarded as a botched job. With a sigh he sat down on the edge of the bed and poured himself a large brandy from the bottle that lived on the packing case which served as a bedside locker. He took a good slug and tried to relax as the fiery liquid burned down his gullet then settled with a glow in his empty stomach. What he'd give for some tobacco in his pipe right now. Hopefully Dr Mason would be in soon, a generous good-natured fellow who would almost certainly share a smoke.

Suddenly restless again, he got up from the bed and went over to the narrow window ledge to inspect the collection of bullets he had dug out of the flesh of British and Russian soldiers alike. He knew from his careful study of ammunition and observation of the effects on the human body that the damage from these weapons was becoming more severe. At the beginning of the war when he was in Scutari you could dig a ball of shot out of a man's thigh and sew him up with little damage – the bullet would literally bounce off the femur. Now the bone would be shattered from top to bottom on impact and the leg would almost certainly need to be amputated.

He was interrupted by a knock at the door and Jones entered carrying a black tin pan containing something to eat – he didn't know what, but thought it might be boiled beef. He instructed Jones to place the meal on the table and then be gone to his other duties. Jones had suffered greatly during their posting to Balaklava. Remarkably, while all and sundry were falling over with typhus fever or cholera back in Scutari, Jones had remained hale and hearty, but as soon as they arrived in the Crimea, down he went with a damned inconvenient fever that left Lampeter without a servant. He knew that the man couldn't help all of that, but with his uniform hanging loose about him Jones now looked for all the world like a pauper from one of those sketches by that chap Dickens.

Lampeter tried to feel something for his poor, downcast servant but increasingly his feelings towards those who were not injured or dying were blunted as they became buried deeper and deeper inside the shell of a man who was required to deal with death and horror on a daily basis.

He was saved from sinking from an angry to a black mood by the appearance of Dr Mason in the doorway. With his cheerful manner and ready wit, his companionship in the evening made a world of difference to John. The meat they were about to eat might be the toughest in the whole world but shared with Mason it would be much easier to stomach.

After supper they both settled with some brandy and a share of Mason's tobacco to talk through the events of the day. When both started to fall asleep through sheer exhaustion the conversation petered out and it was time for bed.

John knew he should check through his clothes and bedding for lice or at least try and remove some of the dried blood on his boots, but sheer exhaustion hit him and after quickly finishing the rest of his glass he fell on to his bed and entered a dark, heavy sleep.

The booming of artillery up the coast continued overnight but nothing could disturb John. Even as a medical student he had had a reputation for being able to sleep through anything and rarely became ill.

His days here at the hospital were intense and so busy it seemed that he could have been here weeks or months or even years. In fact he had arrived on board a steamer from Scutari only a few months ago. That foggy day, as they breached the narrow entrance to the harbour and he saw the dock bristling with masts and the shape of the rocky shore, had felt like the beginning of something he had been craving since his arrival in Turkey last year.

His work at the hospitals in Scutari had gone well enough, but as a young surgeon he was frustrated by the lack of surgical cases and the huge number of chronic medical cases on the wards. Fevers were rampant and often deadly. In fact he had lost two of his colleagues and close friends within the space of a few days, and he too, in the end, had succumbed to an aggressive choleric fever.

He couldn't remember much about that time but was thankful for the ministration of the medical officer's wife at Scutari who had nursed him through the worst. Once able to sit up in bed and take a few steps, he'd known he would at least live, but this episode had for the first time in his life made him feel vulnerable and maybe mortal. The possibility that he might die out here, so far from home, had become real and he now bore the resulting anxiety alongside whatever arrogance he still managed to cling on to.

This anxiety led him to check over himself each morning as a routine. After removing his shirt he would inspect his skin for blemishes; then, trying not to look too closely at his now scrawny frame in the waist-length mirror, he would stick out his tongue to check its colour. Taking up a fine comb he would go through his thick black whiskers and beard to remove any lice and check for scurf. Then, of course, he would check his pulse and the colour of his urine. Sometimes he was concerned by a little irregularity of the pulse and darkness of his water but would put this down to excessive work and lack of fresh air and exercise.

He had devised a short programme of simple exercises in an attempt to build his strength back up following the fever and was quite pleased that this was coming along nicely. However, the quality of food was often very poor and he needed to make strenuous and repeated requests for milk, eggs and boiled beef. A man couldn't live off bread, butter and tea alone.

As he slept, his heart pumped, his muscles relaxed and his guts rumbled on that hard lump of meat and the brandy. Even asleep, his lively mind continued to whir and make plans. After scrounging what he could for breakfast, he would probably make a trip out to Mrs Seacole's canteen for some provisions and his regular glass of cherry brandy before returning to the hospital for the ward round. Once he started with the patients his day would not be his own and this routine allowed the nurses and orderlies to create some semblance of order on the ward and remove any dead before he started asking questions and making demands.

The place was packed out at the moment; mainly with Crimean fever cases, but there were also some interesting war wounds to monitor. One in particular took a great deal of his time. A poor young lad had been hit by a shell full in the face, blasting a hole in his cheek and removing most of his tongue and his teeth. How he didn't die out there in the mud of the trenches they would never know but they were now packing the wound daily and once clear of suppuration he would be attempting to stitch up the hole in the lad's cheek. If he lived to return home his mother wouldn't recognize him but at least he would be a survivor.

Dr Lampeter had been trained not to think or feel too much for his cases but he couldn't help feeling sorry for this boy, who suffered miserable pain, was unable to speak and needed to be fed with slops. Although he still harboured a great deal of resistance to women being out here in the field of war, he had to admit that some of those nurses were doing a damn fine job of looking after his patients.

Mason was always banging on about that pale, thin nurse – Rose something-or-other her name was. Even though her wan face reminded him too much of his mother's drawing room, he had to admit that she was a fairly remarkable young woman. Very beautiful too in an unusual kind of way, with pale freckly skin and strawberry blond hair often wispy around her face after a morning's work. Mason certainly seemed to have a soft spot for her.

Lampeter wasn't sure how that new nurse was going to work out though, fainting away like that during what was, in effect, a routine procedure out here. Even so, he was half hoping that he would see her on the ward again soon.

When he woke, Lampeter felt the new day upon him after what seemed to be nothing more than a short nap, although he had, in fact, slept soundly for eight hours. He was irritated with himself, feeling that he was behind already and not properly prepared for the day. Getting out of bed, he walked over to the bucket and emptied his bladder, taking strange satisfaction in the sound of his urine drumming strongly into the iron pail.

Next he walked over to the mirror propped behind the washbowl and felt the daily shock of his appearance. A wild man with bright blue, blood-shot eyes stared back at him from the mirror with an expression of defiance. He could not believe that this was the same young man that had graced many a ladies' drawing room. His hair was growing back now after it had been shaved off during his bout of fever at Scutari, but still looked stubbly. His beard and whiskers, however, defied all attempts to be trimmed back with scissors and continued to flourish.

With a sigh he turned from his reflection, pulled on his shirt and then tied the bright red sash that served as a cholera belt firmly around his waist. He knew that some thought a piece of cloth tied around the body couldn't possibly ward off cholera, that it was just useless superstition, but he had known one very respected doctor in Scutari who swore by it, and so from his first week in the Crimea he had followed suit and tied the sash around his waist every morning and so far it had worked. Out here, where cholera was rife in the army camps, a doctor needed to use every means that he could to survive.

Once the sash was secure he sat down on his bed and pushed each foot in turn into the sturdy leather boots that he had bought especially for this trip. They had been stiff and shiny for some weeks when he first arrived in the Crimea but now bore the scars of daily toil.

He was not surprised to note the dried blood on the toes of both boots from yesterday's botched job. Steadfastly ignoring these new stains he strode towards the door. 'Let battle commence,' he muttered to himself as he exited the room.

# 10

*'Let us never consider ourselves as finished nurses…We must be learning all our lives.'*
Florence Nightingale

Rose woke with a start, confused about where she was and what she was doing. Rubbing her eyes and then focussing on her surroundings she became aware of the bed and the shape of her patient under the thin blanket. She was a nurse, working in a military hospital – she could smell it now.

Feeling heavy in her limbs and still exhausted, she stood up and leant over the girl to assess her condition. Her colour was good, nice and pink, and when Rose tipped her head and held her pale cheek close to the girl's face she could feel gentle breath on her skin. Looking down the girl's body she saw the slow rise and fall of her chest in what appeared to be a natural sleep. She was alive and seemed to be well, at least for now.

Then she looked across to the other bed.

The hospital nurse had not fared so well.

Rose went straight to the bed and stood for a few moments with her head bowed, saying a short prayer for the woman who had arrived in Balaklava only a few weeks ago. She hadn't known this nurse but remembered she had come up with a group from Scutari. She had seen her on the ward but these hospital nurses who came out to war as paid help already had some experience back home and usually set themselves apart from the volunteers. In fact Rose, when she thought about it, was the only 'lady volunteer' at the hospital at the moment. They'd had chaplains' wives previously, at least two, but they had died of fever alongside their husbands. All were buried in graves not far from the walls of the hospital.

She had heard a rumour that all fever cases were now going into a pit to be covered with lime, but she chose not to think about this. There was so much death from cholera, typhus and Crimean fever that she was forced to accept that this might be the only solution, but she shuddered when she thought of the bodies wrapped in blankets that now had to go out of the back of the hospital and into one big hole in the ground. It didn't seem right that they weren't able to give a proper Christian burial. They didn't even have a chaplain at the moment.

As she stood there, Rose said another prayer for

the woman and then gently pulled the sheet up to cover her face. Taking a deep breath she walked back to the bed of the new nurse. She sat back down for a few moments but was almost immediately disturbed by the sound of Sister Roberts's sturdy boot heels clicking on the floor as she came into the room.

Rose jumped up from the chair.

'Good morning, nurse, you've made an early start,' said Sister, probably aware that Rose had spent the night in a chair. 'Ah, I see,' she said, looking over at the shrouded bed. 'I feared she might succumb during the night. Such a shame ... I'd got to know her and I really liked her. I'll perform last offices; it's the least I can do.'

Sister Roberts stood quietly for a few moments and both nurses listened to the steady breathing of the girl in the other bed. Then Sister straightened her apron and lifted her chin.

'Right, Nurse Blackwood,' she said, noting her tired face, 'get yourself some breakfast and then go along to the wards and see how they're doing. Then as soon as you're done, get yourself back to the nurses' quarters for some sleep.' Pausing for a moment she added, 'I saw Dr Lampeter heading out on his horse earlier so he won't be back for a while but we need the place shipshape before he does his round.'

'Yes, Sister,' replied Rose automatically as she had learnt to do. It was, in fact, no hardship to take orders from Mary Roberts because despite her stern expression and tightly pulled-back hair she was an able and compassionate woman who would pitch in and work hard.

135

The situation with the nurse in charge, Miss Smith, was very different. She stayed mainly in the small room that served as her lodgings and her office. It contained, by all accounts, a small bed and a desk piled high with papers. Once a day she would emerge, stamping and shouting at the nearest nurse, orderly or doctor, and then retreat. It amazed Rose that even the battle-hardened soldiers on the wards who had fought the Cossacks were in awe of Miss Smith.

As Rose approached the ward she became aware of shouting and banging, and then out through the open door ran the biggest rat she had ever seen. Instinctively she drew her skirt tight around her legs as the creature scampered past her. She closed her eyes and was sure she felt the brush of its scaly tail. An orderly was chasing, and she glimpsed his red, sweating face as he ran at the rat with a wooden club. Rose let her body shudder, then, composing herself, entered the ward with a cheerful expression. Opening the door, she never failed to be surprised by the scene – Dragoons, Hussars, Lancers, Riflemen, Guards and common soldiers all mixed up together and closely packed. Some on beds, some on the floor; all bearded and many bloodied and bandaged. Some were still wearing ragged remains of muddied uniforms; some were barely covered, their broken and smashed military hats and helmets cast forlornly beside the beds. And she never got used to the smell; it hit her afresh every single day.

The quietness of the ward sometimes worried her. There could be a murmur of conversation and staff calling to each other but many of the men lay so diminished that speech was difficult. Those who were strong enough were immediately sent back up to the trenches, so inevitably this group of patients were always in an extremely sorry state.

Seeing young Arnold now in the bed by the door, she did her best to smile at him and was sure that his eyes smiled back. Rendered speechless by the bullet penetrating his cheek, and having suffered wounds to both arms, Arnold was a pitiful sight indeed. The wound to his cheek was packed with lint, his head bandaged and both arms immobilized with splints. Communication was difficult but they had devised a system of nods and hand squeezes and Rose always volunteered to feed Arnold when he was able to eat. This was a difficult task as he was liable to choke and liquid leaked out through the hole in his face. She knew that his facial wounds would be reviewed by Dr Lampeter today, so would make sure she was working close by.

The next bed was empty and Rose assumed that the occupant, who had developed an infection following an amputation of the forearm, had died during the night. The orderlies did their best to remove the bodies before the day started in an attempt to keep up morale among the remaining men. The stripped bed now held a stained mattress in testament to the struggles of the many wounded who had occupied it. No doubt it would be filled again very soon. They had tried to make some attempt recently to keep the patients with fever separate from the others because Sister Roberts had observed that the fever cases tended to spread quite readily in close proximity. However, this was impossible at times of heavy casualty.

The nurses and orderlies had got on well with their morning duties, helping men at their toilet and giving out some breakfast. Yet the ward never looked any brighter or cleaner or different. Since they had employed some of the army wives to tackle the laundry there was at least a supply of clean sheets and bandages. These laundresses had constructed washing lines at the back of the hospital which now hung heavy with all the bedding and supplies, but it was almost impossible to keep up with the piles of linen.

Rose preferred to work with the wounded rather than the fever patients, for whom not much could be done except sponging them down and waiting. The dressings were regarded as the responsibility of the doctors but she felt confident enough to attend to those that did not need to be reviewed or would not be expected to require the application of a knife to debride. She took up a basket of clean bandages and looked around for the most needy patient. There were always a number of men moaning in pain and with a very short supply of laudanum there was often no relief for this, but if a change or repositioning of a bandage could help, Rose would give it a try.

The old soldier two beds down from Arnold looked a likely candidate. The bandage supporting his head wound had slipped down overnight and was now obscuring his left eye. Rose had done the dressing a few times for Stanley, and she knew that the bandage was a crucial support for a large flap of skin that covered a mess of bone on his scalp.

She couldn't imagine the daily pain that this man had to endure, and had become an expert at fixing the bandage in a way that could help him.

She approached the bed, spoke softly to him and touched his hand gently. He opened his good eye and smiled through the pain.

'Hello, Stanley, is it all right if I try and fix that dressing for you?' she asked gently.

'You can have a go, miss,' he replied.

They both knew that removing the old dressing would be very painful but then this would settle and be more manageable throughout the day. She felt the man steel himself as she began to unwind the outer layers. Rose recoiled only when she spotted the lice that had worked their way into the dressing.

Then his whole body tensed as she got to the part that was stuck, fabric to skin. Rose had found that using a little bit of water at this time and leaving it to soak could help so she did this now, holding the man's hand for comfort while it was absorbed. She then warned him before the next move, and as always he told her to go quick, get it off, and to ignore his cry of pain. She did this now, praying that the flap of skin didn't come away with the gauze pad. She knew which way to peel the dressing so that the skin moved back into place.

Her experience with this particular wound served them well and the procedure was a success. Her patient visibly relaxed and she knew that re-bandaging would be an easy task now. Rose had been ably instructed by Sister Roberts and it was always satisfying to see the improvement in this poor man's situation. The wound, however, wasn't looking good. Each day the amount of discharge increased and the flap of skin became drier and darker in colour. She would report the deterioration to Dr Mason, rather than Dr Lampeter. She didn't know what was wrong with the man but he always looked distracted, even deranged at times. The patients reported that he did a good job but she just couldn't work him out.

As she looked up from her bandaging she noted that the man in the bed opposite had been watching her perform this duty very closely indeed. He too seemed to be relieved that it had gone well and his comrade would now be more comfortable.

Rose didn't have time to move on to her next dressing because the doctors arrived, chatting away as usual, standing one each side of the first bed. Rose knew that she needed to get over there, to be with Arnold. Dr Lampeter was looking across Arnold's bed, directly at Dr Mason, making little effort to engage with the patient. 'I think we need to remove this patient's dressing and the packing and suture up the wound if it's clean enough.'

Rose saw the look of horror on Arnold's face and slipped in beside Dr Mason. She looked straight at Dr Lampeter, who immediately looked away, and said, 'I'll remove this dressing, doctor, while you see the next patient, then you can come back and suture.'

'I think I need to do that, nurse,' said Lampeter, taken aback by her direct approach.

'I've been packing the wound and know exactly what to do,' said Rose, already starting to unravel the bandage.

Lampeter nodded and muttered something about making sure she did a proper job, and then moved away from the bed with a smiling Mason in tow.

Rose took care with unwinding the bandage, talking quietly to Arnold through every step. As always he managed very well, but Rose saw the tears rolling down his good cheek. She used the large forceps from the dressings basket to remove the sodden packing. She thought that the wound had cleaned up – certainly the amount of suppuration was reduced and there was no foul smell. This might be all right.

As soon as she was ready she called down the ward: 'The patient is ready now, doctor,' standing her ground by the bed. She had no intention of leaving her patient's side.

Lampeter came over directly; he was very interested in this wound.

'Ah yes, looking much better. I think we could proceed to sutures today. What do you think, Mason?'

Mason, still smiling at Rose, nodded his assent as Lampeter called over to the orderlies to come and hold the patient down.

'No!' shouted Rose almost involuntarily, standing by her patient's bed with her fists clenched at her sides. She could not have borne the sight of Arnold being held down while the painful procedure was inflicted and all the men on the ward able to see. 'Arnold can manage this if I stay with him, especially if you give him some drops of laudanum first.'

Lampeter was clearly thrown by her interjection but could see that she wasn't a woman to be argued with. 'This is very irregular, nurse, very irregular,' he muttered as he stomped off to get the laudanum. Mason was now laughing and clearly enjoying the spectacle of the fearsome Dr Lampeter being told what to do.

Rose knew she was right to try this new approach, and only hoped that it would work. While Lampeter was away she told Arnold exactly what the procedure would involve and roughly how many sutures he would have to endure. The black silk they used was thick and the needle had been blunted by much use, but she didn't tell him this. Hopefully, with the laudanum inside him he would manage. Rose also took the precaution of slipping him a nip of brandy from the small flask that she always carried in her apron pocket.

Lampeter came back and Rose administered the drops of laudanum into Arnold's mouth. She then asked the doctors to go and see other patients while it took effect. Again, Lampeter seemed appalled at this suggestion, shaking his head and muttering, but seeing her face he had no choice but to go off down the ward with the smiling Dr Mason.

When they returned to Arnold's bed, Rose was happy to let them proceed. Lampeter produced the needle and thread and, as Rose held the boy's hand and spoke to him quietly, instructing him to take deep breaths as the needle pierced the skin each time, the suturing commenced. Arnold squeezed her slim hand very hard each time the needle penetrated his flesh but he never moved his head. Rose watched carefully as the stitches went in and bright red blood began to run down Arnold's cheek. Lampeter paused when required to deftly swab the blood from the boy's chin.

Despite herself, Rose was forced to admire the sureness of Lampeter's hand and the speed of his work. As the last suture went in Rose smiled to herself and gave Arnold's hand a squeeze in return. When Mason congratulated Lampeter on some fine stitching, she thought that Lampeter looked a bit too self-satisfied and this annoyed her. As they all stood back from the bed they felt or even heard a sigh of relief from the soldiers around the ward.

Certainly Arnold was not a pretty sight with the flesh taken up and puckered at one side of his face, but at least he might live to see home again.

'Thank you, Dr Lampeter,' said Rose on behalf of her patient. He mumbled something in response then walked away. Please yourself, she thought, then quickly turned to find Mason staring at her in a most peculiar fashion. Feeling a little uncomfortable, Rose cleared her throat and said, 'I need to speak to you, Dr Mason, about the patient Stanley Jackson, the man with the head wound.'

Dr Mason was still looking at her in a strange way and his eyes didn't seem to be connecting with what she was trying to say.

'Who, which one?' he said, looking wildly around the ward.

'That patient,' said Rose, calmly pointing to the man two beds down from Arnold.

'Yes, yes, of course. I have seen the wound.

How is he doing?'

Rose indicated that they should move out of earshot of the patients and they walked through the door of the ward to stand just outside. 'Things aren't looking too good,' she said with genuine concern in her voice, and she described the wound. Mason listened intently to what she was saying, standing as close as he could to Rose as she spoke.

'Mmm,' he said when she'd finished. 'Is he delirious?'

'No, not as yet.'

'But if, as you say, the wound is worsening then it's just a question of time before our Mr Jackson deteriorates ... such a shame, he's a nice chap.'

'Yes, he is,' said Rose quietly. 'I will speak to him about last things, see if he wants any letters writing home.'

'Yes, good idea,' said Mason. 'And do keep me informed.'

Sister Roberts appeared next to Rose and smiled at Dr Mason. 'Can I interrupt for one moment please,' she said. 'Rose, you look exhausted. If you're finished here, go and check your patient in the nurses' sick bay, then get some rest.'

'Yes, Sister,' said Rose. She had no strength left to argue.

'I will keep an eye on Mr Jackson for you,' said Dr Mason, watching her as she walked away.

On reaching the sick bay, Rose was surprised to find that the sheet on the girl's bed was thrown back, her clothes and the red shawl were gone and the girl was nowhere to be found. Too tired to worry, she stood for a few seconds and silently queried what might have happened. Not able to find a ready answer, she straightened the still-clean sheet and pillow and went, as instructed, to find her own rest.

# 11

*'Apprehension, uncertainty, waiting, expectation, fear of surprise, do a patient more harm than any exertion.'*
Florence Nightingale

When Ada had woken, fuzzy-headed and still anxious about how close she was to those guns, she was unsure about what she should do but thought that getting up and dressed might be a good start. She had just clipped back her hair with the combs that had been left under the pillow by some thoughtful person, when a friendly face she vaguely remembered from the night before appeared at the door. It was the man who had carried her into the hospital.

'Hello there, miss, my name's Tom Dunderdale, medical orderly,' said the broad, clean-shaven face. 'Would you be free to help me collect more stores this morning? There'll be some breakfast in the bargain.'

'I'm Ada, Ada Houston, but maybe I'd...' She hesitated, not sure what plans Miss Nightingale's nurse, that Sister Mary Roberts, might have for her.

Seeing her hesitate, Tom said, 'That's all right, Ada, don't worry about Sister Roberts, she's too busy to come and find you at present but she would be more than happy for you to be helping out with the stores – they didn't all come up yesterday and we're running short on some food.'

'All right then,' said Ada, grinning as she slipped off the bed and finding, to her great relief, that at last her legs seemed to be working properly.

She followed Tom out of the hospital to a wagon that was waiting out front. He tried to help her up on to the seat but she made it clear that she could easily spring up there by herself. Settling herself on the seat as Tom checked the harness, she looked down and recognized the skinny back of the brown horse that had pulled the cart yesterday.

The wagon lurched as Tom bounced up into his seat and Ada grabbed the side to steady herself. He laughed and told her to hold on, then introduced the horse as Prince, laughing again when Ada gave him a quizzical glance. 'Not any more, but he was once, like the rest of us.'

As Tom flicked the reins Ada noticed that his large brown hands were covered in scars, although clean with carefully trimmed nails. She glanced down at her own hands, still grubby from housework with dirt ingrained around the nails. It would take some scrubbing to get rid of those stains.

'Hold tight,' he said. 'The road is rough.' As the wagon rumbled off, he twisted round in his seat to grab a large bonnet from the back and handed it to her, adding, 'We don't want to make that nose and those cheeks of yours any redder, do we now? Or risk you fainting away again. Then I

146

would be in trouble with Sister Mary Roberts.'

Ada was surprised to feel so calm sat up there, small and friendly beside the hulking frame of Tom Dunderdale, like she had always known this person. Rocking and rolling along the rough track, she noted the barren landscape around her and the dryness of the ground as the wheels of the cart brought up dust. This alien landscape of stubby vegetation, so far removed from the streets of Liverpool, did not worry her at all while she sat with Tom.

As they approached the sparse town that she could barely recollect from the day before, Ada noticed the many ruined buildings. Tom saw her looking around and explained that this was the result of the great November storm last year and, of course, the famous Battle of Balaklava. As she stared at the piles of shot and shells by the side of the road Tom shook his head and with a hint of sadness in his voice said, 'Look at the state of it. Nobody has time to clean anything up.'

Lost for a moment in their thoughts both Ada and Tom were caught off-guard by the sudden noise of a horse and soldier hurtling at full speed towards them, whipping past the wagon so close that Ada could have touched the man's leather riding boot. Prince was, fortunately, only mildly startled and had calmly brought the wagon to a halt in plenty of time.

'Bloody idiot!' shouted Tom after him. 'You could have had us over.' Then by way of explanation, as he seemed to be at pains to make sense of this strange world for Ada, he told her that the rider carried despatches, giving the soldiers at the front their orders, 'God 'elp 'em.'

Prince automatically walked on, showing no concern about a cloud of dust and a loud rumbling and grating noise further down the road. Ada looked at Tom for reassurance but she could tell that he too was trying to make out just what was going on. He didn't seem perturbed and showed no sign of pulling Prince to a halt. As they got closer the heavy dust began to clear and they could make out a team of what looked like bullocks being driven by a group of men wearing brightly coloured cloths of red, white and blue around their heads. The dust got in Ada's eyes and she held the red shawl over her nose and mouth as they went by, but she could make out that these men with bowed heads were heaving and pushing a large cannon.

She looked over at Tom, who answered her questioning look. 'They're moving the cannon now, while the weather is dry, because once that road up to Sevastopol gets a bit of rain on it the mud is so thick and claggy you can't get anything through.' Tom raised a hand to the men as they passed by and shouted to her, 'These Turks are good strong men and used to moving tackle but even they'd struggle in that mud.'

When they were clear of the cannon and moving into quieter territory he continued their conversation. 'The thing is, the army has a train now that could take things up to the camp but, for some reason, the people in charge here make those Turkish soldiers do things that don't make any sense at all.'

As they moved in close to the low walls of the

harbour, Ada sat pondering on the strangeness of this world that she had found herself in. Her reverie was almost immediately shattered by a cart that suddenly shot out of a side street in front of them. They both jumped up out of their seats at the sight of it; though small, it was moving fast and loaded with bread. Catching a glimpse of the driver's futile attempt to pull up, they both knew that they were lucky to avoid yet another collision. The driver glanced back quickly, then shot off even faster, losing one or two loaves on to the dusty road as he bounced away. Tom and Ada stared at each other with their eyes wide. Tom did not call out this time but simply remarked in his dour way, 'You take your life in your bloody hands just getting a loaf of bread round 'ere.'

Ada looked back over her shoulder to see two big dogs, with ribs showing through their rough fur and tails as thin as whips, shoot out from a derelict building, grab the loaves, and run.

There was no time to settle back into her seat because they were drawing up by a low building. Tom jumped down and hitched Prince to a rail, saying, 'That'll stop him firing off into the distance after some young filly.' Then, looking up at Ada, he gestured for her to follow him. Climbing down, she brushed the dust off her skirt as best she could and quickly shook her trusty shawl, before following along behind Tom. As she walked she became aware of the sickly, rotting smell that had greeted her on arrival yesterday and glimpsed through a gap in the buildings pile upon pile of junk and railway sleepers. The place was black with flies and she saw what looked like a moving mound of them, only to realize that this was the abandoned carcass of some dead animal. She felt her empty stomach turn as a wave of nausea swept over her.

Entering the low building, Ada was unable to see at first in the dark interior. When her eyes adjusted she could see a strongly built woman with a pock-marked face behind a makeshift counter. On the other side was a man with muscled arms and a bright red beard, who leered at Ada as he stood swaying with a bottle of ale in his hand.

'Sorry, miss,' said Tom apologetically. 'This 'ere's one of the navvies who were brought in to build the railway up to Sevastopol, and, as you can see, they like their beer.'

'No need to worry on my account,' declared Ada as she stared back at the navvy with an even gaze. She'd had her fill of dealing with drunken men back in Liverpool and knew that she could hold her own. She knew that if he decided to make a move she'd have him good and proper. The big man could not match Ada's gaze and quickly looked away. Then, bidding farewell to the strange proprietress behind the counter, he went on his way, staggering foolishly and grabbing the door frame as he ducked to get through the low door on his way out.

As soon as he was gone the big woman behind the counter seemed to relax. Leaning forward, grinning at Ada, she handed Tom a tankard of beer and pushed over a big slice of bread, thick with butter, and a large mug of tea for Ada.

'Thanks, Ruby... This is Ada, just arrived yesterday.'

'Ada's a posh name – where you from then?' asked Ruby.

'Liverpool,' said Ada, taking a big bite of bread and butter.

'That's not posh,' said Tom, laughing.

'It is,' said the woman from behind the counter, 'compared to where I come from.'

'Where's that then?' asked Tom.

'The arse-end of nowhere, moving from place to place with the army.' And then she told them the story of how she'd come up to the Crimea with her husband, who had gone and got himself killed during the Battle of Balaklava. Ada was shocked at the matter-of-fact way she spoke about such a terrible thing. 'When they brought the bodies back in carts it was difficult to see, but he had yellow boots, a bit unusual, so I spotted him. I was glad I was able to see him that one last time. Some of them are blown to bits and never found.' She paused for a moment, glancing down at the counter, and Ada wasn't sure how best to offer comfort, but before she could do anything the woman looked up and continued her story.

'Then it was down to me to find some way of supporting myself – no pay from the army now. I managed to find a job in this canteen. We weren't paid at first, but our men were suffering through shortage of food. You see, the French have it all organized; they have a woman in uniform called a *cantinière* assigned to a group of men. They provide the food and make sure the men have drinks and are doing all right. We still can't compare to that but at least the great British Army have allowed us to provide something regular. You know what, those French, they have omelettes made with fresh eggs and herbs or mushrooms that they go out and forage. They only have the best, those men, and it shows – they keep much fitter.' She was looking Tom up and down as she spoke and smiling. 'They don't drink as much beer either,' she continued as Tom finished the dregs. 'They have wine,' she laughed, flicking the end of her nose upwards with a finger to indicate a snooty expression. 'Fine wine!'

Tom and Ada laughed as they placed their empty tankard and mug on the counter. Then Tom asked Ada to help them carry the boxes of provisions for the hospital that were waiting stacked up behind the counter.

'Don't worry if they're too heavy,' he said. 'Me and Ruby here can manage 'em.'

Before he could continue, Ada pushed past him and picked up the biggest box she could see. It was heavy, but she was determined to show that she could manage it. Glad to get it safely out and on to the back of the wagon, she turned to grin at Tom as he struggled through the low door, ducking his head and carrying two boxes.

'I may not be a big man,' she said, laughing, 'but at least I can manage the doors round here.'

Tom shook his head as he stowed his boxes on the back. 'Well, miss,' he said, smiling with her, 'one thing I have learnt after working with all those women up at the hospital is to never underestimate a single one of them.'

Ada straightened her back and held her head a little higher at this but then turned, wrinkling her nose in disgust, and asked Tom outright, 'What is that smell?'

'Come with me,' he said, taking her by the arm and leading her to the quayside where she had landed only yesterday – or was it the day before? She couldn't remember.

'Could be any of these reasons,' he said, shaking his head in dismay at the scene that lay before them. 'See all those boxes there? Supplies of food, rotting away while we get clearance for them to be despatched, and while our men are desperate for supplies up in camp and at the front line.'

He led her through the clutter and debris to a point where you could look down at a small beach. As they approached the foul smell became stronger and the air full of strange grumbling noises. She was almost too afraid to look down, dreading what she might find. When she did, it was not the rotting, dismembered bodies of soldiers that she had feared but a sorry collection of painfully thin livestock: some dead, some dying. Those still alive stood precariously on bony legs, all hock and hamstring. There were horses, bullocks and some large, scraggy-looking animals with humped backs and curved necks that Ada had never seen in real life but had seen in illustrations in their Bible at home. She could remember pointing at the strange creatures and asking, 'What's that, Grandfather?' and him replying, 'That's a camel. You don't see many of them round Liverpool. They live in hot countries.'

Standing for a few moments, she allowed herself to linger in that memory from what seemed now like a different lifetime. She felt a warm glow from the presence of her grandfather, as if he was still looking after her. Then she roused herself and glanced at Tom Dunderdale. He was nothing like her grandfather, but somehow managed to make her feel like she had in the early years of her life. It felt strange to have found that so quickly out here, so far away from home.

Ada looked back down to the poor creatures and wondered why they were here. Then, almost as if he had heard her question, Tom said, 'I think these were mainly baggage animals that had been used to haul supplies up to the army camp before the railway was opened. Now there isn't enough fodder to feed them so somebody has herded them down here and left them to die. It's very sad, very sad,' he said, lost in his own thoughts for a moment.

Ada placed a hand on his arm, sensing that this one sorrow was only part of what he had to deal with out here in the Crimea. This made her think of her own situation, so far away from home, with no idea where Frank was. Now that she was here, with nothing that linked her to her own world, she seemed to have less and less idea of how to go about finding him.

And then it hit her all over again: what if he wasn't here, what if she'd got it all completely wrong? She felt like someone had punched her, knocking all the breath out of her. Tears sprang to her eyes and she could not control them. Tom saw her face and put his arm around her, saying, 'I know, miss, it isn't easy seeing all this for the first time. Maybe I should have left you back at the hospital.'

They stood together with their backs to the

harbour for a few moments, then Ada looked up at Tom and said, 'I'm all right now, I'm all right.' Pulling away from him, she wiped the tears from her eyes and took a big sniff. He fumbled for a handkerchief in his pocket but could only produce a piece of ragged cloth. They both laughed and Ada took the rag, saying it was fine. She blew her nose as she had done as a child and then offered it back to him.

'You're all right, miss,' said Tom, laughing. 'Think you'd best keep it now.'

As they walked back towards the cart, they heard the big guns start up in the distance. Suddenly anxious, she grabbed hold of Tom's arm as they made their way through the boxes and debris. Ada began to feel her body shake and knew that she needed to get back to the safety of the hospital. She took some deep breaths and tried to calm herself, knowing already that if she was going to survive out here and stand a chance of becoming a nurse she would probably have to see and smell much worse than this.

Glad to see Prince waiting patiently for them, Ada had to resist the urge to hug the old horse round his neck. They climbed back up on to the wagon and set off at what was, for Prince, a brisk pace.

A rapid salvo from the big guns made her move up closer to Tom on the wooden seat. He told her that they were far enough away for her not to worry at all. But if she was up at the front line, dug in with the British and French, laying siege to the Russians holed up in Sevastopol, well, that would be a very different matter.

As they rumbled their way back to the hospital, Ada let Tom's steady stream of conversation wash over her. He told her that nobody expected the fighting would go on for so long after the big battles at Alma and Balaklava, and the Charge of the Light Brigade. They thought that a siege would be a matter of weeks but it had gone on for months and months and all through the fierce cold of winter. The Russians had batteries of artillery strategically placed to protect their position at Sevastopol. The British and French were all around but struggling at present to make any advance. He told her sadly that this stand-off was costing many lives and substantial injury to small groups of soldiers every day. The fresh casualties were dealt with in the field hospital at camp and he had worked up there as well. 'You need nerves of steel and a strong constitution to work in those conditions. When a bunch of wounded come in there's blood and guts everywhere.'

Ada was so consumed with taking all this in she wasn't able to summon up much of a response but in her heart she felt a deep, deep sadness about all the dead and wounded that must lie in this strange place, so far away from home. Remembering again what had actually led her out here in the first place, she cleared her throat. 'I need to ask you something, Tom,' she said. 'A friend of mine, she thinks her brother may have come out here on one of the ships from Liverpool. She doesn't know where he is but someone told her he could have come out to the Crimea.'

'Is he army?' said Tom.

'No, he definitely isn't army.'

'Is he part of a ship's crew?'

'No, she doesn't think so.'

'All sounds a bit strange then – was he some kind of stowaway or something?'

'She doesn't really know but she thinks that he might have ended up on the ship by accident.'

'Some accident,' said Tom, 'if he's ended up out here.'

'Well, she thinks that he might be here some-where so she asked me to look for him.'

'Right,' said Tom, pondering on it for a few moments. 'That's a very tricky situation, seeing as the army don't even know who's here and who isn't. So I don't even know where you would start to ask. You're sure he's somewhere out here?'

'She thinks so and he would have come on a ship from Liverpool. His name's Frank,' she said, looking at him and hoping there might be some light of recognition on his face.

But there was nothing. 'Nah, sorry... And if he did come all the way up here on a ship and he wasn't army or one of us orderlies, doctors or nurses, then why the hell would hc stay?'

Ada felt the fear that had been buzzing in her head settle like lead in her stomach. Of course he was right; she was clutching at straws, but what else could she do? She felt exhausted now and sat quietly next to Tom as they bumped along, hold-ing on to the side of the wagon. She hoped and prayed that Frank was safe and even if he wasn't here in the Crimea he was somewhere in Scutari or on his way back to Liverpool.

Suddenly Prince pricked up his ears and they both jumped in their seats as a loud voice called from behind, 'Good morning, Mr Dunderdale! And hello to you again, young lady.'

They knew even before they turned round that it was Mrs Fitzwilliam. She was moving at speed astride her black horse and within seconds she was pulling up beside Ada and slowing to the pace of the cart.

Ada had only ever seen the horses that delivered coal or plodded the streets of Liverpool in a steady way, so the sight of this beautiful but fierce-looking creature of Mrs Fitzwilliam's was like something from a story book. It fascinated but scared her all at the same time, chomping and frothing at the bit, with its wild-looking eyes darting around. She could see the tension in the muscles of its silky black neck as it strained to be off, almost dancing on the spot. Mrs Fitzwilliam expertly held it at the right pace, and Ada wondered how anyone could have the courage to sit up on top of such a horse.

There seemed to be no stopping Mrs Fitzwilliam as she launched into conversation. 'On such a fine morning I thought I'd take old Horatio here out to stretch his legs and maybe go and have a look at the camp. Sounds like they're fairly going at it up there today, Tom.' Pausing briefly to draw breath, she went on, 'At least now they're fighting from the trenches the horses aren't in as much danger. I can't begin to describe to you, young lady, what it's like to survey the field of battle and see so many soldiers and horses ripped apart – literally ripped apart. After the last big battle I made sure that I went round with my revolver just in case any of them needed to be put out of their misery.'

'She means the horses,' muttered Tom, just in

case there was some misunderstanding.

'This is a terrible war, Mr Dunderdale, a terrible war.'

Horatio was by this time pulling hard at the reins, starting to snort and dance sideways.

'He needs to be off!' shouted Mrs Fitzwilliam and with a strong squeeze of her legs and a cry of 'Rule, Britannia!' she shot off up the road ahead of them, leaving nothing but a trail of dust in the morning air.

Tom shook his head and smiled. 'She's quite something, that Mrs Fitzwilliam, though. Regularly comes into the ward with boxes of food and treats for the patients. She brought in some flowers that she'd found out riding the other week – some of the old boys nearly wept to see such colour on the hospital ward.'

Tom fell silent for a few moments then said quietly, almost to himself, 'Heart of gold, that woman, heart of gold.'

Back up at the hospital, there was very little brightness but a great deal of agitation from a certain quarter due to an administrative difficulty. Such difficulty, in fact, that Miss Smith had pounded her desk any number of times, causing the papers to jump and the ink pot to spill.

'I know nothing about a new nurse!' she exclaimed to Mary Roberts. 'Nobody told me about a new nurse. What is her name?'

'Ada Houston.'

'Ada who?'

'–ston,' said Mary Roberts. 'Ada Houston,' wishing now that she'd kept the whole thing quiet, particularly since the girl seemed to have disappeared off the face of the earth. 'She has a letter of recommendation from Miss Nigh–'

'I don't care if she has a letter of recommendation from Queen Victoria herself, I have had no correspondence about the appointment, none at all!' shouted Miss Smith. 'Find her, find her now and bring her to me. This is highly irregular. I bet those people at Scutari have something to do with this. Always sending us their flotsam and jetsam.'

Mary had learnt through the months of working with Miss Smith that it was of little use to try and explain or discuss. She nodded and replied, 'Yes, Miss Smith,' and retreated to the door. As soon as she gained the corridor, however, and closed the door behind her there was another shriek from inside the room.

'Sister Roberts!'

'Yes, Miss Smith.'

'Where's my egg? I didn't get my egg this morning.'

'I'll look into it directly, Miss Smith,' she shouted through the closed door before hitching up her skirt and running off down the corridor.

In the end, it didn't take Mary Roberts long to find the girl. She was unloading supplies from the wagon with Tom Dunderdale. 'Ah, Mr Dunderdale, I see that you have made use of our new nurse straight away.'

'Just using my initiative, Sister Roberts,' said Tom with a grin on his face. 'Don't want anybody complaining that we orderlies can't do that, now do we?'

'Indeed,' said Sister Roberts. 'However, Mr

Dunderdale, alongside the use of initiative also comes the issue of communication.'

'Of course, Sister Roberts,' said Tom. 'However, I knew you were busy this morning and didn't want to be interrupted, so again, I used my initiative to get on with the job and thought I'd communicate later at a more convenient time. And that is exactly what I'm doing now, Sister Roberts. It has all gone to plan.'

Sister Roberts couldn't help but smile and Ada saw her face transform. And was that a flush of pink on her cheek also?

'Well, Mr Dunderdale, Miss Smith is stamping mad.'

'No change there then,' said Tom.

Sister ignored his comment and continued, 'You know how she is about staff being sent up to us from Scutari without the proper paperwork. She will probably just send young Ada straight back to Miss Nightingale like she did with the last one, so I'm going to tell her she's disappeared, and I think it's best we all stick to that story. We need all the nurses we can get – you know what it's like on the wards.'

'I do indeed,' said Tom.

Then, seeing the concern on Ada's face, Sister said, 'Look, we need another nurse here right now. We will do all we can to keep you.'

Turning back to Tom, she went on, 'Miss Smith needs to think the new nurse is missing. Let's leave it at that for now, and in a few days' time she will have moved on to another issue. You know what she's like.'

'I do indeed,' said Tom with a smile on his face

and his eyes shining.

'So, Miss Houston,' said Sister, suddenly a little flustered as she turned away from Tom. 'I mean Nurse Houston. We can give you a trial. I know from your letter that you have no training so you will have to start from scratch. I want you learning the right way so I'll put you under the supervision of Nurse Rose Blackwood. Nurse Blackwood trained under Miss Nightingale, as did I, therefore she has the correct standards.'

'Thank you,' said Ada, surprising herself by the rush of relief that came over her. 'I will do my best,' she added eagerly, despite the exhaustion that was setting in again.

Sister Roberts scanned Ada's tired face, with its smudges of dark under her eyes. 'First, however, you need to lie low and get more rest. And I know just the thing. Come with me.' And calling over her shoulder to Tom, she cried, 'I assume that you are able to use your initiative and get on with organizing the supplies without my nurse's help?'

'Yes,' grinned Tom. 'I'll communicate with you later when all the work is done.'

As Ada followed Sister Roberts she saw the movement of her shoulders as she tried to stop herself from laughing.

Arriving at the nurses' quarters, Ada was allocated a mattress that had been squeezed between two of the beds. 'I'll tell all the nurses that you are here and what our plan is, but when you're in here you must try to keep down low so you can't be seen from the door. Miss Smith never usually comes into the room, she only comes here occasionally, and when she does she just opens the door and has a quick scan round.'

'I will,' said Ada, starting to feel more heaviness in her body.

'All right then, nurse,' said Sister. 'You get some rest down there and we will allocate you to some work tomorrow. The others will be in later and they won't disturb you.'

'Thank you, miss – I mean Sister Roberts,' said Ada, feeling strangely pleased despite her exhaustion that Sister was calling her – Ada Houston – 'nurse'.

She lay down on the mattress as instructed, thinking it unlikely that she would be able to get to sleep in the middle of the afternoon. She heard the door of the room close as Sister Roberts left and then she started thinking about Tom Dunderdale and Frank and all she had seen that day. Then she fell sound asleep, and continued to sleep for the rest of the day and all of the night.

# 12

*'Say not "How clever I am!" but "I am not yet worthy" ... and I will live to deserve ... to be called a trained nurse.'*
Florence Nightingale

Ada was woken early the next morning by a woman's voice that she definitely recognized but simply could not place – a very well-spoken voice that seemed to be in conversation with someone who almost certainly was Sister Roberts. The woman's voice was clear with a hint of authority and Ada's health seemed to be the topic of conversation. She was pleased to hear that they thought she had made a good recovery. That's a relief, thought Ada, and it did sound as if they knew what they were talking about.

Then Sister Roberts said, 'She's a bit small but there's something about her. I think she might have some potential, but you never know till they get out there on the ward.'

'True,' said the well-spoken voice. 'I'll wake her now and bring her a bit of breakfast and then we'll make our way to the ward.'

'All right, Nurse Blackwood, and please, please remember that you need to keep her out of the way if you hear Miss Smith coming. She's snowed under with paperwork at the moment and not likely to come down to the ward but you never know.'

'I'll do my best,' said Nurse Blackwood.

'Like I said, keep a very close eye on her; she's had no training whatsoever. Oh, I do hope that she can take to the work on the ward; what with that hospital nurse dying yesterday we need all the help we can get.'

Ada gasped. Dying? What the... Nurses dying on the ward?

Rose, hearing Ada's small gasp, said one or two more words to Sister Roberts then came over to the mattress on the floor.

'Good morning,' she said. 'So sorry, did we wake you?'

Ada looked up to see a pale, concerned face

164

gazing down at her with what could only be described as motherly tenderness. She pulled herself up to a sitting position; she didn't want the nurse to think that she was still sickly and was keen to make sure that she looked like someone who was ready to get to work.

'Good morning,' she said, probably a bit too vigorously. The pale-faced nurse drew back, surprised, her cheeks flushing pink.

'Good morning, Nurse Houston. I'm Nurse Rose Blackwood. Sister Roberts has asked me to supervise you on the ward today.'

'Thank you, Nurse Blackwood,' said Ada, pushing her tousled hair back from her face and hauling herself up from the mattress.

Rose politely turned her back while Ada straightened her skirt and fastened her blouse, and then walked over to the small dresser by the door and picked up an apron. Rose slipped it over her own head and tied it. Ada noticed how tight she pulled the bow and hoped that Rose would be able to breathe.

'I'm sorry, nurse, but we have no spare uniforms up here at Balaklava and the women have to make do with what they've got. However, we do have a fairly ready supply of clean aprons so you can start with this one if you want,' Rose said, turning around and handing Ada a clean pinny.

'Thank you,' said Ada, still feeling a bit sleepy. 'Was it you who helped me when I was sick? I seem to recognize your voice.'

'Yes it was. I wanted to make sure that you were all right,' Rose replied, adding, 'I was just doing my duty.'

'Thank you, Rose,' said Ada, smiling at the pale, worried-looking woman that stood before her. 'Thank you very much.'

'You are welcome,' said Rose with a shy smile.

Before they left the room Rose grabbed a fancy glass bottle off the side, popped off the stopper and applied a generous dab of the contents under her nose. Ada could smell fine perfume, nothing like the soaps that she'd used at home.

'Mmm, that smells nice,' said Ada, going right up beside Rose and having a good sniff. Then, sensing Rose stiffen and get ready to step away, she spoke softly, 'Sorry, Rose, it's just that where I come from we don't smell scent like that every day of the week. It is so beautiful ... do all the nurses use it?'

'No, the others are hospital nurses who've been working on wards up and down the country for years; they're all used to the odours. I do this every day to help me cope. Do you want some?' she said, turning to face her new recruit who had closed her eyes and was continuing to inhale the perfume.

'Yes please,' said Ada, her eyes popping open.

Rose dabbed some on Ada's neck, and she breathed it in again, beginning to feel heady with the perfume.

Rose smiled. 'My mother gave this to me for my birthday last year. If she only knew what use I'd put it to.'

Ada grinned. She was really starting to take to Rose, although it still felt very strange indeed to be looked after by someone so far above her own station – but everything here was new to her, the old rules didn't seem to apply.

On the way to the ward, Ada, still heady with perfume, kept glancing at Rose, trying to read her face, wondering what she had let herself in for. She was glad that Rose turned to her before opening the door and gave her a reassuring smile. 'It's your first day, it will feel grim, just try not to worry and stick with me.'

Ada took a deep breath and steeled herself, but when Rose opened the door she couldn't help but reel back. She stood in the doorway for a few moments, taking in the crowded, sorry sight in front of her. There were rows of beds down each side, tightly squeezed together, all full, mostly men lying down, some groaning in pain. The men had long, straggly beards, and some were wearing ragged military jackets. Everything looked ripped and torn and grey. She didn't know if she would be able to move from that spot but then she saw Rose turn and smile at her and heard her voice.

'Come on, follow me, and let's make a start.'

Ada smiled back even though her face felt tight and her teeth were gritted. She let the door close behind her and took as deep a breath as she could in such a foul-smelling environment.

'All right then, nurse, we'll start with Arnold,' Rose said, pointing to a bed that contained a horrifically injured young man with such a look of pain in his eyes that it made Ada's heart feel heavy in her chest.

Ada followed behind Rose so close that if Rose had stepped back she would have fallen over her new recruit. She stood with her as she made her assessment, but found it difficult to look at the

167

man. His head was bandaged, his mouth looked twisted, both arms were bound up and when he tried to speak in response to Rose's questions he could only make some strange noise.

As she stood watching, taking everything in, Ada could see how Rose showed that she was listening, even though the poor young man was using all of his energy just to try and speak and none of it seemed to make any sense. How terrible it must be, thought Ada, to not be able to communicate properly with another human being. Then Ada followed Rose across the ward to another bed whose occupant was an older man with a long grey beard. The man's head was bandaged and Ada thought that he looked very sick indeed. He was lying with his eyes closed but had a tortured look on his face, a look of sheer pain. There must be some horrendous injury under that bandage, thought Ada, for him to look like that.

The man seemed to come awake as Rose stood over him. He started groaning and moving his head from side to side and pulling at the bandage. Ada was terrified that he would pull it off and do himself even more harm. Then he started muttering something about a cat and asking where the little boy was. She watched Rose place the back of her hand against the man's cheek.

'Mr Jackson,' she said to him gently, 'Mr Jackson, do you know where you are?'

Ada heard the man mutter some more words but it certainly didn't sound like a reply to Rose's question.

'As I thought,' she said quietly, turning to Ada. 'He has a fever and he is delirious. Looks like the wound has taken bad ways and passed poison through to the brain.'

Ada was impressed by Rose's knowledge but appalled at the man's condition. She was even more appalled when Rose said, 'I need to find Sister Roberts. Can you sit with this patient until I get back?'

'Yes of course,' said Ada automatically, feeling out of her depth but hoping she could do something to help the poor man.

'Just watch that he doesn't pull at the bandage, and if he tries to get out of bed you'll have to stop him.'

'All right,' said Ada, praying that he wouldn't do either of those things.

'Oh, and give him some small sips of water from that spouted cup if you can,' said Rose before turning away.

Ada stared longingly after her mentor as she walked away and then looked back at her charge in the bed. So far so good: he seemed to be drifting back to sleep. But then his eyes popped open and he gazed at her. He had such a wild look in his eyes, scanning her face, searching for someone, still muttering to himself. She forced herself to look at him steadily and then he started to murmur, 'Nurse, nurse, nurse.'

Ada glanced around, hoping to see one. And then she realized that the patient was looking at her; she was the nurse. Oh my God, she thought to herself, he doesn't know. He doesn't know that it's my first day and I'm completely useless.

Looking around again, desperately trying to find something that might help, her eyes fell on the spouted cup. Yes, she thought, that's it, I'll try the drink.

'Do you want some water?' she asked gently.

The man just repeated what she had said: 'Do you want some water?' then, 'Does she want a drink, does she?' He wasn't making much sense but Ada picked up the cup anyway. He took it readily at first but then pushed it away, slopping water on the bed. She tried to hold his hand but he was plucking at the bed cover one minute and then at the mattress the next. So long as he keeps those hands away from the bandage, thought Ada, trying to stay calm.

Hearing a strangled moan from the bed behind, Ada twisted round on her chair. The soldier lying there was restless and had started to throw off his blanket. She carefully placed it back over him before turning back to Mr Jackson, but to her alarm she found him trying to swing his legs sideways and get up from the bed. Instinctively Ada swung him back to lie down. She knew, any fool would know, that his legs would never hold him and he would fall. He cursed at her but didn't have the strength to fight.

Ada looked up with relief to see Rose and Sister Roberts coming down the ward towards her. She was so happy to see them she almost got up and hugged them.

'Are you all right?' said Rose.

'Yes, all fine,' replied Ada through gritted teeth as the old soldier tried again to get up from his bed and she wrestled him back down.

She looked up to see Rose smiling at her. 'You're doing a good job,' she said. Ada didn't think so but she managed the grimace of a smile in return.

'I see what you mean, Nurse Blackwood,' said Sister Roberts. 'There is a definite change in his condition. Beyond a dose of laudanum to settle him there isn't much else that we can do.'

'Shall I try to do the dressing and re-bandage?' asked Rose.

'No, I would leave it,' said Sister. 'The bandage is firm; we wouldn't be doing him any favours. Come with me and we'll get him some laudanum and see if he settles.'

'Will you be all right?' said Rose to Ada.

'Yes,' said Ada, not really believing herself for one moment but seeing no alternative other than to run screaming out of the ward.

'I'll be back directly,' said Rose.

As soon as Rose had gone Ada's patient seemed to rouse up again and this time started pulling at his bandage. She moved instinctively to gently but firmly pull his hand down to the bed and then hold it still. This seemed to give the man some ease, just the simple human contact of holding his hand, and Ada felt a swell of satisfaction that she might be doing the right thing, but then he started muttering again and twisting his head from side to side.

As long as that bandage stays put, she thought.

Then the patient behind her gave another groan and when she looked round he was throwing his blanket off again, clearly agitated. She moved to pick up the blanket but as she leant over the stench from his bed made her gag and then she couldn't stop herself from gasping at the sight of the crudely fashioned stump of an above-knee amputation that had worked loose from its bandage. It was stitched up tight with black thread, bright red and swollen, looking like it might burst open. The poor man couldn't keep it down on the bed; it seemed to have a life of its own. She quickly threw the corner of the blanket over him, knowing full well that it wouldn't stay there for long.

Turning back to Mr Jackson she was relieved to see Rose coming back at quite a pace with a small bottle in her hand.

'I'll have a look at him in the next bed in a minute,' said Rose and then Ada watched as she deftly took a dropper out of the small bottle and counted some drops of laudanum into the man's mouth. He seemed to like the taste.

Rose moved to the next bed and set to work reapplying the bandage. She explained that the 'above-knees' required the stump to be weighted down: 'Like this,' she said, showing Ada the thick band of cloth and the two small sandbags that were applied to keep the remains of the leg on the bed. Ada still felt uncomfortable looking at it, but when Rose explained that the soldier no longer had the sheer weight of his leg to hold it down, it made sense and interested Ada. This place still felt like some circle of Hell but maybe there were practical things that could be done to ease the suffering of the poor souls trapped here.

Turning her attention back to Mr Jackson, Ada saw that he was still picking at the blanket but was perhaps a little more settled and drowsy.

'Are you all right to sit for a bit longer?' said Rose. 'Just until he's sleeping.'

'Yes, of course,' said Ada, beginning to feel a bit

172

more confident but still hoping that the man in the next bed didn't start up again.

'When he's properly settled come over and help me, will you?'

Ada nodded and turned back to her charge, praying that he wouldn't try to get out of bed again. She was relieved to see that he was becoming more drowsy all the time. Maybe she could leave him soon. Feeling guilty, she again offered him some water and was glad that this time he took a few sips without any bother. Then slowly his eyes began to close and he seemed to be drifting off, gently murmuring to himself. When she could see that he was settling she started to relax, but she certainly wasn't going to leave him yet, not until he was properly asleep. She didn't want him to try and get up again and fall. That would be terrible.

She stood up and started to straighten the sheet over the patient and then pulled his pillow into what she thought was a more comfortable position, very carefully indeed so that she didn't wake him up again. But she could see that he was starting to slip into a very sleepy state.

'He seems to be settling now. That's good,' said a man's deep voice with a decidedly Scottish accent.

Ada looked up to see the concerned face of the patient in the opposite bed. The man was huge, with a startling beard streaked with red. She had been so preoccupied with her charge and the man in the bed behind her that she hadn't taken much notice of anyone else. The man was so tall that he didn't fit into the bed properly, and although Ada could see that he was quite skinny,

173

as were all the soldiers that she'd seen out here, his shoulders and chest seemed to measure the full width of the bed.

'He's had a really bad night,' said the man, looking at his neighbour with such tenderness that Ada was almost moved to tears. 'I had to keep calling for the orderly on and off all night. He was shouting and seemed to be in a lot of pain and then he kept trying to get out of bed. I was so worried that he'd fall and hurt himself. Poor Stan, things don't seem to be going all that well for him, do they?'

Ada was quite taken aback and she didn't know what to say at first. Then she thought it best just to tell him the truth.

'I don't really know,' she said. 'It's my first day and I don't know much about anything yet.'

'Ah, right, I thought you must be new – not that it really shows all that much,' he said, seeing the anxious look on her face. 'But first days anywhere are hard work, aren't they? You just look a bit tense, that's all. I mean I knew that I hadn't seen you before so I thought that you must be new.'

'I've only been in the Crimea a few days,' said Ada.

'Lucky you,' said the man with a grim smile. 'Me and my lot have been here since the start, since last year.'

'I heard about all those battles, were you...?'

'Yes, every single one of them. But anyway, what's your name and where are you from?'

'I'm ... Nurse Houston,' she said, remembering just in time that Sister Roberts had told her not to use first names with patients.

174

'Welcome to the ward, Nurse Houston,' said the man. 'I'm Duncan Brodie – you can call me Duncan – 42nd Royal Highlanders, and that there is Stanley Jackson, 47th Lancashire Regiment.'

'Pleased to meet you ... both,' said Ada, looking back down to her charge, who was now sleeping soundly. 'I think he's settled now,' she said, standing up from the chair.

'Don't you worry,' said Duncan. 'I'll give you nurses a shout if I see him stirring. I can't go anywhere; once I'm awake that's me, just sitting here for the rest of the day.'

'That must be hard,' said Ada, walking over to the side of his bed.

'Well, it's better than ending up like poor old Stan there and some might think that I'd be glad of this, getting out of the way of those shells, but the thing is, and a young lass like you might not be able to understand, I want to be out there. I want to be with the men. We've come through so many battles... I just wish we could finish this war side by side.'

Ada felt her heart swell. She didn't fully understand what he was saying, of course not, but the passion that she saw in the man's eyes as he spoke, she could feel that all right; it would rouse a fire in anyone's belly. She had to swallow really hard to stop tears welling up in her eyes, but in that moment she had started to understand something about all the men in this ward – they were bound together for life.

Ada gave a nod and put a hand on the man's shoulder. Life here was raw. It was raw and it was real and already her heart was beginning to beat a little faster.

Looking down the bed she saw that the sheet lay flat where Duncan's right lower leg should have been. He saw her looking and gave her a smile.

'Oh, it's the leg ... well, it isn't there any more. It was the leg, but Dr Lampeter kindly removed it for me, so it is no more.'

'I see,' said Ada, her mind flashing back to the horror of the amputation that she'd witnessed at the dock.

He must have seen the look on her face. 'I know, it's a brutal procedure, and the British army don't use chloroform, not like the French, but I did get about half a bottle of whisky first so that took the edge off a bit. Put it this way: it had to be done; it was the leg or me in the end. And now I've got through and things seem to be just about healed, well, I'm on the best side of it. It's strange, though, I can still feel that leg even though it isn't there. I can still feel it and the blasted thing is still giving me jip!'

'How strange,' said Ada, fascinated.

'Doc says that's what they call phantom pain and it might get better or it might not. Anyway, I'm still here and that's all that matters. The wife will have a bit of a shock when I turn up on one leg. I've written to her but the letters take so long I might be back before she gets it. Aye, but she's a strong Highland lass, so she'll be all right with it.'

Ada could have stood there and listened to Duncan Brodie all day. He had a rich voice with a wonderful accent and she had never met anyone who was so easy to talk to. But she knew that she might be needed elsewhere.

'I'd better go and find Nurse Blackwood,' she said, starting to move away from the bed, but then her eye caught a tall, feathery hat with a magnificent red plume on the floor by his bed. She had never seen anything like it.

'That there is a feather bonnet,' he said, 'my pride and joy. That and the red jacket are all I have left of my regimental uniform – the rest was ripped and torn off but I still have the bonnet and I'll be taking it back to Scotland with me.'

'It is magnificent,' said Ada, reaching down to feel the soft, feathery plume. She could see a badge and a tartan headband that the bonnet was resting on. 'What a sight it must be to see a regiment of men like you, all in your red coats and these hats. It must be glorious.'

'We wear kilts as well in the regiment. Do you know what a kilt is?'

'Yes,' said Ada. 'I come from Liverpool and we see people from all over the world in the city.'

'Even Scotland?' said the man, starting to laugh.

'Even Scotland,' she said, smiling back at him. Then, seeing Rose looking anxiously down the ward for her, Ada knew it was time to get going. 'Well, Mr Brodie, it's been nice to meet you but I need to go and help Nurse Blackwood now.'

'Aye, nice to meet you too, lass,' said the man. 'And don't you fret, I'll give a shout if I'm worried about Stan.'

Rose was back at Arnold's bed.

'Is there anything I can do to help?' Ada asked.

'Yes,' said Rose straight away. 'Are the two men down the ward settled?'

'Yes they are, and the patient in the opposite bed said he would shout out if anything more was needed.'

Rose nodded. 'Well then, would you like to give Arnold a drink?'

'Just show me what to do,' said Ada.

Rose demonstrated how to use the spouted cup, making sure the tea wasn't too hot, and not to give too much at once, and then she went down the ward to tend to another patient.

Ada's hand shook slightly as she had a first go, worried that she might choke the poor sod. It was hard to be so close to someone so badly injured and with such a look of pain in his eyes. She was terrified of doing anything that might make him feel worse, but she knew that this was the only way she would learn.

It took her a while to find a technique that worked, and at first she found that quite a bit of the liquid leaked back out of his mouth and on to the sheet. His swallowing didn't seem to be right either and she stood up in alarm when the boy started choking.

Rose came back up the ward to help, explaining that this happened sometimes and showing her what to do. Ada asked Rose what had happened to his arms and was told that he had been shot, but not too badly, and in a few weeks they would be able to remove his bindings and get his arms moving again. Rose made sure that she looked at and spoke to Arnold, including him in this conversation, and Ada followed her lead and did the same. Too many of the staff seemed to assume that because he couldn't speak, he couldn't understand, and treated him as if he was an imbecile.

While they stood by the bed, a figure came up behind them, and Ada turned and gasped when she saw the doctor from the harbour staring straight at her.

Rose shot a glance of concern in her direction. 'Dr Lampeter,' she said, 'this is our new nurse.'

'We've met,' said Lampeter, not even looking at Ada and waiting for Rose to give him a report on Arnold's condition. Ada continued to give Arnold sips of tea. She could tell that he was listening to every detail of Rose's conversation with the doctor. It seemed that they were very pleased with the wound and in a few weeks' time they would be able to take the bindings off his arms. Ada was impressed by Rose's knowledge and compassion, and how she continued to make eye contact with Arnold. She was fascinated by the way Rose spoke and how her eyes shone with enthusiasm for the work.

As Rose was winding up her report, Sister Roberts appeared. She glanced over to Ada and quietly said, 'Are you all right, Nurse Houston?'

'Yes, I think so,' replied Ada, turning back to her patient to give him a few more sips of tea. Out of the corner of her eye she saw Lampeter steal a glance at her before he went off down the ward with Sister Roberts and Rose.

Ada saw them examining a patient further down the ward, and suddenly they were all activity. Rose moved swiftly back to Ada. 'You stay here. We are going to do an emergency amputation. Gas gangrene has set in and the leg needs to be removed as soon as possible.'

Ada nodded, shocked at the speed they were

needing to act. Rose went back down the ward with a tray of implements – including, to Ada's horror, a saw – and the orderlies were there by the bed in no time at all, holding the man down.

The patients on the ward seemed to know what was coming. Ada sensed that they were almost holding their breath. They all winced together as they heard the strangled cry of the man before he blacked out and then, after the procedure was over, the ward was silent apart from one poor soul retching into a bucket.

Before Ada could make a move to see if she could help the patient who was vomiting, she was distracted by the appearance of another man at the bottom of Arnold's bed. He had a mildly amused expression and a very kind face.

'You must be the new nurse,' he said, reaching over to shake her hand. 'I'm Dr Mason. I believe you are already acquainted with my colleague, Dr Lampeter.'

'Yes,' said Ada, 'I am. Thank you,' thinking how pleasant a manner the man had and how good of him to take the time to introduce himself.

Dr Mason gave her a smile and a small bow before he proceeded down the ward to join Lampeter and see what he could do to help. From what she could see the procedure seemed to be more or less over and she was pleased to see Rose making her way back up the ward a little while later.

'First days are very strange,' said Rose. 'I was a terrible mess on mine at the hospital in Scutari. Anyway, I think that you're doing very well so far. If you're done here you can tag along with me and we'll see what else needs doing.'

As the two nurses walked side by side down the ward the doctors passed by on their way up. Ada saw Mason smile across at them, but Lampeter never looked up, staring fiercely at the ground as he walked by. She felt the hairs on the back of her neck prickle; she knew that their paths would cross again and again on the ward and she would need to find some way of managing her feelings of antipathy towards the man. Especially since, even on this her first day, she was starting to feel determined to make a really good go of this work at the hospital. She did not want an arrogant doctor like him to interfere with what could be the start of a new life for her.

Ada followed Rose like a shadow for the rest of that day. In the late afternoon they checked on the poor man who'd undergone the emergency amputation that morning. Even Ada could see that there was a deterioration in his condition. His face was mottled and red, his lips looked blue, his breathing was slow and laboured and his eyes were wide, staring at the ceiling as he lay flat on his back.

Rose lifted the blanket to check the stump bandage. 'I'm checking for haemorrhage,' she said and Ada had a look too, relieved to see that there was no bleeding. Rose looked back at the patient's face and then used the back of her hand to feel his forehead. 'No fever,' she said, then, 'Right, you stay here with him. I need to go and find Dr Lampeter.'

Ada nodded gravely, looking at the man's face and praying that he wouldn't get any worse while Rose was away. One of the hospital nurses glanced over from the other side of the ward, calling over,

181

'Give me a shout if you need anything.'

'Thank you,' said Ada, pleased at last to be making some connection to the other staff on the ward, who were always so busy and always seemed to know exactly what they were doing.

Looking back at her patient, Ada could see that his colour seemed to be darkening and his breathing was starting to rasp in his chest. She didn't like the look of him, not one bit, but she knew she had to just try to provide what comfort she could and wait for the doctor.

Then he started to make a gurgling sound in the back of his throat, a gurgling sound that got worse. Ada looked at him more fiercely, hoping that inspiration might come as to what she could do. Then to her relief she heard the sound of feet running down the ward and Rose was there with Lampeter.

Lampeter pushed Ada roughly out of the way and Rose moved to the opposite side of the bed. Then they rolled the man off his back and over on to his side. The gurgling sound eased instantly and Ada's head sank, wishing she had thought to do that. Lampeter and Rose soon had the man wedged over on his side but his colour still looked bad and he was unconscious. Lampeter felt for a pulse and lay the back of his hand on the man's forehead as Rose had done, but then seemed at a loss himself.

Turning to Ada, he glared at her and said, 'What in God's name do you think you are doing, nurse? Have you no idea at all?' Ada opened her mouth to reply, feeling outraged by his accusation, but he continued to rant at her. 'The other day at the harbour I made allowances for you. You were straight off the ship, you were exhausted, but what about today, nurse, what about today? Are you always so incompetent?'

Ada felt herself bristle and opened her mouth to speak but Rose was in there first.

'Dr Lampeter,' she said with a clear, firm tone to her voice, 'Nurse Houston has not only just arrived, she is a complete novice. She is here to be trained and this is her first day on the ward. Her first day.'

Rose's words stopped Lampeter in his tracks and Ada saw a glimmer in his eyes of someone who knew he was out of line and should apologize. Then he squared his shoulders and looked over to Rose, whose face was now bright pink.

'Well, why didn't someone tell me?' he said.

'I'm telling you now,' said Rose. 'Now, can we get on with treating this patient?'

Lampeter looked back to the man and then spoke quietly to Rose. 'There is no more that we can do. It looks like the amputation this morning was too much of an assault. He might pull through but I doubt it. In the meantime just keep him comfortable and call me back if you need anything else.'

Then Lampeter was gone from the bedside. As Ada watched him stride away up the ward she felt stunned by what he had said and knew that he was right – she was incompetent.

'I want you to be clear,' said Rose, 'none of that was your fault. This man is dying; putting him on his side will ease him, that's all. And you'll soon learn, I can tell. When you see this next time you will know exactly what to do.'

'Thank you,' said Ada, taking a deep breath and trying to find something inside herself that believed this to be the case.

'You are here to learn,' said Rose. 'If you want to learn and you want to become a trained nurse it will be very tough – much tougher than getting told off by some doctor who should know better.'

Ada still felt bad but she took in what Rose had to say.

'That's my girl,' said Rose, seeing Ada's face change as the scrunch between her brows began to relax. 'Now let's make sure that this patient is as comfortable as we can make him.'

Ada helped Rose straighten the bedding under the man and then they sponged his face. 'Should we offer him a drink?' said Ada, noting how dry the man's lips were.

'No, he won't be able to swallow,' said Rose. 'But we can clean his mouth and lips with a sponge soaked in some water.'

Rose showed her how to do this and it felt good to be able to do something for the man that might make him feel more comfortable.

'Do you think you could sit with this patient?' asked Rose. 'We like to do that for the men if we have staff to spare. It's just that they are so far away from home and family, it feels like the least we can do.'

Ada took a moment, and then said yes, of course. She had never sat with anyone who was dying before, but she knew lots of people in the street who had. Mary had sat with her father as he died from consumption and she had talked to

Ada about it. Ada had been terrified for months that her grandfather would get it as well. He didn't get the consumption but that hadn't saved him in the end, had it? Looking at her patient, Ada was glad that, although his breathing was slow and gurgling, he was not fighting. His face looked relaxed and his eyes were closed. Every now and then she stood up to moisten the man's lips with the sponge and to wipe his brow. But mostly she just sat with him and waited.

When the end came, it was more peaceful than she'd expected. Ada quietly stood and crossed herself, wondering who the poor man had left behind at home. They wouldn't know he was gone for months. She didn't spot Rose, who had returned silently to stand by her side, until she heard her say, 'You did well there, Ada.'

She looked at Rose; then she glanced around the ward, and was amazed to see that those men who were awake and not delirious were sitting with their heads bowed in silent respect. She was moved beyond words at this, and stood quietly for a few more moments, feeling the sense of togetherness in that room.

When Rose asked her if she wanted to help with the laying out, she was sure that she did. 'Have you done it before?' asked Rose.

'Yes,' said Ada, 'for my grandfather.' It felt strange mentioning him in this place so far away from their home in Liverpool.

'All right then,' said Rose. 'Now I'll show you exactly what we do here in the hospital.'

As they washed the man's body they saw that a number of his toes were missing from his re-

185

maining foot. Rose had not seen this before but Ada remembered what Elsie the washerwoman had told her in Scutari, that frostbite could make this happen – though it was a shock to see it at first hand. Looking out now at the bright sun, feeling it bake down on the earthen walls of the hospital, Ada found it hard to imagine that this land of Crimea could become so cold in winter. When Tom came to move the soldier's body they asked him about the winter and he told them that Dr Lampeter had a fur-lined coat that he had brought up from Scutari so that, come this winter, he'd be warm and cosy. The story was that it had once belonged to a Russian general.

Typical of him to look after himself, thought Ada.

Evening was fast approaching and the ward seemed to be settling, but when she had time Ada made sure that she went back to check on Mr Jackson.

'He's so much more comfortable,' said Duncan. 'Whatever those drops were they seem to have done the trick. I hope he just slips away quietly; that would be best.'

Ada looked at him, her eyes wide.

'I've been on this ward long enough to know when someone is dying,' he continued. 'We soldiers have to deal with it on a daily basis and I'm telling you now, most would choose a quiet sleep in a hospital bed rather than some of the things I've seen in the trenches.'

Ada nodded, not able to say much to that except, 'Well, you get some sleep yourself tonight. Don't be watching him all the time.'

'Aw, that's all right, I can catch up during the day.'

Ada walked away from his bed smiling and shaking her head; it seemed like they were all in it together here, the nurses, the doctors and all of the patients.

As they continued doing their best to settle the patients for the night, Ada turned to Rose, remembering something she had been meaning to ask all day.

'Where are the lamps, Rose? Do we get one each?'

'The lamps?' said Rose, wondering if Ada was becoming a bit delirious and needed to lie down.

'Yes, you know,' said Ada, not really all that sure of her ground any more. 'The lamps like the one that Miss Nightingale has.'

Rose started to smile, then seeing Ada's serious face she said, 'There are no lamps like that one, Ada. I think somebody must have made it up. You won't find a lamp like that anywhere in Balaklava or Scutari. It makes a nice portrait, though, and of course the "Lady with the Lamp" has a nice ring to it, but no, we don't have those lamps.'

Although it seemed a bit daft to be disappointed by something so trivial, Ada did feel let down; she had imagined that was exactly what they would have. She had been hoping for a proper uniform as well but it was beginning to look like the nurses out here in Balaklava were not provided for as well as those in Scutari. But then she remembered the Sister who had marched her through the hospital and felt grateful to be up here well out of the way. Lamp or no lamp, she was better off here, that was for sure.

'Come on, Nurse Houston,' said Rose, putting her arm around a thoughtful Ada, 'let's get away from this ward and get some rest. Our Miss Nightingale would want to make sure that we're off the ward by eight o'clock sharp, and no one, not even Miss Smith, can break a rule set by the Lady with the Lamp.'

# 13

*'If a nurse declines to do these kinds of things for her patient, "because it is not her business", I should say that nursing was not her calling.'*
Florence Nightingale

The next day the other nurses got up and went down to the ward but Ada slept on. No one wanted to wake her; in fact they were intrigued by her ability to sleep so soundly. Rose kept an eye on her by regularly nipping back from the ward, but didn't want to disturb her.

As Ada slept she had no idea that Miss Smith had opened the door to the nurses' quarters and had a quick look in. Seeing nothing, she had clicked the door shut then moved along to the ward. Bursting in through the door as the staff went about their morning duties, she had prowled down the centre of the ward, glancing closely at each patient and then under each bed.

Seizing on an empty basket, she shouted up the

ward to Sister Roberts, 'Sister, this should be full of clean bandages. Where are they? These men need clean bandages!' Then she threw the basket down on the floor. Some of the men slid down in their beds; others looked away; a brave few risked a smile. Even the delirious patients went quiet.

Sister Roberts came down to Miss Smith and told her in a calm but steely voice that they would send another member of staff to the laundry as soon as someone could be spared.

'Send one now!' shouted Miss Smith. 'Immediately!' Then she strode back up the ward, the click of her heels breaking through the silence.

When she was gone, Sister Roberts breathed out and looked around. They were busy, short-staffed, and already behind with the morning's work. Rose gently touched Sister's arm and said, 'I have an idea.'

Ada was woken by someone gently shaking her arm. 'What time is it?' she mumbled, struggling to emerge from her notorious sleep. 'What time is it, Rose?' she mumbled again. 'I should be on the ward.'

'Don't worry, Ada, we've been letting you rest up,' said Rose, shaking her protégée more strongly. 'Wake up now,' she urged as Ada tried to lie back down. 'We need you to do something different for us today. We need you to work in the laundry.'

'That's all right, I know a washerwoman,' said Ada, turning over and trying to pull the blanket over her head.

'Oh no you don't,' said Rose, pulling the blanket off her. 'Miss Smith has been down and she wants to see clean bandages.'

189

Ada sat up groggily but still had her eyes closed.

'Open your eyes,' said Rose. 'You need to open your eyes.'

Ada slowly opened one eye and Rose started laughing. 'Come on, we need you!'

As they walked along the corridor on the way to the laundry, Ada was still feeling a bit sleepy and trying her best not to yawn. When they came to the back door, Rose stopped and looked at her, then reached over to tidy a few stray wisps of hair. 'Come on then,' she said. 'Sister Roberts is really grateful that you can do this for us today.'

'Tell me later how things are on the ward, will you?' said Ada. 'Let me know about Mr Jackson and Duncan.'

'Duncan?' said Rose. 'Which one is that?'

'The Scottish man in the bed opposite Stanley Jackson, the one with the below-knee amputation.'

'Oh yes, of course, Mr Brodie,' said Rose, looking perplexed.

'Is he all right?' said Ada, seeing the look on Rose's face.

'Yes, of course,' said Rose. 'Sorry, I was thinking about poor Stanley. Sadly he died overnight.'

'Sorry to hear that Rose – are you all right?'

'Yes, yes, of course. I have to be; we still have a ward full of patients to look after ... but there was something special about Stanley.'

'It must be hard,' said Ada. 'I don't know how any of you manage.'

'Well, we have to, and if the men can manage what they have to do out there in the trenches, we nurses back here can do our bit too. That's how I always think about it.'

'Even so...' said Ada, lost in her own thoughts.

'Yes, well, Mr Brodie – Duncan – is doing very well this morning, and in fact Sister Roberts is hopeful that we can have him moving around on crutches fairly soon.'

'That is so good,' said Ada, smiling. 'I hope I can be on the ward for that.'

'We'll try to make sure that you are. But for today they need all the help they can get out here in the laundry,' said Rose as they walked out of the shaded building into an open area full of bright sun.

'Looks like they've got a good drying day,' said Ada, suddenly wide awake and pleased to feel the sun on her face.

'It does indeed,' said Rose, squinting and shading her eyes with her hand. Then she called a greeting to a woman standing by a large, steaming tub. Ada had never seen a more massive woman, not even on the streets of Liverpool. She stood with her reddened hands on her hips, the sleeves of her blouse rolled up to the elbow. When she looked up and saw them, her face broke into a broad smile.

'That's Dolly,' said Rose. 'She'll look after you.' Then, shouting again to Dolly: 'I've brought you some extra help. Miss Smith needs more bandages.'

Dolly gave Rose a wry smile, then gestured for Ada to come over.

'I'll see you this evening,' said Rose as she retreated back into the shade of the building.

Ada nodded eagerly, still enjoying the feel of

the sun on her face, then made her way over to Dolly. As she approached, she heard the sound of a woman weeping, and looked across to see a poor creature sitting on a wooden packing case, rocking backwards and forwards with her head in her hands.

'Come on then,' said Dolly, sensing her concern for the weeping woman.

When Ada stood before the washerwoman she seemed even bigger, almost like a giant. Dolly looked down at her and said, 'Well, you're a bit small but we'll see what we can do.' She saw that Ada was still distracted by the woman's distress, and filled her in. 'That's Ruth; her man was blown up in the trenches yesterday. We're just letting her mourn today and then tomorrow we'll see if she's fit to get back to work.'

Ada didn't think that Ruth would be fit for work any time soon and felt so sad for the woman. She wished there was something she could do to help, but for now she had to make a start on the much-needed bandages.

'We'll start you off at the shitty end – it's always best to get that out of the way,' said Dolly, nudging Ada into action. 'See this big pile of mucky sheets and bandages?'

Ada could not only see them but smell them very strongly indeed.

'Take them over to the washtubs and get 'em into the hot water. When they're all in we'll need you to help work on the sheets with the possers – have you done that before, young lady?'

'I have indeed,' said Ada, laughing.

'Just checkin', that's all,' said Dolly with a

192

smile. 'It's just that you look like you might be a bit la-di-da.'

Ada laughed again. 'Oh, there's not much la-di-da about me,' she said as she walked over to the pile of sheets and got stuck in, gagging at first with the smell. She was glad that Rose had kitted her out again with a clean pinny; at least it would save her only skirt from getting too soiled. The sheets were full of excrement and the bandages even worse, caked with blood and pus.

There was another woman working the tubs with Dolly, Lavinia, an army widow. Ada learnt quickly to pay her little mind but found it hard trying to work alongside someone who never spoke except to pray, which she did almost constantly as she stirred the sheets in the tub. Dolly told her quietly that Lavinia had always been a bit strange, but since her husband had been killed she had become mute, apart from the praying. 'Hard worker, though, hard worker.'

When Ada had finished moving the big pile of sheets she found a basket full of bloodied rags. 'Do you want these in as well?' she shouted across to Dolly, holding up the basket.

'No, leave those till tomorrow. I'll put them in first with the clean water.' Seeing Ada's puzzled expression she continued, 'Those are the cloths the nurses use for their monthly courses. I make sure they're washed and I always have a clean supply if you ever need any.'

Ada blushed. No one had ever spoken to her about her monthly bleeding before, let alone shouted it across to her.

'Thank you, I'll remember that,' she said, busying herself instantly.

Noticing her embarrassment, Dolly instructed Ada to start ferrying some wood for the fires that heated the water. They needed to be kept lively.

'Will do,' said Ada, glad to have something different to do, something that felt much cleaner but just as vital. She took to this very well, throwing the sticks and logs on to the fire and seeing the sparks fly up. It was so hot, though, and she could feel the sweat streaming down her face and between her breasts. Good job Dolly made sure they always had a pot of water on to brew tea or just to give them boiled, cooled water.

The work was hard but it didn't matter because Dolly's hearty laugh and saucy humour seemed to make the day go easily. And the tasks were such that you could get on and do them and have a good natter at the same time. During that first day Ada learnt why Dolly thought Tom Dunderdale kept himself clean-shaven. Dolly had seen Tom, up early in the mornings, over his bowl and in front of his mirror with a shiny cut-throat razor, soaping and scraping away at his chin, never one nick or scratch. Did you ever see any other man taking a shave out here? Not even the doctors or the officers. That whey-faced Dr Mason kept his beard trimmed but the rest didn't bother. So Tom must have some special reason to take the time to scrape, scrape, scrape his skin every morning. Dolly suddenly grabbed Ada's face and rubbed her chin roughly against her cheek: 'So 'e can rub his bristly chin against the smooth cheek of Sister Mary Roberts!' accompanied by great guffaws of laughter. Dolly relished the telling of this story.

When they weren't chatting, Dolly and Ada sang as they worked, to drown out the praying and the weeping if nothing else. Ada felt at home here with these women; it was like being back with Mary and Mrs Regan. They worked on throughout the day, until the light began to change, the fire burned down and they were ready to tip out the dirty water from the tub.

The wash had dried well, strung up on lines and laid out on the grass. They brought it in and folded the sheets, then Ada set to work rolling the bandages so that the nurses could use them tomorrow and Miss Smith would be satisfied by the full baskets. Dolly showed her how to do this and how to keep them tight so they wouldn't unravel.

As she sat, a large ginger cat with light green eyes came to rub and twist its way around her skirt. 'That cat: you know his name, Ada?' She shook her head and Dolly let just the right amount of time elapse before informing her, 'That's Tom Dunderdale, that is,' with a gleeful glint in her eye and a massive laugh to end the working day. Even the silent woman smiled and the weeping woman paused from her grief for just a few seconds as she and Dolly laughed until their ribs hurt.

Then Dolly gestured to Lavinia and told her it was time they were finishing up and they both went over to Ruth and Dolly put her arm around her and helped her up off the box. Dolly set off with them, one on each arm, back to their tent, shouting 'Goodnight,' and 'See you tomorrow!' as they went.

Ada assumed that Dolly's husband was up at the camp or on the front line, but surprisingly she hadn't given Ada one single detail about her own life. When Ada got back to the nurses' quarters she asked some of the hospital nurses about her, and the girls eagerly told her their favourite Dolly story. She'd been at the Battle of Balaklava with a group of army wives and spotted 500 or so Turkish troops running headlong down a hillside straight through the British line towards the port, yelling, 'Ship, ship!' When Dolly realized that the Turks had abandoned a British Army regiment, she brandished a large piece of wood and chased them down the hill, the poor Turks running and shouting with their pots and pans in their hands, Dolly and the Cossacks in hot pursuit.

This story was a favourite in the nurses' quarters and always made everybody laugh. The women thought that all the British Army really needed was a regiment of women just like Dolly – send them in to Sevastopol and the siege would be over in a day.

'You'll be all right out there with Dolly,' they told her. 'Even if the Russians attack, she'll see 'em off good and proper.'

Ada had to admit that she did feel safe out there with Dolly and she would go as far as to say that she was looking forward to another day in the laundry.

Next morning, as they were getting up, there was a knock at the door. Rose quickly finished fastening her blouse and opened the door just far enough to communicate with the person at the other side. Ada could hear some kind of mumbled conversation but she was too sleepy to bother seeing who it was and she was still lying on the mattress, waiting her turn for the commode and the bowl of water.

She heard Rose close the door with a click and then she made an announcement to the whole room. 'They need someone to go up to the army camp this morning to an urgent case. One of the army wives is in labour and running into difficulty and their doctor is sick with a fever. Does anyone have any experience?'

None of the nurses responded. Ada could tell that they didn't want to go, and she knew from her day on the ward how sorely they were needed here.

'Do you have any training, Nurse Blackwood?' one of them asked.

'No, I do not,' answered Rose, looking very uncomfortable at the very idea of dealing with that sort of thing.

There was still nothing coming from the hospital nurses so Ada piped up: 'Well, I have a bit of experience and I've seen the woman who was our local midwife deliver a few.'

Rose looked at Ada, shocked. 'How can that be? You are so young; surely you should not have been exposed to that sort of thing.'

Ada smiled and said, 'Well, it's all part of life where I come from.'

Rose blushed a little at the very thought, then was forced to concede that Ada would be the only candidate. 'Let's get you moving, then,' she said. 'Get ready as quickly as you can; there's a wagon waiting at the front of the hospital as we speak.'

Ada shifted herself and got ready, grabbing her

red shawl on the way out. She was soon down the corridor and out through the front door. Moving at speed, she almost ran into Dr Lampeter, who was standing by the door waiting for something.

Ada mumbled her apologies and dodged around him quickly without stopping, wondering what the heck he was doing lurking outside.

She saw a wagon with the horse tethered but no driver. She was expecting to see Tom Dunderdale for some reason, but there was no sign. She stood for a few moments outside; then someone tapped her on the shoulder. She turned to find Dr Lampeter.

'You're not telling me that they've sent you?' he said.

'Well, I'm waiting to go with someone up to the army camp on an urgent call,' she replied, realizing immediately that he was the person who was going up there, he was the person she would be assisting.

'There must be some mistake,' he said, turning on his heel to go back into the hospital.

'No mistake,' said Ada firmly. 'I'm the only one with any experience.'

Lampeter stopped in his tracks and turned back to her with a scowl. 'Damn and blast it,' he said. 'There's no time anyway. We need to get off.' He walked straight over to the wagon without looking at her, then turned and said, 'We'll see about this when I get back,' before leaping up into the driver's seat.

Ada was frozen for a moment.

'Well, come on then,' said Lampeter. 'No time to lose, nurse.'

# 14

*'I think one's feelings waste themselves in words; they ought all to be distilled into actions ... which bring results.'*

Florence Nightingale

Lampeter did not say a single word to her or even look in her direction during their journey over the roughest road that Ada had ever ridden. It seemed like the longest six miles of her life.

The ground was rock hard and riddled with ruts from all the other vehicles, horses and men that had passed over it during the wet season. It was so dusty that it was difficult for Ada to see much of the terrain they were travelling through and she needed to hold her shawl over her nose and mouth at times. It looked open, empty and barren.

She remembered what Tom Dunderdale had told her about this road, how it could be frozen solid in winter, or, after heavy rain – even in summer – thick with Crimean mud that sucked and dragged man and beast knee-deep to a complete standstill. She knew that things had improved a great deal since the new railway had opened in March to carry supplies up and wounded men down. To think that they'd brought the track, the sleepers and the locomotive all the way out here and built it from scratch in next to no time. It had made Ada feel proud to be British.

As they finally approached the white tents of the camp, Ada saw a soldier waiting for them at the guard post. He gestured for them to stop, then spoke to Lampeter, telling them to be as quick as they could. They both leapt down from the wagon and another soldier took their horse.

They followed the man through a maze of tents until they could hear the sound of what could only be a woman in labour. A blood-curdling scream pierced the air and a terrified-looking man wearing a red jacket winced as he stood outside the tent. The man's eyes widened when he saw them and his face cleared a little; then he begged them to help.

'Are you the father?' asked Lampeter.

'Yes, I am, I am,' said the man with tears in his eyes. 'She's been going on like this for too long, too long. You have to do something, doc.'

Ada saw Lampeter grip the man's shoulder, trying to give some reassurance. Then they both ducked their heads and almost bent double to get into the tent.

Once inside Ada could stand up easily and Lampeter had more room than expected but it was still very cramped. Ada was shocked, not only by the darkness and heat inside such a confined space but by the salty, pungent smell of childbirth. The woman was lying flat on her back in an area inside the tent that was dug down into the ground. She was lying on the bare earth with only a filthy blanket under her. Another woman was in attendance but she was panicked and crying.

Ada took off her shawl and asked the crying

woman what had been happening.

'Well, she was labouring all day yesterday and her waters broke this morning but the baby won't come.'

Another strong pain came over the mother. She grabbed her friend and started to scream. Ada glanced across at Lampeter for reassurance but he was looking thoughtful and didn't seem to have much else to offer. And then he said, 'Get the history. Ask them more about what's been happening so far.'

Ada nodded. As soon as the pain had subsided and the mother had lapsed back into an exhausted state, she said, 'So the waters broke this morning?'

'Yes,' said the friend. 'It's her first, see, and I've only helped with those who've had babies already before. This is different, see. It's not going right. She keeps wantin' to push and she's pushin' and pushin' but nothing comes. I've never had anything like this, see. Somethin's wrong.'

Ada saw the worried look on the mother's face as her friend was speaking and she knew that she had to move quickly.

'Right,' she said to the friend. 'We can take over from here. You go and get yourself something to eat and drink.' Ada could see that the woman looked relieved as she leant over to give the mother-to-be a kiss and said, 'You'll be all right now, lovey, the doctor is here.'

Ada looked over to Lampeter and wasn't sure that was the case; he looked nowhere near as comfortable in this army tent with a labouring woman as he had on the ward and she knew that she would have to take the lead for now. She remembered that one of Mrs O'Dowd's women had been struggling with her first and she had given birth on all fours. She couldn't think of anything else that might help and looking again at Lampeter she knew that he had no clue.

'Right,' said Ada, outwardly calm but inwardly terrified, stroking the woman's arm as another pain started to build. 'I need you to turn over on to all fours.'

'What the bloody hell!' snarled the woman. 'Get off me!' she shouted, pulling her arm away and screaming in Ada's face.

Ada let her ride through the pain once more and then as soon as it was subsiding she said again, more firmly, 'You have to move. You have to move so the baby will come.'

Exhausted and slurring her speech, the woman started to wail and cry, 'I can't move, I can't!'

'You can if we help you,' said Ada, indicating to Lampeter that he needed to assist. 'Now, before the next pain,' she said, but the woman's face was already starting to contort. 'Right!' shouted Ada, hauling on the woman's arm and pulling her up. 'Now, turn over. Dr Lampeter, help us please!' she almost spat at him.

Together they pulled and heaved the woman over on to all fours as another huge pain swept over her. Ada grabbed her red shawl off the ground and placed it down under the woman between her legs. Ada's instinct had told her that the baby needed to move down. And down it would bloody well come with the next pain.

'Right,' said Ada, helping to support the woman,

'when the next pain comes, try not to push; pant like a dog.' She had just remembered that piece of advice from Mrs O'Dowd.

Within seconds another strong pain was racking the woman's body. Ada shouted, 'Pant, pant!' and panted herself, showing the woman what she meant.

Lampeter clearly didn't have any other ideas and this seemed to work better than the agony of watching the woman lying flat, bearing down and bearing down. The next pain came. 'Pant, pant!' shouted Ada, and then again, and again, and again, the pains coming one on top of another, piling up. The woman was holding up but only just. In the short time they had together between pains, Ada tried to soothe her and establish eye contact, then maintain that contact as the woman's face contorted in agony.

The woman had her skirts bunched up around her middle now and with the next pain something seemed to change. There was no way that she could resist the urge to push, no way on earth. And as her body contorted with a huge contraction, the black sticky mass of something appeared between the woman's legs and then slipped back.

'Good, good!' said Ada, inwardly terrified. 'Baby's coming, baby's coming.'

Looking round at Lampeter for support, she saw that he had started to explore the contents of his medical bag.

With the next contraction the black sticky mass appeared more and with the next and the next it didn't slip back. Ada had shouted to Lampeter to get ready: the baby was about to come. Then another pain came and as the woman started to push she saw the baby's face appear with a tiny blue hand squashed against its cheek. The head was out now but Ada could see the thick, twisted cord wrapped round the baby's neck. She moved round to support the woman, telling Lampeter calmly what she had seen.

'Leave it to me,' he said, 'I know what to do with that,' and Ada was so relieved she thought she might faint. She moved back while he came to look and without hesitating felt gently round the tiny neck and pulled at the cord, stretching it over the baby's head just in time for the next huge heave of the woman's body that delivered the shoulders. Then with the next pain the rest followed, out on to Ada's bright red shawl.

Ada looked down, almost shocked to see a baby. 'It's a girl,' she said to the exhausted woman, who was now hanging her head, unable to speak. 'It's a girl,' repeated Ada.

For one still moment they all waited, panting, pouring with sweat. Waiting for that first cry, but none came.

Ada looked down at the sticky bundle on her shawl, all arms and legs, fingers and toes and a scrunched-up face. But no breath, no breath entering its small body. She took the shawl and rubbed the baby's body, moving it around, rubbing its back. Still nothing.

By this time the woman had lain down in exhaustion, too far gone to even look, with tears streaming down her face. Ada looked at Lampeter for help but knew without him saying that he had as much idea about what to do with that baby as she did. He had turned his attention to the thick blue-veined cord, using a length of the woman's apron string to tie it firmly in two places before taking some big scissors from his bag and cutting it. Ada was surprised to hear how gristly that sound was.

At least now she had the baby free to try and stimulate some sign of life.

She continued rubbing at it; she held it upside down in the hope something might drain from its nose and mouth. Still nothing.

Next she cradled it in her left arm and then with the index finger of her right hand felt round inside its tiny mouth, pulling out slime. She then grabbed the corner of her apron and used it to wipe inside the tiny mouth. Still nothing.

The baby's colour was darkening and she thought that she could feel the small body starting to cool. She began to feel real panic building inside her.

In desperation, as she cradled the tiny body in her left arm, she bent over, held its face with her right hand, covered the small nose and mouth with her own mouth and gently breathed out her own warm breath of life. Gently, so gently. Still nothing.

Again she bent over the tiny face, tasting its salty, sticky new-born coating. Again she breathed out over the baby's mouth and nose, this time more strongly. Still nothing.

She gave the baby's body another rub and, in a blind panic but determined not to show the woman or Lampeter, gave one last breath over the baby's face.

Suddenly she felt a small movement, like the stirring of a gentle breeze. Then the sound of a small bubbly snort and a cough. Instinctively she turned the baby's body over on to its side as it coughed a bit more, and then came a feeble cry; it drew in some more air and gave a stronger cry.

A loud cheer came from those gathered outside the tent.

As she held it she felt the movement of a tiny chest and then her own tears started to flow freely down her face. Keeping her back to Lampeter she checked the baby over. It seemed to be all right; she could see that the baby girl had all the parts that it was meant to and looked like the other babies that she'd seen just born. Then, wrapping the baby in her red shawl, she handed her to the woman, who was crying nearly as much as Ada.

Lampeter coughed and muttered something but the women couldn't make out what he was saying. Ada looked across and saw that he was waiting for the afterbirth to be delivered and she knew, from the story of her own birth, that this was a dangerous time too.

He asked Ada to help the woman put the baby to the breast, which they did, although both looked too exhausted to feed or suckle. However these movements must have helped complete the task of delivering the afterbirth, as suddenly there was a slipping, plopping sound and Lampeter was massaging the woman's abdomen. Ada could see a small pool of blood developing beneath the woman and hoped that this was nothing to worry about.

Lampeter didn't seem to be too concerned but

206

kept massaging the woman's abdomen. Then he asked Ada to find as clean a piece of linen as she could. This happened to be the woman's underclothes, which she was asked to press between the woman's legs while Lampeter wiped up the blood and wrapped the strange meaty, flat disc of afterbirth, straggled with membranes, in a filthy blanket. He then disappeared out of the tent and Ada heard him telling the father of the baby and what sounded like a large group of people gathered outside that all was well and they had a baby girl.

Ada and the woman had a few silent moments together. The woman looked at Ada and quietly said, 'Thank you, nurse,' and then, 'What's your name?'

'It's Ada. My name's Ada.'

The woman looked disappointed. 'I can't call her that,' she said, starting to laugh. 'It's his mother's name and we fight like cat and dog.'

Ada started to laugh as well. 'What will you call her then?'

A couple of army wives were coming in through the flap of the tent.

'Call her Alma,' piped up one of the wives immediately. 'A baby girl born in the Crimea should be called Alma.'

Ada looked at the woman, puzzled for a moment, and then she remembered Tom Dunderdale mentioning a battle.

'It was the first big battle of the war, last September, and our men fought like red devils. We fought with the French and the Turks and we won. At least we won that one.'

'I'll call her Alma then,' said the new mother,

cutting her friend short. 'After all, she had to fight to get into this world,' she went on, looking down at her new baby's face.

Seeing the tears that were welling up in the mother's eyes her friends started with their congratulations, hugging and kissing and then crying as well.

Ada was overwhelmed; she didn't know what to say and so she quietly left the tent.

Once outside she was shocked to see such a large group of soldiers and wives. This seemed like one big family. Alma's father already had a large cigar and they were all clapping and cheering.

No sign of Lampeter, though; he seemed to have disappeared very quickly.

As she came through the crowd outside the tent, she saw someone standing quietly at the edge of the group. She recognized him instantly: the groom she had seen on the ship. As she walked by him, she felt his eyes on her and sensed a small smile on his face.

Ada never caught up with Lampeter but was informed that the doctor had decided it was too late for them to set off back that night, and that he'd gone to the cabin of an officer he knew.

The mood in camp was one of celebration. Uncertain as life was for all those required to live there, and especially for the new baby delivered in the midst of war, it seemed that this made it necessary to celebrate all the more. That evening there seemed no end to the number of soldiers and women patting Ada on the back and congratulating her, offering her rum, which she refused, and a pipe of tobacco, which she tried but made her cough her guts up, much to the amusement of the group. She felt welcomed and warmed by the camaraderie and the hospitality of this group of rough-looking people – the men with their long beards and tattered uniforms, the women with their unruly hair and patched-up skirts.

Amidst the booming of the guns they continued to celebrate, and as night fell, the flare and sparkle of the shells in the sky seemed almost like fireworks.

Finally, exhausted, Ada was allowed to find space in a tent next to the looming marquee that was the field hospital, and fell sound asleep on a blanket on the ground.

She woke in the dark, early hours of the morning to the sound of gunfire and a loud bugle. Someone ran into the tent, shouting, 'Get up, get up! It's a turn-out.' She didn't know what that was but jumped up off the ground immediately, and after hitting her head on the tent pole and falling over a box managed to stagger outside.

The whole camp was alive. Lights were moving and bugles blowing. She asked someone what it meant and they told her that the Russians had attempted a night attack. Staring up at the beautiful night sky full of stars, Ada found it hard to believe that they were all in the midst of war.

When the firing died down after about an hour, she was shocked to learn that there had indeed been an attack that night, with at least three British soldiers killed. Once the 'All clear' was sounded she was told to go back to her tent. No more sleep would come, though, and she was more than glad when light began to show through the seams of the tent.

When the sun had risen, she went to find the tent of the new mother and baby. It was easy to spot because someone had attached a large pair of pink bloomers to the top that flapped in the breeze.

Ada hovered outside the tent for some time, unsure of how to enter. You couldn't knock on the door and you couldn't see who, if anyone, was inside. She listened through the canvas and thought she could hear the small sounds of a baby, but amidst the noise of morning camp and the shelling at the front line, it was very difficult.

Suddenly the flap of canvas that served as a door was thrown back and the new father darted out. 'Morning, miss,' he said as if it was the most natural thing in the world to see her there. 'Go on in and see them.'

On re-entering the shaded interior she was relieved to find a much calmer scene than that of the day before. The woman sat nursing the baby, still wrapped in Ada's red shawl, her gaze fixed on the small bundle that had caused so much pain and so much trouble. The baby was feeding well at the breast, with small bubbles of milk at the side of her mouth.

The woman looked up and smiled at Ada, thanking her again for what she had done. Ada smiled, enjoying this moment of calm. Then she realized something. 'What's your name?' she asked. 'We didn't have much time to introduce ourselves yesterday, did we?'

'I'm Miriam,' laughed the woman. 'No, we didn't have much time for some reason.'

'How are you today?'

'A bit sore down there,' said the woman, 'but my friend's had a look and she said that it all looks like what you'd expect after pushing a baby out.'

'Must be more than a bit sore,' said Ada. Even after seeing it a number of times, she had no idea how any woman's body could recover from such an incredible feat.

'She's worth it,' said Miriam, looking down at the baby. 'She's worth every bit of it.'

Ada gently stroked the baby's head, wondering if her own mother had got to hold her just once on the day that she was born, and whether she had looked at her the way Miriam was looking at her baby now. She felt sadness creeping in, as she always did when she thought of Maggie.

'What will you do now? Will you stay here?' she said, leaning away from the mother and baby. 'Is there anywhere a bit safer that you could go?'

'Oh yes, I'm leaving as soon as I've got the strength. I mean, don't get me wrong, I came out here to be with my man and it will be hard to leave, but now that this little one is here, well, I need to do what's best for her. So, yes, I'll be heading back to Scutari just as soon as I can. I never thought I would want to go back there though, what a terrible place it was for us army wives when we first arrived. I mean, they ordered us to stay there but they didn't provide us with any accommodation. The only space we had was a filthy basement and it was soon full of women and children who were sick and dying. There was no proper food and not much water. No hope.'

Miriam stopped for a moment and lowered her head.

'It must have been terrible,' said Ada, not able to believe that the British Army would have treated their own women so badly.

'If I hadn't left when I did, me and this one here, we'd both have been dead. We had the money to secure a passage up to Balaklava, but most of the women, they were spending all their money on drink, trying to blot things out. They were living like animals.'

'So why do you think you're better off back there?' said Ada anxiously.

'Well, I wouldn't even have considered it before, but I've been told that there's some English lady in Scutari now who's set up a home for army wives and they've got a clean place to live with food and clothes and even a school for the children.'

'Are you sure?'

'As sure as I can be when it comes to the British Army,' said Miriam. 'And don't you worry, I'll make sure that I do the best for this little one now.'

'I know you will,' said Ada, stroking the baby's head again. 'Can I ask you something?'

'Anything for you,' said Miriam, sensing that Ada was troubled.

'Well, it's just that I've come out here to look for someone, to look for my brother. Do you know if there've been any new men in the camp in the last couple of months?'

'None that I know of. And we all know everything there is to know about what's going on. That's what it's like here.' Seeing the disappointment on Ada's face, Miriam continued, 'But he might be in Scutari? Which regiment is he in?'

'I don't even think he's in the army.'

'Right,' said Miriam. 'Well, that makes it more difficult then. I mean, it's chaos out here with people coming and going. But we definitely haven't had anybody new here in camp for ages.'

And then, as she sat in that tent with Miriam and the baby, it was as if something clicked inside her and she almost knew in that moment that Frank wasn't here in the Crimea. She had come prepared to turn over every boulder to find him if need be, but she knew it wasn't as simple as that and she felt it, she felt it in her bones that he wasn't even here.

'Are you all right, Ada?' asked Miriam, gently putting a hand on her arm.

'Yes, yes, I'm fine,' she said, trying to smile as that leaden feeling settled again inside her.

Then with one last stroke of the baby's head she roused herself. 'Well, I could sit here all day with you and Alma but I really need to get going.'

'I know,' said Miriam. 'Now don't you worry about us two; we'll be gone from here as soon as we can. I will always remember you, Ada, and we'll raise a glass to wish you well every year on this one's birthday.'

Stepping outside the tent into full sun and trying to adjust her eyes, Ada was startled by a tall, wiry figure advancing towards her down the line of tents. It was Dr Lampeter, stamping mad and shouting, 'Where the blazes have you been? I've been looking for you everywhere! We need to get back to Balaklava.'

213

Ada thought he had a nerve, given that he'd been the one to disappear last night. As he came close she was pleased to note that his face looked pale and his eyes were bloodshot, probably from some over-indulgence with his friend last night.

'Come along, come along, nurse!' And then, quickly turning back to her, 'By the way, you did a fine job with that woman and baby yesterday.'

Ada tried to contain her shock at this hastily flung compliment as she ran after Lampeter, who was moving at speed with his long stride.

As they neared the centre of camp they saw a group of soldiers gathered round two sorry-looking men, their heads hung low, their hands tied. Ada didn't know if they were captured Russian soldiers, but she felt for them. Lampeter had stopped and was looking at the group, trying to make sense of the situation. An officer spotted him and summoned him over.

'Hope you don't mind giving us a bit of your time, doc, but as you know, our doctor is down with a fever, and regulations require us to have a medical man here while we see to these men.'

'What for? What are you doing?' asked Lampeter.

'Oh, they're to be flogged, for drunken insubordination. We need you to be here in case one of them collapses; don't want the buggers dying on us.'

Lampeter seemed a little taken aback. 'So these are our soldiers then, not prisoners captured last night?'

'That's right, sir. These fine fellows were too drunk to take up their guns during the night attack. They're lucky not to be facing a firing squad.'

'I see,' said Lampeter.

Ada must have shown her horror because Lampeter nudged her and muttered, 'Routine procedure, nurse, routine procedure. They need to maintain discipline and these men deserve to be punished.'

However, as the first man's hands were untied, his shirt ripped off and he was led over to a large cart wheel then lashed to it, she sensed Lampeter's resolve weaken as he looked away, coughing nervously.

A thick-set soldier then took off his jacket, rolled up his sleeves, spat on his hands and rubbed them together before picking up a leather whip. A punishment of thirty lashes was ordered for each man and without further delay it began.

Ada felt the impact of the first lash as it bit into the man's flesh, and saw the man's face contort, although he made no sound. And at first no mark could be seen across his back. Then the next lash fell, and the next and the next in quick succession, and by this time bright red welts were showing. It went on and on, and with each stroke the man's body slumped further down on the wheel and he began to make a short grunting noise. By the time they got to the final ten lashes the man's back was a mess of red stripes and was bleeding freely. How could any civilized nation allow this to happen to a member of its own army? Ada's head was reeling. Lampeter stood silent and tense.

When they took the man down from the cart wheel, Lampeter was asked to go over and check him. Two soldiers dragged the man to the side

215

and laid him face down on the ground. He was in agony but seemed to have gone beyond being able to show this. He was barely conscious but still breathing. Lampeter looked up and nodded to the officer while one of the army wives liberally applied some kind of greasy salve to the soldier's ripped and torn skin. The man's back would forever bear the scars.

The procedure was then repeated for the other man. Ada could not watch. Lampeter stood with clenched jaw and balled fists.

By the time Lampeter and Ada were able to leave they could not speak; moving like machines they retrieved their horse and wagon, anxious to get going. As they moved off Lampeter simply said, 'My friend at camp has a nest of rats living under his hut.' Ada looked at him, wondering what he was talking about but sort of understanding why he had said it. She couldn't think of anything to say in reply.

Then, as if on cue, almost as if they'd paused to allow the floggings to take place, the big guns started up for the day.

The road home was just as rough, just as dusty, and there was just as little conversation between them; but on this return journey Ada felt a certain unity with Dr Lampeter. She sensed there was some common ground between them now and felt easier in his presence. So much so that she had no qualms about lifting up the hem of her skirt to cover her nose and mouth as the dust began to thicken around them. It wasn't that she was abandoning all consideration of propriety, she was simply missing the red shawl that had served her so well. Even though she'd had no choice but to leave it there with the baby, she couldn't help but feel a pang at the loss of the only thing that had been her mother's. She felt sure, though, that Maggie would have been glad of the way that it had been put to good use, swaddling a baby girl born so far away from home. They'd had so little in the tent in the way of blankets or provisions, it had been the best thing she could have done, and it made her feel glad to know that baby Alma would be resting snug in that shawl right now.

After they'd been on the road for some considerable time, Lampeter told her that they were going to make a bit of a detour to the British Hotel at Kadikoi, where he needed to pick up some supplies. Ada didn't know what this British Hotel was and she didn't have the strength to ask or to object.

Within minutes of turning off the main road, a few buildings became visible in the near distance, and with what seemed like renewed energy their horse ploughed a path over to them and pulled up outside what looked like a large shed. Lampeter slipped down from the wagon without looking at her and told her to follow him.

Ada was surprised to find that the interior of the building was lined with shelves of tins and bottles and what seemed like a wealth of provisions. The place had tables and chairs dotted about and some armchairs and an old sofa with the stuffing poking out.

A group of officers sat round one of the tables with their red coats unbuttoned and an open bottle of wine in front of them; talking, laughing and smoking cigars.

They stared over at Ada but she paid them no mind.

Lampeter had gone straight to one of the tables and slumped in a chair. She stood just inside the doorway, exploring this new place with her eyes and fascinated by the collection of full hams and dried meats suspended on ropes from the ceiling.

As she was staring up at this aerial feast, a quiet voice spoke kindly to her in an almost sing-song accent that she had never heard before

'We have to keep them up there so the rats don't get to them.'

Looking down, Ada saw the most beautiful young woman. The girl was so lovely that Ada found herself unable to speak. She looked younger than Ada, with soft, light-brown skin and a mass of black hair curling to her shoulders. A certain lightness shone out from the girl's beautiful dark eyes, and her curved, smiling mouth offered welcome. She had large looped gold through her ears and a red neckerchief tied around her slender neck.

Stretching her hand out to Ada, she introduced herself as Sally, Mother Seacole's maid, and welcomed her to the British Hotel. The name Seacole seemed familiar and then Ada remembered what the washerwoman in Scutari had told her.

Without hesitation Ada replied, 'Pleased to meet you. I'm Ada, a nurse at Balaklava.' That's odd, she thought, she'd never referred to herself as a nurse before. Maybe she should have said she worked in the laundry or she was Dr Lampeter's assistant. No, not that. Looking across at him now she was loath to be associated with someone who, with his demeanour of entitlement, was already drinking a large glass of something and ordering a plate of ham with the sort of air that Ada didn't like and would not tolerate.

Did he just click his fingers and call for the girl to come over?

Ada would have left and gone to sit back in the wagon immediately if it hadn't been for Sally's teasing laugh and the way she turned her back on Lampeter and rolled her eyes at Ada. They both laughed and Ada followed the girl to the counter.

'Now, nurse,' she said, 'while Mrs Seacole's away I'm in charge, so what can I get you, on the house?'

Close up the shelves were full of many delicacies – potted meats, pickles, bottled beer, roasted coffee, tins of biscuits, chocolate, cigars, tobacco, spirits and even bottles of champagne.

Ada couldn't take her eyes off the chocolate, and without asking Sally brought some down and broke off a good chunk. She then presented Ada with a small glass of dark red liquid, saying with a smile, 'Cherry brandy – try a sip, it's sweet.'

Then Sally was gone, moving over to the frowning Dr Lampeter with a plate of ham and pickles and a full bottle of wine.

Ada stood at the counter with her back to Lampeter while she savoured the melting chocolate in her mouth. Then she tried a sip of the drink. It was sweet and definitely alcoholic, but with the chocolate it tasted delicious and for the first time Ada enjoyed a spot of the strong stuff. Wanting to make this moment last for as long as possible, she ate slowly and sipped the drink and gazed at the shelves. She felt the warm liquid soothing and relaxing her – no wonder people used this stuff to get through hard times.

Suddenly Sally popped up behind the counter and they both laughed. 'I think your friend might be tired or very cross about something,' she said in a low voice.

'He's not my friend and he's always like that,' whispered Ada. 'But he seems to be enjoying your lovely food – maybe that'll put him in a better mood.'

'I'm not sure,' said Sally, 'but a lot of them who come in here are like that. We just let them get on with it.'

'Do you open up here every day?'

'Yes, except Sunday. That's our day of rest but we still work anyway, getting ready for the next week, and if there are casualties Mrs Seacole will go out to the front line.'

'To the front line?' said Ada, her eyes wide.

'Yes,' said Sally. 'She takes her medical bag with needles, bandages and medicines and off she goes on a horse or in the cart. It's what she does. If there are injured soldiers, Mrs Seacole will get to them somehow. She treats all wounded soldiers, the Russians as well.'

Ada was shocked. 'But the Russians are vicious barbarians,' she said. 'That's what I was told back home. How could Mrs Seacole treat them? Would they not try to kill her?'

Sally smiled; it felt like she was used to answering that question. 'The Russians are just men with mothers, wives, children too. Soldiers just like the

British, the French, the Turks, and if they need help, Mother Seacole will give it.'

'Really?' said Ada. 'Isn't that dangerous for her?'

'Yes it can be – she sometimes goes out there when the troops are under fire – but usually she will wait for the ceasefire and for the truce.'

'The truce?' said Ada, scrunching her brow. 'You mean when they put up the white flag and no one is allowed to kill the enemy?'

'Yes, that's right.'

'And do they stick to it?'

'Yes they do, and if there are dead or injured men lying on the ground between the two sides – what they call no-man's-land – they're allowed to go and treat the injured or remove the bodies without fear of attack.'

'I never knew that,' said Ada. 'So our side will mix with the Russians during the truce and nobody will get killed.'

'Correct,' said Sally. 'Sometimes they help each other or share a smoke or try to chat.'

'And then once the white flag goes down, bang, they start trying to kill each other again?'

'That's exactly the case,' said Sally.

Ada's whole view of the world as it had been given to her, mostly by her grandfather, seemed to be turning upside down. She was amazed by this other side to something that she had thought was very straightforward: us against them.

'But we also treat the wounded and sick who come to the door, here at the British Hotel. We open up every morning except Sunday, and we serve coffee, and by that time we usually have a line of men waiting to be treated. We see each one in turn.'

'So Mrs Seacole can do this herself; she doesn't need to work with a doctor?' said Ada.

'Yes. She has done that kind of work for many years. We are from Jamaica and she is called a doctress there. Mrs Seacole knows all about herbal remedies too. Have you heard about the cholera powder?'

'No, but I've heard about the cholera,' said Ada. 'Is the powder a cure?'

'Not always a cure,' said Sally, 'but it can help sometimes. Mrs Seacole is famous for it out here in the Crimea.'

I hope I don't find myself having to try some of that famous powder, thought Ada, terrified at the thought. They lived with cholera constantly in Liverpool, and she knew that many, many people had died from it.

As she stood there, pondering the number of ways that a person could die out here, she didn't at first hear Lampeter calling over to her. He had finished his bottle and it was time to leave.

When she turned he had already got up from the table and was weaving his way across to her. How much has he had to drink? she thought, outraged at his behaviour.

''S time to leave,' he slurred, before turning and weaving his way back through the tables and towards the door.

'Wish me luck,' said Ada, smiling at Sally.

'Don't worry,' she said, 'the horses know their way back to the hospital. And don't forget, Ada, come back up and see us again soon. Mrs Seacole would be very pleased to meet you. She likes to

222

meet all the new nurses.'

'I will,' shouted Ada as she ran after Lampeter, who was struggling to open the door. Then she grabbed his arm to steady him as he stumbled across to the horse and wagon. Once she had him loaded, Ada jumped up beside him and sat for a moment catching her breath. As she sat she noticed a woman standing against the wall of the building wearing a bright red dress, tattered at the hem. Something about the woman's appearance worried her. She tried to smile at her but the woman just looked down at the ground.

'Who is that?' she asked Lampeter as he leant against her, smelling of drink.

'Oh, she's a *vivandière*, waiting for the officers,' he replied with a slur in his voice. Ada thought he must mean they were like the women of the streets that she had seen in Liverpool, the women that Mrs Regan had warned her to stay away from and told her that she might become if she didn't find the right fella.

Lost in her own thoughts for a moment, Ada was startled as Lampeter grabbed her arm and started talking at her again.

'You see, there's always a need amongst the soldiers for that sort of woman – away from home, away from their sweethearts and wives. And unfortunately some of the women who come out here fall on hard times when their men get killed, or some of them come out here to make money in that way anyway and there's always the trade to be had, you see, because men will be men and they are a certain way.'

Lampeter then let go of her arm but grabbed her

thigh to steady himself as he slumped to the side, and Ada was quite glad that he seemed incapable of any further explanation. She removed his hand from her thigh, making sure he was wedged in and not going to fall out of the carriage, then took up the reins and flicked them across the horse's back. She did this gently, not wanting to hurt the creature. The horse didn't move. She flicked the reins again. Still nothing.

Looking over, she saw the woman in the red dress staring at her. Ada began to feel flustered and could feel her face going red. How the hell does anyone get these things to move? she thought. When she looked up again she could see that the woman was miming a flick of the reins but doing it more strongly, like she meant business. Ah, she thought, I need to give it a bit more. So she flicked the reins hard across the horse's back and they shot off very fast.

Lampeter lurched to the side, and if she hadn't grabbed him he probably would have fallen out. As they hurtled away Ada put her hand up to thank the woman in the red dress.

She prayed that Sally had been right and that the horse would take them back towards the hospital and not the army camp. She certainly didn't fancy another night there with all those shells and night raids. It made the hospital feel like the safest place in the world. Ada couldn't wait to get back there and curl up in her new bed on the floor next to Rose.

# 15

*'I am ready to stand out the war with any man.'*
Florence Nightingale

The next day Ada found herself back in the laundry.

Miss Smith had been on a rampage yet again and caused uproar by entering the ward, stripping sheets off the men, moving beds and insisting that floorboards were taken up to try and get rid of the rats and fleas. Consequently there was an enormous pile of washing to be done. Thankfully most of it was reasonably clean and not foul-smelling.

Ada got stuck in to the work alongside her silent companion. The upturned box was empty today and Dolly explained that Ruth was resting in the tent. She'd cried every last tear out and was now lying exhausted. Dolly was hoping that they might be able to tempt her with a morsel of food later in the day, but she was still in a terrible state. As Dolly spoke, Lavinia started praying and this became louder and louder until they were forced to change the subject.

Working together with the women at their simple tasks, Ada felt a certain contentment; she could relax and let her mind wander. She kept thinking about Alma up at the army camp and Sally at the British Hotel. She spent most of the day in some kind of reverie, but doing her best at any opportunity to show some kindness towards Lavinia, a woman who Dolly said had been as chatty as you please before her man was killed.

'It takes people different ways,' said Dolly with a look of sadness in her eyes.

Later in the afternoon, as Ada straightened up from the washtub to stretch her back, she looked around and found that she was completely alone. Dolly must have gone to check on Ruth and she wasn't sure where Lavinia was. There was just the ginger cat stretched out in the sun on the up-turned box, flicking its tail.

It felt a bit odd. Since arriving in the Crimea she had very rarely been on her own; all work and activity here was communal. For a few moments all she could hear was the soft boom of artillery in the distance and the twitter of birds in the bush by her side.

She breathed in the hot air, feeling the trickles of sweat run down her face, her back and between her breasts. She took pleasure in the moment of solitude.

Then, from nowhere, two arms shot around her from behind, clamping her in a strong, vice-like grip. She tried to struggle and kick back with her heels but couldn't shake off this fiend who had come out of nowhere.

'Don't struggle or I'll really hurt you,' said a man's voice up close to her ear. She couldn't see him; she couldn't turn to face him and kick him in the balls. The voice, now wheedling, began to whisper in her ear: 'Well, nursey, or should I say little Miss Laundry, what are you doing out here all alone, eh? Want to spend a bit of quiet time with me – is that the plan?'

Ada kicked and struggled harder but still couldn't shake him off. She could smell his foul breath as he panted in her ear and feel the bony hardness of his body against hers. He had started to move with her, to try and drag her away.

'You best not struggle, Nurse Ada. I saw you back in Scutari with those army wives. I knew you weren't one of them; you came up from Liverpool. I know you–'

'You know nothing, Cedric Wilson!' shouted a woman's voice.

Instantly Ada's assailant released her and staggered back with a cry of pain. A woman's voice shouted again, loud and clear:

'Don't you dare touch her again, Cedric Wilson, don't you dare! And you know nothing about her life and who she is. Nothing!'

Ada turned to find Lavinia with a savage look on her face and a large piece of firewood in her right hand. Cedric Wilson lay helpless on the ground, rolling from side to side and nursing the back of his head.

Ada was shocked, her head reeling. She couldn't speak, just stared at the scrawny man on the ground trying to make sense of the situation. Then she felt relief wash over her and began to register her amazement at Lavinia who, now that she had found her voice, continued to chastise the man, tapping him on the legs with the piece of firewood and calling him a cowardly bastard, until with an angry growl he jumped up and staggered off, holding his head.

Ada was stunned. Lavinia grinned at her, then

227

said, "'The Lord is my shepherd, I shall not want,'" before laughing and coming to Ada with a concerned expression, asking if she was all right, telling her not to worry about him, he would stay away now, she'd see to that.

Ada stood in amazement and then hugged Lavinia, saying, 'Thank you, thank you!' The women clung together, aware that in very different ways they had both been rescued that afternoon.

Breaking away at last, Lavinia said, 'I've been wanting to do that to him for such a long time. He was in the same regiment as my husband but they chucked him out and sent him back to England. Now he's come back here to be an orderly. My Robert always used to say that Cedric was a good-for-nothing, deceitful coward. Unfortunately they're not all good men and true.'

When Dolly reappeared she was amazed to find Ada and Lavinia chatting away over the washtub, as if no one had ever had a problem talking.

'What you two lasses been up to then?' she enquired with a puzzled look on her face.

Without hesitation Lavinia replied, 'We've been chasing the biggest rat we've ever seen out of the laundry.'

Ada laughed. Dolly said nothing but went over to Lavinia and gave her a big kiss on the cheek.

Lavinia never stopped talking all day, as if a river of words had been dammed up inside and needed to pour out. She told Ada about her Robert and the town they had both grown up in, her brothers and sisters, Robert's mother, who must be heartbroken at the loss of her only son, the church they were married in, her best friend Iris who worked as a seamstress, life in the army, what she thought about Miss Smith, Dr Mason and that other bad-tempered one, and that beautiful well-spoken nurse they called Rose. They laughed again at Dolly's jokes about Tom Dunderdale and complained about the extra laundry. It was good to talk and moan with Lavinia. Ada was almost glad that she'd been accosted by Cedric, as it had given Lavinia a way out of her silent world.

That evening they folded the dry washing, rolled the bandages and emptied out the washtub, but instead of letting the fire die down Dolly found a bit more wood and built it up again. She then said her goodnights to Ada and Lavinia and headed off to spend time with Ruth.

Once she'd gone they went together to find their food from the kitchen: the stew, mostly potato and onion, that was served every day, some bread and butter and a cup of tea for Ada and a measure of rum for Lavinia. They sat by the fire watching the wood spit and burn while they ate their meal. Then, in a more measured way, Lavinia began to talk again, to tell Ada more about Dolly. Not the oft-repeated story of her chasing the Turks but this time how she came to the Crimea in the first place. Lavinia knew because their husbands had both been in the same regiment and while Lavinia had been picked out of the ballot to go to war with her man, Dolly's name had not been drawn. So Dolly was not 'on the strength', as they called it.

'So the women can't choose if they go or not?' said Ada.

'No they can't. And the army only allow a few

from each regiment to go with the men. The names of those without children go into a hat and get drawn a few days before the men leave and that's that. It was a terrible time for us women, especially those with children – they were left behind starving for food and without any money.'

'That can't be right,' said Ada, the sense of it burning inside of her. 'How can that be allowed to happen?'

'It's the army, they just seem to be able to get away with it,' said Lavinia. 'Dolly was distraught, so she devised a plan based on stories she'd heard about other women. She got hold of a full uniform for her man's regiment, bound her breasts flat to her chest, cropped her hair and embarked with the men disguised as a soldier.'

'Really?' said Ada. 'That's incredible. And no one knew that she was a woman?'

'Well, they knew in the ranks, but none of the officers cottoned on. She lived with the men and fought with them too. Just look at the back of her neck if you get the chance; she has a scar from a wound that she got at Alma. Dolly is the kindest, most gentle person I've ever known, but she's big and strong and can fight like a man.'

Ada sat quiet for a while taking it all in, and then Lavinia continued with a story of another woman, a story that had made everybody in the ranks laugh. 'One of the officers couldn't understand how, that first winter, one of his men was getting fat as the rest were getting thin. This soldier's belly was growing and growing. Then one day the soldier disappeared for a while and came back carrying a baby boy. All the men cheered and celebrated and the woman was allowed to stay in camp with her child. The army are fickle; sometimes you can do something that seems quite small and get a good thrashing; other times, if the officers are in favour or if it feels like a good omen, they let you get on with it.

'They were good with me when they told me about my Robert,' she went on, her voice suddenly sombre. 'They knew he was missing but didn't find his body for days. By that time he was difficult to recognize, just a letter from his mother in his pocket to show who it was. Dolly's husband was killed at the Alma as well. That's when she had to come clean to the officers and tell them who she was. She'd fought with courage alongside her man during the battle and they admired her for that, so they brought her out of the regiment and found her work as a laundress. She's strong, strong and clever, so she'd do well anywhere.

'I mean, without people like Dolly I don't know how any of us would have survived that first winter here. It was terrible. We weren't told, you see, how cold it would be. Nobody had thick clothing or enough blankets. The men's backs were never dry and they were going down to the trenches in rags, wet to the skin. Then they had to lie there in mud and slush till morning. There wasn't enough wood or charcoal for fires so they couldn't dry their boots or clothes. Men were dying from cold and frostbite in those trenches and they were ordered to dig more trenches, digging into hard ground in freezing temperatures under constant enemy fire. Somebody told us that every yard of trench was at the cost of one man's life.'

Ada felt the sorrow seeping out of Lavinia and put an arm round her shoulders to try and offer some comfort.

Lavinia smiled at her then continued with her story. 'We didn't get enough food either because before the railway was open there was only that road, deep in mud and impassable. Starved baggage animals had no strength to wade through that mud; they were so weak that many of them were dying from cold every night. The men were starving and then when the rum ration ran out... I mean that was the only stand-by that kept them on their legs at all. There were rumours that men were deserting, going over to the Russians for food and a bit of warmth.'

Lavinia paused for a moment, lost in her thoughts. Ada didn't try to speak, just continued to listen.

'The officers made sure that they were all right, though; they made sure of that. They had their own horses so they could go down to Balaklava for supplies and they had the money to pay for them. We had bugger all that winter, bugger all... Terrible times. Ruth's husband, he survived all that, only to get struck by a shell when he was peering over the trench to look for his dog. He always liked a dog did George Bell, seemed to have a special way with them. This one he'd picked up as a stray in camp, skinny little thing it was, left behind by some of the locals when they moved out. He kept it and fed it from his rations and the officers didn't mind because it was good for morale. Anyway, they said he woke up that morning and the dog was gone. He just poked his head up to have a quick look and bang, that was it. At least it was quick for him. They never did find that dog – Boney, he called it, little brown Boney.

'I was glad that me and Dolly stuck together at camp and then down here. She looked after me that winter and she's looking after me now,' said Lavinia, wistful and beginning to yawn.

Ada drew in all this information as they sat by the fire watching the embers glow then turn grey. She began to feel tired but was reluctant to leave until Lavinia was ready, worried that she might lose her voice again.

As darkness fell, the temperature dropped and Ada felt a bit of a shiver without the red shawl, though it gave her a warm glow to know that it was keeping that baby warm.

Sensing that Ada was tired, Lavinia said, 'I'll walk you back to the nurses' quarters, young Ada, just in case there's any big rats lurking in the shadows.'

They both laughed and got up together to walk through the hospital. And that night, as they parted with a kiss on the cheek, Ada felt the closeness of a sister.

# 16

*'Mrs Seacole was with the British army in the Crimea... This excellent woman has frequently exerted herself in the most praiseworthy manner in attending wounded men, even in positions of great danger, and in assisting sick soldiers by all means in her power.'*
Lord William Paulet,
British adjutant-general in the Crimea

Early next morning there was another knock on the nurses' door, and Rose was not surprised to find Dr Lampeter standing there, mumbling about asking that nurse to come with him again up to the British Hotel.

'Ada,' said Rose in a low voice, turning from the door and holding it to, 'Dr Lampeter wants you to go out with him again, up to Mrs Seacole's place this time.'

Ada felt herself bristle. She really didn't fancy doing anything with him again. He'd probably just want to get blind drunk and then expect her to get them home like last time.

'Well?' said Rose, still holding the door and indicating with her raised eyebrows that Ada really had no choice – she had to go; an order from a doctor was an order.

Ada nodded and Rose opened the door just far enough to say, 'Nurse Houston will meet you out front in five minutes.'

Ada heard the door click shut as she scurried into her clothes. Then Rose came over to help her fasten up, saying, 'I'm going to miss you again today, Ada. I was hoping we could work together on the ward but you'd better go with his lordship.'

'I'll be back soon, don't worry,' said Ada, and then, thinking about what Rose had just said, 'Do you really think I'm some use on the ward?'

'Of course,' said Rose. 'Sister Roberts and I are very pleased with you. You have the makings of an excellent nurse.'

'Really?' said Ada, beaming at Rose.

'Now go on,' said Rose, smiling back. 'You don't want to keep the great doctor waiting.'

As she walked through the hospital Ada was pleased with the thought that she might at least be able to see Sally again. She was fully expecting to have to travel in complete silence, but she could manage that; it might even be easier than trying to make awkward conversation.

Lampeter was waiting on the wagon, ready to get going, and barely acknowledged her as she scrambled up on to the seat beside him. She sat upright and held on to the side, expecting them to leave at some speed. However, he flicked the reins gently this time and they moved away at a slow pace. Almost leisurely, thought Ada, settling herself for a long, bumpy journey with a silent companion.

Then she heard him speak and out of the corner of her eye saw him turn in her direction. She was so shocked that she didn't take in what he was saying. He hadn't seemed to think her worth his

235

time of day before, but now she thought he sort of smiled, though she wasn't really sure if it was a smile or some kind of grimace. She noticed how blue his eyes were but felt a bit unsettled by the way they seemed to burn into her. She also noticed that he had been attempting to trim his beard. It was a bit lopsided but certainly not as wild as it had been. She wondered what he looked like under all that hair.

She returned a sort of smile and they reverted to their usual silence as they rocked and bounced along. Maybe he was sick or going down with a fever. She glanced across at him again quickly. He looked his usual self, and now he seemed to be lost in thought, staring at the horse's back end.

In due course their pace slowed and Lampeter sat back a little and turned to Ada as if to speak, but then, thinking better of it, looked at the horse again. A few moments later he said hesitantly, 'You settling in all right at the hospital?'

'Yes, very well,' she blurted out, looking at him only to find that he was still staring at the horse's back end.

'Are you comfortable enough?'

'Yes of course,' said Ada with a small smile at the corners of her mouth, thinking of the hard, narrow bed under the stairs in their house on the street. What did he think she was used to: a feather mattress?

He opened his mouth to respond but then no words would come. At long last he managed to say, 'You homesick or anything?'

Wanting to put an end to this strange, stilted

conversation, Ada replied with a simple 'No.' It was of course a complete lie; now that she was further away from Liverpool than she had ever imagined she would be she thought about the place constantly. It was mainly tied up with how much she still missed her grandfather and Frank, of course it was, but she was amazed by how much the city itself kept calling to her and how much longing she had for it. Sometimes when she woke she thought she was back at home. She missed the smell of the city and the rhythm of the people in the streets and their accents, but most of all she missed the roll and clank of the docks and the little house that she would never go back to.

Now that her grandfather was dead and gone and Frank was missing it almost felt that the city had become more to her; it gave her a sense of who she was. She had never thought of it like that before but she did now, all those miles away and with no idea of when she would be able to get back to it. She realized she would always feel tied to Liverpool with some unseen thread; that was the reality.

But she sat up there on that wagon with Dr High and Mighty and told him an outright lie, just to shut him up and end their awkward conversation.

'Well, not many people get to see a place like this,' he said.

Strange man, she thought. Very strange. No, they don't get to see a place like this, probably because most people don't want to risk life and limb visiting a war!

Later he turned again to her and said, 'You still

have a lot to learn, you do realize that, don't you?'

Before she could reply, he turned back to look down at the horse and she lost her opportunity to respond.

Of course I know that, she thought, what is he going on about?

When they approached the British Hotel, Lampeter sat up in his seat and became instantly alert as they saw a line of soldiers waiting outside the door. Ada remembered what Sally had told her about the emergency treatment that Mother Seacole gave to the troops. It looked like this would be a good opportunity to learn from a woman who by all accounts knew what she was doing.

Lampeter pulled up the horse and jumped down in a lively fashion. Turning to Ada he said, 'Come on then, nurse, let's go and have a look at what they're doing.'

Jumping down from the wagon, she only just caught up with him. As they went through the door he was explaining that he had promised Sally that he'd bring the English girl back. Ada wasn't listening but got the gist of it. She was distracted by the sight of an older woman – in a bright green dress with feathers in her hair and large shiny earrings – bending over a young soldier with a towel soaked in water wrapped around his head.

The woman looked up with a broad smile as they walked in and Lampeter greeted her warmly. 'Good morning, Mrs Seacole. You've made an early start today.'

With a full, strong voice she replied, 'Yes, doctor, this young man couldn't wait in line. He was bleeding everywhere, and I mean everywhere.'

The lad looked up with pain in his eyes and Mother Seacole spoke to him gently, telling him not to worry, that these head wounds always bled freely and looked a lot worse than they were. He wasn't going to die; he just needed to keep still and then she could sew him up as quick as anything and he'd be perfectly fine to go back with his friends.

Ada noticed two other young soldiers who sat to the side, spattered with blood.

Mrs Seacole shouted over to the counter, 'Sally, bring this young man some of the best brandy and then we'll get started.'

Sally smiled at Ada and then came over with the spirit in a flask so the lad could swig it easily. Ada couldn't help but notice that seeing Sally that morning was a real pleasure for the lad, despite the nasty head wound that had brought him here.

'Can I take a look at the wound?' said Lampeter, interested as always in gaping flesh or broken bones. Satisfied that the situation was as Mrs Seacole stated, he let her get on with it, telling Ada, much to her surprise, 'This woman can suture a wound better than any surgeon I've ever worked with.'

The woman in question looked at Ada and simply said, 'Many, many years of practice. Many years.' Then added, 'You must be the young nurse that Sally told me about. Pass me that needle over there, please, then you don't need to do anything 'cept watch and learn.'

Ada was instantly fascinated by this woman who had the same rich brown skin, dark eyes and

239

black hair as Sally. She could have been Sally's mother.

Lampeter was quite right; Mrs Seacole's nimble fingers were quick and adept with the needle and thread. So quick in fact that the lad who was still staring at Sally didn't seem to notice the stitches going in, even as small rivulets of blood from each one began to stream down his face Ada made a move to lift a swab but Mrs Seacole told her to let the blood flow freely. It would help clean the wound. After the final suture Mrs Seacole pressed the wound firmly; this she told Ada was to squeeze out any residual blood from inside the wound so it didn't turn to infection. She then asked Sally to apply a dressing and a firm bandage.

'I'll have a break now, Sally,' said Mrs Seacole as she wiped the blood from her hands. Then she went over to Dr Lampeter's table. 'Please, Sally, when you've time can you bring us over a pot of coffee with three cups. I need a pick-me-up before I can see the rest of them.'

Once Sally had brought a steaming pot of freshly brewed coffee and three cups over to the table, Mrs Seacole beckoned for Ada to join them. The conversation between Mrs Seacole and Lampeter revolved around the number and type of cases they were seeing, the recent improvement in medical supplies and then predictions of what might happen next in terms of the siege.

'I think the Russians are weakening,' said Lampeter, cradling his coffee with both hands, 'but then we failed last time and who knows if another assault will be any more successful.'

'That's the thing,' said Mrs Seacole. 'There they

240

are, holed up in Sevastopol, and I've heard that conditions are terrible for them in that city. Just terrible, I really worry about those Russian soldiers.'

'I can't worry about the enemy soldiers like you do,' said Lampeter, smiling at her, 'I've got too much to do worrying about our own.'

'The thing is,' said Mrs Seacole, 'they're all just wounded soldiers to me. They're all brave men and if they need help, I will treat them, in the trenches or when that white flag goes up and we can get into no-man's-land during a truce. I will do my best to help them if I can.'

'Well of course, I know what you mean, especially during a truce. I had an encounter with a Russian officer soon after I came up here. I'll never forget it.'

'What happened? Did he try to shoot you?'

'No, not at all.'

'He should have done,' said Mrs Seacole, laughing and nudging Ada with her elbow. 'Don't you agree, nurse? A short-tempered, bloody-minded doctor like him deserves to be shot.'

Ada opened her mouth to reply but Lampeter was there first, clearly not picking up on Mrs Seacole's light-hearted tone.

'I'd only been up in the Crimea a matter of days, but a truce was signalled. I didn't know what to do or how to do it but went forth with the men to try and help. Most of the Allies were dead or dying but I did find a Russian officer who was struggling to hobble back to his own line. He looked a bit worried when he saw me approaching, must not have realized I was friendly...'

241

No surprise there, thought Ada, trying to stop herself from smiling.

'When I did manage to make him understand that I just wanted to help, he showed me his leg, which had a nasty wound below the knee. I gestured for him to sit down on the ground, and used one of our field bandages to try and staunch the blood, gave him a drink of water from my flask, then helped him across to his own territory. By that time they were just about to sound the end of the truce and lower the white flag.'

Lampeter paused for a moment in his story-telling and took a swig of his coffee. He looked lost in his own thoughts and when he spoke again his voice was charged with emotion.

'As I turned to go back to our line the Russian signalled for me to wait. He undid the top buttons of his uniform and reached up around his neck to remove something. It was a pendant, a leather pendant embossed with the image of the Madonna and Child. The Russian held it in the palm of his hand for a few moments before kissing it and insisting that I take it... We parted with a handshake.' Lampeter took another swig of his coffee.

Mrs Seacole sat smiling at him, before reaching over to pat his hand. Then Lampeter fished between the buttons of his shirt and brought out the pendant to show her. Ada wasn't quite sure, but was there a hint of a tear welling up in his eyes? Maybe there was more to this Dr Lampeter than she thought.

'Well now, John,' said Mrs Seacole, dropping her voice, 'who would have thought that a man like you with such a stern expression would be capable of such an act of humanity. And by the sound of it he gave you his most treasured possession. I pray for an end to all wars but if they can't end then let's hope that they'll always have truces so that those who fight can see each other for what they are, man to man, just human beings.'

Ada felt a tightness in her chest when she saw that Lampeter's eyes had now definitely filled with tears and he was sitting with his head bowed. Mrs Seacole put out a hand and gently touched his arm. 'It's hard, it truly is, to go out there and try to patch people together, people who shouldn't be blowing each other to bits in the first place. But we have to keep doing it. We have no choice.'

Lampeter nodded and then ran his hand over his face, trying unsuccessfully to wipe away the tears before they were noticed. Ada didn't see it as a sign of weakness at all; she had been very moved by his story and had become aware that maybe the man's arrogance and hard exterior were a face that he showed to the world. Behind that it was just possible that he was a man who had feelings.

'Are you going to spend some time here with us today, John?' said Mrs Seacole, clearly aware that the man was struggling.

He wiped his face with his hand again and then said, 'Not today, I'm afraid. We need to get on up to the army camp. There's another wave of cholera sweeping through the soldiers and they're asking for some more of your cholera powders – that's if you have the supply.'

Cholera, thought Ada. Nobody told me there'd

be cholera involved.

'I have indeed but I thought that you British swore by the cholera sash, even though I've told you many times that they are a useless superstition,' she said, laughing and pointing to the piece of red cloth that he wore tied around his waist.

'Well, we British like to employ all means when it comes to cholera and we are willing to try your powders as well,' he said.

'Because you know for a fact that the powders are the only thing that stand a chance of helping.'

'Well, I'm not sure about that. After all, what you call useless superstition has worked well for me so far,' Lampeter replied, looking down at the red sash, making sure that it was secure.

'I'll get you the powders,' said Mrs Seacole, laughing again. 'You need to get them up there as fast as you can cos those pieces of cloth are useless.'

As they got up to leave Ada looked across and saw Sally still busy with the soldiers. She wished that she could stay here and keep well away from the cholera yet she had no choice but to follow along behind Lampeter as he made for the door.

Scrambling back up beside Lampeter, she held on tight to the side of the wagon once more, sensing his urgency. Ada remembered her grandfather telling her the story of the cholera epidemic that had hit Liverpool hard before she was born. In those dark days almost every family in her local area had been hit by it as it swept through the city. She began to feel a bit sick as they lurched away towards the plague, hoping that she wouldn't catch it.

Lampeter seemed twitchy. Ada sensed this was about the cholera, but with him you could never be sure. She was racking her brains for some topic of conversation that would distract them both, but nothing would come, so she sat quiet, swaying along beside him as they lurched towards the camp. As soon as she saw the white pointed canopies of the tents her heart started to pound a bit faster. Her anxiety was fuelled even further as an orderly came running over to them, shouting, 'Stay back, stay back! The cholera is bad here.'

Lampeter pulled the wagon up sharp and called to him from a distance: 'How many dead?'

'Six men this morning in one tent alone. Don't come any closer. Leave the supplies on the ground and I'll pick them up.'

'Of course!' shouted Lampeter, even more twitchy now and eager to be off.

He gave Ada the cholera powders and she clambered down to leave them on the ground; before she was fully back in the wagon they heard a second voice shouting and saw another orderly running towards them.

'We have a soldier just brought in with an injury – not bad but he'll need a bit of stitching. The hospital tent is full of cholera so we don't want to put him in there. Can you take him back down to Balaklava?'

'Has he had any contact with anyone affected by cholera, any contact at all?' asked Lampeter, clearly worried.

'No, not yet, he's just arrived from the front line.'

'All right then, send him down as quick as you can.'

In a matter of minutes the orderly reappeared with a lad at his side, his arm in a sling. Before she even saw his face, Ada recognized the brown tunic and the upright posture of the young man she had first seen on the ship, the one who looked so much like Frank.

Her heart missed a beat as she watched him approach their wagon with a confident but apologetic air. As he came closer she realized that he had something tucked into his tunic. It was a small dog.

Lampeter got down to give the bandage and sling on the boy's arm a quick check and help him into the back. Then, much to Ada's surprise, he gave the small scruffy white mongrel with a brown patch over one eye a friendly stroke before handing it up to Ada.

'Keep it safe, will you? This young man will have enough to do holding himself steady without having to worry about this little one as well.'

'I will,' said Ada, not really sure about what to do with dogs and hoping that she would be able to keep hold of it. Fortunately the creature seemed to know what was best and easily settled on Ada's lap. She rested her free hand on it just in case but it seemed to be used to travelling by cart.

Once they were moving Lampeter spoke quietly to her. 'The boy seems to have a nasty flesh wound in his upper arm but it looks like the shell hasn't touched the bone so it should be a reasonably straightforward procedure to dig it out and stitch it up.'

He then reached across to stroke the dog that was curled up on Ada's lap.

The sleepy dog wagged its tail and Ada smiled to herself. At least the dog seemed to like him. She glanced round to check on the young soldier who was wedged in the back of the wagon. She could see the back of his head, and his dark blond hair was so like Frank's it almost made her want to cry.

By the time they reached Balaklava, Ada was exhausted. She didn't dare look around at the young man in the back; though it was nice to see someone who reminded her of Frank, it was also painful. She was glad when Tom Dunderdale appeared to help the lad out.

Lampeter told Tom to take the new admission straight into the ward and that he would be there directly. He then took the dog off Ada's knee, jumped down from the wagon with it and walked towards the hospital. Looking back, almost as an afterthought, he said, 'Get your apron, nurse, and come and assist with our new patient.'

'Of course,' she said, not needing to be asked twice.

She found the patient sitting quietly on the edge of a bed with his bloodstained jacket still draped around his shoulders. Tom had already supplied him with a large glass of rum, knowing that he'd need it in the next few hours.

Ada, masking her disquiet at seeing the boy who looked so much like her brother in such a vulnerable state, adopted the no-nonsense tone that she'd heard Rose and Mary Roberts use:

'What's your name?'

'Billy Collins.'

She heard herself giving him instructions: 'We'll need to get you out of that shirt so the doctor can have a proper look at the wound. Then I'm going to very carefully start to remove the bandage,' she said, 'but if the wound starts to bleed I will have to put it back on again.'

'Understood, Sister,' said Billy, smiling.

Ada held her breath as she carefully unwound the bandage and then they both looked at the blood-soaked pad covering the wound.

In the very moment she decided to leave this undisturbed until Dr Lampeter was with them, she heard his voice behind her. 'Leave that where it is for the time being, nurse. The wound will have started to clot under there and we don't want to disturb it just yet.'

Ada stepped back and allowed Lampeter to come and have a closer look. He didn't look at the patient's face or ask him any questions, but told him that the shot was still in there and they'd have to dig it out.

Ada told Billy to lie down, doing her best to soothe him. Lampeter knelt by the side of the bed and quickly removed the dressing pad. There was an immediate trickle of blood that made Ada catch her breath. 'That's fine, just a bit, nothing to worry about,' Lampeter said almost to himself. 'It must have missed the major vessels because he hasn't haemorrhaged,' he continued. 'Can you move your hand?'

Billy did so with some pain but not much difficulty.

248

'Looks like the nervous connections aren't too disrupted either,' Lampeter muttered before sticking his finger into the wound, making the lad nearly shoot off the bed.

Lampeter looked irritated and told him that he really needed to be able to examine the track of the shot. Billy, white as a sheet, nodded. 'I understand that, doc, but if you could go a bit careful, like.'

Lampeter almost, but didn't, tut.

Ada grabbed Billy's hand and glared a warning at Lampeter. This time, the lad was prepared, and although he squeezed Ada's hand in pain and sweat broke out on his forehead he was able to manage while the doctor completed the examination.

Before Billy and Ada had time to think, Lampeter had a long pair of forceps in his right hand and was back in the wound. After a bit of digging around, which Billy managed by almost breaking Ada's hand, the forceps came out clasping the piece of shot. Then Lampeter was straight back in the wound with the forceps, nearer the surface, this time taking out pieces of cloth and debris that had been carried in at the moment of impact.

'It's important to get as much debris out of the wound as possible,' he said. 'I have observed that those where it's left in are much more likely to suppurate, which can kill the patient.'

Ada saw the look of alarm on Billy's face and tried to reassure him. 'But you seem to have got it clean.'

'Yes, yes,' replied Lampeter impatiently.

'That's good then,' she said, smiling at Billy.

Lampeter then told Ada that they'd pack the wound with iodine overnight; they'd found this also helped prevent suppuration and seemed to improve the patient's chance of survival. Ada smiled at Billy again and told him that this was just routine procedure; he was going to be fine.

While Lampeter went off to find iodine and lint, Ada sat holding Billy's hand. They didn't speak but it seemed the most natural thing in the world for them to do this. They were almost re-laxed now that the wound had been treated.

Lampeter was soon back with a big bottle of the yellow-brown liquid. As he poured it generously on to the lint, its sharp distinctive smell met Ada's nostrils and it seemed somehow comforting. It smelt clean; it smelt medical. However, the next step caused Billy to almost leap off the bed again: Lampeter poured iodine directly into the wound, saying, 'It will sting now but you'll find that it will help in the long run.'

While Billy was struggling to manage the pain, Lampeter quickly packed the wound with the lint and then applied a pad and a firm bandage.

'We need to leave the packing in overnight. I'll be back in the morning to suture the wound,' he said as he walked away from the bed.

Billy managed to shout after him, 'Where's my dog?'

Lampeter replied, without checking his pace, 'He has been fed and I'll have him sent to the ward directly.'

Ada stayed with Billy until the intense pain had settled and she was still there when Tom appeared with the dog under his arm.

'It's nearly eight o'clock, Ada,' he said. 'You'd best be getting yourself off the ward or there'll be trouble – Miss Nightingale's rules.'

'Oh, I forgot about that,' said Ada, then, turning to Billy, 'I'll be back tomorrow to check on you.'

Tom put the dog down and it jumped on to the bed and scrabbled up to Billy, wagging its tail and trying to lick his face. Billy soothed the dog and quietened it with his good hand, and the animal soon found a comfortable spot on the bed.

Ada didn't want to leave. Even though she could see that the lad was fine, she would have sat by him all night if she could. Sensing this, Tom chivvied her along. 'He'll be all right, miss, truly.' And she knew that she would have to trust that he would.

Ada slept badly that night. She felt that she'd somehow left a part of herself back on the ward, and fretted that Billy's wound might open up and bleed, that suppuration would set in with fever overnight.

She dreamt about Frank and saw again the room in the Dock Traffic Office and her grand-father's face as he told her he was missing. She woke with a start, covered in sweat, her heart pounding, sitting up on her mattress on the floor not knowing where she was for a moment. And then remembering... She had come out here to look for Frank but now she felt herself being dragged into all kinds of other things and she was no nearer to finding him. All she had to hold on to was that feeling in her bones that he was still alive, her brother was still alive somewhere – but increasingly that feeling also told her that Frank wasn't out here in the Crimea; he had never been out here.

She got up from her bed on the floor. It was still early and the rest of the nurses were sleeping, but she needed to get on and do something; she needed to get to work on the ward, and she wouldn't be able to settle until she had checked that Billy was alive and well. If she couldn't find her brother she could at least try to make sure that Billy was safe.

# 17

*'The grateful words and smile which rewarded me for binding up a wound or giving a cooling drink was a pleasure worth risking life for at any time.'*
Mary Seacole

'Don't worry, nurse, he's up and about – he's only gone out for a smoke,' said the old soldier in the bed opposite Billy's, just before his entire body was convulsed by a fit of coughing.

'Thank you,' said Ada. 'Are you all right? Can I do anything to help?'

'No, no,' he wheezed between coughs, 'my chest's buggered, that's all.' And then he was coughing again and needing to spit in the bowl beside his bed.

Ada stood for a moment and made sure that he

252

could get his breath before moving over to the window.

She glanced outside to the bench where the men sat for their smokes. Billy was there with the little dog beside him. Thank goodness.

She turned back to smile at the old soldier, but he was hawking up phlegm again, his face dark red and his nose purple. Some of the respiratory cases suffered terribly and there was little anyone could do. Poor man, she thought. She would come back to him later when he was able to speak.

From there Ada went straight to check on Duncan Brodie. He was fast asleep and she didn't want to disturb him. She knew that today would be a big day for him; he would be trying out some crutches and she wanted to make sure that she was there to help.

It was time now to go to Sister Roberts to see what her duties would be that morning. She made sure to ask if they would give her a shout when Duncan was ready to move.

There was plenty to do before then, however, and even more than usual because Miss Smith had insisted that they continue to strip beds, scrub floorboards and root out vermin wherever they could. While the nurses were going about their duties – helping the men wash, giving them breakfast and the morning ration of rum – Tom and, much to Ada's disgust, Cedric Wilson, were moving beds and lifting up floorboards. He made her blood run cold, that bastard. Ada shuddered as he looked over and nodded good morning to her, turning her face away and feeling her cheeks burning red. He tried to say something to her, something smart, but she glared at him. Shut up and keep away, said the expression in her eyes.

She was glad just then to see Billy come in with the little dog trotting at his side. He had distracted her at exactly the right time; a few moments longer and she might well have gone over to Cedric and punched him right on the nose.

Ada gave Tom a small smile then looked away as Cedric walked past her, much closer than he needed, almost but not quite brushing her clothing. She could feel his eyes boring into her back and felt the hairs on her neck prickle as he passed by. Once he had gone past and Ada felt satisfied that Tom would keep an eye on him, she went in search of Rose.

She found her with Arnold.

Yesterday, the doctors had told them that they could remove the bandages and splints from his arms and see how it went. Ada was pleased to see that the wound on his cheek had healed well and had not broken down since the stitches were removed. His smile was lopsided and he couldn't speak or eat properly, but he had beaten suppuration and at least he was alive.

Trying not to think about what the future might hold for someone like Arnold, Ada gave him a bright smile and asked him if it was all right for her to help Rose remove the bandages on his arms.

He nodded and tried to form the words but only noise would come.

Ada smiled reassuringly and then set to. There seemed to be miles of bandage and padding on each arm and as they worked away, unravelling layer after layer, they forced themselves to ignore the lining of black lice that had woven their way into each fold. The bandages were alive with them.

At last they got down to the thin arms that had lain for so long in their cocoon of bandage. At that moment of their uncovering they looked like they might never be of any use again. But the wounds on both arms seemed to have healed well, the scars ragged-looking but with no signs of suppuration. Then Arnold tried to move his arms but they wouldn't respond.

Seeing the panic in his eyes Rose said quietly, 'They've just got used to being still, that's all. You need to go slowly and start by moving your hands. They will work again,' she reassured gently. 'Just give them time.'

Arnold looked at Ada then, as if seeking another opinion.

'Nurse Blackwood is right,' said Ada. 'Of course it will take time to get moving; you just need to do a bit more each day, starting from now. When we've gone, start gently, but don't try and move at first, just get used to having your arms free without the splints.' Ada glanced at Rose to make sure she approved of what was being said and then she thought of something else. 'It will take a long time but you might be able to hold a pencil. Do you know your letters?'

Arnold nodded, and when he tried to smile she knew that he had realized what that meant.

'And if you can write, well then, you can spell words out on paper to help you communicate.'

He nodded again more vigorously.

'Good idea, Nurse Houston,' said Rose, smiling.

As they turned away from Arnold's bed, Ada could see Sister Roberts down the ward. She was holding a pair of wooden crutches and gesturing for her to come.

'You go,' said Rose straight away. 'I can carry on here for the time being.'

Ada was straight there with Sister at Duncan's bedside. He was sitting up in bed and smiling away as usual, but she could tell from the fixed expression on his face that behind all of that he was terrified of getting out of bed and trying to walk for the first time. After all, he had been lying there for weeks waiting for the stump to heal and now he was going to stand up with the crutches and feel how things would be for him for the rest of his life.

Ada gave his hand a squeeze and then helped Sister Roberts move him to the side of the bed, where he sat resting his one leg on the floor. Sister stood in front with the crutches.

'Now, Mr Brodie,' she said, 'we need to go carefully at first. I want you to push up with your leg as hard as you can. I and Nurse Houston will be on either side of you and will help pull you up, but we need you to push as hard as you can. When we have you standing – and you will feel very unbalanced – Nurse Houston and I will put a crutch under each side.'

Duncan nodded, Sister Roberts handed Ada one of the crutches, and they were all set. 'Ready when you are,' said Sister and Ada felt him use all the strength he had and she pulled and pulled under his arm with all her might, but he only managed to move a few inches up off the bed before sitting back down. He could not stand.

Ada saw the anguish on his face.

'That's fine,' said Sister. 'You need to give yourself time. The muscles in that leg haven't been doing any work for weeks. Just give them time. Have one more go when you're ready.'

Duncan braced himself again and then pushed and pushed and Ada pulled and pulled under his arm until she was quite red in the face. He got a little bit further up off the bed this time but then fell back again with a cry of frustration. He sat there with his shoulders slumped, shaking his head. Ada could see that he was about to give up. She had to think of some way of helping him.

'Sister Roberts,' she said, looking across at her, 'can we try something?'

'What do you have in mind?'

'I was just wondering, if we had one more person, maybe somebody stronger than us like Tom Dunderdale, and you and he went to each side and then I stood in front so Mr Brodie doesn't feel like he's going to fall flat on his face...We do the whole thing again like that except, Mr Brodie, if you could lean forward as well as push up that will help.'

'That might just work,' said Sister with a gleam in her eye. 'I'll go and find Mr Dunderdale.'

She was back in no time with Tom in tow and then they were set for another go.

'Right,' said Ada firmly, 'now, Mr Brodie, lean forward and as soon as you start pushing with that leg Tom and Sister will help as much as they can. Look up at me, push up, and then stand as tall as you can.'

She glanced at Sister to make sure she approved, then said, 'I will count to three and on three you stand up and I've got you.'

Duncan nodded and Ada was relieved to see that he was starting to get some life back in his eyes.

'Are we all ready?' she said, looking from one to another. 'Right then, on three, you count with me, Mr Brodie. One, two, three!' Duncan pushed with all his might and Tom and Sister pulled, and at last he stood tall.

'Put your hands on my shoulders,' said Ada. 'Steady yourself.' And she was so small and he was so tall that it seemed to work. He was standing and she could see the proud look on his face. He was standing at last.

Sister Roberts quickly placed a crutch under one arm and Tom did the same at the other side.

'Now just get your balance,' said Sister. 'Are you all right there, Ada?'

'Solid as a rock.'

'Now, Mr Brodie, when you're ready, let go of Ada one side at a time and put each hand here on the crutches.'

Ada saw a momentary look of fear cross his face and she said quietly, 'I'm here. I'm still going to be here.'

Slowly he let go of her shoulders, one hand at a time, and found the hand-holds on the crutches. And then very carefully Ada stood back and there he was, supporting himself with the crutches.

'Now,' said Sister, 'you have done very well, and let me tell you it will take some time to get used to moving around on those things, but a big, strong man like you will do it easily. If you want to try one step now, put the crutches forward and then move. Tom and I will stay right by your side.'

Duncan nodded and Ada stood ready, her heart pounding, anxious in case the crutches slipped and he fell.

'So, one, two, three again,' said Ada, and he moved the crutches forward together and then, with the strain showing in his arms, he moved his body forward as well. The man moved for the first time in weeks. It was clumsy, it didn't look safe, but he moved. And as he stood there with Tom at one side and Sister Roberts at the other he started to cry, big tears rolling down his cheeks and into his rough beard. Ada moved forward and stood close to him, patting his arm until he was able get back some control.

'Now move back one step, Mr Brodie, and sit back down when you're ready,' said Sister. 'That's enough for one day. Just take it slowly.'

When he was back on the bed, Duncan hung his head for a few moments, taking it all in.

'Thank you, Tom,' said Sister Roberts. 'You can get back to what you were doing.'

Then she sat down beside Duncan on the bed and spoke softly to him. 'This will not be an easy road for you, Mr Brodie, but with time and determination you will get used to using the crutches and you will find some way of making a new life for yourself. You just have to keep going, and if you start to waver, give yourself some time, but then get back up again. It is the only way. I know you can do it, Mr Brodie, I know what you lads out here in the Crimea are capable of. And you are a 42nd Highlander! You might not be in the ranks any more, but you will always be a 42nd Highlander.'

Ada felt tears welling in her own eyes, but she knew that wouldn't help her patient, so tried to distract herself by glancing to the side of his bed to check that his regimental hat was still there. It was, of course; most of the men had some kind of hat or other piece of uniform next to their beds, and no one would move Duncan's feather bonnet.

When she looked back to Duncan, Sister Roberts was telling him that now he had been up on the crutches he would soon be able to leave the ward and go home on a troop ship out of Balaklava harbour.

With that news he was crying again, more big tears rolling down his cheeks. Sister Roberts got up from the bed and put a hand on his shoulder, then gestured to Ada. She knew exactly what Sister was asking. Of course she would sit with Duncan – she would sit with him for as long as he needed.

As she went, Sister whispered, 'Well done, Nurse Houston,' and Ada felt herself glow with satisfaction. When she sat down next to Duncan he had stopped crying and all he could say was, 'Thank you, nurse, thank you for what you did. I thought I was never going to get up off that bed.'

'That's absolutely fine,' she said, smiling at him. 'All part of the service. Good job I'm so small, just the right height for you to lean on.'

'I need to take you back to Scotland with me,' he

260

said, starting to laugh. 'My wee lassie from Liverpool.'

Ada put a hand on his arm again, gave him a pat and stood up from the bed. Then, before she could move away, he grabbed hold of her hand as if he'd just remembered something. 'Just in case I don't get to see you before I go, there's something I want you to have. Reach me that box from under the bed, will you?'

Ada crouched down, pulled out the box and handed it to him.

'This is for you,' he said, taking off the lid and fishing around inside. He pulled out a piece of paper and unfolded it. 'My lucky heather. It's kept me safe all the time I've been out here – well, I know I lost the leg but I could have been dead – and I want you to have it.'

'No, honestly, I couldn't, it's–'

'Take it,' he said, pressing it into her hand. 'I'm off back to Scotland. I'm going back to the heather: I want you to have it.'

'Thank you,' she said quietly, moved beyond words. Slipping it into her pocket, she managed somehow to keep her voice steady. 'Now, let's get you comfortable in this bed.'

When he had swung his leg back up on to the bed and moved back to sit up, Ada made sure that his pillow was wedged in comfortably behind him and then gave him a final reassuring pat on the shoulder before picking up the new crutches and propping them against the wall, side by side, next to his feather bonnet.

Ada had no time to find her next patient before a man's voice directly behind called loudly for a nurse to assist with some suturing. It was Lampeter.

She glanced up the ward for Rose but saw her look down immediately at a basket of bandages. Ada knew that it was up to her; somehow she felt herself step forward without any bother. And of course she wanted to be there to assist with Billy, which is where Lampeter was most likely heading.

Ada could see him now by Billy's bed with the suture tray in his hand. Billy was sitting on the edge of his bed, ready and waiting. The small dog sat next to him, almost leaning against him. Strange, thought Ada, it's as if the animal knows exactly what's going on.

Billy looked up at her and smiled, and Ada stood for a moment and watched Lampeter at his work. As he knelt on the hard floor beside Billy, unravelling the bandage, she couldn't help but notice the nape of his neck and the curve of his spine. For the first time he seemed vulnerable, exposed to her in a way that made her feel a moment of sudden tenderness towards him.

She came to with a jolt as Lampeter called impatiently for her to take the packing, which he had cleanly removed from the wound. Ada smiled again at Billy and reassured him. 'The wound looks good.' He smiled back, his shoulders relaxing a little now that the first stage was over.

Lampeter examined the wound carefully before being satisfied enough to go straight into the suturing. Then Ada saw him looking over his shoulder and she knew he was about to call the orderlies over to hold Billy down.

'This patient will be fine, Dr Lampeter,' she

said, looking him straight in the eye. 'He managed well enough last night when you poured iodine into his wound; he will be able to stay still without being held.'

Lampeter huffed a little but then gave in. 'If you say so, nurse.'

Ada sat next to Billy, steadfastly holding his hand and talking to him all the time as Lampeter stitched up the hole in his arm. Each time the needle went in his eyes closed and he grimaced with pain, squeezing Ada's hand very hard. But each time he opened his eyes, there she was, calm and reassuring. Ada watched Lampeter very carefully during the procedure, grateful for his skill and the accuracy of his strong slender fingers as they wielded the needle. Even after he had completed the task she continued to hold Billy's hand, lost in her own thoughts, almost mesmerized. In the end Lampeter had to cough politely and ask her to apply a dressing and bandage to the wound. He told her that the sutures looked good and even patted Billy on the shoulder as if to say well done.

Ada started to apply the dressing and bandage as if her life depended on it. Never was such tender care taken. The men in the surrounding beds even started calling across the room with 'Ah, how sweet,' and 'How nice,' but Ada was completely oblivious. Lampeter held the pad in position while she applied the bandage. Her fingers brushed his as she secured the dressing, and she expected him to withdraw his hand, but he didn't.

'You seem to have done a good job there, nurse,' said Lampeter.

Ada drew her breath in and felt her face begin to

flush as she tied the bandage to secure it. When she glanced up Lampeter was looking into her eyes, and just for a moment it was as if a bubble had enclosed the three of them, muffling the outside world. Ada had to force herself to look away, look back to the bandage and check again.

'Right, Billy, you rest up for today and we'll see how you are tomorrow,' she said, still puzzling over what had just happened.

Before leaving the bedside Lampeter picked up the dog and held him close, stroking his head and giving him a bit of a scratch behind the ears. The dog seemed to like him. 'I think there's a bit of Jack Russell terrier in this one,' he said. 'I used to have one at home. What do you call him?'

'Well, I call him Bob,' said Billy, 'but the fellas who gave him to me after his owner was killed in the trench, they said he was called Jock. He seems to answer to anything.'

Lampeter gave the dog another stroke, looking thoughtful. 'He must have seen some sights though ... and had to deal with all sorts on the front line. The noise for a start – it must be terrible for a dog. You're a special little fella, aren't you, Bob?' he said, giving the dog one final scratch behind the ears. Then he placed him carefully down on the bed next to Billy and went on his way.

Ada and Billy exchanged an amused glance and then both shook their heads as Lampeter moved up the ward. But when Ada looked back up she saw Cedric's thin face and hard eyes turned in their direction. She glared back at him for a moment, trying not to feel uncomfortable, and then looked around for Rose. Spotting her down the ward, she patted Billy on the shoulder, said she'd check on him later and then moved away to join her friend.

When their work was done on the ward, Rose wanted to sit with Arnold and help him try to move his weakened arms. Ada decided to leave her to it. She felt sure that Lampeter would be back soon to check on some of the patients before they settled for the evening and she didn't want to see him again just yet. As for Billy, she felt much better about him now that the wound was sutured up. Ada knew that getting close to a patient like Billy or Duncan Brodie probably wasn't a good idea, and she knew that she should try to avoid it but, inevitably, this work brought nurses close to their patients. Look at how Rose was with Arnold.

She was bound to be drawn to Billy. He looked so much like her brother and spending time with him reminded her of why she had come out here in the first place. But then she began to feel guilty at starting to feel satisfaction from the work, the work that she was doing simply because she had wanted to find Frank. And he was not found and maybe – yes, she had to admit this to herself – maybe he never would be.

Was it right for her to enjoy working with Rose and even Lampeter, who she had felt sure, when she first landed in Balaklava, was an absolute monster? Was it right for her to be involved with all of this and starting to feel at ease with a man like Lampeter, who was clearly from a different class, while Frank was still missing? She knew exactly what Frank would say about Lampeter –

exactly. And she also knew how well he would get on with Billy. Who wouldn't like Billy, with his calm manner and his gentle blue eyes? He was lovely.

Leaving Rose on the ward, she headed out to the laundry but was amazed to find the place deserted. Could the women be ahead with their work and already finished up? There seemed to be nothing more to do out there, everything was straight, so she sat on the upturned box staring at the fire with the cat mewing at her feet and rubbing himself against her legs.

Then she heard a noise, someone moving quietly behind her. She knew it wasn't Cedric; she knew how he moved. It turned out to be Lavinia, who'd seen her sitting alone and wanted to check that she was all right.

Ada smiled at her friend and held an arm out to her.

'I've come to give you some good news,' said Lavinia. 'We've just heard, on good authority, that our man Cedric is being moved out. He's being sent up to Sevastopol, to the front line. Some issue with patients' belongings.'

Ada felt relieved to hear this. 'That's good,' she said quietly. 'I did see him on the ward today acting suspiciously. I'm so glad that he's going.'

'You sound tired,' said Lavinia, taking Ada's hand. 'Are you sure you're all right?'

'I'm fine,' said Ada, seeing the concern on Lavinia's face.

I have to be, she thought to herself. I have to be fine and I have to stay fine. That's why I need to steer clear of any complications and make sure that I put all my attention into the work. She had made all the enquiries she could about Frank and found nothing. There had been no word from the army wives, and she'd got to know them well enough to trust that they would send word if there was any news from Scutari. What more could she actually do? It was killing her that she couldn't do more.

But she knew in her heart of hearts that Frank would understand; he would be the first to urge her to focus on the work. He would want her to take the chance to do something different, to make a new life for herself.

'Are you sure?' said Lavinia again, still concerned for her friend.

'I'm sure,' said Ada.

# 18

*'War, I know, is a serious game, but sometimes very humble actors are of great use in it.'*
Mary Seacole

Ada had begun to feel that she was shaping up to be a decent nurse, and the work on the ward was something that she had started to enjoy. So when Sister Roberts asked her to help out in the laundry the next day she was at first a little disappointed. Then again, at least I'll be able to spend some time in the sun and catch up with Dolly, and Lavinia, she thought. Maybe I need a bit of a break from all the mayhem on the wards.

She buried the creeping thoughts of Lampeter and Billy, and the knowledge that she would miss seeing them. 'Oh for goodness' sake,' she muttered under her breath, 'I just need to get on with the work. I don't want any complications.'

Dolly and Lavinia were already well into their work when she arrived at the washtubs with a scrunch between her brows and a serious face.

'What's up with you?' said Dolly.

'Oh, nothing,' said Ada. 'I'm just a bit tired, that's all.'

'Mm,' said Dolly smiling to herself. 'Well, you'll soon get over it when you put your back into that,' she said, pointing to a huge mound of washing.

They were still overloaded with extra laundry and now seemed to be working their way through all of Miss Smith's linen, including some fine tablecloths. Dolly was chatting away and Ada only listened vaguely at first, her thoughts elsewhere: rumour had it Smithy was in bed herself at the moment. 'It looks like she's sick in the head,' said Dolly. 'Mary Roberts went in there the other day and she was sat up in bed, wearing her night cap, with papers scattered all around. She couldn't speak but she kept pointing to the papers and shaking her head, saying, "I'm in despair, I'm in despair," over and over again. Mary Roberts had asked that young Dr Lampeter to go in there and take a look at her but nobody knows what he said.'

'Really?' said Ada, suddenly latching on to the conversation when she heard Lampeter's name.

'Well, who knows what's going on with the woman?' said Dolly. 'We don't really like her but you wouldn't wish her any harm.'

Ada agreed and then got stuck into the work. She began to feel good about being back in the laundry, where she could relax and be herself and just listen to the banter and the stories around her. Her body could work hard without much thought doing this kind of task. Dolly had found another box and an old chair so they could all sit together for a break, and as they sat in the sun with a cup of tea a figure appeared and sat himself down next to Ada.

'Oh, hello,' said Ada, surprised but pleased to see Billy away from the ward.

'Hello,' he said. 'I was looking for you on the ward and that Sister, the one with the stern face and the nice voice, she told me that you would be out here. Sister thought it was a good idea for me to come out and get some fresh air. She said I could even help with my good arm if there was anything for me to do. And I wanted to say thank you for yesterday,' he added simply.

'Oh, you're welcome,' said Ada warmly, delighted to see him looking so well. 'How's it doing today?'

'Still feels sore and I need to be careful with it but the sling really helps. The good doctor came by to have a look and he's happy. Didn't say much; you know what he's like.'

'I do,' said Ada, laughing and feeling slightly uncomfortable all at the same time. 'So you really think you're up to helping us with all this?'

'Course you are, lad,' said Dolly. 'As you can see we're piled up with stuff at the moment and we could do with a hand, even if it is only one.'

Billy laughed, moving to take his place among the women.

'Where's your dog?' said Ada.

'Oh, he's really taken a shine to Dr Lampeter, so he's trotting round after him today. Really seems to like him.'

Somebody has to, thought Ada, apart from Dr Mason and me.

'Right,' she said, standing up and suddenly anxious to get on with the work. 'Let's get crackin'.'

Billy stood up too but wobbled a little, off balance with his arm.

'Whoa,' said Ada. 'Are you sure you're going to be all right?'

'Yes, I'm sure,' said Billy with a grin.

So they got on with the work and as Ada brought the wood for the fire, Billy chucked it on with his good arm. When they had finished stoking the fire he passed her the clean bandages to roll and put in the basket. Then they went to fetch some more firewood from the big pile of scrap timber that had been brought up from the harbour to supply the hospital. The day was sunny and glorious in every way.

Ada and Billy gathered wood into a pile and then sat together for a quick breather on a pile of sleepers that served as a bench. Ada didn't want him over-exerting himself – she knew that rest was important for healing, and she didn't want anything going wrong with that arm. It was still too early to tell if suppuration would set in and she prayed that it wouldn't. If it did he would probably lose the arm or die. A shudder went

270

through her at that thought and she needed to distract herself.

'What did you do back home?' she said, swinging her legs backwards and forwards as she sat.

'I live out in the country,' he said. 'I worked on a farm with the horses.'

So that's why he's so good with the animals, Ada registered.

'And then you got called up?' she asked.

'One day the army turned up to requisition some of the horses to take out to the Crimea and when they saw me with them they asked if I wanted to join up. I said yes on the spot, without even thinking about what it'd do to my mother, but by then it was too late. I had to go.'

'Must have been a shock for her,' said Ada, noting his momentarily haunted expression.

'It was. She couldn't stop crying,' he said, his voice going quiet.

Gently trying to steer him away from a subject that was clearly painful, she asked him what life was like up at camp.

'When I'm not needed as a groom, I sometimes have to fight in the trenches as well.' He paused then and Ada sensed that there was so much that he wanted to tell her about that experience but just couldn't.

'You men must see terrible things out here, when you're in battle,' she said. 'I don't know how you get through it.'

'Well, we do,' said Billy. 'But mostly people don't talk about it. They just get on with things and get ready for the next battle.'

Then he fell silent for a few moments and Ada

271

let him sit, lost in his own thoughts, sensing that he needed time.

'It is bad sometimes,' he said at last, his voice quiet. 'I had no idea what I was signing up for. I mean who would have thought that a groom would be expected to fight in the trenches. All I'd ever done before was use a small gun to shoot rabbits on the farm.'

Ada put her hand on his to show her sympathy for him and all the other men who had ended up out here in the thick of it.

'I mean it's much the same for the real soldiers as well, you know; none of them have seen battle before. The last time we were at war was with Napoleon. What was that, forty years ago?'

'Thereabouts,' said Ada.

Billy took a smoke out of his pocket, and Ada sat quietly waiting until he had got the tobacco alight.

'So many fine men and horses have been maimed and killed out here,' continued Billy. 'The officer I work for, Lieutenant Goodman, he lost his own mount following a direct hit by cannon fire in that Charge of the Light Brigade. The poor horse fell instantly, didn't stand a chance. Goodman had to battle his way out from beneath it, grabbing his sword and dagger and going straight into hand-to-hand combat with a Cossack.'

Ada felt a shudder go through her but was determined to sit and listen to what Billy had to say. She thought that it was probably good for him to talk about this stuff.

'He told us that the floor of the valley was so thick with dead and dying men and horses that he could hardly climb through it. He described a scene I hope I never have to see – blood everywhere and men crying out for help and for water.' Billy hung his head for a minute, silenced by the horror of it, then took a long drag of his smoke while Ada sat beside him with her head bowed.

She felt winded by Billy's story but then, as she sat taking it all in, she began to feel glad that she had come out to this place, to do this work. Never had she felt more needed. She raised her head and looked at Billy sitting next to her in his very ordinary way, little more than a boy, and felt proud of him and all the other men out there on the front line. He looked at her and smiled as he dropped his smoke on the ground and crushed it under his boot.

Then he was ready to lighten the tone, telling her that thankfully Goodman had got himself another horse. 'Oh yes,' he chuckled, 'he has Captain Jack.'

'What's so amusing about Captain Jack?' said Ada, intrigued.

'Well, Captain Jack is an old horse – strong and stubborn but not expected to survive the winter. He isn't really the kind of mount that Goodman would have ever chosen. I mean, he's only got one speed and he certainly couldn't move up to a gallop. But I bloody love that horse.'

Ada laughed, glad to see him looking more relaxed again. 'Well, let's hope we don't have any more charges of the brigade,' she said.

'Too right,' said Billy. 'Jack would only move fast if there was some fodder to be had!'

Ada could tell he had a real affection for the

horse. 'Do you ever get to ride Captain Jack?' she asked.

'Yes I do. I take him out, try to keep him in as good a shape as I can. Only recently we went out when the guns were quiet. I stopped at a stream to let him have a drink and as he dipped his muzzle into the water, for some reason it really made me think about home. I stood by that stream for ages watching him drink, watching the drops of water fall back into the stream, and that was one of the most peaceful days I've had out here.'

'You must really miss home,' she said, her eyes searching his face.

'No more than anybody else, I suppose,' he replied with a shrug.

'Come on, we'd better get back,' said Ada, taking his hand and helping him up before he could start asking any questions about her home. She didn't want to have to go through all that had happened to her, and risk triggering the grief that she knew was always there, lying in wait just beneath the surface.

'Thank you,' he said. 'Thank you for helping me and looking after me.' Then he let go of her hand.

'Come on,' she said, 'we've been gone long enough,' and she started to walk ahead, her arms full of wood, leading the way back to the laundry.

When they got back, the women were just finishing up the work and Rose had arrived. Ada could tell immediately that something was wrong and rushed straight over.

'There's been a call for a team to go up to the

front line,' Rose said.

'Right,' said Ada steadily, giving her friend time to calm herself.

'We've been chosen,' she said. 'You and I are going with Dr Lampeter.'

'When?' asked Ada, her heart racing.

'Next week,' said Rose. 'We are to go next week. Dr Mason thinks they're probably planning a big push.'

'But what about the cholera?' asked Ada anxiously.

'They say there haven't been any new cases for a few days, and so by next week it should be all right. We don't have any choice anyway: we're needed. We're to go up there with any of the soldiers who are fit to travel.'

'I should be all right by then,' Billy said.

'No,' said Ada instantly. 'You need more time than that.'

Billy didn't reply and she knew that he had made up his mind. She felt sick to her stomach.

# 19

*'I thought the end of the world, instead of the war, was at hand, when every battery opened and poured a perfect hail of shot and shell upon the beautiful city which I had left the night before sleeping so calm and peaceful beneath the stars!*

Mary Seacole

Ada worked extra hard for the next week, throwing herself into it and trying not to think about their trip to the front line. She spent as much time as she could with Billy, trying to persuade him that he needed to stay back at the hospital, let his arm get fully healed. But he just smiled at her and she knew she was wasting her breath.

On the day of departure she was busy helping Rose to organize supplies and pack up the dressings and bandages they would need. Just before they were about to leave Dolly popped her head round the door of the storeroom. 'You all set then, young Ada?' she said.

'I think so,' said Ada, 'but you know what it's like.'

'I do that,' said Dolly, putting her booted foot up on a wooden box and pulling up her skirt. Ada watched, intrigued. Dolly was unfastening something, which she then held out to Ada. It was a small dagger in a leather sheath with a strap to fit around the leg.

'What the heck...?' spluttered Ada. 'What do you think I'm going to do with that?'

'You're going to protect yourself,' said Dolly. 'You need all the help you can get out there, Ada, believe me.'

'Well, I'm not fixing to be fighting in the trenches,' said Ada, but she could see by the way Dolly stood her ground, holding the dagger out to her, that she had no chance of refusing it.

'Pull up your skirt,' said Dolly and Ada did as she was told. The strap was miles too big for her leg so Dolly measured it, then took a corkscrew from her pocket and made a new hole. She thinks of everything, thought Ada.

'Pull your skirt up again,' said Dolly, this time fixing the strap around Ada's thigh, making sure it was firm and that the dagger was positioned where she could reach it. 'It's served me well, that little knife,' she said.

'Thanks,' said Ada. 'I sincerely hope I don't need it.'

'I hope so too, but at least you've got it now.'

Dolly said no more but blew her a kiss as she went through the door. Ada stood for a moment feeling the strap firm around her leg. It did make her feel stronger somehow.

When Ada and Rose emerged from the hospital building, Lampeter was already up on the wagon, ready to be off. He glanced down at Ada, gesturing for her to sit up front with him, but she made it clear that Rose would be best suited up there with her long legs and she would fit better in the back with Billy.

As they were about to set off, Billy's little dog came scampering out of the hospital straight towards the wagon, yapping away at the side, wanting to come with them. Ada started to climb down to lift him up but Lampeter said, 'No, leave him, he'll be safe here.' She glanced at Billy and he nodded his agreement.

She got down, picked up the dog, and carried him, struggling against her, back inside the hospital. She just couldn't bear to leave with him yapping away and then maybe trying to follow them. She saw Tom Dunderdale and thrust the dog into his arms. 'Keep him safe,' she said.

'I will that,' said Tom assuredly. 'The lads on the ward wouldn't be without this little fella. The rats won't be all that happy to see him stay though.'

When she walked back out to the wagon she could see how tense Lampeter was and thought he glared at her but, as she was desperately trying not to look in his direction, she couldn't be sure. As soon as she got back in next to Billy, the wagon lurched away, two horses pulling this time due to the heavy load.

Ada and Billy bounced along in the back, not saying much, each aware that after this day of travelling they would go their separate ways and it was entirely possible, given all that was going on, that they might never see each other again. Billy winced with pain as they went over a particularly large rut and Ada shot a look at him.

'I'm fine,' he said. 'Just caught my arm on the side, that's all.'

She shook her head and tried not to think about what would happen to him if he was sent into the trenches. She had tried so many times to persuade him not to go but he was having none of it. There was nothing else that she could do.

Ada felt her mind and body fall into some kind of steady rhythm as they rocked along the road to the army camp. As they approached the pointed canopies of the tents, Billy reached across and squeezed her hand and then smiled. Her heart lurched as she saw again, in that moment, how like Frank's his eyes were. She tried to smile back but her face was tight and all she could feel was the misery she'd held inside since the day her brother went missing. She carried it with her all the time; it just seemed to vary in intensity. She sat without moving, the pit of her stomach heavy.

When the wagon ground to a halt, Ada and Billy scrambled off and stood together for a few moments. There didn't seem to be anything else to be said and so Ada reached for Billy's hand and gave it a squeeze. He opened his mouth to say something but in that moment they both saw a man in uniform marching in their direction.

'That's Sarge,' said Billy. 'I'd best get moving.'

Ada let go of his hand and tried to smile, but then she heard the sergeant giving Billy his orders. He would be going to the trenches; he would be on the front line. Ada felt her heart tighten and tried to suppress the feeling of dread that had started to creep through her body.

Already Billy was starting to move away, following the sergeant, and then he turned and gave her one of his smiles and she called to him, 'You take care, Billy. I need to see you on the other side of all this, do you understand?'

'Yes, Sister!' he shouted back and gave her a final wave. The big guns started up and she moved instantly, hurrying along to find the others, who had already disappeared inside the hospital tent.

As she came through the door her body felt heavy and she still had that leaden feeling in the pit of her stomach. The now familiar smell met her, hanging in the air even though the tent had been cleared and the sick and wounded shipped out, and she knew she had to get on with the job in hand.

She saw Lampeter deep in conversation with a good-looking man with glossy brown hair and a quick, pleasing manner. She noticed Lampeter look up and glance in her direction. Their eyes met for just an instant before he looked down and she went over to Rose, but in that instant she felt a surge of connection with him. It made her feel annoyed and excited all at the same time.

'What do you want me to do?' she asked Rose who was bending over a large box on the ground.

'Oh, if you could help me move all this stuff and get organized I would be most grateful,' she said, sounding rather breathless. 'They say that there's going to be a big push and a heavy bombardment, and then the men will go over the top,' she added, straightening up from the heavy box that she was trying to move.

'Right,' said Ada. 'Where do you want this?'

'Over there,' said Rose, standing by still slightly out of breath while Ada manhandled it across to the appointed position.

'They expect heavy casualties,' said Rose as Ada stood up.

'Right,' said Ada, feeling a tightness in her chest as she thought of Billy in amongst that lot. Then she looked at Rose and she could see her hands shaking.

'We'll be all right back here, Rose,' she said. 'The guns don't reach this far.'

'But what if the Russians–'

'No what ifs, Rose. The Russians are all in Sevastopol; we are pushing towards them. I really don't think they will be coming up to us.'

'But that doctor said they had some Russians attack camp only last night.'

'Well, they didn't get far with that, did they?' said Ada, knowing that she was not really sure of her ground and needing to change the subject fast. 'Where do you want this box of bandages?'

'Over–'

They both jumped at a heavy explosion from the front line. Ada grabbed Rose and they clung together until the noise had died down.

'No need to worry,' called the doctor. 'They won't reach us up here.'

'See?' said Ada. 'What did I tell you?'

'Well,' said Rose, 'he also said that we are all right when the guns are sounding, it's when they go quiet ... that's when the wounded will come.'

'I've heard that too,' said Ada as she bent over the box to explore the contents. She saw that Lampeter and his new acquaintance were still deep in conversation. Not much preparation going on there by the look of it, she thought, annoyed. Maybe they're discussing our plan of action. Then the guns fell quieter for a few minutes and she caught the gist of their conversation. It seemed to be about the larger, heavier rifle bullet that the Russians had been using since the spring. They were now equivalent to the British and French ammunition and left a bigger hole in the body.

His new partner laughed grimly. 'It's time I got some more practice with the knife.'

'I think this might be your opportunity,' said Lampeter, 'but I wish we could do this somewhere further out of reach of the shelling.'

'True,' said his companion. 'And another thing, the Russians can resist attack so well – they are adept at building bunkers and protecting them with thick timbers and earthworks. And the speed at which they can repair those defences – it's quite incredible.'

Doesn't sound like we stand much of a chance, thought Ada. We need all hands on deck here. She looked up again to see Lampeter pulling a pistol and some bullets from his doctor's bag. 'Oh for goodness' sake,' she muttered under her breath. 'What does he think he's going to do with that?'

'What was that?' asked Rose, still a bit shaky and distracted.

'Oh, nothing.'

'Right,' said Rose, sounding like she was trying to calm herself down, 'when the casualties start to flood in we need to treat only those who have a chance of survival. Those who are fatally wounded we will have to leave, I'm afraid.'

'Understood,' said Ada, terrified of what that might be like in reality.

Lampeter and the new man were now moving trestles and boards around, making them into tables to take the wounded in need of treatment. Ada heard Rose suggest that they erect some rope with sheets draped over to act as a screen for any surgery, so as not to distress the other men.

Good idea, but it won't do anything about the noise, thought Ada, remembering so well the sound of the saw.

Trying to keep busy was the best way of coping but they were coming to a point when there were only so many times that you could count bandages or wipe down a table.

Finally the big guns fell silent.

Lampeter and his new friend looked at each other and then came over to the nurses to check that all was set. They knew it wouldn't be long.

'Hello, I'm Nurse Houston,' smiled Ada, extending her hand to Lampeter's handsome friend.

'George Rossiter,' he said, taking her hand and firmly shaking it. 'I'm the medical officer up here at camp.'

'Pleased to meet you,' said Ada, enjoying the feel of his dry, warm hand. 'Oh, and this is Rose, Nurse Blackwood,' she said, looking around for her friend. Rose nodded to Rossiter but chose not to take his hand.

There was movement at the door of the tent and they all looked up in expectation of their first casualty. It was, however, a young man wearing a dog collar who stepped nervously in through the door.

'Ah, Chaplain,' said Rossiter, 'glad to see you could make it. I fear we will be in need of your services very soon.'

Ada instantly felt sorry for the young man. He

looked terrified. He tried to smile at them but his face was twitching nervously. She was glad to see Rose step over and take his hand.

'Now, Chaplain, why don't you say a prayer with us before we all get too busy,' she said.

The young man, sweating freely in his starched collar and black wool coat, seemed to be pleased with that idea and his shoulders relaxed a little. Still holding Rose's hand, he was just opening his mouth to start when they heard a shout from outside the tent.

The chaplain closed his mouth as two orderlies ran in carrying a man on a board.

'Help, help!' they shouted. 'This man has been caught by heavy fire. We're losing him fast.'

Lampeter was there first and it didn't take him long to assess the situation. The man had been shot through the belly, a big gaping wound visible only briefly to Ada and Rose as he lifted the grey blanket covering him. Ada thought it looked very bad and she could tell by Rose's face that this man must be one of those they would consider fatally wounded. He is dying in front of our eyes, thought Ada miserably, and there is nothing we can do about it.

The doctors tucked the blanket round him and soothed him as best they could, telling him that he was going to be just fine. The patient was beginning to draw his legs up in pain and his face was contorted. 'Give him some laudanum,' said Lampeter, his voice steady, 'and take him over to the far side of the tent.'

Rose swiftly went to find the laudanum. After she had administered a few drops she asked the stretcher-bearers to move him. Ada went with her. Rose took a low stool and sat by the man.

'I'll be all right,' she said to Ada. 'I'll just give him some sips of water. If you could go and find me a bowl of water and a sponge, so I can wipe his face?'

'Yes, of course,' said Ada, her heart swelling with pride for her friend, whose only concern was to stay with her patient.

While Rose sat, Ada continued to check that all the supplies were in place and that the tables were ready to receive the wounded.

After about an hour, Rose called her over. The man had stopped breathing and his unseeing eyes now stared up to the canvas roof of the tent. When Rose stood up from the stretcher there was a smudge of bright red blood on her white apron. She looked down and muttered something about changing it but then the chaplain was back in the tent and came over to say a prayer with her.

As Ada went to find a clean apron for Rose, another stretcher was coming through the door. This poor man had apparently blown away the side of his own face. Dr Rossiter quickly explained that he had seen these cases before: men driven mad by months of constant bombardment and night raids; men not able to face another foray into enemy territory; men who felt their only option was to turn their guns on themselves.

Lampeter leant over to have a closer look. 'He must have put a musket in his mouth and pulled the trigger, but his grip on the gun has slipped and he's taken out the left side of his face,' he pronounced grimly. 'Get me a wet towel,' he added.

'All we can do for now is cover it. If he survives then we can look at some kind of surgery. But unfortunately in seeking a quick end to his daily suffering I think this man has ensured a protracted and painful death.'

'I'll get him some laudanum,' said Rose, frowning at Dr Lampeter and then assuring him that they could manage the patient. 'I do wish he wouldn't pronounce like that over the patients,' she muttered to Ada. 'The man can still hear him.'

They administered a dose of laudanum but the poor man was becoming agitated and starting to rant about getting his gun. He kept shouting out that he wanted to die, begging that they just let him go. Ada stayed with him, trying her best to soothe him, but he was beyond all comfort. The guns had started up again and each time a shell exploded the man screamed out.

The chaplain came over and started to say the 'Our Father'. This caught the man's attention and he started to calm. The chaplain, visibly shaking, continued to pray and recite psalms. This seemed to be the only way to comfort the poor soul.

Now that the guns had started up again Rossiter thought there might be a break before the next lot came in, and suggested that they step outside for refreshment and leave the chaplain to his work.

Ada was amazed to find that he had arranged for a tray of tea to be brought over and they sat, incongruously, on wooden chairs outside the tent, taking tea as if – just for a moment – they were on some picnic or church outing. As they sipped tea, the guns continued to sound, and all except Rossiter flinched each time the shells seemed a bit too close. Dr Rossiter was lively and talkative as he sat next to Ada. She thought that he was probably much more nervous than he was letting on, and that the talking was a sign of that. At least it was a distraction, especially for Rose, who was still very shaky.

When Rossiter at last fell quiet Ada got the opportunity to ask him a question that had been burning in her mind since she had arrived at camp.

'Do you remember the army wife, Miriam, who gave birth to a baby?'

'Yes, yes, I remember them very well. Only baby born in camp. I was down with a fever at the time and they had to summon Lampeter from Balaklava to deliver it.'

'Well, it was more Nurse Houston who delivered the baby,' said Lampeter, seeing how Ada glanced at him.

'You did it?' said Rossiter. 'What a fine thing, Nurse Houston – a midwife as well as a nurse.'

'Well, we worked together,' said Ada, seeing how uncomfortable Lampeter looked.

'Teamwork,' said Rossiter. 'Even better. That's exactly what we need here in this tent today, teamwork.'

Ada smiled and looked over at Lampeter again, but he didn't meet her gaze and was shifting around restlessly. Then he jumped up from his seat and walked back inside the tent as if he'd just remembered something that he urgently needed to do. Ada noticed that after he'd gone Rose kept looking across to where he'd been, as if trying to work something out.

The chaplain had fallen silent inside the tent. After a while he emerged to tell them that the poor man who had tried to kill himself had just died, and was out of his misery at last.

The big guns were still sounding and it looked like there would be even more waiting before the inevitable casualties filled up the tent. Ada saw Lampeter pacing up and down; none of them could settle. She just wished that it would all start – this waiting was becoming unbearable.

In fact the bombardment continued all night and it would not be until the next day that the full horror of war would be revealed to Ada.

As soon as first light came, the casualties started to pour in through the door of the tent.

'Let's split up into two teams,' said Lampeter to Rossiter. 'Nurse Houston and I will deal with emergency surgery, you and Nurse Blackwood stay outside the tent and separate those who should go in for treatment from those who have no hope of survival. Those poor devils need to be left outside with the chaplain.'

'Righto,' said Rossiter, turning to Rose. 'We'll put the dead round the back of the tent.' Ada felt a shudder go through her as they all nodded in agreement of the grim plan.

Before she was separated from Rose, she went over and gave her hand a squeeze. 'Good luck,' she said. 'Just keep going; we'll get through this.' Ada didn't know where the words were coming from; she was terrified and shaking inside, but somehow seemed to be able to appear calm on the outside. She could see that Rose was trembling, so she gave her a quick hug and then it was time to get cracking.

Lampeter was shouting for her, and as she moved swiftly to join him, she called back over her shoulder: 'Watch out for Billy, will you?'

'I will,' promised Rose.

They were quickly swept up in the first batch of casualties: men with faces blackened by gunpowder, uniforms torn to shreds, bloodstained, battered and mangled, with bandages wrapped around heads, limbs, bodies. Men crying out in pain, writhing on the makeshift stretchers, or lying still and moaning, or silent with a deathly pallor.

Rossiter took charge, quickly excluding those who were too far gone.

Two cases were deemed fit for surgery: a soldier with a horrific wound on his right lower leg and another with an arm blown away to the elbow.

Ada was in the thick of it now, no time to even think about feeling faint. 'Move this one round behind the screen,' she instructed the orderlies, indicating the leg injury and quickly picking up some scissors to cut away the remains of the man's uniform. She couldn't avoid cutting through strips of skin as well, but she did her best to expose the injury and Lampeter was quick to make his assessment.

'He's already lost a good deal of blood,' he said urgently. 'We need to move swiftly.'

Ada quickly applied a leather tourniquet to the man's thigh, and Lampeter moved to make an incision just below the knee. With the first cut of the knife the man shouted out and tried to get up, but the orderlies were on hand to hold him fast.

Lampeter worked away with fierce concentration. 'Pass me the saw,' he said, then, 'Hold the leg.'

Tooth snagged bone as the strokes went through cleanly.

'Pull away the limb,' he said and Ada did, shocked by how much it weighed.

She made sure that Lampeter had enough swabs and was able to proceed with tying off the blood vessels. She then handed him the needle and suture thread and he expertly stitched up the stump.

Ada calmly held the dressing pad in place while one of the orderlies wrapped a firm bandage round the stump, then in record time the man was moved back out into the body of the tent. They had no time to clean up properly. Ada just had to do the best she could, knowing that another patient would be brought through straight away. As she quickly wiped down the wood of the makeshift table, the soldier with his arm blown off was brought through and placed on the trestles. This man was awake and cursing with pain. Ada swiftly administered some laudanum drops while Lampeter looked at the wound.

Ada had thought she was prepared for anything after all she'd already seen, but this was the worst so far. When the field dressing was removed, strips of flesh hung around a lump of raw meat and bone. Most of the arm had gone. Blood was dripping down freely.

The soldier looked over to what was left of his right arm and simply said, 'Well, doc, I suppose I'll have to learn to write with me other hand now.' He then slumped back and told them to get on with it.

Ada and Lampeter worked well together and she was proud of what a neat job Lampeter managed to do. She couldn't help but marvel at the way that they were working on casualty after casualty, keeping going, striving to do their absolute best for each and every injured soldier. Lampeter took a big swig of brandy from his flask then offered it to Ada. She took it without hesitation and didn't even splutter. But there was little time for celebration before the next case came through.

This man was shot through the shoulder. Lampeter told him it looked like he'd been hit by ball shot because it had bounced off the bone and lodged into soft tissue. It was outside of the chest cavity, thankfully, and had missed the large blood vessels, so he might do well.

Before they started extracting the shot, they gave the man some brandy and Lampeter poured some of his trademark iodine into the wound and over the medical instruments, wiping them clean on a rag. Then he took up a long knife and some forceps, first gently exploring with the knife while the man groaned in pain, and then going in with the forceps to pull out the ball shot, showing it to the soldier with a flourish before dropping it into a tin pot.

The man managed a hoarse, 'Thank you, doc,' as Ada cleaned him up, deftly applying a bandage before the patient was carried away.

Back outside the tent Rossiter and Rose were struggling to keep up with the number of men needing assessment. They worked well together:

Rossiter making the decision as to which direction the men would go and Rose dealing with any dressings or laudanum or instructions to the chaplain.

Some were an easy decision. Those with holes blown through the abdomen were often awake and coherent but stood no chance of recovery. Rose and Rossiter worked together to tie some kind of covering over exposed wounds, then reassured the patients and told them that another doctor would be seeing them soon. Rose would give laudanum and ask the stretcher-bearers to take them over to the chaplain.

There were many with head wounds. Those who were awake and able to communicate would have the wound dressed and then be taken into the tent. But some came in with injuries too severe for recovery and these again were sent over to the chaplain.

Rose told Ada later that she soon realized that those who arrived shouting and screaming were the ones who were most likely to do well. The quiet ones were the most worrying and either needed to go straight to the surgeon or straight to the chaplain.

Many times the wretched men, covered in black dust and blood, grabbed at Rose and held on to her for dear life. As they pressed into her body she would smell the gunpowder and feel the rawness of their injuries. She tried to stay calm but often found herself struggling with the soldiers, waiting for Rossiter to come and help her break free.

The whole team worked side by side throughout that long day, never tiring until the flow of casualties started to wane. Only then did they begin to feel their aching backs and the weight of exhaustion. Only then did they see each other's stained and bloodied faces and clothing.

The chaplain had prayed with and prayed for dying men all day, and he now sat on a wooden chair looking desolate. Around him lay four men, very quiet. One had laboured breathing and was starting to sound the death rattle. The exhausted chaplain went over to where he lay to say the final prayer.

The stretcher-bearers took the body round the back of the tent shortly afterwards to lie with the others.

When Rose and Rossiter finally entered the hospital tent, it was crammed with men, moaning, groaning, some calling out names trying to check if their mates had made it.

Rose went behind the screen to find Ada and Lampeter just finishing the final amputation. They were covered in blood, iodine and black gunpowder residue and Lampeter's tin pot was almost full of shot.

They were beyond conversation.

Rose went over to stand by Ada's side in case she needed anything and then, when the operation was finished, they all helped clean up the surgical area.

Then the whole team went out amongst the wounded to check that bandages were secure, if anybody needed laudanum or if any had died. All the bandaging was good. There were many needing laudanum, but not enough supply, so they had to save it for the worst cases. They found one man dead and Ada recognized him with sadness as the first soldier they had treated, whose leg they had had to amputate.

When they were done Lampeter stood by the door of the hospital tent, his head down and his arms drooping by his sides. Ada knew to just let him be. She saw Rose sitting on one of the boxes, completely wiped out with exhaustion, and flopped down beside her. Neither of them could speak but Rose reached over to take Ada's hand. Both of them closed their eyes and drifted off somewhere just for a while. Ada's body ached with tiredness and sorrow. She didn't think that she would ever be able to get up off that box and move around again. And then she became aware of the sounds around her, the murmuring and groaning of the mass of injured men inside the tent. She needed to get up and check around again, make sure that there was nothing more that she could do, but she was so exhausted. And then one of the patients from outside the tent began to scream in pain. Ada felt Rose squeeze her hand and they both stood up together, Rose going to the screaming man and Ada checking what was needed inside the tent.

Rose came back in with the chaplain when the screaming had stopped. 'He's gone,' she said, bleakly. 'That's the last of them outside.' Ada didn't know what to say. There were no words. The chaplain was crying and covered in gunpowder and blood, Rose looked so thin and frail with exhaustion that she could barely stand, and where was Lampeter?

Ada looked round for him. He was nowhere inside, and then she caught a glimpse of him through the door, standing a short distance away, with his back to the tent. As she walked outside she saw Lampeter's shoulders heave for a moment and then he slowly shook his head and started to pull a pipe out of his pocket. She stood beside him without speaking as he began to fill the pipe with tobacco. His hands were shaking and stained with blood and when she looked at his face she saw a single tear make its way down his cheek, leaving a fine, clean line.

# 20

*'I attended to the wounds of many ... and
helped to lift them into the ambulances... I
derived no little gratification from being able to
dress the wounds of several Russians; indeed,
they were as kindly treated as the others.'*
Mary Seacole

The next day a truce was called to allow both sides to treat their wounded and remove any dead from no-man's-land, and two members of the medical staff were ordered up to the front line.

The team decided that it was best for Lampeter and Ada to go, and Rose and Rossiter would stay to deal with the wounded in the tent. Rossiter still hadn't gained any extra surgical experience so he was hoping that he could get some practice.

Ada was so exhausted that she really didn't care

who she was working with and felt that after being with the wounded and seeing all that suffering for a full day, nothing really mattered any more.

That morning, early, she had gone through the whole tent looking for Billy. Even though Rose hadn't seen him come through as a casualty, it had been so busy that Ada wanted to be absolutely sure that he hadn't been missed. And all the time she had that gnawing, restless feeling in the pit of her stomach. It gnawed at her so much that she checked all the men in the tent once again and, finding nothing, she went round the back of the tent to take on the grim task of checking the dead, praying she would catch no glimpse of a brown tunic.

As she stood in front of those poor souls, the stark reality of any war, she felt that restless feeling in her stomach expand to fill her whole body and her legs went from under her. She collapsed on to her knees, her head hanging low, and began to weep.

Ada had no idea how long she knelt in front of the bodies of those men who had given their lives for some cause that most of them probably didn't really understand. She had no idea how long she cried for them, for all of them and for herself and for Frank and her grandfather and even her poor dead mother. She wept and wept and it felt like there would be no end to her grief.

Her weeping was broken in the end by the sound of Lampeter's voice through the thin wall of the tent, calling for her. 'Where the blazes has she gone now? We need to get off.'

For some reason, his ridiculous tone made her

smile. He was still himself, she thought, after all he'd done yesterday and how he had looked last night. He was still himself, muttering and grumbling, and he was right – they did need to 'get off'.

Ada wiped her face and stood up, her legs able to hold her again, and called back through the tent, 'I'm here, I'm coming.' Hearing him mutter, 'About bloody time!' she smiled again and made her way back around the tent, ready to do whatever was required.

As soon as she was in through the door of the tent he passed her a bag of supplies and barked, 'Come on. We need to be off.' She nodded and they joined the back of a platoon who were marching to the front line.

As they walked over grass and through bushes they became aware of the quietness around them. No guns sounding. They could hear and see small birds and then they came up to a stream that gurgled and trickled along.

The world was so different without the sound of war.

Ada found herself looking around and then gazing up to the sky as she walked.

Soon they saw trenches that were occupied by the British and the French and surrounded by huge ragged shell holes. And then they saw the white flag of truce flying and were soon scrambling up from a British trench into no-man's-land.

The area was thick with fallen men, some lying face down, some with their arms flung wide looking up to the heavens. There seemed pitifully little that a surgeon or a nurse could do here.

As they helped the soldiers move the bodies and

pile them on to stretchers, Ada stifled a small scream as she saw rats running from underneath the bodies. Lampeter made a strangled noise in his throat but neither of them had any choice but to continue their grim task. As she worked, Ada became aware of different coloured uniforms and strange accents and realized that they were standing in the midst of British, French and Russian men, all trying to do the best for their fallen comrades. She saw enemy soldiers offering tobacco or shaking hands with their counterparts. Lampeter saw her face and said, 'These are the rules of war. When the white flag is taken down they will start trying to kill each other again but while it is raised they are all men together.'

'Well, why can't these men together sit down and sort out their differences,' she almost shouted.

Tragically there were no living casualties to be found on the battlefield, just piles of dead bodies, some literally blown to smithereens by a direct hit. Ada saw a man's foot still in its boot lying incongruously on its side. She continued to help clear the bodies, feeling more exhausted and more helpless than she had ever done in her whole life.

As they worked, spots of rain began to fall, the first rain they'd had since Ada had arrived in the Crimea. Spots soon became large drops and Ada turned her face up to the sky and let the rain run down her dusty, blood-stained clothes. It felt like the world was weeping.

'Come on,' said Lampeter in a voice thick with emotion. 'We need to go and find some shelter.' And with that he grabbed her arm and she put up no resistance as he led her back down into the trench. The place was full of splintered wood and as they walked along Ada felt a deep shudder run through her body.

At last they found a bunker that looked like it might be waterproof and even had somewhere to sit. They went inside and sat down on some empty ammunition boxes. As they looked out at the trench, the rainwater was collecting and causing the earth to soften. It would soon be a sea of mud.

Suddenly two men bobbed in through the door.

'Sorry,' said Lampeter, jumping up from his seat. 'Is this your place?'

'No, just looking for shelter,' said one. 'I'm Captain Richard Townley and this is my servant, Jenkins. You are welcome.'

'Thank you,' said Lampeter, standing up to shake the man's hand and introduce himself and Ada.

'Not many out there for you to rescue today, doctor,' said the officer grimly. 'A very sad state of affairs … very sad. But let's hope that this is the final push and it will take us nearer to breaking the siege at Sevastopol.'

Despite the officer's attempt to rally to the cause, his voice was full of weariness and far from hope. Sensing this, perhaps, he moved on to more immediate concerns. 'Are you hungry? Do you fancy a bite to eat and a sup of something? I'm sure Jenkins could rustle something up.'

Jenkins didn't wait for the order; he was straight out through the door, splashing his way down the trench in the mud and rain. When he came back, dripping wet, he was carrying a bundle of provisions which he laid out on one of the munition boxes. He had managed to find some cheese, flatbreads and half a bottle of brandy, which he produced with a flourish from inside his coat.

'Well done, Jenkins, good man,' cried Townley. 'Well done.'

By this time they had managed to light a few candles and discovered a bed with blankets towards the back of the bunker. There was a charcoal burner that was still lit and they had made some tea, using a couple of tin cups that had been discarded by the previous occupants. They sat round on the boxes, eating what they could with their fingers and taking turns to swig from the bottle. Despite all that was going on around her, in that hole in the ground, with the rain falling outside, Ada felt safe and almost content.

After their makeshift meal, Townley and Jenkins bade them goodnight and moved on up the trench to try and rejoin their regiment. Ada felt some concern as she heard them splashing away. It seemed a bit too quiet without them.

It was still raining and too late for them to head back to camp, so they would need to sit tight in the trench overnight. Ada was glad of this – she didn't want to leave this place of comparative safety.

'We should try to get some rest,' Lampeter said. Ada looked over at the bed and wondered how that was going to be done. Sensing her concern he said, 'We can take turns on the bed, so we each get some sleep.'

Ada readily agreed, relieved he wasn't suggesting that they snuggle up together. 'You lie down first,' she said, not wanting to fully submit to his plan until she was sure that it was acceptable.

Lampeter tried to argue that she should rest first, but soon gave in and gratefully lay down on the bed, turning away from her. There were two blankets so he took one to cover over himself and she took the other to put around her shoulders while she sat. Ada was amazed at how quickly he fell asleep and how still and quiet he was. She would have thought, given his restless demeanour, he would have tossed and turned in bed. But there he was, out like a light.

She sat with the blanket around her, keeping herself warm beside the charcoal burner. It seemed the most natural thing in the world to be sitting there with him sleeping in the bed. She yawned a few times but didn't feel all that sleepy.

When the burner began to die down and the air became cooler, she pulled the blanket more tightly around her and felt a small shiver run through her body. She sat for some time with images from the field hospital going through her head, things she didn't want to remember. But she decided it was best to let them run through her mind – maybe that way they would eventually leave and not come back to haunt her.

In the end tiredness did start to wash over her and she began to feel her eyes closing. Forcing them open and sitting up straight before they started to shut again, she was just thinking she would need to wake Lampeter up when: Boom!

The world erupted; the ground shook; the shelling had started again.

Ada leapt up from her box and Lampeter jumped up from the bed. Instinctively she grabbed

301

him and they clung together as the sky outside the bunker lit up with bursting shells.

'So this is what it feels like up close,' he said, raising his voice so that she could hear him above the roar of shells. Ada pressed her body closer to him as another shell landed very close. She couldn't speak. She felt his arms around her, squeezing her tighter. Then another shell burst with a flash that lit up the trench, and grit showered down from the roof of the bunker.

Ada could feel both her and Lampeter's hearts pounding as one. They continued to stand, covered in dust, waiting for the next shell, but then things went quiet.

Pulling away from him, and dusting herself down, Ada walked gingerly to the door of the bunker to look out, breathless, her heart still racing. Lampeter came and stood by her at the door. She glanced up at his face; his eyes were full of life.

As he tried to put an arm around her shoulders she pulled away. 'I'd best try and see if I can get some sleep.'

He nodded at her with a smile and she moved over to the bed.

But the shells started falling again, not as close now but still loud and shaking the ground. She felt the bed quake with every detonation and could feel the vibration through her whole body. She pulled the blanket up over her head to shield herself from bits of grit and earth that fell from the roof. This was Hell! How could the men endure this day after day?

It was loud, so loud.

The rain had stopped, but each time a big shell fell close by, small clumps of earth would fall from the trench wall with a splash into the water that now filled the bottom. Ada shuddered as she glimpsed a huge rat, slicked with water, skim past the door of the bunker. Lampeter had moved over to the charcoal burner, where he was taking the lid off the teapot. 'It's still warm,' he said, 'but we'll have to share a cup.'

She watched him pour the tea and then bring the cup over to her.

'You go first,' he said.

'Thank you,' she said, taking the cup from him gratefully and sipping the warm liquid. It was very stewed but seemed like the best cup of tea she'd had in a long time. As she sat she felt a shiver run through her body. She gripped the cup with both hands, trying to stop herself from shaking, but it didn't help. Then her whole body started to tremble uncontrollably.

Lampeter grabbed the other blanket off the bed and wrapped it around her. She pulled it close but knew that these shakes were only partly due to the cold. She felt that her whole body was reacting to all the emotions that were colliding and sending out shock waves within her. All the fear and the pain and the loss and, yes, in an odd way, the excitement as well.

She could not stop shaking and her teeth were chattering. She felt Lampeter sit down close beside her, pulling her to him, rubbing her arm, talking to her, telling her it would be all right. She couldn't speak because her teeth were chattering too much, but she wasn't too convinced that he believed what he was saying – she could feel his body flinch every time a shell exploded. Then he put his arm behind her and gently pulled her down so her head was nestling against his chest. She felt so safe as she rested there, she had no inclination to move, and at that moment, when the world was exploding around them, it felt like it was the only place to be.

He continued to hold her close but she was still shaking, so he started to talk again, raising his voice above the noise, telling her about the different types of shell. The crackling, fitful bursts of fire that lit up the sky were a 'bouquet', a shower of small shells enclosed in a bomb. The shot that buzzed along like a covey of birds was grapeshot. Round shot made a shrill shriek as it rushed through the air. And large mortar shells rose proudly and grandly up into the air, leaving a fiery trail of burning fuse then swooping down with a birdlike noise.

It was nice to hear the sound of his voice and she understood that he was trying to distract her – although his strategy seemed a bit flawed, drawing even more attention to what could kill them. As he continued, she began to feel her body relax and her teeth gradually stop chattering, and she started to smile to herself inside. Fancy being stuck here, in this dark, dangerous cave, with a crazy man ranting about ammunition.

Just as she was starting to feel calm there was an almighty commotion outside the bunker and the splashing sound of soldiers' feet running down the trench. A man was shouting: 'They're coming over the top! They're coming over the top, get your guns!' and others were running around in what seemed like chaos.

Ada started to shake again.

'Stay there,' said Lampeter, striding to the door.

But Ada followed him and they both peered carefully out, she looking one way down the trench and he the other. A soldier was coming towards them, walking fast, splashing through the water with his gun at the ready. They both drew their heads in fast.

'It's all right, all right,' he shouted at them, 'we think it's a false alarm.'

He disappeared around a corner; then they could hear him coming back, much more slowly. They both peered out again.

'No need to worry,' said the soldier. 'Looks like it was just one of our lads. When you've been down 'ere long enough you start to see and hear things that aren't there. He must have thought the Russians were coming over. We all go a bit mad down 'ere,' he went on with a grim laugh. 'You two get back to bed. You'll soon know if summat's up.'

'Thanks,' said Lampeter as the soldier continued on his way; then another big gun sounded, the earth shook and more soil fell into the trench. They heard the soldier shout, 'This'll go on all night,' just before another big one fell even closer.

They both pulled right back inside the bunker and Ada asked nervously, 'What kind of shell was that then?'

'A damned big one,' he answered quickly, and before they knew it they were both laughing so hard they had to hold on to one another. Then his arms found their way around her, pulling her body close against his, almost crushing her. She felt her breasts squashed against him and could hardly get her breath, but her heart was pounding and her body felt alive. In the next moment he leant down and pressed his lips to hers, so gently that she almost wanted to cry. She never imagined that this man, who had always seemed so brusque, could have such tenderness inside him. Then he drew back from her a little and stroked her face with his fingers. Ada felt her lips tingle and shivers went through her whole body.

As the world outside exploded again and lumps of grit fell down on their heads, he kissed her again, hard this time. She pulled away for a moment, gasping a little, then she was kissing him back, giving like for like, feeling a hunger in her body that she never knew she had. She pushed herself against him and he stepped back against the wall of the bunker. It didn't seem to matter where they were and what was going on outside. They broke away from each other for a moment and she looked up but couldn't see his face properly. She could just feel the pounding of his heart and hear his breath coming fast. When the next big shell exploded, showering them yet again with grit and earth, they both dived for the bed and pulled the blankets up over their heads.

At some stage they must have fallen asleep. Ada woke with a start, instantly feeling for him by her side. Finding him gone, she sat up in bed, her hair tousled and her lips feeling bruised. She saw him – thank goodness – just outside the door, standing in the trench enjoying a smoke.

In the same moment that she wondered if it was safe for him to do that, she heard the shriek of a shot and saw Lampeter drop his pipe and fall into the bottom of the trench.

She felt a sharp pain sear through her body as if feeling his pain, and quick as a flash she was up and at the door.

'I think I've been hit!' he said with a look of surprise on his face. Then, feeling at his right thigh, 'I have been hit. You'll have to help me, Ada.'

'Can you move?' she asked, a renewed burst of energy surging inside her. 'I need to get you inside.' She grabbed his arm and, half dragging, half crawling, got him back into the bunker. 'Wait there,' she said as soon as he was in through the door. Then she went to the back of the bunker and pulled the bed over.

'What are you doing?'

'It's too dark over there. We need to see,' she said. 'Now, get on the bed.'

He scrambled up on to the bed and lay with his hand clamped over his right thigh. She looked anxiously at the hand fiercely pressed into his flesh, bright red blood seeping out between his fingers.

'We need a bandage first,' he said, 'just in case there's torrential bleeding.'

'Of course,' said Ada, already pulling a bandage and a lint pad out of her bag. 'Right, as soon as you move your hand I'll compress with the pad. Ready? Now!' He lifted his hand and Ada was quick to press the lint down as if her own life depended on it. She couldn't help noticing that Lampeter had gone white, having seen the wound, and knew she was going to have to continue to take the lead in treating his injury.

She held the pad in place for a minute or so, and when there was no seepage and no blood running down his leg she eased the pressure slightly so she could lift the edge of the dressing to take a look. His breeches were torn, just a small slit, so she carefully moved the fabric away and peered closely at the injury.

'What do you think?' said Lampeter. 'How bad is it?'

'Well ... it looks like a scratch,' she said, starting to giggle. 'Just a scratch!' The relief was making her giddy.

Lampeter shot up in bed to get a closer look himself, and then stood, and there and then unbuckled his belt and dropped his breeches. Ada laughed even louder.

He moved over to the doorway and scrutinized the small wound in daylight. 'Yes, nurse,' he said, clearly amused, 'I agree with your diagnosis. Just a scratch. Bugger must have skimmed by me. What a stroke of luck.'

'Pull your breeches up,' said Ada, laughing so hard now that tears were streaming down her face and her ribs were hurting. 'I can hear someone coming down the trench.' But he was laughing as well and seemed incapable of any action. In the end she went over, grabbed them and pulled them back up. 'It doesn't even need a dressing,' she said. 'I'll just give it a clean with some iodine.'

She buckled his belt for him, still laughing and crying at the same time.

'Thank you, nurse,' he said with a grin. 'Now,

could you pass me the suture please... I need to stitch up my breeches; they're the only pair I've got.'

As they were laughing, a soldier came to the door and looked into the bunker in amazement. 'Everything all right in here?'

'Yes,' they said together, laughing even harder and needing to sit down on the bed.

The soldier went on his way, muttering, 'It takes people different ways, being under fire all night.'

Sober at last, they went over to the bed and gratefully crawled back under the blankets, lying close together, their arms around each other, and must have fallen back to sleep because the next thing they heard was the sound of Captain Townley's voice.

'Glad you two made it through all right,' he said. 'We've arranged for you to move out with a party going back up to camp in about ten minutes. Is that suitable?'

'Yes, yes,' said Lampeter, scrambling up from the bed.

'At ease,' said Townley. 'Be ready to leave in ten minutes.'

When he'd gone, Lampeter looked down at Ada and repeated, 'At ease, Nurse Houston,' and they both snorted as they tried to stifle their laughter. Then he leant over and gave her one last kiss before they had to get up and start to resume their previous lives.

As Ada stood by the door waiting for the order to move, she felt the morning air on her face. Closing her eyes for a moment she breathed in the smell of the earth made fresh by rain. When she opened her eyes she saw a black and white bird sitting on top of the trench looking down at her with what seemed like a puzzled expression. It was a pied wagtail.

'What do you want?' she said. 'Get lost, you cheeky bugger.'

As they made their way back towards camp, Ada walked by Lampeter's side. His leg was a bit sore but it didn't slow him down, and she kept smiling to herself as she thought about their night in the trench. As they covered more and more ground she began to look around her and see the colours that had emerged from beneath a layer of dust. Even the black of the earth was more satisfying, and the newly washed plants, the few that remained, stood out with a green so fresh she could have bitten it. And there were red flowers coming up through the cracks in the ground, beautiful red poppies.

# 21

*'Although there might be only a few short and sullen roars of the great guns by day, few nights passed without some fighting in the trenches ... and when I awoke in the night and heard the thunder of the guns fiercer than usual, I have quite dreaded the dawn that might usher in bad news.'*
Mary Seacole

The pointed canopies of the army tents began to

emerge clean against the bright blue sky and Ada caught a glimpse of one or two soldiers in their red coats. She looked again at Lampeter and he smiled at her, his eyes twinkling. Then his face straightened and he started to frown a little as he became, once again, Dr Lampeter.

They found the hospital tent almost empty and Rose busy packing up their supplies. She leapt up as soon as she saw them. 'Thank goodness!' she said. 'I could hear those shells going all night long and I've been praying that you were both safe.'

'We're fine, we're fine,' said Ada, not wanting any fuss. 'Where have all the patients gone?'

'They were moved out yesterday and this morning. Some have gone down to the hospital and others to the harbour to await transfer to Miss Nightingale in Scutari. They moved them all by train.'

And what about the stack of bodies behind the tent, thought Ada, are they still there?

'Are you all right?' asked Rose, giving Ada the once-over. 'You look a bit flushed. You're not coming down with something, are you?'

'I don't think so,' said Ada, knowing exactly what had caused it but not ready to share that with anyone, not even Rose, just yet.

'It's just that Dr Rossiter has been taken ill with some fever. We don't think it's cholera, but he's put himself into isolation just in case.'

'What's that?' said Lampeter, coming over to stand by Ada. 'Rossiter?'

'Yes,' said Ada. 'Some fever or other.'

'I must go and see him, check him over.'

'No,' said Rose. 'He gave express orders that no

311

one was to see him, just in case the fever is catching. He doesn't want it spreading.'

'Ah, I see,' said Lampeter, frowning. 'Right then, let's get this stuff into the wagon. Ada, I mean Nurse Houston, help me with this box, will you?'

Rose could sense a strangeness that had come over her two colleagues but had no idea why. She assumed that being down at the front line over-night had been a harrowing experience for both of them.

As they began packing up the boxes and clearing the tent, Ada felt the exhaustion that she had been holding at bay hit her with some force. Somehow it felt so sad, so sad just to tidy up and leave the tent empty, almost as if nobody really cared about all those who had passed through over the last few days, or all those dead bodies that had lain out behind. As if they too had just been cleared away, swept up and disposed of, ready for the next lot of dead and wounded as the inevitable cycle of war continued.

By the time the last of the boxes were ready to go, they were flagging and needed to sit down together and eat the remains of the food that had been provided. As they ate, Lampeter produced his flask and offered it round. Rose declined, but Ada accepted some eagerly. She didn't just want it, she felt that she needed it and took a good swig before handing it back to him. In her exhausted state even that small amount made her light-headed and a bit fuzzy, but she felt better; it softened the tightness in the pit of her stomach.

Watching Lampeter drain the dregs, she started

to feel annoyed with him – he could have offered her a bit more. And now that they were back in camp she could feel him stepping further and further away from the easy intimacy that they had shared last night. It had been less than twenty-four hours and already she felt that what had happened between them was forgotten or didn't even matter. She started to seethe inside. It looked like her grandfather and Mrs Regan had been right all along: a man of his standing, from his class, would only be looking at a woman like her, from the streets of Liverpool, for one thing and one thing alone. And when that was done, the woman would be thrown aside, discarded. Yes, it certainly felt like that.

Progress along the road back to Balaklava was slow and as they moved further from the camp Ada's heart began to feel heavy; it just didn't feel right for them to be going back without Billy as part of the group.

They were heavily loaded and all exhausted, even the horses. In the end they all got down to walk, Lampeter leading the horses by the bridle, Ada and Rose each resting a hand on the side of the wagon, lost in their own thoughts. By the time they got to the turn-off to the British Hotel, the light was beginning to fade.

'We'll call at Mrs Seacole's place,' said Lampeter. 'Have a bite to eat before we go back to the hospital.' Ada saw the concern on Rose's face and it mirrored her own, but hot food and a glass of that cherry brandy would certainly be welcome.

'Must we, Dr Lampeter?' said Rose. 'They'll be

busy at the hospital with all the new admissions. We need to get back and see if they need any help.'

'We'll be late back anyway; it will be almost curfew time and you two won't be allowed on to the ward till tomorrow,' said Lampeter firmly. 'And I don't know about you but we're not in much shape to help out tonight. We need to get some sleep then come at it fresh tomorrow.'

'I suppose you're right,' said Rose, 'but I don't think we should stay long.'

Ada kept quiet. She had another reason for wanting to call at the British Hotel – she was going to ask Mrs Seacole if she could stay there. Then she would be closer to the front line in case they needed help or there was any news of Billy; and further away from Lampeter. She knew that going back to work on the ward with him now would be awkward and she was feeling increasingly irritated with him. She had no reason to feel ashamed of what had happened between them last night, but the way he'd been acting made her feel that they should keep the whole thing secret, that he was ashamed of her in some way. According to Lampeter himself, there would continue to be skirmishes in the trenches for the next few days and a big push towards Sevastopol was imminent. So she would speak to Mrs Seacole and let her make the request. She felt sure that Lampeter wouldn't say no.

It was warm and full of colour at the British Hotel that evening. They had good food and Lampeter and Ada both had a strong drink. She lapped up the cherry brandy and as she drank she stopped thinking about all she had seen in that hospital tent and in the trenches. Dr Lampeter had plenty of drink inside him by the time he stood up, a bit unsteady, ready to leave. Ada had already had a quiet word with Mrs Seacole, and when she asked him if Ada could stay, he paused, taken aback momentarily, before agreeing readily.

'First-rate idea, Mrs S,' he said, his words slurring, unable to meet Ada's eyes. 'Big push coming.' Then he frowned, as if he was trying to work something out, and tried to smile.

Ada looked away. She didn't want any fuss and wanted to stay with Mrs Seacole, but she thought he would at least have put up more of a fight. Then a harsh voice in her head told her: For goodness' sake, Ada, as if he really cares anyway, so long as he's got some nurse at his beck and call.

Rose came over to say goodbye with a worried look on her face. 'Are you sure that you want to stay? This is dangerous work up here close to the front line. Can I not persuade you to change your mind?'

Ada looked down momentarily, touched by Rose's concern and feeling a little guilty that she hadn't been able to share the full story. 'I'll be fine here with Mrs Seacole and Sally,' she said, at last able to look Rose in the eye. 'Truly, I think with all the experience I've had in the last few days I can really help up here, and I'll have the opportunity to learn more as well from Mrs Seacole. I will be fine – please don't worry.'

Rose sighed. 'Well, it looks like I won't be able to do anything to convince you to come back with me and Dr Lampeter seems to have approved it,' she said, gesturing in Lampeter's direction as he made his way unsteadily towards the door. 'Promise me you'll stay safe though,' Rose said, hugging Ada and then giving her a kiss on the cheek. 'Just keep away from the trenches and don't take any risks. I don't want anything happening to you...' she added as she hastily made her way out through the door that Lampeter had left ajar.

'Don't worry!' called Ada after her friend, then more quietly to herself, 'I'm sorry, Rose, I just can't go back yet.'

There was no line of injured soldiers at the door the next morning, just a couple of what looked more like boys in uniform standing quietly, leaning against the wall, sharing a smoke. Ada watched as Mrs Seacole opened the door and shouted, 'Come on then, you two!'

Ada couldn't work out what the matter was. They didn't look injured; they just looked a bit shifty.

The boys stood staring at the floor until Mrs Seacole said, 'Come on then, spit it out. They'll be needing you back in the trenches.'

'The officer told us to come. We need a remedy – we've all been down to Balaklava and picked something up.'

'Yes, and what would that be?' said Mrs Seacole, staring directly at the one who had spoken, who immediately looked down at the ground.

Then the other lad piped up, 'We've been drinking and seeking some bawdy female company in Balaklava and now we're pissing pins and needles.'

'You have the clap,' stated Mrs Seacole in her straightforward manner. 'Let me get something

316

for you to take by mouth and something to put on the affected area.'

When Mrs Seacole came back she gave each man one of her remedies to mix and take with plenty of water. She then gave them a pot of powder to shake freely down their breeches.

'You've got off lightly this time,' said Mrs Seacole. 'The pox is much more serious – it can kill you. Make sure you check for sores and come straight back to me if you find any. Now, off you go.'

The lads scuttled off through the door and Mrs Seacole turned to Ada and Sally. 'What with the cholera and the fevers and the venereal diseases going round that lot I'm amazed that they have any men left to fight! Now, you two girls, take heed, you make sure that you choose a man carefully and make sure that he is clean and that he stays clean.'

Ada was already blushing at the information, but when Mrs Seacole added, 'And try to find a man with his own French letter so you won't be having babies all the time,' she felt her face go even redder and looked down at the floor.

To everyone's surprise there were no other customers that day, but Mrs Seacole said that she could feel in her bones that something was about to happen. And almost as soon as she had spoken those fateful words the big guns fell silent and they all stopped in their tracks and looked at each other. Ada felt the skin prickle at the back of her neck.

'We need to pack the bags,' said Mrs Seacole. 'I know exactly what's happening. They're fighting in the trenches as we speak, hand-to-hand fighting with small-bore guns and bayonets. There'll be injuries from the shelling as well. Sally, you stay here in case we get walking wounded at the door; you know what to do.' Sally nodded. 'Ada, you come with me,' she said, grabbing a medical bag and leading the way out of the door. 'You can take Sally's pony.'

'What?' said Ada. 'Take it where?'

'Ride it, of course!'

'What! But I can't ride. I've never ridden a horse in my life.'

Mrs Seacole laughed, seeing Ada thunderstruck. 'Well, this is your chance. What's wrong with you, girl? I'm not asking you to ride to the very gates of Hell.' Then, thinking about what she had just said, she shrugged and muttered, 'Then again... Anyway, there's no need to worry, Sally's pony is as tame as a lamb and I will take you on the lead rein.'

She mounted her own horse, showing Ada what to do, and once Ada was sitting astride the pony she thought to herself that the animal seemed, so far, to be very accommodating. Mrs Seacole turned in her saddle to instruct Ada to hold on to the pommel, and they were off. Ada lurched to the side but managed to right herself, clinging to the saddle as they creaked along. When they broke into a trot she grabbed tighter as she bumped up and down, up and down, behind Mrs Seacole. This would have been terrifying at the best of times, but in the middle of a war it seemed like unbelievable madness.

She had to admire Mrs Seacole though, off in

front with her medical kit. There really was no stopping the woman. As they rode along, Ada kept her eyes steadily on Mrs Seacole's back and tried to keep her balance as the old saddle moved and creaked beneath her in time with the movement of the pony.

They travelled through a rocky valley that was strewn with cannonballs and the bones of some large creatures, probably horses. Mrs Seacole twisted round and shouted, 'This is the Valley of Death where the Charge of the Light Brigade took place. A famous English poet called Mr Tennyson wrote a poem about it.' Then she started reciting: '"Half a league, half a league, half a league onward, all in the valley of Death rode the six hundred. 'Forward, the Light Brigade! Charge for the guns!' he said: into the valley of Death rode the six hundred."'

Ada was pleased to have some distraction as they moved through this desolate place, although the words gave her a shiver right down her spine and made her hold on to the saddle even more tightly as she bobbed along behind.

As they came out of the valley they started to hear the sound of gunfire in the distance. This grew stronger and stronger as they moved closer to Sevastopol. Ada was surprised to see a group of well-dressed men and women up on the heights overlooking the city, sitting on horseback with telescopes.

Mrs Seacole turned to tell her that some rich people thought it useful to come out on a trip to view the war. 'They are looking for battles or skirmishes and hoping to see some action,' she

319

said simply.

Ada couldn't tell if Mrs Seacole approved or dis-approved but she felt herself that this kind of practice was abominable. What if one of those fancy ladies with a telescope was watching a soldier, somebody's son or brother, someone like Billy or Frank, being shot or blown to bits by shell fire? There could be nothing right about this and she half wished that a stray mortar would fall in their direction.

As they left these visitors behind and came closer to the trenches, Mrs Seacole instructed Ada to dismount. 'We'll leave the horses here,' she said. 'They're easily spooked by the noise of guns or the smell of blood.' Ada felt her stomach lurch as the reality of where she was heading hit home.

Mrs Seacole handed her a bag of medical supplies which she slung across her shoulder and then, just as they were trying to find their bearings and make sure that they were heading in the right direction, they heard the sound of a horse and cart behind them.

They both looked round, and Ada was shocked to see that it was John Lampeter. What the hell was he doing here? And not only that, he had come out here with the little dog. He was jumping down from the wagon with it in his arms. What the...?

'Good morning, Dr Lampeter, come to join us on our sortie into the trenches?'

'I have indeed,' said Lampeter, looking past Mrs Seacole towards Ada.

'And you've brought your little friend as well,' she said. 'Not sure that's entirely a good idea, but we'll have to get moving and we can't leave him here.'

As she spoke, Lampeter put the dog down and it scampered over to Ada, wagging its tail.

'Well, I was just coming back to the hotel to see if you needed anything,' said Lampeter, still looking at Ada, 'and Sally told me that you'd gone out to the trenches, so I thought I'd come along and see if I could help out.'

'Right, let's get on,' said Mrs Seacole, turning and leading the way.

When the party reached the British line they found a stretch of trench that appeared deserted. But as they got up closer, they could see the dead bodies of many soldiers in their ragged red tunics lying in the trench. They continued to step over bodies, some with heads blown off, others sitting back against the walls of the trench with their arms flung wide almost in a gesture of surprise.

Suddenly they heard the shriek of a big shell and, as it dropped close by, the earth shook and dust and grit flew everywhere. By this time they were all in the bottom of the trench covering their heads with their arms. Ada could feel her heart racing and smell gunpowder. Strangely, she did not feel afraid.

'Where's Bob!' she shouted.

'It's all right, he's here with me,' replied Lampeter.

'All all right?' said Mrs Seacole, standing up after the dust had settled.

'Yes,' said Ada and Lampeter at the same time.

The trench further up was full of thick smoke, and they could hear men shouting. Coming closer they saw two soldiers slumped against the wall. Lampeter went straight to examine one while Mrs Seacole saw to the other, but there was nothing they could do for either of them. There was more shouting and screaming and as they moved along, keeping as close to the ground as they could, Ada saw the dog prick up his ears and put his nose to the ground. That's strange, she thought, I wonder if he's got the scent of something.

There was more smoke ahead and more yelling, and they stopped to make sure it was safe to proceed. Bob was keen to keep going and struggled against Lampeter as he held him. 'He must be spooked by the noise,' he said.

Then it was time to move again and Lampeter put the dog down. He shot off, running like fury.

As they came to a bend in the trench they could hear the little dog barking and barking. 'He must have found something,' said Mrs Seacole.

Ada started to feel a lump in her throat and her heart was racing. She had heard Bob making that noise before and she had an idea why he was making it again. As they rounded the corner into the next section, they saw the dog beside a soldier lying on the floor of the trench, barking as if his life depended on it. All three rushed forward and as Ada got closer she could see what she had feared: a brown tunic. She felt her heart lurch. She had been right: the dog had found Billy, and he didn't look in good shape at all.

'It's the lad from the hospital,' said Lampeter, rushing to the boy. 'I fixed his arm – do you remember, Ada?' Then, seeing her face, he knew that she did. 'He's still alive. I can see that he's breathing.' But opening up his shirt he saw the extent of his injuries and turned to Ada with a look on his face that told her all she needed to know.

'It's the lung,' said Mrs Seacole. 'See here, Ada, two holes in the chest.'

Ada knew exactly what that meant for Billy; he was surely one of those with 'no hope of survival', one of those that would have been left outside the hospital tent. She sank to her knees and cradled the dog in her arms. He had stopped barking now that they were there with Billy, but he kept trying to go over to lick his face.

'We can give him some laudanum,' said Mrs Seacole. 'That's all we can do.'

Ada nodded. She fully understood the situation and sat there motionless as Lampeter administered the drops. Then Mrs Seacole held a hand out to her.

'Come on, Ada, come closer, come and sit with him. It won't be long now.'

Ada put the dog down and did as she was told.

As she sat down next to Billy he opened his eyes and tried to smile at her. Always so good-natured, thought Ada, even when he's dying. He is dying.

'You stay with him, Ada,' said Mrs Seacole, 'while me and Dr Lampeter go further up the trench to see if we can find any more casualties. Can you do that?'

'Yes I can,' said Ada. 'Of course I can.'

So Ada and the little dog stayed with Billy as he lay dying in the bottom of the trench, covered in soil. He didn't open his eyes again but he did try to speak, though Ada couldn't tell what he was saying. She sat there holding his hand as he quietly slipped away. She could hear his chest bubbling and just before the end he gave a small cough and a gobbet of blood came out of his mouth. Then he was gone, as easy as that.

When Mrs Seacole and Lampeter came back they found Ada sitting there, the little dog lying next to the still warm body and Billy's dusty face stained with Ada's tears.

'Come on now, Ada,' said Mrs Seacole. 'We have to get going. There's nothing more we can do here today.'

'What about Billy? We can't leave him here.'

'He's gone, Ada; you did all you could. You gave him comfort when he needed it most. But there's nothing more we can do for him now.'

'But we need to take him with us, give him a decent burial,' pleaded Ada, her face wild with grief.

'We can't do that,' said Lampeter firmly. 'You know that. The body needs to stay here.'

'What do you know?' said Ada, almost snarling at him. 'We can't leave him here – it's not decent!'

Mrs Seacole took her hand and said to her gently, 'Look around, Ada, look down the trench: how many bodies do you see?'

'Lots. I can see lots.'

'We can't take just this one and leave the rest now, can we? This is where the lad has fallen, next to his comrades, and it's right and proper that we leave him here.'

Ada knew she was right. Reluctantly she nodded, stood up and started to walk back down the trench, her head hanging low. Mrs Seacole and Lampeter exchanged a glance and then Lampeter shouted to the little dog, who was still lying next to Billy's body. He didn't move at first but when Lampeter shouted again more insistently he came straight to him.

'I'll take Ada back with me,' said Mrs Seacole to Lampeter, glancing with concern at the girl as she walked in some kind of trance. 'There's nothing more that I or Ada can do here unfortunately, but you might want to stay on for a while with the dog – he seems to have a knack for finding wounded soldiers.'

Mrs Seacole wasn't sure that the doctor had taken in what she had said. He was staring at Ada, but then he said, 'Yes, yes, of course. But you make sure that you get Ada back to the British Hotel. She had a special bond with that young lad in the trench and she's still learning how to manage these things. You know how it goes.'

'I do, I do,' said Mrs Seacole quietly. 'Some just get to you more than the others and each one of us has to learn how to manage in our own way.'

# 22

*'I saw Mary Seacole ... at the fall of Sevastopol, laden not with plunder, good old soul, but with wine, bandages and food for the wounded or the prisoners.'*
William Howard Russell, *The Times*

They were up early the next morning at the British Hotel; no one could have slept with the noise of those big guns – they were almost shaken out of their beds. Ada had fallen exhausted on to one of the couches and Sally had covered her with a blanket. She had slept all night and when she woke she felt empty inside. She knew that she needed to keep going: the war wasn't over yet; she had to find the strength from somewhere, so she made herself get up and help Sally with the morning duties.

'You all right?' asked Mrs Seacole.

'I'm fine,' said Ada with the sound of her own voice echoing in her empty head.

'That's good. We need to get going again, this time up to Sevastopol. There are no soldiers at the door and as far as I'm aware that can only mean one thing. The big push is on, and they will break the siege at Sevastopol today.'

It seemed strange to close the door on a completely empty British Hotel but the guns were still pounding and all Hell seemed to have broken

326

loose in the world. Mrs Seacole had hitched some mules to a wagon and had packed up food, wine and medical supplies, and now they were heading towards the noise of the guns, Ada in the back, helping to secure the boxes and keeping a look-out behind, Mrs Seacole and Sally up front.

Ada was glad to be on her own in the back. She didn't feel that she could make conversation. Her mind was blank and her body felt numb after what had happened yesterday. She didn't feel afraid; she didn't really care.

Mrs Seacole was giving the impression that she knew exactly where to go and what they should be doing, but Ada understood the situation in Crimea well enough by now to know that no one knew; most of it was guesswork. Certainly they had not received any order or instruction from the military. Despite this, they were going to Sevastopol and not even the big guns and the shells shaking the ground would stop them.

As they rocked and lurched along the pot-holed road, Ada listened to the gentle murmur of conversation between Sally and Mrs Seacole. It didn't matter that she couldn't hear properly because all she needed was something that might help her feel right, and for some reason that murmur of voices was helping her mind to start functioning again. She began to think about the hospital and how busy Sister Roberts and Rose would be preparing for a wave of new casualties. She knew that, in due course, one of the doctors would be sent up to the front line. She wondered, but then knew instantly, which one would go. Of course it would be Lampeter.

Suddenly the noise of the guns stopped.

Mrs Seacole halted the mules and looked round to check on Ada. 'I don't know what that means, but it could be that the Russians have retreated and the city has fallen,' she said, a smile spreading across her face. 'If the city has fallen,' she continued, 'I want to be the first woman in there.'

With that Mary Seacole urged the mules forward.

Rocking around in the back of the wagon, Ada didn't know what they would find. All she could do was sit tight and watch the rugged road disappear beneath them as they moved away from relative safety towards Sevastopol. After a while, the wagon stopped again and Sally turned round to her. 'We are on Cathcart's Hill now, Ada. You can see the city from here.'

Ada stood up on the back of the wagon and faced front. There was no city to see, only smoke. She had never seen so much thick, grey smoke pouring up to the sky. The city was burning below them. Mrs Seacole sat, speechless for once, then said to them quietly, 'Only the other night I was up here and I saw the city so calm and sleeping beneath the stars. The beautiful white city.'

There were others around them now, officers and civilians, watching and waiting. 'The city is about to fall,' they said.

'We need to get in there and help any soldiers that we can find. British, French, Turkish or Russian, we will help,' said Mrs Seacole.

'You can't go yet,' said one of the officers. 'There's too much smoke and we have heard that the Russians have left the city booby-trapped with mines.'

Almost on cue, they heard a loud explosion.

Ada was relieved that Mrs Seacole was taking this advice on board, at least for the time being. Of course they couldn't head into the city just yet. Mrs Seacole opened up some of the provisions and they sat and watched, looking down on the city like the tourists on the hill that had so infuriated Ada on her first trip out towards Sevastopol.

In fact they were forced to sit and watch throughout the whole of that day and into the night. They saw fire after fire break out in the city and a great ship alight in the harbour casting a beautiful but terrible light all through the long night. They slept in the back of the wagon when they could, thankful of the good supply of blankets that they had brought.

The next morning was cold, much colder than the previous day, as if the events of the war had caused a sudden change in the early autumn weather. Fires still burned and cannon sounded all morning as the besieged city's defences were bombarded. Then around midday the big guns quietened and they could see a surge of troops moving towards the city.

'We can get going now; the Russians have withdrawn from the city,' said Mrs Seacole, urging the girls forward.

Ada's mind seemed to be fully alive again and she was terrified of leaving their place of safety. With her heart racing, she settled in the back of the wagon next to Sally. Mrs Seacole wanted to sit up front alone to reduce the risk of a stray shell

329

catching the younger girls, but also, they thought, so that she could lay better claim to being the first woman into Sevastopol.

They were stopped many times by sentries, who tried to persuade them not to go on, but Mrs Seacole was having none of it.

They got down from the wagon a number of times to treat casualties – a man with wounded hands and an officer with a throat injury – all the time stray shells falling around them. One fell so close that they all threw themselves down to the ground and waited until they could hear conversation and laughter around them before they got up. Mrs Seacole found a piece of the stray shell and put it in the wagon.

'A souvenir,' she said, seeing Ada's puzzled look.

This time, when they were all back in the wagon, they were able to pass through the last line of sentries. Ada could tell that if the men hadn't known Mrs Seacole so well she would not have been allowed to pass.

And so they proceeded into the fallen city. There were men lying dead in the streets, buildings were blown open, fire and smoke everywhere, but somehow some of the beauty of the place still remained.

They stopped many times as they progressed along the street to give provisions to the soldiers. A sudden explosion sounded down the street as a mine went up and they saw a man fall. Mrs Seacole raced to him but the man was dead, almost blown apart. Then, even before the dust settled, a British soldier appeared before them, staggering and drunk, wearing a woman's dress and bonnet.

He lurched over to Ada and tried to grab her but she was quick enough to dodge out of the way. Then Mrs Seacole and Sally were called further down the street to attend another casualty, and Ada was suddenly alone, lost in the dust and needing to escape those soldiers, shamefully drunk and looting what they could from the houses of Sevastopol.

She headed down another street, hoping to find safety, and heard a man's voice calling for help, almost sobbing. Through an open door she saw what looked like a hospital. This could be familiar territory, she thought.

The scene that met her eyes as she stepped through that door would come back to haunt her in nightmares for the rest of her life.

In a long low room lay the bodies of men. She could see that they were Russian by the remains of the uniforms that they wore, and at first she thought they were wounded; but then she saw that they were hundreds of corpses piled up on top of each other. She covered her nose and mouth with her hand but there was no way that the sickly sweet stench of death could be blocked. She gagged and her eyes streamed as she scanned the mound of bodies looking for some sign of life.

There was no life in this room. The voice she heard must have come from elsewhere.

Ada staggered into another room, and this time there was a low murmuring of voices and groaning so Ada knew that at least some of the men were alive. The room was quite dark but she saw a sudden movement in the corner. There must be someone alive over there she thought, or maybe it's a rat. She felt a shudder go through her.

There were heavy curtains at the window that had been nailed into place. Her instinct was to let the light in so she could see if she could help any of the poor souls in there. She pulled at the heavy curtains, but they were full of dust and tightly held. It took all of her strength to drag them down but in the end she managed to rend one of them and pull it away from the window, letting a shaft of light into that dark, fearful place.

There were many dead in this room too, but in the bed nearest to her she was sure that the soldier was breathing. Then she caught movement in the corner of the room again, where it was still dark. As her eyes adjusted she saw that there was, at least, someone up on their feet, someone who could help. And he was wearing a British army tunic. Thank goodness, she thought, someone who can help me with these wounded men.

As her eyes focused more clearly on the figure, he looked in her direction. He looked familiar and for a moment her heart lifted – but then with a shock she realized that this man would be no help. It was Cedric.

He was looting from the poor defeated Russian soldiers, taking what valuables he could find.

'Well, hello there, missy,' he said, moving quickly in her direction.

Ada was too shocked and unsteady to move.

'Hello there,' he said again, standing in front of her now, leering down at her.

She took a step back. 'Stay away from me,' she said.

'Well, I'm not sure I can do that,' he said. 'After

all, we're old friends, aren't we? From back in the laundry and on the ward. Old friends.'

She took another step back but now she was against the wall. She tried to dodge to the side but his arm shot out and he grabbed her. He held her tight and she remembered how strong he was as his bony hand bit into her flesh.

'Let me go,' she spat at him.

But he was shaking his head and moving closer.

'Let me go!' she said again, trying to stop her voice from wavering. But he had her now with both arms and was dragging her down to the floor.

What could he be thinking of? Surely not! Not here in this place full of death and suffering?

Even as she thought it she knew, sick with horror, that was indeed what he was thinking. He wanted her. He held her fast and pushed his face towards her, trying to kiss her, grazing her lip. She could taste the blood. Then he pushed her down on to the floor and before she knew it he was on top of her, pulling up her skirt, pushing her legs apart with his knee. He was like a man possessed. A demon.

She had had the breath knocked out of her but she would not succumb without a fight. She tried to move her legs or get her arms free but he had her pinned to the ground, well and truly pinned. But in pulling up her skirt, he had reminded her of the dagger, still strapped to her leg. She wriggled against him, managed to get her right arm free and felt for it with her hand. While he was ripping at her underclothes, she felt it and tried to grasp it, but couldn't quite get a hold on it. She needed him to shift position, so, defying all of her instinct for survival, she let her body relax a little. And in that moment he responded. She didn't look at his face but she could tell that he was smiling, thinking that he had her now. She had to move fast and in the next second she grasped the knife from its sheath and plunged it into the top of his leg.

He jumped back with a howl of pain.

She took advantage and pushed him off violently, scrabbling up from the ground and preparing to run. But he moved fast, easily ripping the dagger out, and then he was back at her again before she had a chance to get away.

She kicked out at him and screamed but he was so strong. She bit his face when he tried to kiss her and then it felt like it was becoming too late for resistance. Ada had no strength left to fight. She would have to let this happen, she thought, utterly wretched, as she felt him pawing at her underclothes again.

Then, suddenly, there was a loud bang and Cedric fell back. She almost expected to see Lavinia there behind him with a piece of firewood in her hand. Instead she saw a tall Russian soldier, swaying unsteadily, a revolver in his hand.

Ada gasped, desperately trying to take in what had just happened. Cedric was not moving; he must be dead. The Russian was trying to speak to her, his voice quiet. She didn't understand the words but he didn't seem threatening. He had helped her, after all; he had helped her.

Before she could gather herself, another man's voice shouted, a familiar voice. What on earth? It sounded like Lampeter! It *was* Lampeter. He was advancing towards them with a pistol in his hand. And he was raising the pistol in the direction of the Russian.

Suddenly realizing what he was about to do, Ada screamed, 'Stop, stop! This man has saved me. He saved me!'

Lampeter continued aiming the pistol, close enough now for Ada to see how much his hand was shaking.

The Russian had both arms raised in surrender.

Lampeter's hand was shaking even more and he looked wildly from her to the Russian.

Ada shouted again, 'Don't shoot, John, this man saved me. He saved me!'

Then and only then did Lampeter seem to realize what had happened. He dropped the pistol and grabbed her.

The Russian breathed out and then sagged in the middle, slumping down on another man's bed. The revolver dropped from his hand to the floor.

Lampeter tried to hold on to Ada but she pushed him back. Her clothes were torn, and her flesh was scratched and bruised from what had just happened. She stood gasping for air, holding out her hands to him, telling him that she would be all right but she didn't want him too near, she didn't want him to touch her.

Lampeter looked round for the Russian and, now that he knew that Ada was safe, walked over to him, stepping over Cedric's lifeless body.

The soldier was crying and shaking his head, looking around in shock. Lampeter placed a hand on his shoulder and said, 'Thank you, thank you.'

The man just nodded and then looked at Ada and shook his head, trying to say in broken English that no man should be allowed to do that to a woman, no man anywhere ever.

Lampeter fished a flask of water out of his pocket and urged the man to drink.

'Thank you,' the soldier said in English. 'Thank you.'

Lampeter patted him on the shoulder again. 'I will go and get help for you. We will bring in some men and try to help.'

'Thank you, thank you,' said the man again. 'Two days, no help, no water.'

'We will help you now,' said Lampeter. 'But first I have to take this woman to safety.'

The soldier seemed to understand.

'I can stay, I can help,' insisted Ada.

'No, Ada, please, for once just listen to me. You need to get away from here, you need to go back with Mrs Seacole. She will take care of you.'

And for once Ada didn't have the strength to put up a fight. She felt that she had been hit by something very heavy, something that had taken all of the strength that she had left.

'But please, please, you must get these men help.'

'Of course I will,' said Lampeter. 'But first I need to make sure that you are safe.'

Ada nodded, still reluctant to leave but knowing that he was probably right. 'You win...' She stooped to pick up Dolly's dagger from where it had been thrown on the ground. Without thinking she pulled up her skirt, wiped the blade on the hem and then slipped the dagger back into the snug leather sheath fitted to her thigh.

Lampeter saw her torn underclothes and understood immediately what must have almost taken place.

'Let's get you out of here, Ada,' he said quietly, reaching out towards her. 'Let's get you home.'

'Just a moment,' she said, stepping away from him, unsteady on her legs but determined. She went over to the Russian soldier, who sat quietly on the bed. 'I just need to say thank you,' she said, her voice starting to break on a sob. 'You saved me.'

The man looked at her, not understanding her words completely but knowing what she was saying. He tried to smile; then he grasped her hand for a moment before gesturing that she should go.

Lampeter was there as she turned away from the soldier, still unsteady on her legs. He was about to sweep her up into his arms, but saw the determination on her face and seemed to understand that she would insist on walking.

Outside the hospital building it felt like the world had gone mad. There were British soldiers everywhere, some drunk, others carrying furniture, candlesticks, pieces of Russian army uniform and anything they could get their hands on.

They heard Mrs Seacole before they saw her, berating the men for their unseemly conduct. 'And no, I do not want a sofa for the British Hotel, or a fine painting. No!' Then they saw a drunken soldier walk up to her swinging a parasol. He made her laugh and in the end persuaded her to take it.

'Another souvenir,' she told Ada, seeing her approach the wagon, and then, noting the look of the two of them, immediately grabbing hold of Ada and hauling her up on to the seat. Mrs Seacole knew that this was not the right time to start asking questions.

'Right, John,' she said, 'we were just about ready to head back now,' indicating a couple of injured men in the back of the cart. 'Do you want to come with us?'

'I wish I could,' he said looking anxiously at Ada, 'but there are so many Russian soldiers in there who need help. I have to stay on.'

The ground shook again as another mine exploded somewhere. Mrs Seacole shouted to Sally to get back on the wagon and within minutes she had turned the mules and they were heading out of the city.

Ada looked around through the dust but she couldn't see Lampeter. He was already gone.

She didn't remember much of the journey back to the British Hotel. Images from inside the hospital kept coming back to her and then she would gasp with fright as she felt Cedric grab her time and time again. Then she would see Billy's face again and hear the little dog barking and see her grandfather lying on his bed with two pennies on his eyes. Everything was fresh and jumbled up and going round and round in her head.

Alongside this she had that gnawing feeling still in the pit of her stomach. She didn't know any more if it was for Frank or Billy or Lampeter or Rose or for all of them. The feeling had been there for so long it had become part of her. The only things that could make it feel better were strong drink and her work, her work at the hospital. She realized, there and then as she travelled on the back of Mrs Seacole's wagon, that when she was nursing on the wards she didn't feel that lead weight in her gut.

Ada couldn't properly grasp what time of day it was but it felt like late afternoon when they got back to the British Hotel. She was able to walk in through the door but as soon as she felt the warmth and safety of the place and heard Sally's voice her legs started to feel weak and Mrs Seacole was straight there, leading her to one of the sofas and insisting that she lie down.

At some stage Tom Dunderdale arrived for supplies of food and herbal remedies. He was shocked to see Ada's bedraggled form asleep on the hotel sofa.

'What's happened to her?' he asked Mrs Seacole, his face full of concern. 'She looked right as rain last time I saw her.'

'She's been through a great deal since then, Tom. We've been out in the trenches and that's where she found that young lad, Billy, the one she nursed at the hospital. He had no chance. Then we went into Sevastopol.'

'You went in there? From what I heard it was terrible. That hospital full of dead and dying Russian soldiers – what an awful thing!'

'Ada was in there as well, I think,' said Mrs Seacole. 'She hasn't spoken about it to me but that was the direction she came from as we were leaving, and she was with John Lampeter. I think she's still in shock. She needs to be back at the hospital in Balaklava, needs to be given some care by those she knows best. She's a young woman who's been through a great deal in the last few days and she's already had other things in her young life. She's told Sally about some of it, what with her grandfather dying and her brother missing.'

'Her brother missing, you say?' said Tom, remembering the strange questions that Ada had asked on her first day.

'She'll be all right, I think,' said Mrs Seacole as she gazed at Ada and smiled. 'Her spirit is very strong and determined, you see.'

Tom nodded.

'Now, you get her back to the hospital, Tom. Take it slow over that rough road; she will need to be treated very gently for a while and you will have to watch her very carefully. Speak to Mary Roberts about it. I've heard about her and the good work that she does down at the hospital – she will know what to do. I hear she trained under Florence Nightingale.'

'She did that,' said Tom. 'Mary will look after her; I know she will.'

Then, looking again at the girl still sleeping on the sofa, he said quietly, 'Right then, let's get our Ada sorted.'

After what felt like a long and slow journey back, Tom lifted Ada out of the wagon and carried her into the hospital just as he had done that first day she'd arrived up from Scutari. Sister Roberts saw them come through the door and was there immediately. 'She looks exhausted, Tom. Let's get her into bed and we'll let her sleep as long as she needs.'

Walking ahead, Mary Roberts held open the door of the nurses' quarters. 'Put her in this bed here. I'll speak to Rose – she won't mind sleeping on the floor.'

Mary pulled back the cover and Tom placed Ada in bed. Ada opened her eyes for just a moment, saw their two faces looking down at her and knew that she was safe. She tried to smile and say thank you, but her face wouldn't work.

She remembered hearing the door click shut, and then she was lost in a sleep so deep she couldn't even dream.

The next day – or maybe it was longer, she would never know – she woke to find Rose sitting on the bed next to her, a cup of tea in her hand.

'What time is it?' said Ada. 'I need to be on the ward.'

'Not today you don't,' said Rose. 'And besides, we are managing. It was unbelievably busy for a few days but things are much calmer now. And you haven't heard the news – Miss Smith is gone. She has left the Crimea.'

'What?' said Ada, sounding a bit groggy and not having the strength to sit up. 'Really?'

'Well, of course she hasn't been right for some time and she'd taken to her bed, but after the fall of Sevastopol she came out to the ward and told us all that she was no longer required and would be leaving on the next ship. You should have seen the faces of those men. Some of the new ones didn't know who she was but the ones that did, well, they had to try and keep a straight face.'

'Oh, Rose,' said Ada, grabbing her friend's

hand. 'That means I can stay on here without any trouble ... and is Dr Lampeter back? Is he safe?'

'Yes of course he is,' she said. 'He's been desperate to come and see you, but Sister Roberts would not shift on it. No men in the nurses' quarters.'

'Is he all right? Was he injured?'

'No, you know what he's like; I think he'll live forever.'

'Oh, thank you, Rose, thank you,' said Ada, feeling herself trying to smile but not sure if she could.

Then she felt something nipping her thigh and wondered at first what on earth it could be. She pulled back the covers and saw the small dagger in its sheath. She unbuckled it from her leg and slipped it out from under the covers.

'Ada, what on earth are you doing with that? Give it to me,' said Rose, horrified by the sight of it and then not knowing what to do with it. 'I'll put it... Ada, Ada, are you all right?'

But Ada could not speak. She had slipped down under the covers, pale and shaking. Seeing the dagger again had brought back the moment that she'd been forced to use it.

'Are you all right? You've gone very pale. You're not sickening for something, are you?' said Rose, putting a hand on her forehead.

But Ada still couldn't speak.

'I'm getting Dr Lampeter,' said Rose.

She found him on the ward doing his round with Sister Roberts and walked straight over to tell him her concerns. She was somewhat taken aback by how he reacted, looking instantly worried, and this made Rose more concerned than ever.

'I don't understand,' he said, turning to Mary Roberts. 'I thought that she was just exhausted and needing to sleep ... but this sounds like some kind of collapse. What do you think, Mary?'

'Tell me exactly what happened,' said Sister Roberts to Rose.

'Well, we were chatting and she was all right, and then she undid a strap around her leg and pulled a dagger out from under the bedclothes. I took it from her, and when I looked back she was pale and shaking and couldn't speak.'

'Do you think she has a fever, or could she have had an apoplexy?' said Lampeter, starting to look even more anxious.

'I'm not sure,' said Sister Roberts, clearly struggling to make sense of the situation.

'Wait a minute,' said Lampeter. 'What you said about the dagger sounds like it was some kind of trigger. I think she's suffering from shock. I've seen the men have all kinds of reactions when they come out of the trenches – what they've started calling trench madness. After all that happened to her in Sevastopol it would be no surprise and I know for sure that she did need to use that knife. She picked it up off the floor after I found her.'

'How do you know that she used the knife?' asked Rose.

'When I went into the hospital she was there, and she was fighting off an attacker. I think she must have needed to use it, but it was all a bit confusing–'

'Those Russians,' said Rose.

'No,' said Lampeter, firmly. 'It wasn't the

Russians. Her attacker was one of ours. He had the uniform of an orderly. It was a Russian soldier who shot him, who saved her.'

'Oh my!' said Sister Roberts, utterly shocked. 'What a thing to happen to her ... and from one of our own. We need to go very carefully with her now. Give her plenty of time to rest and if she needs to talk, let her. Let her talk as much as she wants... That's the way she'll get better. She will be all right,' she added, seeing their worried faces. 'That girl is made of strong stuff. She's the sort that will get up no matter how many times she's knocked down. She will come through; just give her time.'

A few days later, Lampeter had special permission to go and see Ada in the nurses' quarters, but only while Rose was there. He took the little dog, Bob, with him but even when it jumped up on the bed wagging its tail, trying to lick Ada's face, they still couldn't get her to speak. She would absent-mindedly reach out a hand to stroke the animal but that was as far as it went.

Lampeter was becoming desperate to hear the sound of her voice; although he gave some cred-ence to his own theory of trench madness he was still unable to exclude some physical condition. And so he kept checking her for fever or disrup-tion of the nervous system. He even asked Rose to hold open Ada's mouth while he had a look down her throat, thinking there might be something mechanical obstructing her speech. But he found nothing. It was as if she had simply stepped away somewhere and left her body lying in the bed with basic functions only.

Dolly and Lavinia visited regularly. They were worried about Ada but they both knew what Lavinia had been through after her husband died and it felt like something similar. They sat on the bed and chatted to her every day and even brought the cat, Tom Dunderdale, in as well sometimes, but the cat was restless and wouldn't settle and needed to be let back outside to lie in the sun.

Dolly had taken back the dagger. Rose had told them the story of what had happened in Sevastopol and Lavinia had a good idea who Ada's attacker might be. Of course it was that rat Cedric, good riddance to him, she had said. Dolly was so pleased that she'd given the dagger to Ada – who knew what might have happened to her if she hadn't been able to use it? And she *had* used it – Dolly was certain of that.

So Ada continued to lie in Rose's bed and Rose slept on the floor. Rose looked after her friend and gave her every opportunity to talk, but day after day, nothing came. Sister Roberts kept reassuring Rose, telling her to keep going, to continue gently caring for her friend, repeating over and over, 'Just give her more time. With the right care she will come to.' But even Rose was hard-pressed to keep faith with that theory, despite Mary Roberts's years of experience. What if she was wrong? What if Ada never came back and never spoke again?

Rose had found that Ada would eat and drink if she left food and water on a small table by the bed and then closed the door on her, and she could prompt her to get out of bed to the com-

345

mode. If she brought a bowl of water she could wet the cloth, wring it out and give it to Ada and she would wash her own face, then Rose would do her hands, wiping them gently and patting them dry. She brushed Ada's hair, telling her how thick and beautiful it was, and then she would put her hair up, making her look like the woman that she was. Ada only had one nightdress so Rose made sure that she always had a clean one by using her own supply, beautiful soft cotton with delicate lace trim. And then she would make sure that the mother-of-pearl brooch was pinned to her nightdress, not knowing who had given it to Ada but knowing that it was very special. And last of all she would take her bottle of eau de cologne that they now shared, and make sure that her friend had a good dab on her neck. It was only a bit of perfume, but Rose thought that it made all the difference. She loved to be able to do these things for her friend and she would continue to do them, but Rose missed so much the sound of Ada's voice and her laugh, and prayed that her friend would start talking soon. She would do anything to try and make it happen.

# 23

*'You little know how intensified anxieties
become to those who have no change;
how the very walls of their sick room seem
hung with cares; how the ghosts of their
troubles haunt their beds.'*

Florence Nightingale

The soldiers on the ward now had spent months in the trenches. Tom reported that the nights were lively, with the poor sods shouting out and trying to get out of bed. He regularly found a young lad huddled in the corner of the ward, clawing at his legs, weeping and completely disorientated.

Most of the men were sensitive to noise and movement, and Sister Roberts stressed to the nurses that they must move around the ward as carefully and quietly as possible, looking out for signs of trench madness in the men and reporting it to her immediately. She had seen a number of men with dangerous suicidal or murderous intent while working at Scutari and knew that this was a serious issue. She also knew that the men couldn't help their disturbed behaviour. Their senses had been bombarded and overstimulated for far too long and they had been existing in a state of high anxiety.

Rose had just been to check on Ada and was pleased because she'd seen her friend try to smile, something that might be a glimmer of her coming back to life. Going in through the door of the ward, she was struck by how restless the current group of soldiers were. They weren't getting patients with new injuries now, except those who shot themselves. Most of the admissions were fever cases and those with old, sometimes minor injuries. But this lot had spent a long time in the trenches and they were nervous and restless.

The other nurses were well ahead with the work, so Rose took a walk down the ward to check on everyone. She walked slowly, taking in each patient: some in their beds, some standing at the top of the ward, some sitting on their beds. As she reached the top she glanced out of the window to check if any patients were sitting on the bench outside.

Before she had a chance to turn back, she was grabbed from behind. She knew instantly by how rough her assailant was that she was in danger and she let out a terrified scream. Her assailant tightened his hold, his arm around her neck. She couldn't breathe, and thought he was going to strangle her there and then.

He swung her round to face the ward and she could see her colleagues frozen in time, terrified looks on their faces. Lampeter, Mason and Sister Roberts all stood down the ward, holding their breath. She felt the man – it must be one of the patients – loosen his grip and move his arm down her body and she started to breathe a little more easily, but then she felt the sharp point of something against her neck.

'Oh my God, he's got a knife!' shouted one of

the hospital nurses. 'He's going to kill her!'

'Shh, quiet now,' said Sister Roberts. 'Everybody keep still and stay quiet.'

But Mason couldn't help himself and took a step towards them, hoping that he wouldn't be seen.

Instantly the man pressed the knife in harder against Rose's pale neck, making an indent in the flesh. Rose screamed again and Mason took another step.

'Stop!' shouted Lampeter as they saw a trickle of blood flow down Rose's neck and on to her white blouse.

Mason was in anguish as he stood like a statue, terrified of making any further movement. The soldiers on the ward had all stopped in their tracks. The whole ward held its breath.

'It's all right,' said Lampeter, keeping his voice steady. 'It looks worse than it is. It's just a flesh wound. But nobody move.'

Lying in her bed down the corridor, Ada heard what sounded like a scream, and then she thought she heard people running. She felt like she'd been sleeping for a long, long time; it must be time to get up. As she stood up out of bed she was surprised to see that she was wearing a fancy nightgown, and when she glanced in the lopsided mirror on the wall she could see that her hair was neatly pinned up. Also, she fairly stank of that expensive perfume of Rose's. Funny that, she thought, she couldn't remember putting any on. She was just thinking of getting dressed and heading to the ward when she heard another scream, a scream that pierced her heart.

That's it, she thought, there's definitely something up. She headed out into the corridor in her nightie.

'What is it?' she asked a hospital nurse who was skulking in the corridor.

'It's one of the patients! He's gone crazy and he's holding Nurse Blackwood with a knife.'

Ada didn't need to hear any more; she was already striding towards the ward. She had no idea what she was going to do but she had to do something.

She opened the door as carefully and quietly as she could and saw straight away a soldier with his left arm tight around Rose's body and his right hand holding a knife to her throat. Rose's eyes were wide open and her breath was coming quickly. She had a trickle of blood down her neck.

Nobody was doing anything – why wasn't anybody doing anything? She could see their backs, see how still they were, Lampeter, Mason and Sister Roberts, but if they didn't make a move it looked like the man was going to kill Rose with that knife. It would be easy, thought Ada, easy as anything. She had learnt enough in her short time as a nurse to know about the big vessels that carried blood in the neck.

So quietly, with her bare feet on the ward floor and the nightie lightly brushing her legs, she walked forward, through those who were standing. She walked through like some ghost from a different time.

The soldier saw her moving towards him and seemed transfixed, thrown off from what he had set himself to do.

'Lizzie?' he said. 'Is that our Lizzie?'

Ada had to think on her feet. 'Yes,' she said, making eye contact with him and maintaining it as she continued to walk carefully towards him.

'What are you doing here?' he said.

'I've come to see you,' said Ada, still keeping eye contact and trying not to look at Rose's terrified face. 'I've come to see you. How are you doing?'

Then she saw the man look from side to side, unsure. She saw him tighten his grip on Rose again, who gave a muffled sob.

'It's all right,' said Ada. 'It's all right, don't worry about this lot in here. I've come to see you; we need to talk.'

Ada's heart was racing and she could feel her breath coming quickly as she got closer and closer to the man. His eyes were still all over the place and she stopped and waited and then spoke to him softly again. 'Come on then, let's see what we can do to help.' He didn't look at her at first and then she said again, 'Remember me? It's Lizzie,' and he dropped the knife and released Rose and came over to her.

'Lizzie! Lizzie, my own sister!'

He grabbed Ada in a hug and started crying. Ada patted him on the back, saying, 'There there,' all the time looking over his shoulder and seeing Mason go straight to Rose and lead her away, and then Sister Roberts indicate that Ada should try and release herself from the man's grip. And she could see Lampeter with a fierce look on his face ready to tackle the man and drag him away if need be.

'All right then,' said Ada, 'let me have a look at you,' and she stepped out of the man's embrace and stood back.

Then Sister Roberts and Lampeter were by the man's side and helping him over to a bed. 'Let's get you some medicine,' said Sister Roberts. 'You can see Lizzie again later.'

The whole ward breathed a sigh of relief and in the next moment Rose was by Ada's side with a dressing and bandage on her neck and Dr Mason holding her hand.

'Ada,' she said, 'you can speak! Oh, Ada,' and she grabbed her friend in a hug.

'Never mind that,' said Ada with a grin. 'You're alive. That's all that matters.'

'Thanks to you,' said Rose. 'Thanks to you.'

'I'm not quite sure why I'm wearing this get-up,' said Ada, 'and stinking of your perfume.'

'It's a long story,' said Rose, 'a long story.'

Just then the ward door swung open and Mrs Fitzwilliam appeared, her arms full of poppies. 'Hello, everyone!' she said, and then seeing Ada she cried warmly, 'And hello again to you, young lady,' not even remarking on Ada's appearance.

Mrs Fitzwilliam gave the poppies to one of the nurses, asking her to set them out in jars around the ward, and then she fished in the large bag she was carrying for the chocolate and biscuits that she had brought for the soldiers. Ada could see how the patients loved to see her and how her visits must make such a difference to them. She remembered what Tom Dunderdale had said that first day they went out for supplies. Yes indeed, she was 'quite something', that Mrs Fitzwilliam.

Then Mrs Fitzwilliam came back to Ada and stood holding her hand while she related to the whole ward the story of their meeting that first day on the harbour and the botched amputation. Ada was grateful that she spoke quickly so that not many could follow her. But then she concluded by asking loudly where that ghastly doctor had ended up – 'What was his name? Lambeater or some such?'

She turned then to find that very same ghastly doctor standing right behind her. Ada gasped but Lampeter simply held out his hand to Mrs Fitzwilliam and said, 'Dr Lampeter, as a matter of fact.'

Mrs Fitzwilliam didn't flinch, just stuck out her arm and gave him a strong handshake before making a smart exit. Lampeter smiled and shook his head, then went over to the nearest jar of poppies and carefully withdrew the choicest bloom. Coming over to Ada, he bowed and gave her the flower. 'This is for you. You are truly the bravest nurse I have ever worked with ... but maybe you need to think about getting yourself dressed.'

'I'd forgotten about that,' she said, starting to smile.

'And there is one other thing as well, Nurse Houston,' said Lampeter in a formal voice, and then he took her hand and whispered in her ear, 'I want to kiss you.'

Later that day the ward seemed quieter, almost as if, after all that had happened, the rhythm had somehow been restored. The patients seemed to be resting easier. Even the man who had grabbed

Rose was sleeping on his bed, his troubles left to one side for the time being. Rose was there, insisting that she could carry on and not wanting to rest up as Mason had ordered, and Ada had dressed and come on to the ward in a clean pinny, slowly getting back into the routine.

It was early evening and the windows had been cranked open as wide as possible. A light breeze was just about stirring the air inside the ward and the sun was slanting in, catching the red of the poppies and making them glow in even greater contrast to the grey blankets and the white bandages. Now that Ada was back at work, she could breathe more easily; she felt calm. She had no idea if the feeling would last, but for now, she was at peace.

# 24

*'And yet all this going home seemed
strange and somewhat sad.'*
Mary Seacole

## *Balaklava, 1856*

It was April, the world was slowly coming back to life, birds were singing in the broken trees, flowers grew around the edges of the shell holes out on the Crimean plain and the graves that had been dug in the autumn were covered with fresh blooms. All those months ago Tom had taken Ada

354

out to the grave that contained Billy's body and she had stood beside it with her head bowed as the autumn leaves blew around her and the first cold of winter came in off the sea. That had been a bleak day and Ada had felt the nip of that wind around her face for weeks after, but she was glad that she had gone out there to pay her respects before the ground froze solid.

And now it was spring and, at last, the war had been declared over. It was time for the army to clear what they could, pack things together and start to leave.

Most of the soldiers and medical staff had stayed on during the winter. It had been very cold, but this time around the army had been housed in wooden huts on the heights above Sevastopol. They had plenty of food, warm clothing, and now that hostilities had ceased the only real concern had been to find diversion through their time of waiting. Bars and shops had been packed full, there'd been gambling, billiards, hunting and even horse-racing. Mrs Seacole had done a roaring trade at the British Hotel and the Christmas celebration she'd provided there had been legendary. They'd even had boat-loads of tourists arriving from Britain, wanting to see the famous battle sites, collect souvenirs and stand on Cathcart's Hill looking down on the ruined city of Sevastopol. Ada would have nothing to do with these people in their fine clothes; she'd found the whole thing detestable.

Ada and Rose had had time to get to know each other even better, and in the quiet of the ward where they still had patients – those with chronic wounds or fever cases – Ada had been able to spend more time with Sister Roberts: listening and learning. She had soaked up so much knowledge and had even pushed Lampeter for all that he knew of anatomy and physiology, devouring the information in the medical books that he had given her. In the biting cold of winter he had also given Ada his Russian fur coat and she had felt very special indeed snuggled up inside it.

But now they all knew that the war was over, Lampeter had been driving Ada crazy, constantly asking her what she wanted to do when she got back to England. Would he see her? Where would she go? They had been spending stolen moments together around the hospital, but with the eyes that seemed to be forever on them, they hadn't ever had the chance to really talk things through.

And then he simply stopped asking and she was finding it more and more difficult to track him down. It felt like he was trying to avoid her and she started to think that she had been right all along – they'd had something that was of its own time out here in the Crimea and now that they were getting ready to go back home he was feeling differently, and maybe she was too; she didn't even know any more.

It seemed like a lifetime ago that she had set sail from Liverpool, so eager to get away. Yes of course she had needed to do everything in her power to find her brother but, if she was honest, she had also been running away. Running away from the pain of grief and from what others might be expecting of her. She had known what they were thinking, that she should be getting married or looking for a job as a housemaid. But she had wanted none of that. She couldn't have gone straight from that special world of imagination she had had with her grandfather to the cold reality of life as a young woman from the street where she had been born. She knew that she'd wanted something else back then, and that had not changed. The difference was that now she seemed to have found what she wanted and it was to carry on with the work. The work had become a calling and that calling was so strong that, in a way, she didn't have a choice any more.

She didn't know how any of this would fit with Lampeter or what he had imagined they might have together. He didn't know anything about her, had never asked any questions. The last time they had properly spoken she had been trying to tell him about Frank and he'd said, 'I didn't even know you had a brother.' And she'd thought to herself: Exactly, you don't know anything about me. And then she had realized, fully realized, that, yes, she had come out to the Crimea to find her brother but she had found other things instead: friends who were like family, a sense of purpose, work that she loved, the promise of a new life ... and love. She had not wanted to love John Lampeter but she had ended up with it. And the thing was, they were from two completely different worlds. It could never work, not back home. He'd asked her about going to live in London, hinting at some kind of life that they could have together, but she knew straight away that she couldn't do it. It was easy for the likes of Rose and Mason, they were as good as engaged, but they were from the same class and they spoke the same language. They would get married and then Rose would give up her nursing to be a wife.

Ada had been shocked when she had first heard this from Rose, shocked to hear that Rose had been told a married woman could not work as a nurse. It didn't seem right to her – where she came from many of the women went out to work alongside their men; they had to earn money. But for the better off, and apparently for the Nightingale Nurses, they could not carry on working once they were married.

Ada was still glowing with pride after a visit to Balaklava from Miss Nightingale herself, and ever since had known that she could not, would not, give up her nursing now. Miss Nightingale had come on to the ward and spoken to Mary Roberts; then she had done a round of the ward. And, much to Ada's amazement, she had stopped in front of her and fixed her with those bright eyes that Ada remembered so well from her meeting with the great lady in Scutari. She had said, 'You're that nurse who came to see me at the hospital, the one without any qualifications.' Ada had felt her knees go a bit weak, wondering what was coming, and had just about managed a mumbled response. Then Miss Nightingale had broken into a smile and said, 'Sister Roberts tells me that you have done exceptionally well here, that you have met all the criteria to be a trained nurse, and therefore I am recommending you. You can use the title of Nightingale Nurse and we will be sure to find you employ at one of the new Royal Infirmaries.'

Ada, quite overwhelmed and not knowing whether to bow, curtsy or shake the woman's hand, managed to stumble out another reply before Miss Nightingale continued, 'Speak to Sister Roberts. She will advise you of a position in due course. Congratulations, nurse, excellent work. I must admit when I saw you in Scutari I really didn't think you'd amount to much but you have proved me wrong.'

Ada had stood there on the ward, speechless, as Miss Nightingale swept on.

The rest of that day Ada was turning over all the things that Miss Nightingale had said. She still couldn't believe that she had a recommendation. She would have to speak to Lampeter. There was no time to lose; she would speak to him that evening.

'I need to tell you something,' she said, finally catching up with him in the corridor outside the ward. She knew by the way that he looked at her that he had some idea of what was coming.

'So at last you come to speak,' he said with a strained smile on his face.

Although Ada had come to him knowing exactly what she wanted to say, seeing him standing there now pretending that he couldn't care less about her or anything else, she felt her resolve weaken a little.

'Well?' he said, starting to sound impatient, and that did it, something clicked inside her and she came straight out with it.

'The thing is, I know what I want to do when I get back. I want to carry on with nursing and I will be going back to Liverpool.'

Lampeter looked down at the ground and then lifted his head and shrugged his shoulders. 'So, are you telling me something I don't already know?'

'Well, I thought I was,' she said, raising her voice a little, 'given that you've been asking me over and over about what I was going to do.'

He shrugged his shoulders again. 'Have I?' he said, seemingly distracted.

'You know you have,' she said, wanting to take hold of him and give him a good shake.

'Where you go, Ada, is your business. Where I go is mine. We both have our work and our lives to lead.'

She stood and glared at him. He looked down at the floor.

'Is there anything else?' he said. 'It's just that Mason has a good bottle of brandy and he is waiting for me to join him.'

'Yes, that is definitely all,' she said crisply, turning on her heel and striding down the corridor without looking back, bitter tears of frustration beginning to stream down her face as she walked.

She went back to the nurses' quarters burning with fury and not able to speak to anyone. She tossed and turned on her bed, unable to settle, and then she had to make some excuse to go outside to the now empty laundry to sit on a box and look at the sky full of stars. She still felt fury and energy coursing through her body, and in that heightened state her mind was able to see things more clearly than she had ever been able to before and she knew that there was nothing more that she could do about John Lampeter. She would have to leave him be and wait, see if he came to her, to know that what they had shared in this strange world of war was something that was strong enough to take back home. Ada knew that she could be strong and that she would wait for him. And she also knew that there was every chance that he might not come.

Lampeter didn't come to find her the next morning. She saw him pass in the corridor and could tell just by the look of him that he was probably sorry for what he had said the day before – but he didn't speak. And then as the days went by she saw the way he looked at her when he thought she couldn't see him, and all the time she could sense that strong connection that buzzed between them, something drawing them together. But the more it seemed to draw, the more they both resisted. There was nothing more that she could say or do; she would just have to bide her time.

Yet there was little time left. The sense of leaving was bubbling through the hospital, and out on the road up to Sevastopol it felt like everybody was making preparation to leave and soon there would be no time left at all. Ada had been saying good-byes over the last few weeks and had asked Tom Dunderdale if she could go with him to the army camp and the British Hotel on his next trip. There were a couple of things that she still needed to do.

Bumping along the dusty track beside Tom Dunderdale as they headed towards the army camp, Ada began to feel some lightness; she felt free.

'Have you heard about Mrs Fitzwilliam?' Tom said, trying to stop laughing as they swayed along together over the rugged road.

'No,' said Ada. 'What now?'

'The story goes that after the fall of Sevastopol she was seen riding Horatio through the French camp and swigging from a bottle of champagne.'

Ada started laughing and Tom launched into another story. As she sat she let his stories wash over her and when she glanced at his profile as he steadfastly drove ahead she knew that she was going to miss him terribly. She already missed Dolly and Lavinia. They had been moved out by the army a few weeks ago. And she knew that Rose and Mason would be going soon.

'When are you going back, Tom?' she said.

'Don't know yet. The army don't give much notice. One day they'll come along and say, you, get on that ship, and that's it really. What you going to be doing, Ada?'

'I'm going to nurse,' she said.

'That's good work, Ada, and you have a real talent for it. Mary is so proud of you.'

'Thanks, Tom, that's really nice of you to say so.'

'I'm not being nice,' he said. 'I mean it: you are going to do great things. I know it.'

Ada smiled. 'I hope you're right,' she said. 'I've still got a lot to learn and I'll have to work hard but I really want to do it.'

'Good for you, Ada. And I hear that Dr Lampeter's going to a hospital in London.'

'Really?' said Ada, pretending that she wasn't bothered in the slightest.

'So they say. I mean, he has to, he is such a fine surgeon and he needs to be working with the best.'

'Well, I've heard that there are some fine surgeons in places like Liverpool as well.'

'I would think there are,' said Tom, giving her an amused glance.

'What?' she said. 'What's that for?'

'Nothing,' he said, still smirking.

'Stop it, Tom.' And then, desperate to change the subject, 'Have you heard about Dr Mason?'

'No, what's he up to?'

'Well, I've heard that he's got himself a supply of those herbal powders from Mrs Seacole. He says he's going to study them and make himself a fortune.'

'He needs to an' all with the amount of champagne he drinks,' said Tom.

Ada laughed.

'And it's good to hear about him and Rose, the engagement and everything. It's nice, that.'

'Yes, yes, it is,' she said, feeling a flush on her neck and not wanting to get into any talk about engagements or weddings.

As soon as Ada jumped down from the wagon at the camp she found herself taken back to when she had said goodbye to Billy, that last time she had seen him. It made her feel sad for him and for all the rest who'd lost their lives out here, so far away from home and family.

'I'll meet you back here in an hour or so,' said Tom, his voice breaking through her thoughts. She didn't realize that he'd been waiting, leaving her to think, standing by the wagon, until he could see that she was ready to make a move. He knew how much she had been through and wanted to make sure she had a chance to come to terms with things.

'Thanks, Tom,' she said. 'I'll just go and have a look at the hospital tent.'

'Righto.'

She found Dr Rossiter sitting all alone in the middle of the tent surrounded by packing cases. 'Hello,' he said warmly. 'Do you want a drink?' and he raised a half-bottle of brandy to her.

'No, but thank you,' said Ada. 'I've just come back to have a look at the old place before it's time to leave.'

'I know, quite right,' said Rossiter, sounding a little drunk. 'Don't think any of us will ever forget that couple of days we spent in this tent in the thick of it,' he went on, taking another swig from his bottle.

'We certainly won't,' said Ada, almost catching again the smell of gunpowder and the screams of pain and feeling a shudder go through her. 'Think I might just have a swig of that after all,' she said, stepping over to take hold of the bottle.

'Help yourself,' said Rossiter. 'I spent all last night with Lieutenant Goodman. Don't think I can take much more liquor after that lot.'

Lieutenant Goodman, thought Ada as she took a good swig of brandy from the bottle, that sounds familiar. And then she remembered the story that Billy had told her all those months ago. Of course, Goodman was the officer that Billy had worked for as a groom.

'That's strange,' said Ada, handing the brandy back to Rossiter. 'Lieutenant Goodman is the man I've come to see.'

'Really?' said Rossiter. 'Do you know the fine fellow?'

'No, but I've heard of him, and, in fact, I need to call and see him if you can tell me where he is.'

'I can indeed. He has a hut two rows along. You can't miss it; it has a line of champagne bottles against the wall.'

'Thank you,' said Ada, making to leave.

'Come and sit with me, Nurse Ada,' said Rossiter. 'I have something to ask.'

'I can't really,' said Ada. 'I've got to get back to Balaklava soon.'

'Well,' said Rossiter, 'all I was wondering was, what are you thinking of doing once you get back to Blighty?'

'I want to nurse,' she said firmly. 'I don't want to give it up.'

'And you shouldn't give it up. You are a fine nurse and there is so much more out there for you to learn. The foundations of the new nursing have been laid, very firmly laid, by our Miss Nightingale. The time is ripe, Ada, the time is ripe.'

'I do believe it is,' she said, smiling at him as he took another swig of brandy.

'Anyway,' he said, wiping the back of his hand across his mouth, 'I have a proposition for you, young Ada.'

'Oh, well, I'm sorry, I need to get going,' said Ada.

'No, no, not that, not what you're thinking,' he said, laughing. 'I was wondering if you would be interested in a position at one of the new Infirmaries appointed by Queen Victoria. They're crying out for nurses like you who've had experience in the Crimea and I think that you have a valuable contribution to make.'

'Do you really think so?' said Ada, surprised by how forcefully Rossiter had spoken.

'Yes of course,' said Rossiter, smiling at her. 'Would you be interested?'

'Well, yes,' she said, her eyes shining, 'and as a matter of fact I have a recommendation from Miss Nightingale herself for the very same thing.'

'Excellent,' said Rossiter. 'That is excellent indeed. You're from the north, aren't you? I've heard that there's one in Manchester. A fine establishment by all accounts. They say that the new buildings are heated by hot water in pipes and lit by gas.'

'Really?' said Ada, her eyes widening. 'That sounds impressive but I need to go back to Liverpool. That's where my people are.'

'In that case you need to look at the Liverpool Royal Infirmary on Brownlow Street. Not as modern as the hospital in Manchester but there's a lot of good work going on there.'

'Thank you,' said Ada, 'I might just do that.'

'Well, good luck with Lieutenant Goodman. He's a luckier man than me,' he said with a bit of a glint in his eye that she chose to ignore. 'Don't forget, the hut with the champagne bottles. You can't go wrong.'

Ada emerged from the tent and followed his directions, but the camp was still an absolute maze of tents and huts and it took her some time to find the right place. Finally she saw the champagne bottles and knew she was there. As she approached the wooden door she could hear the sound of voices and laughter and hesitated a moment before knocking.

366

'Come in!' shouted a voice and she pushed open the door to find a group of three or four officers inside, smoking, drinking and playing cards. The room was stacked with boxes of food and bottles of drink, and there was a foul stink of rotting flesh that made Ada's nose wrinkle.

'Hello,' she said. 'Could you tell me where I'll find Lieutenant Goodman?'

A man stood up, smiling and swaying and saying that maybe it was his lucky day.

She smiled, but was careful not to encourage his advances. 'It's not actually you that I'm here to see, Lieutenant Goodman. I wondered whether I could see Captain Jack. Could I see him please?'

'That's my horse!' said the officer as the other men burst into laughter. 'That's my damn horse!'

'Yes, I've heard a lot about him. Could I see him?' Ada repeated, calmly.

'He's tied up round the back of the hut, I think. That's where I left him at any rate.'

Ada nodded her thanks before turning to leave.

'Oh look, now she's leaving, she's leaving, it must be the foul stench in here,' he said. 'It's not us, we don't smell that bad. It's the rats, they nest under the hut. We poisoned them and now they're rotting away under the floor. Horrible stink, so sorry.'

Ada smothered a laugh as she heard the last of it and closed the door on them.

She soon found Captain Jack, who appeared to be a very ordinary-looking horse, brown in colour with a dark mane and tail, and with a bit of a belly on him. Ada went over to him timidly at first. She'd never had much to do with horses. Jack didn't seem to mind her presence, so she ran her hand down his neck. Then, moving in closer, she laid her cheek against his neck and felt the warm smoothness of his coat. As his big ears flicked backwards and forwards, she told him that she had known Billy and that she had been with him when he died.

The huge animal twisted his big head round to look at her and she instinctively stroked his velvet muzzle, smelling that special horse smell and feeling his warm breath on her hand as she cupped it around his nose. Then, giving him a final pat, she said, 'Goodbye, Jack,' and left him there tied up behind the hut.

When Ada saw Tom sitting quietly on the wagon, ready to move, she knew exactly where they would be going before heading to the British Hotel and then back to the hospital. It was somewhere that he and the other soldiers regularly visited themselves, knowing that they would have to leave them soon, their comrades who would lie forever in Crimean soil. Ada was glad that he let her stand by the war grave alone, to say her own goodbyes. The last time he had brought her here, she had felt weak and the day was bitingly cold. She had left feeling empty inside. At least this time she could feel the spring sun on her face and she had the colour of the flowers to warm her soul whilst she paid her respects and said her final goodbye.

When they reached the British Hotel they could hardly get in through the door. The place was packed with officers and loud conversation, Mrs

Seacole at the centre of everything, dressed in her bright yellow silk, talking and laughing. When she saw Ada she came straight across and gave her a hug. Holding her at arm's length, she cried, 'You're looking so well!' Taking a bright orange feather from her hair, she stuck it in amongst Ada's dark brown curls.

Sally was busy at the bar and Ada went in behind the counter to give her a hug and say an emotional goodbye.

'What are you going to do when you get back to England?' Sally asked.

'I'm going to be a nurse,' said Ada proudly.

'That is so good, Ada, so good,' said Sally, beaming. 'Mother Seacole has always said what a good nurse you will make.'

'Where will you go?' said Ada.

'We don't know yet, but we have time to get something organized,' said Sally, looking over at Mrs Seacole. 'We would like to go back to England but we're not sure. We need to make a living, you see, we need to have more money. But don't worry about us; we will be all right. You know what she is like.'

'I think I do,' said Ada, looking over again at Mrs Seacole in her fine silk.

Ada walked back over to Mrs Seacole and they hugged a final time. 'Goodbye, darlin',' Mrs Seacole said. 'I hope you stay with nursing: there is no better work.'

'I plan to stay,' said Ada. 'I will stay.'

'I know that you've been through a great deal here, Ada, but never forget, all of those experiences are important for you; they make you the person that you are. No experiences, even the bad ones, are wasted. Always remember, darlin', every woman is the sum of all she ever did and all she ever felt.'

Ada stood for a moment taking in Mrs Seacole's words. She was right. All of Ada's experiences were part of who she was now, part of her story, and she knew that she would go on to have more experiences, good and bad, and no matter what happened she swore that she would always try to keep learning and to keep going, no matter what life threw at her.

That night she dreamt that she was back in Liverpool with her grandfather and Frank. She saw again her yellow silk bed curtain with its pattern of flowers, butterflies and exotic birds. She ran her hands over it like she had done the first time when her grandfather had brought it back home from the docks. She saw her grandfather's face smiling down at her once more. And she heard his voice, telling her as he had done so often, 'You are here for a reason, Ada, you are strong and clever and one day you will tell your own stories.'

# 25

*'Let whoever is in charge keep this simple
question in her head ... how can I provide for
the right thing to be always done?'*
Florence Nightingale

Ada stood on deck as the ship pulled out of Balaklava harbour. She had not seen Lampeter for
days. She had stayed strong, waiting for him to
come to her, but in the end he had not and she
had certainly not been inclined to chase after him
just to say goodbye. She had held her ground and
waited ... but he didn't come and now the ship was
leaving.

As the ship began to move further out she
looked back at the harbour and the group of buildings that had been so strange to her when she
arrived last year. The quay was clear now, but back
then it had been packed with people and horses
and wounded soldiers. She thought about the first
time she had seen Lampeter, covered in blood.
How he hadn't even seemed like a thinking, feeling person. How she had detested him. And now
... well, now, she knew that he thought and felt
more than anyone could imagine. As for leaving
without a goodbye — well, she would get over it.
She had her sights firmly set on Liverpool and
working at the Infirmary. And maybe, just maybe,
there would be news about Frank. As she thought

about her brother she felt that old, familiar tightness in the pit of her stomach and she took a deep breath to try and settle it down.

Still looking at the harbour, thoughts and feelings flowing through her mind, she saw a dark figure come into view. They were still close enough for her to make out who it was. Even if they hadn't been, she would have known instantly who it was. It was Lampeter, with the little dog beside him. He had seen her up on deck, her face turned to the harbour, and raised one hand in farewell. She knew then, in that moment, that he had, at last, given her a sign. She raised her hand back without hesitation and then she saw him wave properly to her, and he continued to wave as he stood there with the little dog, watching her go, until he was just a small mark in the distance.

Ada turned to go below deck, feeling sure now that what had happened between them was strong. This wasn't the last of it; there would be more to come.

Ada spent most of the voyage home quietly below deck, rocked by the ship, sometimes seasick, but mostly just rocked. On the day they arrived off the shore of Liverpool, waiting for high water so they could sail in, she could feel the excitement buzzing through the whole ship until at last they were ready to move. And for Ada, it felt spectacular as they came in up the Mersey under full sail amidst any number of other ships. As the sails billowed and the ship cut through the water she could feel a fresh breeze on her face and felt exhilarated, like she was riding the crest of a wave.

A massive cheer went up around her as the magnificent harbour and the first line of the dock buildings came into view and she felt a surge of pure joy go through her body. She was back home in Liverpool at last and desperate to feel the ground beneath her feet. She waited impatiently on deck, her heart pounding, as the ship manoeuvred through the harbour, bristling with masts, and finally squeezed in between two other ships to moor. As soon as the gangplank was in place she was walking down, making her sea legs steady up, and then she was there, back on dry land and amongst the people of Liverpool.

Almost the first person that she saw after disembarking was a young woman wearing a shawl, carrying a large bag and looking flustered, probably heading for one of the passenger ships. As Ada walked by, she felt as if she was passing herself that day she'd left Liverpool for the Crimea. She smiled at the girl and then looked down, seeing her new self for the first time. She realized that she was wearing the good skirt and hat that Rose had given her, and her hair was swept up and pinned in the way that Rose had shown her. Curls still escaped on to her face, but she was able to keep it a bit tidier. She didn't look like that young woman wearing a shawl any more.

As she made her way to Mary Regan's house she walked back up her old street. It still felt familiar but by this time she had no sense of her grandfather by her side and she didn't see one person that she knew. As she passed their old house she noticed that the paint had started to peel from the windows, and remembered that it had always happened in the heat of the summer sun, and her grandfather always made sure that the windows were repainted before winter came. But the house had new tenants now and things would be done differently.

She carried on through the city, enjoying the sights and sounds of the place that she knew so well but now felt so unfamiliar to her. The noise of the people and the sound of the accent felt like home, but at first almost grated on her, and the smell of the streets was quite different from what she remembered.

As she stood on Mary's doorstep she listened for the sound of the screeching baby but all was quiet inside. She wondered what she would find, what news there would be, and prayed that all would be well.

Hearing voices inside the house, she tapped on the door and waited, but no one came. So she knocked again a bit more firmly, and finally heard Mary's voice and footsteps.

The door opened and Mary stood there, looking at Ada, but clearly not recognizing her under the hat.

'Yes? Can I help you?'

'You can indeed,' said Ada, removing her hat.

'Ada!' Mary clapped a hand over her mouth and no other words would come. Then she grabbed Ada and hugged and hugged her on the doorstep.

Finally letting her go, Mary looked distracted. 'Did you get my letter?'

'No, what letter?'

'About Frank!'

Ada felt her stomach lurch. 'Frank? You've

news?' she whispered. 'Is he alive?'

'Yes, yes,' said Mary quickly. 'You really didn't get my letter? I'm so sorry. I've so much to tell you. But yes, he's alive,' she beamed. 'He turned up back here a couple of months ago and he, well, I think he will be all right. Come in, come in. Let's not stand on the step. Come and sit down.'

When they were sitting at the kitchen table, Ada looked across at Mary and started to feel worried, despite such wonderful news.

'Well then,' she said, 'you need to tell me. There's more, isn't there?'

'Oh Ada, it was so sad. I felt so sorry for Frank when he got back. He'd been to the old house, of course, and the new family there had told him they didn't know anything about you or your grandfather. So, of course, he'd gone straight round to Mam's and she'd had to tell him... He took it very bad, Ada. He was heartbroken about your grandfather, and then of course all he wanted was you – but you were gone looking for him and, not only that, you'd gone out to the war. What with the grief and the worry, poor Frank didn't know what to do with himself.'

'Is he all right now? Where is he, Mary? Is he at work? Can I go and see him?'

'Well, he did try going back into work, but he was a mess, he couldn't work, and ... well, he's taken to drink, Ada, that's what he's done. He's taken to drink and he won't listen to me or to Mam.'

'So where is he living?' said Ada, urgently. 'Where can I find him?'

'He was staying at Mam's but she had to ask

him to leave a couple of weeks back. He was coming in at all hours, so drunk, knocking things over, she couldn't manage him, and I'm sorry to say we don't know where he's sleeping now.'

Ada sat quiet for a minute, staring at her hands, then she looked back at Mary and reached a hand out to her.

'Look, Mary, don't you worry. I know you've done your best for Frank. He's not easy to manage, but I'm back now and I will find him.'

Mary nodded and gave Ada's hand a squeeze, knowing that Ada was more than capable of sorting Frank out.

'You look good, Ada. You look well. I know you won't have time just now but you must tell me everything, everything that's happened to you.'

'I will that,' said Ada, knowing that she would have to leave chunks of it out, parts that she didn't want to go back to herself just yet, but she would talk to Mary; she always could. 'Just as soon as I've sorted Frank out. So what did happen to him, has he been able to tell you? Did he get knocked on to another ship?'

'No – well, not in the way we thought he had. He went off that morning to work as usual and then somebody begged him to make up the crew on a passenger ship leaving for Australia. The ship was leaving there and then, so he went.'

'Australia? He just got on the ship without leaving any word, without letting us know?' she gasped.

'Well, he told Tommy Simpson, who was overseeing that day. He told him to tell you and your grandfather, to make sure that he told you. But then Tommy was killed soon after and nobody ever knew.'

'What?' said Ada. 'All that time I was thinking he was dead or fallen on to some ship going to the war and he had willingly gone as crew, willingly gone. Who was it that persuaded him to do such a thing? Or did they force him?'

'Well, the thing is, Ada, apparently it was his father, your birth father, Francis...'

'What?' said Ada, utterly shocked now. 'Frank found him and he didn't tell me?'

'He had got to know him through working on the docks, apparently. I don't know why he didn't tell you. I'm sorry, Ada,' she said, giving her friend's hand a squeeze. 'Anyway, Frank had always said he wanted to go on a ship, not thinking it would happen so fast, so when he got the chance he went.'

Instantly Ada was back in their house on the street with Frank and Grandfather. She'd always known how interested Frank had been in their father, whereas she had felt differently; she hadn't wanted to know him. So perhaps that was why Frank didn't share anything with her. And then she remembered that note in her grandfather's tin, the note making it clear that this Francis already had a wife and a child.

So Frank had found their father, and had got to know him. And if he knew him, did he also know that woman, that Marie, and her child? Did he know them too?

'So does Frank know Francis's wife then too?' she blurted out. 'Or their child, the one that could be our half-sister or -brother?'

Seeing Ada's face and knowing her of old, Mary hesitated a moment, then said, 'I don't know if he knows the woman, I'm not sure of that ... but he does know the daughter.'

Daughter, thought Ada, her head reeling. Daughter. So I have a half-sister.

'I think he sees her sometimes when he goes out drinking. I think she's called Stella.'

'Right,' said Ada, almost to herself. 'Right. So she's called Stella, is she? She must be about my age, I suppose, or maybe just a bit older.'

Ada sat for a while staring at the cup of tea that Mary must have put in front of her at some stage. And then she looked up and reached a hand across to her friend and just smiled at her.

Suddenly realizing how quiet it was in the house, she said, 'Where's the baby?'

'Oh, he's fine, he's sleeping. He's toddling around now, he doesn't have the gripes any more and he doesn't scream the place down.'

'Thank goodness for that,' said Ada, gulping down some of the tea and then getting up from the table.

'Can I leave my bag here for now, Mary?'

'Of course you can. And you can stay as long as you like, until you get yourself sorted.'

'Thanks,' said Ada, giving her friend a hug before putting her hat back on and fixing it with a long, brutal hat pin. 'Now, what pub will our Frank be in? I'm going down there to drag him out by the scruff of his neck.'

Ada knew exactly where the pub was: directly opposite Lime Street Station, one of the areas of the city that Mrs Regan had always told her to stay clean away from. She marched through the city, but once she was outside the pub door, hearing the noise and the tinkling of a piano from that other world inside, she started to feel nervous.

She knew that the longer she stood there with butterflies in her stomach the worse it would get. And then thought, after all the things she'd seen and done in the Crimea, that this was ridiculous. Her brother was in there, she had been worrying about him for a full year, and here he was ... right now.

She took a deep breath and pushed the door open vigorously, nearly knocking a couple of men over on the other side. She had never been in a pub before, and was in no way prepared for the noise and the smoke and the press of bodies. But she had to get through, so she pushed and she shoved until she could see the counter with a row of men hunched over their tankards. They were all wearing caps and dusty jackets, and all looked the same. She felt like screaming out Frank's name but nobody would hear over that din.

There was some drunken man singing to a melancholy tune at the piano. She shot a glance at him, wishing that he'd shut up. Then her legs nearly gave way as she saw that the man standing next to the piano was Frank. His hair was long and straggly and he had a bit of a scruffy beard – but it was Frank! With a final burst of energy, Ada pushed her way through the circle of men and then she was there, right next to him. He was swaying all over the place, but when he looked down at her she saw his face light up and he started shouting her name. 'Ada, Ada! You've come back, Ada!' Then he was crying uncontrollably as she held on to him for dear life.

'Frank!' she shouted over the din. 'Come on, let's get you out of here!'

He started to move but then stopped dead and turned towards the handsome-looking woman playing the piano. He tried to speak but his voice was slurred. ''S'just … let me, Ada, let me intro, intro … dush you to Ste–'

But it was too late. Ada wanted him out of there and she pulled on his arm as hard as she could, dragging him out and on to the street, where she hugged him and hugged him as he swayed all over the place, stinking of beer.

Ada marched back through the city, hauling Frank along, to Mary's. It was no easy task – she barely came up to his shoulder and he was much stronger than she was – but she was determined, and so she pulled him through the crowds of people as he swayed along behind. She didn't really want to take him back to Mary's in that state, but there was absolutely nowhere else that they could go, and as far as Ada was concerned, Mary was the only family that they had left in Liverpool.

In the days that followed, when Frank was stone-cold sober, Ada started to ask him about Francis and their half-sister Stella, but each time, as soon as he started telling her, she just got angry and told him to stop.

'Well, you asked me,' he said each time.

'I know, I know, and I do want you to tell me,

but as soon as you start saying the words and their names, well, it just feels too much. I will want to know, I have to know, but I don't want you to tell me too much...'

'Can I just tell you two things then?' he said at last.

'All right,' she said, looking at a spot on the floor, steeling herself to hear what was bound to come.

'You know when you found me in the pub?'

Ada nodded.

'Well, that woman playing the piano in there, that was Stella.'

Ada held her hand up. 'Don't tell me any more about that woman just yet.'

'But she's a good–'

'Not yet,' said Ada. 'What's the other thing?'

'The other thing is ... well, on that voyage to Australia I got to know our father, Francis, and ... well, he wasn't the man that I thought he would be.'

Ada looked at Frank, his head down and his shoulders slumped. She put a hand on his arm and he looked at her and then he said, 'And I never saw him again after he went ashore, and I was glad that he stayed there, that he didn't come back to Liverpool.'

Ada hooked her arm in his. 'I'm sorry, Frank,' she said gently. 'I'm so sorry that you didn't find what you were looking for.'

Frank sighed heavily and didn't seem to want to say anything else.

'But I'm back in Liverpool now,' said Ada gently, 'and you and me, we'll soon get ourselves sorted out.'

Frank looked up at her again then.

'You'll soon find a job on the docks, not unloading ships this time, a better job, and I've already got a letter for work as a nurse at the Liverpool Royal Infirmary.'

'You have?' said Frank, starting to smile. 'I always knew you were clever, Ada. I never would have told you, not when we were young, but I always knew.'

'We'll be all right, us two,' said Ada, tightening her hold on Frank's arm. 'We'll be all right. We're Padraic Houston's grandchildren, that's who we are.'

A few days later Ada was tapping on the polished wood door of the superintendent's office at the Liverpool Royal Infirmary, waiting to be called in. She had only been standing there for a few moments when the door was opened by the woman herself.

'Come in,' said the superintendent. 'You must be Ada Houston. I've been expecting you. Sit down, sit down.'

Ada sat herself down on an upholstered chair and the superintendent went around the other side of the desk and leant forward, smiling at Ada.

'I had a lovely letter about you from Sister Mary Roberts,' she said. 'You come very highly recommended and I believe you have a letter from Miss Nightingale as well.'

'I do, yes,' said Ada, somewhat taken aback by the welcome she was receiving. She had been expecting a grilling from a stony-faced woman.

'Well,' said the woman, 'given all of your experience out in the Crimea, working with a Nightingale Nurse like Mary Roberts – and with Mrs Seacole too, I believe – after all that experience, there isn't much we need to say here except we can definitely offer you a position.'

Ada's mouth dropped open.

'There is a great deal to do at the Infirmary and we want to move with the times here. We need to have Nightingale Nurses like you on the wards ensuring that our patients are cared for to the right standard. There is so much that needs to be done, but I think with your experience and the grit and determination you have shown out in the Crimea, you are ideally placed to do that work.'

'Thank you,' breathed Ada. 'Thank you so much.' She was incapable of saying more.

'So I can offer you a position straight away.'

Ada was still unable to speak. She had expected that the superintendent might be interested in her experience but thought that she would have to volunteer on the wards first and show what she could do. But she had been offered a position straight away!

'So,' said the superintendent, standing up from her chair and smiling even more, 'Nurse Ada Houston, may I welcome you to Liverpool Royal Infirmary?'

When Ada was out of the hospital and on her way back to Mary's she finally let herself smile – a smile that made her face ache. She still couldn't believe it: she had been offered a post at the Liverpool Royal! She couldn't wait to get back to tell Frank.

And then, immediately, the sadness hit her in the pit of the stomach. Because she realized that the person she really wanted to tell, above all others, was dead. He was dead and gone. Why did she keep having to remind herself that he wasn't there? It had been well over a year since Grandfather had died, but these thoughts still came to her. Would they always come, forever?

Ada stood for a few moments with her head bowed, trying to steady herself. She took a few deep breaths, trying to push the thoughts away, but they were too strong. She could see his face and he was smiling. She tried to clear her head but he was still there. She couldn't shift him; she probably never would. She was comforted by that, knowing that he was there with her, but sometimes it did make her feel a bit jangled, having him in her head, always smiling and trying to give her advice, for goodness' sake... And then she began to see the funny side of it and she started to smile. Of course he was in her head, because she knew that he would have been proud of her. And he wouldn't have wanted her to feel sad. He would have said something like, 'Well, Ada, it won't be plain sailing, you'll have to work hard and there'll be times when you'll just want to come home ... but you can do it, Ada, you can do it. You show 'em.'

'I will,' she said to herself softly. 'I will, Grandfather.'

Then she lifted her head and started to walk steadily towards the house where she knew that Mary would be waiting with the baby and Frank would be lounging in a chair and even Mary's husband might be pleased for her. As she walked she started to think more about the job and what she might be facing. No, it wouldn't be easy, and it would be far different from the work at the hospital in Balaklava. But you know what, Ada? she thought. You just remember what the women in the street used to say when things were tough – and they often were very tough. They used to say, 'Where there's a will there's a way.' Ada smiled as she heard Mrs Regan's voice in her head: 'Come on now, Ada, where there's a will there's a way... Where there's a will there's a way.' Repeating this in her head like a song, Ada walked back from the Infirmary with her head held high.

# Acknowledgements

First and foremost, thanks to my family for their unwavering support and enthusiasm.

Thanks also to my agent, Judith Murdoch, and my editors, Eve Hall, Clare Bowron and Rebecca Hilsdon, and thank you to Eugenie Todd for the copy-edit.

Finally, thanks to the patients and staff I have worked with over many years of nursing, especially my team at St. Catherine's Hospice.

This book has grown out of a lifetime of work that has been very rewarding. And for that I am grateful.

The publishers hope that this book has given you enjoyable reading. Large Print Books are especially designed to be as easy to see and hold as possible. If you wish a catalogue please ask at your local library or write directly to:

**Magna Large Print Books**
Cawood House,
Asquith Industrial Estate,
Gargrave,
Nr Skipton, North Yorkshire.
BD23 3SE

This Large Print Book for the partially sighted, who cannot read normal print, is published under the auspices of

## THE ULVERSCROFT FOUNDATION